DECISION OF FATE
A NOVEL OF ARMOURED COMBAT IN THE
GREAT WAR

by
Steven B. Howery

Author of Without Reserve: A Novel of the War on Terror

Khukuri Publishing, LLC
Littleton, Colorado

To my extraordinary wife and three incredible children, who've borne with me the honor of serving our country in two wars.

With gratitude to my father in law, James K. McCloskey, for his Irish gift for story-telling; my step-father, Dr. Bruce N. Bastian, for his enduring support and enthusiasm; to my mother, Miriam B. Bastian for instilling in me a love for the English language; and to my mother in law, Anna Marie McCloskey for her editorial wisdom and encouragement.

Dedicated with greatest respect and admiration to the people, intelligence services, and armed forces of the United Kingdom, whose loyalty and dignity as steadfast allies have earned my everlasting respect and affection.

—

While Decision of Fate is based, in part, on actual events and living historical individuals, it is a work of fiction. The words, thoughts and actions of historical figures described in this story are also fictional. The remaining characters are completely fictional and serve merely as a vehicle to tell an extraordinary story. Similarity to any single individual, living or dead, is purely coincidental.

Cover: "The first tank-versus-tank action, near Villers-Bretonneux, 24th April 1918" is used with permission of artist David Rowlands, who retains the Copyright thereto.

No Copyright is claimed as to B.G. Hugh Elles' communique at the Battle of Cambrai or the portion of Seigfried Sassoon's "Poet as Hero" cited in this work, the Copyright to which remains with the original owners.

ISBN 13: 978-0-9793274-1-4 ISBN 10: 0-9793274-1-5

Library of Congress Control Number: 0000000000

SAN: >>>>>>>>> 0 0 0 – 0 0 0 0 <<<<<<<<<<

"The war was decided in the first twenty days of fighting, and all that happened afterwards consisted in battles which, however formidable and devastating, were but desperate and vain appeals against the decision of fate."

- Winston S. Churchill
Lieutenant Colonel
Royal Scots Fusiliers
1916

FOREWORD

British development of the tank during the Great War is a story of great triumph and needless tragedy. It was a triumph for men of vision who recognized the same industrialization that brought stalemate to the Western Front could provide the means to overcome it. However it played-out as tragedy because an intransigent military establishment failed to grasp the utility of the new weapon in time to properly employ it before the war ended in an inconclusive peace that French Marshal Ferdinand Foch propheticly described in 1919 as "an armistice for twenty years."

True to Foch's forecast, the peace would be broken just over twenty years later by another veteran of the Great War, a man who drew on his own visionaries to exploit the combined arms theories of British strategist Colonel J.F.C. Fuller. They created an irresistible force that swept into Poland in 1939 and engulfed France and the Low Countries in 1940. The veteran was Adolph Hitler. The visionaries were Guderian and von Seeckt. The tactics became known simply as, "Blitzkrieg."

This work is a historical novel. It follows the development of tank warfare through the eyes of a young man wounded at the Battle of Loos in 1915. Suffering what we would now recognize as Post-Traumatic Stress Disorder, he's drawn-into the development of the tank as a means to break the defensive stalemate on the Western Front and finds himself playing an ever-increasing role in the tumultuous battles that result. But it is also a coming of age story about a young man that discovers love and comradeship among the most tragic circumstances. As such it is the story of all wars, at once brutal and hateful, yet filled with moments of beauty and simple human decency.

Heavily researched, I've done my best to remain historically accurate throughout. Having crawled inside the Mark IV, I've contemplated the misery of fighting a battle from its hot, cramped, fume-filled confines. Many of the characters in this story are real. Having read their writings, I attempt to portray their personalities and contributions to tank warfare as faithfully as possible. Other, equally important, contributors to tank warfare are omitted for the sake of keeping a complex story as simple as possible. Their exclusion should in no way be viewed as an attempt to diminish their exceptional accomplishments.

To help ensure the most realistic setting amid the fog and misery of war, I drew on my own experiences and those of close friends who served alongside me in Afghanistan, Iraq and other lesser-known theaters of 21st Century conflict. To provide immediacy to a war that began more than a hundred years ago, the entire story is written in present-tense, using traditional English spelling. Finally, as an American author writing a uniquely British story, I attempt to lend authenticity by enlisting the excellent editorial skills of two distinguished British colleagues with whom I served in Afghanistan, Bea Walcot and Michael Osman, both scholars in their own right. Any errors or omissions are mine alone.

Note

The vernacular of the Great War was unique. A glossary is provided at the end of the book to define acronyms, phrases and terms with which the reader may not be familiar.

Steve Howery
Denver, Colorado, 2015

PROLOGUE
France
September 1915

A line of sweating, khaki clad Tommies shuffle blindly through darkness along split wooden duckboards. It's a starless night, lit intermittently by the pop of distant flares painting the ground with an eerie yellow glow that highlights the craggy contours of shattered trees, distant slag heaps, and stagnant water-filled shell holes. As the light fades, Maxim guns claw into the darkness, bullets ricocheting lazily off the barbed wire and expiring in the distance.

"Come on, you lot," rasps Company Sergeant Major Adkins. "We've only got an hour before dawn!"

Behind him, Private John "Jack" Mallory, head crowned by a soft, "gor-blimey" service cap, staggers wearily beneath 60 pounds of kit. Suddenly, the soldier in front curses, rifle clattering against the duckboards as his foot submerges into a bottomless sea of mud. Mallory grasps the man's pack strap and drags him from the mire.

"You okay, mate?"

"Yeah. But it's so bleedin' dark I can't see me hand in front of me face."

Sergeant Major Adkins looms before them. "By the time you can see it, Fritz will be able to see it too. Now keep moving."

Squinting into the darkness, Adkins peers down the line of recent replacements from England. "Bloody hell," he murmurs.

The skinny, half-trained rabble is part of "Kitchener's Mob", citizen soldiers recruited to replace the ranks of England's professional army - an army decimated in all but name during the first Battle of the Marne and subsequent "race to the sea" that resulted in a quagmire the length of the Western Front, from the North Sea to the Swiss border.

Mallory shifts his aching shoulders beneath cutting pack straps and leans into the march, willing his way forward despite growing exhaustion. After six months of grueling training, he's finally inching toward his first battle. Though his excitement was tempered earlier in the day by the sight of wounded men slogging rearward, heads and shattered limbs swathed in bloody bandages and whimpering, gas-blinded soldiers led like docile sheep by only slightly less wounded comrades.

As the new army stared in muted shock at the remnants of the old, the "Old Army" seemed barely to notice the reinforcements. Friendly gestures were ignored. No welcome was extended. The hollow stares of shell-shocked men seemed to look right through the fresh, young replacements. Even the unwounded veterans appeared numb, displaying indifference bordering on hostility.

"Sir," whispered Mallory. "What's wrong with them?"

Adkins glanced impassively at the passing soldiers. "Wounded, mostly," he replied with a shrug.

"But their eyes... I mean, *look* at them."

"The war," sighed Adkins. "It's just... the war."

Mallory began to suspect what is being touted as "The Great War" is not going to be the glorious fight he anticipated.

Now, as they trudge through the darkness, a single question arises. "Where the hell are we heading?" he asks no one in particular.

From behind comes a whispered response. "Loos".

CHAPTER 1
The Battle of Loos, France
September 1915

"You're *late!*" snaps Lieutenant Chilcott.

Sergeant Major Adkins sighs, his gaze sweeping the line of fresh, scared faces before returning to the lieutenant.

"Right," grumbles Chilcott. "This lot will be replacing 6th platoon out on the left wing. Try and get them into position before the morning hate." He glances at his wristwatch. "Pick a dependable man and have him take 'em down. We have a meeting with the new battalion commander in a few minutes."

Adkins points at Mallory. "You're acting corporal."

"Why me?"

"Because you're the only bloody fool that didn't fall on his face coming into the line, tha's why."

"Yes, Sir. What shall I do?"

"Fifth Brigade holds this section of the line. C Company is deployed between 'Deadman's Trench' and 'Berkeley Street' – just watch for the trench signs. Take these men down there and tell Lieutenant Ashdown you're to relieve first Platoon. Lieutenant Chilcott and I will be along shortly. Do you have that?"

"Yes, Sir," responds Mallory, his spine a little straighter now that he's been entrusted with responsibility.

"Off with you, then."

Chilcott watches the young soldiers depart. "Good God, they're *so* young."

"You were a ranker before the war, Sir. Youth makes good soldiers - young men believe they're invincible."

Chilcott rubs his bloodshot eyes. "I suppose so. I just hate being the one to teach them otherwise."

"We all learn eventually, sir. This lot will learn a bit earlier than their mates back home, that's all."

A runner dodges down the trench toward them.

"Sir! The colonel is ready for the brief."

"Right. On our way," replies Chilcott tiredly. He motions for Adkins to follow and together they trudge down the communication trench to the support line a hundred yards to the rear. Nearing the battalion dugout, they step aside to allow a wiring party to pass the opposite direction, their faces darkened with burnt cork and carrying wire-cutters to clear lanes through the barbed wire for the upcoming attack.

Arriving at the battalion headquarters, Chilcott draws aside a worn canvas flap. He and Adkins descend fifteen feet into the damp, earthen dugout.

The battalion commander looks up at them and glances at his watch. "Didn't your mother teach you about punctuality, Lieutenant?"

"My apologies, sir," responds Chilcott. Clearly, his commander is in no mood for excuses.

Lieutenant Colonel Woodward nods curtly. "As I was saying, the Hun in our sector has been drawn-off by French action on our right. General French believes this is an opportune time to punch through the line here at Loos." He points to the map with an unsheathed bayonet and traces the proposed line of advance.

"The Hun has already introduced gas, so we are going to reply in-kind. At oh-five-fifty on the morning of the twenty-fifth, the engineers are going to unleash 140 tonnes of chlorine into the Hun lines – you've probably already noticed canisters appearing in your trenches. The liberal use of gas and a rolling barrage should lay-low any Hun in the first two lines."

An engineer captain in the front row shifts awkwardly and clears his throat.

"Do you have something to add, Captain?" asks Woodward, annoyed.

"Well… Sir. We're not yet certain about the wind direction the morning of the attack…"

"Nonsense! I was just outside and the weather seems to be cooperating splendidly."

"Yes, Sir. But this time of year the wind is a bit iffy. You see, it can be blowing steadily to the east all night then suddenly… well… reverse itself first thing in the morning."

"Hmph. We can hardly plan for the unforeseeable," snorts Woodward. "Besides, everyone's been issued smoke hoods so I expect there'll be no problem in any case."

Chilcott glances discretely at Adkins who appears wholly untroubled by the course of the conversation.

"As I was saying," continues Woodward. "We'll smash him with a barrage and release the gas to keep him hunkered down when the barrage lifts."

"How long a barrage, Sir?" asks a lieutenant from another company.

"Three days."

Officers and NCOs from the new units nod sagely. Those who've been in the line for more than a few weeks know better.

"Jump off is at oh-six-thirty on the twenty-fifth. But have your people ready before we release the gas. Don't want anyone caught unawares by any blow-back, eh?" He peers imperiously around the dugout. "Questions?" His eyes survey the group, searching for any sign of weakness. "Well, then. If there is nothing else, I'll see you on the field."

The officers and NCOs file from the dugout and fan out into the trenches to return to their platoons. Certain he's clear of the other officers, Chicot whispers to Adkins.

"My arse, he'll see us 'on the field'. He'll be right there in that bloody dugout while we go over the top!"

The stoic Adkins remains mute.

Chilcott pulls him into a traverse. "Come on, Sar' Major," he insists. "You know as well as I those smoke hoods are useless. *If* you *can* breathe through them, the lenses get so fogged you can't see where the hell you're going!"

Adkins stares impassively back at his platoon leader.

"And a lousy three day barrage?" continues Chilcott. "What bloody good will *that* do?"

"Sir," responds Adkins finally. "Sar' Major Bedford tells me we ain't got the shells necessary for a proper barrage. Whatever reserve ammunition we have is goin' to be needed when Fritz counterattacks – and he *will* counterattack."

Mallory rests on the fire step, Short Magazine Lee Enfield rifle across his lap as he picks mud from the cleats on his boot using a detached bayonet.

"Blimey, what is the stink?" asks his friend Private Miller, a sour expression on his boyish face.

Mallory sniffs tentatively. "Dunno. Somethin' rotten."

"Gas?"

"If it was, we'd already be dead, wouldn't we?"

Miller takes another sniff and wretches. "I hope it passes soon. I wouldn't want to live with that!"

"You'll get used to it," comes a voice from behind.

Mallory and Miller turn to see Chilcott coming up the trench followed by the Sergeant Major. Mallory springs to attention, right hand snapping smartly to the brim of his cap.

"Sah! The men are posted!" he barks a bit more loudly than intended.

Rather than returning the salute, Chilcott casually lowers Mallory's hand back to his side. "We don't salute at the front, Corporal. Rather tends to draw fire. You don't want to get your lieutenant killed, do you?"

"Sir? Of course not! Uh, Corporal? Sir, I'm just a private."

"Turning down the promotion?" asks Adkins kindly.

"No Sir!"

"Sir," asks Miller. "What did you say we'll 'get used to'?"

"Putrefied corpses," responds Chilcott. "After a couple of days, a body begins to decompose and lets-off a hell of a stink."

"Why don't we bury 'em?" asks Mallory.

Adkins shrugs the rifle from his shoulder and fixes the bayonet. "Give me your cap, Mallory." he snorts. Mallory hands over his gor-blimey. Adkins places it on the tip of his bayonet and raises it above the sandbags.

Within a few seconds a shot rings-out, knocking the cap to the bottom of the trench. Adkins retrieves it and pokes his finger through the hole through the crown.

"Do I have to spell it out?"

Mallory's face pales. "N-no Sir."

"Good man," replies Chilcott. "Now we've resolved you're not insane, so why don't we get out of this pissing rain so we can discuss the upcoming show?"

Mallory follows Chilcott and Adkins into a small dugout burrowed into the side of the trench, its roof layered with corrugated iron and logs beneath several feet of damp earth. The door is covered by a gas cape trapping humidity inside the stale chamber.

As they enter, an orderly pours tea into battered tin cups. He passes one to Chilcott and one to Adkins.

"And for him too," nods Chilcott and the orderly grudgingly shares the last few dregs.

"Mallory, I'll be forthright," announces Chilcott. "This is a new platoon cobbled together from replacements. We've not yet received any experienced NCOs, so I'm going to have to count on you to recommend men of skill and character."

"Sir?"

"What the Lieutenant is saying, Corporal, is he wants you to recommend three other men from the platoon to become acting NCOs," explains Adkins.

"Sir, I'm not qualified to choose…"

"Damn it all!" curses Chilcott. "We jump the bags in three days. I need your opinion of the men you've trained with for the past few months. Step-up, son. Sar' Major Adkins and I will make the final call."

Mallory sits up, his face flushed. "Going over the top, sir? Are we really? So soon?"

"Soon enough," replies Chilcott. "Why? Are you scared?"

"No, sir!" blurts Mallory, squaring his shoulders. "We'll give 'em hell!"

"Anxious to get at 'em are you?"

"Why, yes sir!"

Chilcott turns to Adkins. "Perhaps the Hun *isn't* our worst enemy."

"Sir?" asks Mallory in confusion.

Adkins shakes his head discretely.

Chilcott sighs. "Nothing, son. As you say, we'll certainly give 'em what-for. Now, the names?"

"Notting, Sir. He's a big guy. Calm, steady. Everyone respects him. And Smith. He used to be a boxer and knows how get men to behave. And there's Fisher, sir. Jewish chap, but a right smart bloke who can handle a bayonet. They're probably the best of the lot, Sir!"

Chilcott smiles benignly. "Excellent. Run along and fetch them for me. We'll see what kind of men they are."

Rising to leave, Mallory glances forlornly down at his half-empty cup of tea.

"Go on, go on. Take it with you," encourages Chilcott.

Mallory smiles gratefully and disappears through the gas cape, cup in-hand.

"This is a hell of a way to run an army, Sar' Major," sighs Chilcott.

"By the end of the week, sir, they'll all be veterans," responds Adkins. "One way or the other."

That evening, all hell breaks loose.

A thrill races through the men as artillery rounds scream overhead, the ground shuddering as the first rounds impact on the German trenches. Mallory inches onto the fire step to peer through a vacant firing loop.

"Wassit like up there?" shouts Miller.

"Bloody inferno," reports Mallory. "No one could survive such a thumping!"

A cheer erupts within the trench.

"Shut up, you blighters!" barks Adkins. "You'll be sick enough of the shellin' before it's done."

As predicted, after several hours, the rumbling artillery begins to lose its novelty. Nearly deafened, hands and feet numb from constant vibration, those on sentry duty stand to their posts. The remainder of the men shelter in dugouts in search of comparative peace.

Mallory reaches into his pocket and retrieves a deck of cards. "Anyone for a game 'a Whist?" he asks as he limbers-up the cards.

"Count me in!" Miller plops an ammo crate beside the table and takes a seat across from Mallory. Two others wander over, dragging cots and upending crates as they gather around the rickety table.

The man to the left shuffles the deck and hands it to Mallory. Mallory finishes dealing, turns the last card face-up, and places the deck on the table. The men recover their cards, fan-open their hands and begin laying down cards.

"Any news on when the show will start?" asks Miller.

"Couple of days, the lieutenant says," reports Mallory. "Why? You in a hurry?"

"Not me. The longer they pound the bastards, the easier it'll be to walk right over 'em."

"Do you really think so?" asks Mallory with mild interest.

Miller glances up at the dirt ceiling, vibrations shaking loose a cascade of dust. "Don't see how anyone can survive *that!*"

Adkins pulls-back the gas cape and descends into the dugout. "Glad to see you're putting your free time to productive use."

"Hullo, Sir," replies Mallory and the men begin to rise as a group.

Adkins waves them back to their seats. He leans his rifle in the corner and removes his cap.

"Sentries posted?"

"Yes, Sir."

"Good. I want you to check your men's equipment tomorrow. If they're missing anything, get me a requisition immediately. Make sure their rifles are clean, bayonets sharp, and make damned sure they've not been at their iron rations."

"Yes, Sir."

As the game proceeds, Adkins wanders around behind Mallory and peers at his cards, indicating one to play. Mallory glances up at him questioningly. Adkins nods. Mallory places his card on the table and completes the trick.

"Shit!"

Miller beams and nods at his partner.

"Not fair!" protests a soldier. "The Sar' Major coached you!"

Adkins glances at the soldier's discarded hand. "You never had a chance, Morse. Where the hell did *you* learn to play?"

Morse shrugs indifferently. "Don't know how. I just wanted to keep busy, so I joined this lot."

Everyone laughs.

"Sir," asks Miller. "What's it like?"

The burly Adkins leans casually against the mud wall and shakes a Woodbine from its pack, eyes searching the ceiling as if deep in thought. "Well, the first time is always awkward," he replies, hesitating to light the cigarette and exhale the first breath of smoke into the dingy room.

The men lean forward in rapt anticipation.

"You know, not really knowing how to do it, but itchin' to have a go," he continues. "But it's worth it just to get the first time out of the way."

"So it gets easier after the first time?" responds Miller, encouraged.

"Second time's definitely better than the first, more so if you find a pro. She'll show you everything you need to know and won't mind you're inexperienced."

"*She*, who?" asks Mallory.

"The bird. The chippie."

"What are you talkin' about?" asks Miller.

"Sex," Adkins responds innocently. "Ain't it what you was askin'?"

The cramped dugout echoes with laughter.

"I meant the first time 'over the top'," Miller explains in exasperation.

Adkins shrugs, a twinkle in his eye. "Same thing."

More laughter.

"You'll do fine," promises Adkins. "Just maintain your intervals and keep moving. You'll be in Fritz's trench in no time, ready to put 'em to the bayonet."

"But…"

"Look, son," explains Adkins. "Nothing in this world can prepare you for your fist step into no-man's land. Just remember your training, stick with your mates and watch out for one 'nother."

"But it *is* exciting, isn't it?" interjects Mallory hopefully.

"So is Hell," replies Adkins. "Don't mean you want to go there."

In a pre-dawn downpour, the newly appointed Corporals take charge and spread their men throughout the muddy length of trench. The day before, sappers distributed wooden plank ladders. Now, the first line of Tommies balance precariously on the lip of the decaying fire step, the remainder lining the water logged trench awaiting the whistle to send them over the top.

Chilcott climbs onto the fire step and raises a dampened finger cautiously above the lip of the trench. A breeze licks his finger on its way east. He nods down at Adkins.

"Hoods!" barks Adkins over the roar of the guns.

The order is met by an annoying clank of rifles and bayonets colliding as soldiers struggle to balance their weapons while pulling the baggy sacks over their heads, lining-up the eye pieces and tucking the hoods inside their collars.

Placed at intervals along the trench are huge 190 lb. "ooja" cylinders manhandled into place by engineers over the past week. Today, men in awkward head-to-toe chemical suits stand ready to initiate the attack at the prescribed time.

The engineer officer-in-charge of the nearest string of canisters stares intently at his wristwatch. He gives the signal. An engineer climbs onto the fire step and twists a handle on the valve. From the tube extending into no-man's land, a greenish vapor hisses from the nozzle and expands into a cloud drifting languidly toward the German lines.

Chilcott moves over to the ladder, cap beneath his arm, gas hood pushed back on his head, rain-spattered face exposed. A burnished brass whistle dangles from his lips, its chain entangled with the lanyard leading from around his neck to the .455 caliber Webley Mark VI pistol in his hand.

Time passes slowly. Finally, "one minute!" he shouts. "One minute!"

The ground trembles as mines tunneled beneath the German positions explode in rapid succession. Anxious Tommies nearest the ladders strain forward like a surging tide.

The tenor of the barrage changes, the gunfire lifting to the Germans' reserve line. Chilcott blows the whistle with all his might.

Mallory scurries up the ladder and emerges atop the sandbags. Having seen nothing but the drudgery of the trench since arriving, he hesitates momentarily, taken aback at the panoramic view of the swampy battlefield.

Waist-high barbed wire entanglements were dragged aside into piles during the night. The vista beyond is void of trees but for the few lonely shattered stumps standing forlornly amid the destruction. Several hundred yards away, the German line stands shrouded in an eerie mix of gray mist, white smoke, billowing black soot, and translucent green chlorine. Tall, black conical-shaped slag heaps rise in small hillocks across the landscape, dominated in the center by an iron mining structure homesick Tommies refer to as "Tower Bridge".

Mallory lurches forward, heart pumping as he wheezes through the stifling gas hood, lenses fogging as he staggers half-blindly across the pockmarked earth. His rifle at high-port, he weaves beyond the last of the defensive wire and emerges into the swampy field: no-man's land.

Thousands of Tommies, unidentifiable in shapeless gas hoods, surge forward on his flanks, small clumps of men forming as they seek solace in proximity to one another.

Beside Mallory, a soldier trips and lands face-first in the gooey mud. The brim of his cap sticks in the earth as he staggers to his feet. Flinging his gas hood to the ground, Miller screams, "I can't breathe!" He inhales the smoke-filled air. "There's no gas! It's moved-on!" He jerks his cap from the mud and clamps it back onto his sweat-soaked head, smiling broadly.

Others push-back their hoods, broad grins erupting on their faces as they recognize friends. Cries of "Hello chum!" and "Wortcher, mate" fill the air.

Chilcott raises his hood. "Keep moving! Keep moving!" he yells. "And put your bloody hoods back on!"

"But sir...," begins Miller.

"We must reach the Hun line before they man the machineguns!" growls the lieutenant. "Now put on your damned hoods and MOVE!" He jerks his hood back over his face, tucks it beneath his collar and continues leading the platoon forward.

Mallory follows his lieutenant toward the German lines, barely able to make-out the hazy form ahead as moisture condenses on his lenses. Enemy wire floats into view, thirty yards deep and largely uncut by the barrage.

Through the smoke and mist, flashes erupt across the wire, the supersonic snap of bullets passing close-by as the dreaded German Maxims open fire. Tommies begin falling around him. Some spin violently to the ground. Others sink pitifully into the mud as if sleep has suddenly overtaken them.

Ahead, Chilcott glances back at his flagging troops withering beneath the hail of machinegun fire. His arm rises, pistol in-hand, as he waves his platoon forward. At the apex of the arc, the arm freezes. Knees buckling, he collapses like a rag doll and disappears from sight beneath the haze.

Mallory freezes. "*Sir!*" he screams like a lost child.

"Keep moving!" bellows Adkins, propelling Mallory forward. Gasping for breath, boots heavy with caked mud, Mallory struggles to the edge of the German wire, miraculously alive amid the mounting glut of twisted bodies blocking his path.

Bullets tug at his sleeves. A near miss rips the cap from his head, the wind of its passing knocking him senseless. He stumbles into the wire. Boots slipping in the blood and mud, he flails helplessly against the barbs holding him firmly in their grasp.

"Help!" he screams. "*Help me!*"

Adkins' strong hands grasp Mallory's pack straps and drag him from the wire. Shoving him toward a gap, Adkins shouts, "Keep moving, son! We're nearly there!"

The world goes suddenly dark. Mallory drops his rifle and gropes frantically around him. "Sar' Major! Sar' Major! *Where are you?*" he screams in terror.

A hand grips his ankle and tugs insistently. "Get down, Jack! Get down!"

Sinking to his knees Mallory allows himself to be dragged into a water-filled crater. Hands slap at his smoke hood and the lenses begin to clear. He cups his hands and splashes muddy water from the bottom of the crater onto his mask. Blood flows from the lenses as Miller's boyish face swims into view.

"What happened? Where's Sar' Major?"

"He's dead," yells Miller.

"No... he was just..." Mallory edges up over the crater and spots the twisted remains of Sergeant Major Adkins, his head shattered by shrapnel. Mallory glances down and realizes he's spattered with Adkins' blood and brain matter.

"Oh my God!"

"I've got to get out of here!" Miller screams and claws his way to the opposite side of the hole.

Mallory seizes his friend's belt and drags him back. "Stay down, you moron! There's a machinegun up there!"

"I... I can't!" shrieks Miller. "Gas!"

"What about it?"

"It's coming back!"

Mallory rolls onto his back and peers up into the sky. Through smeared lenses, he notices the green sheen drifting back over them. The wind has shifted against them.

"Where's your mask!?"

"Out *there!!!*" screams Miller and renews his struggle.

"If you go out there, you'll be killed!" yells Mallory.

"If I stay here, I'm dead!!!" wheezes Miller as gas settles into the shell hole.

Mallory releases Miller's belt and watches him disappear from the crater and slither through the mire back toward British lines. German bullets churn the earth around him.

"He won't make it," breathes Mallory. "Oh, mother of God, *he's not going to make it!*"

Abruptly, his training comes flooding back. Recovering his rifle from the mud, he thrusts the barrel onto the edge of the crater and begins snapping-off rounds toward the German machinegun, aimed rapid fire one shot after the next. Brass shell casings accumulate in the mud as he snipes for the loophole from behind which the Maxim is firing.

Each time he jacks the bolt rearward to chamber another round, he glances despairingly over his shoulder. With each glimpse, Miller seems to be moving slower, slower, slower. Finally, a string of bullets rip over him. His shoulders shudder and with a last, gasping breath... he dies.

"Bastards!" shrieks Mallory. "BASTARDS!"

The "taka-taka-taka" of the Maxim pauses.

Leaping from the crater, Mallory dashes headlong toward the German trench, bayonet thrust forward as he bounds over a path of dead Tommies fallen across the wire. Around him, men emerge from their muddy refuge and join the charge. A swelling cry of anguish and fury rise from the Tommies as they rip their way through the wire to break like a wave into the first line of German trenches.

Mallory drops into the trench, startling a machinegun crew. Caught reloading, they abandon their weapon and scatter. "No, you bloody don't!" blurts Mallory and chases-down the nearest German, bayonetting him and twisting his rifle to draw the bloody blade from the man's back.

He raises his rifle to fire at the remaining Germans fleeing down the trench. "Click!" With shaking hands, he jerks-back the bolt. An empty shell casing 'pings' past his ear as he chambers a fresh round and again raises his rifle. A punch to the chest knocks the wind from him; his rifle drops to the ground.

"Bloody hell..."

Confused, he bends down to recover his rifle.

A German appears suddenly from around the traverse, eyes wild inside the alien gas mask. He hurls himself upon Mallory. They grapple against the mud wall, each clawing for advantage over the other. Finally, Mallory locks his fingers around the German's throat and rips the gas mask from his face. Massive yellow teeth yawn before him, bloodshot eyes bulging from their sockets as the two men slide to the floor of the trench. A cloud of misty green chlorine envelopes them.

"Nein!' gasps the German. "Bitte..." he wheezes, drool oozing from his lips as blisters form within his lungs and begin to burst. Finally, his eyes roll back into his head as he lets out one, last pathetic wheeze.

Then there is silence.

Mallory glances up, cramped fingers still locked around the German's throat. He's alone in the trench with the dead. Looking down in horror at the blistered face of his dead enemy, he releases his grip. Head swimming, he staggers to his feet and stoops to recover his weapon. Blood trickles down his arm and drips from his sleeve onto the rifle's stock. His eyes follow the stain on his tunic to the torn fabric and mud-red tinge spreading across his chest.

"Oh, God…"

Darkness closes around him.

CHAPTER 2
Calais, France
October - November 1915

A white blur hovers overhead. Faint hissing echoes in his ears.

"*Gas!*" He claws violently in search of his smoke helmet.

"No! Stop it! You're all right. It's okay!" Strong hands press him down. "Doctor, help me!" cries a disembodied voice.

"Young man! Young man!" booms a deep voice. "It's all right. It's all right. You're in hospital!"

Slowly, agonizingly, Mallory awakes from the nightmare. Standing over him are a doctor in a white surgical gown and a blue-clad nurse in a bloodied white apron.

"What... where?" he rasps.

"Get him some water," orders the doctor. The nurse hastily pours water from a pitcher and kneels beside Mallory, placing the cup to his lips. As he gulps thirstily, the nurse runs her long fingers gently through his hair as if caressing a child after a nightmare. When the cup is empty, he collapses back into the pillow.

"Where am I?" he croaks through a parched throat.

"Duchess of Sutherland Hospital, Calais," explains the doctor. "You're badly wounded, young man," he explains as he reexamines Mallory's sutures. "When you're stable, we'll get you on a ferry back to Blighty. That sound all right? Until then, you must remain still so the wound doesn't reopen."

"I... I thought heard gas," replies Mallory, feebly.

The nurse blushes endearingly. "I'm sorry," she replies. "We were whispering. We didn't wish to wake you."

Still trembling, Mallory smiles weakly with relief.

"You're quite the special young man," announces the doctor.

Mallory presses his eyes closed. Images of his friends, his leaders, his company, lying dead in the mud crowd his mind.

"There's nothing special about me," he mumbles. "I'm just a survivor."

"And quite the survivor, it seems! You were left for dead at a casualty clearing station. Some chap on the burial detail heard you groan and got the M.O. to take a second look. A bullet through the lung nicked your heart and the other one broke your clavicle and passed right through your back. With a collapsed lung and loss of blood, I'm frankly surprised you made it back here to Calais."

"They should have left me," mumbles Mallory.

"That's just the after-effects of anaesthesia talking. You'll feel better soon, what with the decoration and the trip home..."

"Decoration?"

The doctor reaches in to the bedside table and withdraws a medal. "A major from General Haig's staff dropped-by several days ago. You've been awarded the Distinguished Conduct Medal for leading some sort of bayonet charge. Isn't *that* something?"

"No," insists Mallory. "It must have been someone else."

"Isn't it marvellous," beams the nurse. "Such modesty."

Mallory examines the silver medal adorned with crimson and blue. The ribbon flows over his hand like a stream of blood.

"No. It's not mine," he growls and flings the award across the room.

The next three weeks are a blur of repeated surgeries and recovery, of nightmares and flashbacks and faces of dead and dying friends. Little-by-little, Mallory's strength returns and the prospects of returning home become increasingly attractive.

He imagines a home posting, serving out the rest of the war in a respectable desk job. Before the war, he studied economics at university. Perhaps he can obtain a position as a clerk in the War Ministry.

Sure. That'd be all right. Wouldn't it?

The mere idea they might return him to the trenches seems absurd. How can they return someone to battle when he's seen his entire platoon slaughtered? *There must be a regulation or something... No. Inconceivable. I'll be posted home.*

After several weeks, the doctor arrives to examine him for the last time. "Yes, yes. Healing fine. I'll certify you to travel, but you mustn't over-exert yourself chasing skirts 'round Piccadilly," he scolds.

"Will I be fit for active service once this heals?"

"That'll be up to the Medical Review Board, of course. Anxious to get back up to the front with your mates, eh?"

Mallory smiles weakly. *I have no mates at the front.*

After several weeks convalescing in the City of London Red Cross Hospital, Mallory finally earns home-leave.

"Come back in two weeks and the medical board will provide your disposition," he is told.

But his young body is healing much faster than expected and he knows the demand for troops in Flanders grows daily. Deep down, he realizes he will be declared "fit for active service" and returned to the trenches.

The thought horrifies him.

Searching for solace, he takes the train to Wallingford, fifty miles west of London, to visit his last surviving family member. A spinster at 28, his older sister, Adelaide, works as a secretary at St. Mary Le More and St. Leonard Parish.

He crosses the medieval stone bridge and wanders into town, the cobblestone street glistening with morning dew. Inhaling the fresh, humid air, he feels a rare sense of inner peace.

As he strolls past the Corn Exchange, the clock on the church tower strikes 9 a.m. He crosses the street and leans against an empty planter in front of the Post Office. Elderly men and women, young mothers and children, spill from the church and disperse down the street - apparently weekday prayer services have increased in popularity with the advent of war.

A young man is last to leave. He closes the church doors, shoves his hands into threadbare pockets and starts across the street. Mid-way, he glances-up and spots Mallory, arm in a sling, dressed in the thick woolen khaki 1902 Pattern Service Dress uniform, puttees and peaked cap of a field soldier. The young man turns abruptly and shuffles away, head down, shoulders in a cringing slouch.

"*Jack!*"

He glances up to see Adelaide and the vicar, waving to him. As he crosses the street, Adelaide takes a running leap and throws her arms around his neck.

"Bloody Hell!"

"Oh, my!" she squeals and releases him.

"No. No. It's okay." He gently takes her in his good right arm and kisses her on the cheek. He feels her warm tears against his face as she clings to him.

He releases her and she beams. "Father Hall, this is my brother, Jack."

"Good morning, my son. Glad to see you looking so well."

Mallory glances down at the bandages bulging beneath his tunic. "I wouldn't say 'well', Father."

"If you can walk away after a fight, you're well enough," responds Fr. Hall with a paternal wink. "How long will you be in town?"

"Yes, how long?" squeals Adelaide.

"I... I dunno. At least until the review board decides my status."

"Have you a place to stay?"

"I thought I'd grab a room...," begins Mallory, motioning vaguely toward the pub on the corner.

"Nonsense! I've got a guest room at the rectory. And Adelaide lives close-by. It would be my pleasure to have one of our boys in uniform as my guest. Save you a bit of money, too."

"Please *do*," blurts Adelaide.

Mallory smiles at his dowdy older sister. "That's very kind of you."

Glancing over his shoulder, he spots the young man still shuffling down the street. "Father, can I ask...do you know him?"

"Ah, young Jimmy Dalton. He wasn't rude was he?"

"No, more like... afraid."

"Well, I shouldn't be surprised. At this stage of the war, any young man not serving is assumed to be either medically unfit, a munitions worker, or a coward. In any case, seeing you probably embarrassed him."

"If it bothers him so much, why isn't he serving?"

"He's the last surviving son of three boys lost during the first weeks of the war. His mother forbids him to join. I imagine he's ashamed to be left behind while his mates are all at the front."

"But *I* don't care."

"It *is* complicated, isn't it? Young women are distributing feathers to men who aren't serving. It's all rather humiliating," explains Fr. Hall.

Jimmy rounds the corner and disappears from sight.

"Shall we go?" Fr. Hall asks.

The three of them stroll casually down the cobblestone street toward the rectory. Removing the key from his waistcoat pocket, Fr. Hall turns to Adelaide. "Why don't we drop-by The Swan for a bite to eat in celebration of Jack's safe return."

"Wonderful!" responds Adelaide. "I'll put on a clean dress and be back directly." She kisses Jack on the cheek and scurries away.

"Lovely young lady," sighs Fr. Hall. "Wish there was some worthy young chap to cast a glance her direction."

"Perhaps after the war," responds Mallory tersely. "If there are any young men left."

"Hmmm. Yes," mumbles Fr. Hall as they enter the foyer. "Why don't you wait for me in the study? I'll get out of my vestments and we can go for that meal."

The echo of Fr. Hall's footsteps disappear into the stairwell as Mallory wanders into a small, musty room lined with sagging book-laden shelves and shabby, fading wallpaper. Beside the window are two threadbare, but comfortable-looking, chintz armchairs and a reading lamp, its yellowed shade cocked to one side.

As he begins to sit, something draws his attention across the room. Rising abruptly, he approaches what turns out to be a sun-bleached pith helmet dangling from a hook on the wall, a straight-bladed cavalry sword hanging beneath. The display is surrounded by framed photographs, tarnished regimental badges, and other mementos of a war gone-by.

"The Transvaal, 1902," announces a voice from behind.

Mallory examines one of the photos. "That's *you?*" he asks, pointing to a young officer standing beside his mount.

"Yes. I was a lieutenant in Paget's Horse, 19th Battalion, Imperial Yeomanry."

"*You* were in the Boer War?"

"The second one, yes."

"Cavalry, eh? Not of much use in this war."

"Well, not horse-bound variety, anyway."

"What other kind is there?"

"You'd be surprised."

"Would I?"

Standing, smiling at one another, Fr. Hall clearly has no intention of elaborating.

"So," he declares. "Let's retrieve Adelaide and see what kind of trouble we can get into, eh?"

The ancient inn reeks of history. Its dirt floors and low, smoke-stained ceilings seems host to the ghosts of a thousand weary peasants, of barristers and bankers and King's tax-collectors. Patrons glance-up in surprise as Fr. Hall enters the room with Mallory and his sister at his side.

The innkeeper waddles over and offers a pudgy hand. "Welcome," he belches and shakes Mallory's hand enthusiastically. "Back from France, are you?"

"Yes sir."

"Second Battalion, Ox & Bucks," announces Fr. Hall. "Recovering from wounds received at Loos."

"Well then, lunch is on me," insists the innkeeper as he drags a filthy rag over the table's scarred surface and motions for the three of them to sit.

Adelaide slips onto the bench beside Mallory and locks her arm through his. "So tell us about the war!" She insists eagerly.

Mallory's face falls. "Not much to say, actually. I wasn't in it very long."

"Long enough to earn a medal!"

"Only because I was the only lamb to survive the slaughter."

"*Jack!*"

"It's okay, Adelaide, he's just not ready to talk about his experiences yet. *Right,* Jack?" Fr. Hall's kindly eyes narrow in warning.

"Yes, of course Adelaide. Sorry. I'm just tired and these bandages itch like hell."

As the inn fills, people drop by the table to pay their respects.

"Givin' the Hun what for?" asks a man.

"Yeah, sure," responds Mallory with a non-committal shrug.

"Why, if I was a few years younger, I'd be over there showin' 'em how it's done!"

"Well, I'm sure they'd take you."

"Both my sons are over there right now," announces a frail woman in a trembling voice. "Do you know Bill or James Davies?"

"No, mum, I'm afraid not. There are a lot of blokes over there I don't know."

"Hmph!" snorts a farmer. "Bloody capitalist conspiracy, if you ask me. Just another way for the bourgeois to get rich off the backs of the proletariat."

"I wouldn't know. I'm just a soldier."

As visitors rattle-on with senseless comments about the war, Mallory's attention wanders. Across the room, he spots a woman, not old, but aged in a manner caused only by tragedy. Slumped over her meal, she picks at her food and casts him furtive glances.

"Mrs. Waddington," whispers Fr. Hall. "Lost her only son at Mons."

Weariness settles over Mallory. He gulps and doesn't reply.

"Well, young man!" comes a booming voice from behind. A pudgy hand settles on his shoulder. "About got this thing wrapped up, eh? The Hun can't hold on much longer!"

"Oh, yes. They can."

"Nonsense! If General French had a bit of moral fortitude, the Boche would be out of Flanders by now!"

Sweat beading on his forehead, Mallory hooks a finger inside his collar and tugs, stifling a sudden urge to thrust a bayonet through the bellicose banker's protruding gut.

"It's not about moral fortitude," responds Mallory. "It's about entrenched positions, machineguns, barbed wire, artillery…" He glares up at the man and announces sharply, "It's about how many men you are willing to murder to gain a few hundred yards of worthless damned dirt!"

"Oh, I say!" scoffs the banker.

Mallory stands abruptly. "Excuse me. I have to visit the lavatory." He darts out the back door, eyes desperately sweeping the garden in search of the outbuilding. Jerking open the door, he steps inside, closes it and collapses against the wall, pulse racing as he gasps for air. He braces himself over the toilet and vomits, the tension flowing out with the contents of his stomach. Throat raw, he collapses against the wall, buries his face in his hands and weeps silently.

A knock at the door startles him.

"You 'bout finished in there?"

"Um, yes. Just a moment." Mallory drags a scratchy wool sleeve across his eyes, straightens, and opens the door.

A gnarled old man glances up at his uniform. "Been overseas, eh? Rich French food's givin' you fits?"

Bloody bully beef and biscuits...

"Yes, sir," lies Mallory and stalks quickly back toward the inn. Entering, he realizes he's been gone long enough that Adelaide and Fr. Hall have finished their meals. As he takes a seat, Fr. Hall motions to the innkeeper, who goes into the kitchen and returns with a warm plate.

"Thank, you," mumbles Mallory.

"Are you all right, Jack?" asks Adelaide, her brow furrowed in anxious concern.

Mallory pokes indifferently at his food. "No. No, I don't think so."

"Adelaide, why don't you go across to the chemist and get something for his stomach," suggests Fr. Hall. "Jack's suffering the lingering side-effects of anesthetic – plays havoc with the digestive tract." Pressing a few pence into her hand, he nods for her to leave. With a worried glance over her shoulder, she departs.

"You know what it is?" asks Fr. Hall once they are alone.

"What *what* is?"

"Battle stress. You've been living under tremendous pressure since arriving in France, never knowing when you or your friends might be killed. And then finding you're the only survivor amid the carnage".

Mallory nods woodenly. "I killed a man," he mumbles. "Several, actually."

"Yes."

"I *didn't* like it."

"I should hope not."

"But now I'm back here, everyone wants to congratulate me - like I should be proud of it."

Fr. Hall fingers his half-empty glass as a question forms in his mind. "Jack, how did you feel when all those people were pummeling you with questions?"

"Alone."

"Why?"

"I dunno. I guess because nothing I could say could possibly explain what I feel."

"You're more perceptive than most young men," admits Fr. Hall. "In the beginning, wars are always about King and Country. But once you've seen your mates die, killed a few of the enemy yourself, you're no longer a patriot serving his country, you're a man trying to survive. That which motivated fails to sustain."

"I don't want to go back, but ..." Mallory's voice fades.

"It's only natural. You know what's going on in Flanders. You feel alone here because the only people who *understand* what you are going through are still *over there*." Fr. Hall wipes his mouth and drops the napkin on the table. "I was a bit older than you when I returned from the Transvaal. My war was wildly unpopular in this country and left us all with a sense that a war's end doesn't necessarily justify its means."

"Are you a pacifist?"

"Not at all, actually. Our army has a proud tradition of service to King and Country. If we don't respond when called, we substitute our will for that of the people."

"But what if the politicians are wrong? What if the *King* is wrong?"

"Do you really think we were mistaken to come to the defense of France? Should we let the rape of tiny Belgium go unavenged?"

"No, I suppose not." Raising his eyes to the ceiling, Mallory shakes his head in frustration. "But the way we are fighting the war *isn't working!*"

Time passes quickly as the dreaded verdict nears. Despite long hours of solitude in Fr. Hall's study thumbing through the teachings of The Bible, the theories of Plato, the writings of

Clausewitz, the biting humor of Punch, Mallory still finds no perspective on the war.

One morning, as he thumbs disinterestedly through the Times, Fr. Hall enters the dining room, a wicker picnic basket dangling from his hand. "I thought we'd take lunch by the river. Interested?"

Casting aside the paper, Mallory sighs. "Ok. Why not?"

It's a cool, humid day. The Thames is not far from the rectory and they quickly reach a shady Willow overhanging the river. Fr. Hall spreads a checkered table cloth across the grass as Mallory unpacks the basket.

"Father, how can a benevolent God allow what's happening in France?" Mallory asks.

Uncorking a ginger beer, Fr. Hall hands it to Mallory. "A test of free will, I suppose."

"What's *that* mean?"

"Some believe in pre-destiny - God has determined how our lives will unfold before we were ever born. If that's true, those men were dead before they ever reached France. So nothing is to be done about it..."

"My *God...!*"

"But," Fr. Hall interrupts, raising a cautionary hand. "Others believe – as I do – that God placed an imperfect world in motion and we are all judged by how we react to the random challenges we encounter. How we deal with those encounters is an exercise in free-will."

"God makes a man before he kills him, eh?"

"If you wish."

"You don't seem too certain for a man of God."

"What do you *want* from me?" asks Fr. Hall. "Certainty? I can't provide that. But I *believe* in a greater purpose to life and am willing to pursue answers." He takes a swig of ginger beer before continuing. "But I do know one thing with absolute certainty - running away is *not* the solution."

"Sorry?"

"You know what I am saying," responds Fr. Hall as he focuses on slicing an apple. "You don't want to go back to the trenches and you rationalize it thus? 'All my mates are dead, so I owe them nothing'? Or how about, 'I've done my bit'? Thin gruel, my friend. You run away now and you'll be running for the rest of your life."

"I don't know what you're talking about…"

"You're packed already, aren't you?" asks Fr. Hall.

"I… I've got to go back to London for the medical board."

"Then why are there no uniforms in your kit?"

Sputtering, Mallory grapples for words. "Look… just because I'm a guest in your house doesn't give you… you… the *right*…"

"Balls! I invited you to stay with me because I once felt *exactly* the way you do right now!"

"Then you know I can't go back to that…that… slaughter!"

"Then don't!"

"But you said…"

"I said don't run away. I never said 'go back !'"

"Well… what the *hell* does that mean?"

"It means you have a duty to help end the slaughter and you can't do it by deserting."

"Then how?"

Slicing off a piece of apple, he hands it Mallory. "There's someone I want you to meet."

Next day, Mallory is packing - uniforms this time - to return to London. There's a knock on his bedroom door.

Shrugging-on his khaki jacket, he opens the door. In the hallway beside Fr. Hall stands a tall, thin middle aged officer with a crooked smile and sprawling mustache.

"Thought I'd come by and make some introductions," announces Fr. Hall as he ushers his guest into the room. "Jack, I'd like you to meet Lieutenant Colonel Swinton."

"Sir!"

"I see you're packing. Don't let me interrupt," insists Swinton and takes a seat on the edge of the bed.

Mallory resumes shoving uniforms into his kitbag.

"Mike and I served together in the Transvaal," announces Swinton. "Before he became a man of God he was a pretty fair horseman and deadly chap with a cavalry sword."

"My arse!" scoffs Fr. Hall. "Lost my bloody sword at Paardeberg Drift. Had to fight it out bare-fisted. Nearly got my whole section wiped-out."

"Yes, well. He's also a pretty fair liar," Swinton adds dryly. "Didn't earn a VC by stumbling around the battlefield looking for his sword, did he?"

"Well, I suppose not," replies Mallory.

Victoria Cross?

"Look here, young man. I'll come straight to the point," announces Swinton. "A while back I was in France as a correspondent and noticed an artillery tractor dragging supplies up to the front. It occurred to me that putting armor around the bloody thing and slapping some guns on it might be a damned sight better than sending men trudging across no-man's land to soak-up Maxim bullets."

Mallory pauses packing as the colonel's words sink-in.

"Michael tells me you led a bayonet charge at Loos, lost most of your platoon," continues Swinton.

"I didn't do anything."

"No, you *didn't*," snorts Swinton, somewhat unkindly. "Did what the brass hats told you to do and it didn't work, *did it?*"

"I'd say not."

"Right. So I sent a letter to the Secretary of the Committee for Imperial Defence – a politician, of sorts, but a man with considerable influence…"

"Sir, may I ask why you're telling me this?" asks Mallory.

"I'm getting there, young man. Of course, Lord Kitchener poo-pooed the idea. But the secretary got the proposal in front of the First Lord of the Admiralty – a rough and ready chap named Winston Churchill. He thought it a splendid idea and provided naval funds to build the prototype."

"Naval funds?"

"Hmph, strange isn't it? Well, Churchill isn't the type of chap to let branch of service get in the way of a good idea. Point is, I was appointed to the Landships Committee to look into how to build a trench-crossing armored vehicle to protect the crew and make these forays into no-man's land less costly."

"Is that possible?"

"The prototype's ready. I just need a crew to help prove the thing. Thought you might be interested in coming aboard to help us iron-out the wrinkles and get her into production."

"Why me?"

Rising to his feet, Swinton brushes the lint off his cap then settles it on his head. "Because you've seen the alternative. I need people who understand the consequence of failure. I need men with… commitment."

Glancing at Fr. Hall, he continues. "And Michael saved my life in the Transvaal. I owe him at least one life in exchange. It seems *that* life will be yours."

Mallory stares at Swinton in disbelief for a moment before glancing at Fr. Hall and back.

"So what is this new weapon?"

"For security purposes, we just call it a 'Tank'."

CHAPTER 3
Tank Proving Ground, Hertfordshire, England
January 1916

A late-night winter rain drums steadily on the roof as the Austin staff car crawls down a narrow country road in Hertfordshire.

"Sir, may I ask where we're going?" asks Mallory.

"Hatfield Park," responds Swinton

"What's there?"

"Well, for one thing, Lord Salisbury's golf course."

"And for another?"

"It's where 'Mother' awaits."

"Mother?"

"Mother is the name of our prototype," explains Swinton. "I want to get you trained for the crew so we can demonstrate it next month to the Minister for Munitions, Lloyd George and First Sea Lord, Arthur Balfour."

"I thought Churchill was First Sea Lord."

"Not any more. He took blame for the Gallipoli disaster and had to resign. Headed off to the Somme as a major with the Grenadier Guards."

"Seems rather odd for a politician."

"Yes, well. He's a rather odd politician," chuckles Swinton. "But his funding got this project moving so we ought to get these weapons to France and help-out the old-boy, eh?"

The staff car rolls to a stop before heavily armed guards at the grand stone entrance. Swinton presents his pass. With a stamp of feet and slap of flesh on wood, the sentries bring their rifles to present arms and pass them through the gate.

The car continues into the depths of the park to where a large tent stands beside a grove. The headlamps sweep a pair of sentries marching the length and breadth of the large, green tent.

30

Leaving the lights on and engine idling, Swinton slides from behind the wheel. "Come-on," he exclaims. "Let's have a look at her."

As they drag aside the heavy canvas flap, in the headlamps' beam emerges a massive, gray, steel, rhomboid-shaped box, easily eight feet tall and thirty feet long, with caterpillar tracks encircling its body. With a nautical shape and riveted steel hull, it does indeed look like a "landship". On either side sprout large steel blisters from which cannons protrude.

"My God," breathes Mallory as he surveys the machine. "How heavy is she?"

"Twenty-eight tonnes all-in," replies Swinton proudly as he walks around the beast. Knocking on the sides he announces, "Mother is built from boilerplate, but production models will have ten millimeters of armor plate in front, six on the sides. That should stop Jerry bullets, eh?"

"How fast is it?"

"Moves along at a *blistering* four miles per hour."

"It's not very fast."

"Really? How fast were you moving at Loos?"

"Across broken ground? Not so fast, I suppose."

"Mother's job is to shepherd her chicks across no man's land, sweep aside wire entanglements, and cross enemy trenches, while enfilading the Germans with cannon and machinegun fire." His hawk-like eyes lock with Mallory's. "If we do this right, it can be a war-changer. The tank will brush aside defensive strength and reintroduce manoeuvre to the battlefield."

Walking the length of the sleek steel ship, Mallory runs his hand lightly along one of the gun barrels, staring in wonder at the sheer size and bulk of the contraption. It seems nearly inconceivable something this large can even move, much less cross a trench and penetrate the German lines.

On the back of a sponson he discovers a hatch. "May I look inside?"

"Probably a bit dark," observes Swinton. "There's no interior lighting, but..." He retrieves a lantern from its hook and passes it to Mallory. "Try this."

Mallory wrenches-open the hatch and accepts the proffered lantern. He leans inside and floods the whitewashed interior with yellow light. Just inside the door, he spots the gun's rectangular breech, an odd push-bar and pistol grip fitted as if the cannon were merely a large caliber pistol.

In the center of the compartment rests a massive engine, its manifold exposed to the interior of the vehicle, exhaust pipes protruding through the ceiling. His eyes follow the drive shaft to a bulbous drive differential at the rear of the vehicle. As his eyes sweep forward again, he can just make-out two raised seats and a steering wheel surrounded by gear shifts and braking levers.

"How many crew?"

"A commander, driver, and two gearsmen to manoeuvre, add two gunners and a pair of loaders to fight her," replies Swinton. "Eight, total."

Peering around the interior, Mallory notices it's not quite tall enough in which to stand and doesn't appear to be a comfortable place to sit.

"A bit prison-like, eh?" scoffs Swinton. "It'd be a war crime if we locked German prisoners inside it," Swinton chuckles. "But at least it *is* bullet-proof."

Mallory smiles. He backs from the tank and pushes the door closed. "When can I start training?" he asks eagerly.

"Tomorrow morning. One of the original designers, Lieutenant Wilson, is coming 'round to work with the crew."

It's nearing midnight when they arrive in the billets at Hatfield Workhouse.

"Don't strain your shoulder. I'll get your kit from the boot. You get inside and find a place to sleep," orders Swinton.

The rain continues to fall as Mallory dashes from the car to the building's front door. As he enters, the Duty Sergeant glances up with annoyance from his desk in the hallway. "See here, Corporal. It's too late to report tonight."

Swinton appears behind Mallory and flings the dripping duffle bag into the hallway.

"Sah!" shouts the NCO and snaps to attention, boots thumping on the wooden floor.

"This is Sergeant Mallory," explains Swinton. "Hasn't had a chance to sew-on his new stripes yet. But he's here with me and my chaps for the trials. Be sure to find him accommodation suitable for his rank, will you?"

"Ah, yes sir," replies the sergeant. He returns to Mallory. "Identification?"

Mallory fishes through the breast pocket of his tunic and presents his Pay Book to the sergeant, who dutifully enters Mallory's name, rank and service number in the duty log and hands it back. He retrieves a scratchy woolen blanket and lumpy pillow and passes it to Mallory. "Jes down the hall, third room on the right. Take care you don't wake your mate."

"Right," responds Mallory and turns to Swinton. "So I'll be seeing you tomorrow, then Sir?"

"No. I've got to go to London for a few days," announces Swinton. "You take a few days with Lieutenant Wilson and his crew. Get familiar with dear 'Mother' and show me what you can do with her when I return."

"Yes, Sir."

Swinton turns on his heel, strides out the door and disappears into the rainy night.

Mallory lifts his kitbag, bedding tucked beneath his arm and shuffles down the hall to his billet. As he opens the door, the room fills dimly with light from the gas lantern in the hall. Amid the sliver of light, he spots an empty bunk. Entering the room, he pushes the door closed behind him and gropes his way through the darkness and takes a seat on the edge of the bed.

Unraveling his puttees, he unlaces his boots and slides them beneath the bunk, then shrugs-off his tunic and hangs it on the bedpost. Reclining onto the mattress, he falls quickly asleep.

"CLANG!"

His eyes blink open. The ground shakes as artillery rumbles overhead. Dirt sifts between the beams, showering him with chalky dust. He jerks upright, strangely alone in the airless room, lit solely by a dim lantern swaying from the ceiling above.

He glances around. *Where is everyone?*

"Boom! BOOM!"

His eyes cut to the ceiling. The timbers creak. He springs hastily to his feet. "Miller? Sir?" he calls anxiously. "Anyone there?"

He gropes for his rifle and retrieves his cap from a peg on the wall.

The mournful groan of straining wood rapidly escalates into the crack of timbers as dirt cascades from the ceiling.

Ripping aside the gas cape covering the dugout's entrance, he encounters a solid wall. Casting aside his rifle, he claws at the dirt with bare hands, fingers bleeding as he attempts to dig his way out of the collapsing dugout. A shoring timber snaps, the splintered board striking him in the face and knocking him to the floor.

As he lay, stunned, the ceiling collapses over him. He raises his arms in a vain attempt to avoid being crushed beneath several metric tonnes of dirt and timber.

"No! NO! *NOOOOO!*"

"Bloody hell!' croaks a voice.

The light from a gas lantern fills the room. A soldier stands beside Mallory's bunk, staring down at him in horror.

"You all right, mate?"

Mallory bolts up-right. "What?" he gasps.

"Are you all right?' asks the soldier again.

"I'm...," Mallory begins before noticing a stain on the front of his shirt. Dragging his forearm across his face, he finds it smeared with blood.

"Tha's a nasty nose bleed," announces the soldier as he helps Mallory to his feet. Leading him to a small wash stand, he hands Mallory a towel and pours water from the pitcher into the enameled basin.

"I... I don't know what happened," lies Mallory.

"It's all right. Jus' a nightmare," replies the soldier. "Almost time for reveille anyway. Let's get you cleaned-up and I'll take you over to the mess. You got a clean shirt in yer kit?"

"Yeah," gags Mallory as blood flows thickly down his throat. He pinches the bridge of his nose and tilts his head back. The soldier unties the duffle and rolls-out Mallory's kit. As he sorts through Mallory's clothes, he spots the uniform jacket hanging on the bedpost, a wound stripe stitched to the sleeve., DCM ribbon above his pocket.

"Been in France, have you?"

"Yes."

"You must be Mallory. The colonel said you'd be joinin' us." He walks over and pulls the towel away, notices Mallory's nose is still bleeding, and replaces it. "Name's James," he announces by way of introduction.

"Hullo, James. Uh, is James your first or last name?"

"Last. Don't use my first name."

"Which is?"

James just smiles. "You know what it is, don't you?"

"We just met. How would I know?"

"Not talkin' about my name, I'm talkin' about your nightmare. It's like grievin'. Yer body has to bleed off stress a little at a time. It keeps ya from losin' your bleedin' mind. Had the same problem myself - still do sometimes."

Mallory nods silently.

"Here, let's get that thing off you," advises James and begins unbuttoning Mallory's shirt. Mallory continues to pinch his nose, alternating hands to free-up a bare arm as James peels the bloody shirt off him.

James whistles. "You must be a bleedin' vampire."`

"Sorry?"

Nodding to Mallory's scars, he explains. "Never seen a bloke take one through the chest an' live to tell about it."

"I'm afraid it takes a wooden stake to kill me – bullets don't count," snorts Mallory. "What about you?"

James tosses him a clean shirt. "Got mine at Mons." He points to his right hip. "Came in 'ere and exited 'ere," he explains, pointing to his right bum cheek.

"Shot in the arse, eh?" Mallory chides.

"Shot in the hip, exited my arse. I prefer to say I was shot in the 'thigh'. It's more dignified."

Mallory smiles. He likes this new mate. "So how'd you wind-up with this lot?"

"Same as you: the Colonel. While I was recoverin' from me wounds, I was assigned to drive 'im to see one of his officers in hospital. 'How tall are you?' he asks me. A bit cheesed-off, I says 'five foot five, Sir. Wha' about it'?"

"He laughs and says, 'How'd you like to learn to drive a bullet-proof caterpillar that can go anywhere and knock down trees and things?' Figured it'd be okay, so 'ere I am. Course 'e didn't tell me he expected I'd drive the beast through the German lines! Now he's recruiting crews by running ads in 'The Motorcycle' magazine. Says he's lookin' for men with *mechanical abilities*."

"Yeah, mechanical abilities and balls of steel," snorts Mallory. "I'm afraid I don't know enough about a tank to be in charge of a crew."

"Oh, tha's all right. Lieutenant Wilson will be in-charge. Great bloke. He designed Mother 'imself. Brilliant man! O' course, bein' a Royal Navy officer, 'ees a bit odd."

Mallory finishes dressing and pulls on his jacket.

"Come-on," announces James. "Let's get some grub and I'll introduce you to the crew."

By the time they arrive at the mess, the crew has already been driven off to the test site. After a quick meal, Mallory and James trek through the morning dew to where "Mother" awaits.

In daylight, she looks even more absurd than the night before. With the canvas awning rolled back, she's been moved into the field and stands, hatches open, crew members swarming over her like bees on a hive. It appears a two-wheeled trailer has been attached to the rear. As they approach, a tall man in greasy tan overalls unfolds himself through the rear door of one of the sponsons.

"Ah, James! Good to see you old boy," he announces. "Got a bit of moisture in the carburetor last night. Devil of a time getting her awake this morning." His gaze shifts to Mallory. "And who's this?"

"Sergeant Mallory," announces James.

"Yes, yes! Colonel Swinton said you'd be joining us. Glad to have you aboard." He returns his attention to James. "Got to find some ether to stir the carburetor. Have her running in a jiffy," he announces then bolts away.

"Who the hell was that?" asks Mallory.

"Lieutenant Wilson," chuckles James.

"My God! I didn't even salute!"

"He didn't notice," replies James. "Says he likes to keep an 'informal tank'. 'Can't work together as a crew if everyone's saluting all the time', he says."

Mallory watches the officer disappear into the tent. "Interesting..."

"Well, come on and meet the rest o' the crew," announces James and leads Mallory beside the tank. "Hey, lads! Gather 'round and meet the new sergeant."

Men converge around them wiping greasy hands on smudged overalls, faces dripping with sweat.

"This 'ere's 'The Crew'," announces James formally. "Gault and Michaels are me gearsmen."

"Mornin', Sergeant."

"And this 'ere's Devers and Fredricks, me gunners. We just call Fredricks, 'Freddy'."

Mallory nods to each.

"I thought there was a crew of eight," concludes Mallory.

"It really only takes four to drive 'er. Since we ain't actually shootin' at anything for the trials, Devers and Freddy are helpin' out with the mechanics. O' course we ain't close enough to combat yet to need loaders."

He glances back toward the tent where Wilson disappeared in search of the ether. "Between you and us, this thing can't go two miles without throwin' a track or stallin'," he explains conspiratorially. "But for the demonstration, she'll do. Our job is to make 'er look good."

"What if the trial fails?"

"Then it's back to the PBI for the lot of us."

Wilson returns with the bottle of ether. "Sergeant Mallory, I want you to train as alternate driver. Sergeant James here is quite good, but if these trials are successful, we're going to need more qualified drivers to teach the others."

"Right."

"Good, good! James will teach you everything he knows."

"That won't take long 'cause I don' know much," announces James cheerfully and motions for Mallory to join him.

They enter through the rear of the right sponson. Edging around the 6-pounder and squeezing past the engine, they approach the seats at the front of the cabin, placed slightly higher than the rest of the crew's positions. James occupies the right hand seat and directs Mallory to the left.

"Right. Pay attention, my boy, and someday all this will be yours," announces James grandly.

"For drivin', ya got two vision ports, one large, one small. Use the large one whenever you can. With these great bilges on the sides, driving this thing is like steering a pregnant hippo." He grasps the lever to his right and raises the port. "Smaller one's for when the fightin' starts. Makes for a smaller target. If we get bullets rattlin' around inside, someone's goin' to get 'urt.

"Now, the controls may look like a motorcar, but it drives completely diff'rent." He points to the levers on either side of Mallory's seat. "Since we ain't got no wheels, most of the turnin' is done by adding power to the track on one side while slowing or stopping the other." He makes a motion with his hands indicating how the tank will turn in each scenario.

Working his feet on the pedals, he explains. "I got a clutch and brake down 'ere." He places his hands on levers beside his seat. "And 'ere I got the hand throttle and primary gear box. Two forward gears, one reverse."

He points to the levers on either side of Mallory's command seat. "Those levers are the steerin' brakes. You'll work those in cooperation with me."

"What about the steering wheel," asks Mallory with a nod toward the device.

"Ah, yes. Well as far as I'm concerned, it's just something for me to brace myself against when I'm feelin' wobbly." He points vaguely toward the rear of the tank. "You saw those wheels in-back? Think of 'em like a rudder on a ship. When the rudder goes right, the ship turns right. To go left, the rudder turns left."

"So you *can* drive it like a motorcar," concludes Mallory.

"Not really. The wheels don't have enough 'bite' to turn twenty-some-odd tonnes o' steel, so the turning radius is bloody awful. Start your turn in Flanders and you might be in Berlin before you complete it. I'm tryin' to convince the boss we don't need it. But he's obsessed with the idea a 'landship' needs a 'rudder'.

"Now, yer job as commander is to tell me where you want to go and then work the brakes to help me get her pointed that direction, right? So if you tell me to veer left, you'll brake the left track and I'll goose the engine. That'll turn us left. Turn right? Just the opposite. Once we're headed the right direction, just release your brake and we'll go straight again. Got it?"

Mallory nods.

"It'll be noisy as hell in 'ere, so when you want me to move a particular direction, just punch me on the arm and point. I'll acknowledge and you use your brake to start the turn."

"Okay. That doesn't sound too complicated."

"Yeah, well. We ain't out of the woods yet. If we're gonna turn real tight – like to change directions – we 'ave to stop, clutch, and one of the gearsmen in the back will drop us into low gear. I'll goose the engine and swing 'er around. Then we gotta stop again and reset the gears before continuing. We'll need to do the same thing when crossing large barriers. We gotta have the torque to get thorough some of the nastier German obstacles. Got it?"

"Right. I think it'll make more sense once we're moving."

"Well, that's next, so let's get everyone aboard and start this thing." He rotates the 'pigeon hole' in the side of the cab. "Next version will have a hatch on top, so we don't get trapped inside if something goes wrong."

James calls and waves through the opening. The crew converges on the machine. Gault and Michaels take seats at the rear of the tank, while Devers and Freddy position themselves on either side of the engine.

"Ready!" calls Devers.

James flips a switch on his dashboard and slips the tank into neutral. "Contact!"

Devers and Freddy grasp the bends in a crank located between the engine and differential and begin turning it. The engine sputters twice and dies.

"Wait a sec!" calls Wilson and climbs into the machine. He places a few drops of ether in the carburettor. "Okay, give 'er another crank!"

Three more cranks and the 6-cylinder Daimler engine coughs to life. Black smoke belches from the exhaust, smoothing to white as the cold engine warms-up.

Vibrating in his seat, a faint smile creases Mallory's lips.

James nudges him. "Release the brakes!" he yells over the rumble of the engine. Mallory squeezes the hand locks and shoves the brake levers forward.

James slips the tank into low gear and slowly releases the clutch. Mother lurches a few inches, hesitates, and rocks forward again, engine groaning as 28 tonnes of steel claws its way forward.

CHAPTER 4
Tank Proving Ground, Hertfordshire, England
February 1916

Mallory sits leaning against the trunk of a spreading willow, the light mist captured by its upper branches. A dozen yards away sits Mother, her unpainted armor shimmering fish-like in the dampness.

While the crew eats lunch at Hatfield Workhouse, he takes advantage of the peace to collect his thoughts. He thumbs through a pamphlet, returning yet again to a recently published article. He re-reads it, the words speaking to him like a close friend, someone who has shared the deep, dark feelings haunting his sleep.

"Whatcha' readin?"

Startled, he glances up to see James standing over him. He quickly closes the pamphlet. "Nothing," he blurts unconvincingly. "Just passing the time."

James reaches out with his great paw. "Gimme."

Mallory reluctantly passes up the pamphlet. James thumbs through it and glances sharply at Mallory. "*Poetry?*"

"Just a little something I picked-up in town," explains Mallory. "The writer's a lieutenant in the Royal Welch Fusiliers – chap named Sassoon."

"Siegfried Sassoon? Sounds like a bloody Fritz to me."

"He's a serving British infantry officer," replies Mallory defensively.

"Hmph! You went to university, didn't you?" James announces disapprovingly.

"Two years," replies Mallory. "I dropped-out to enlist."

"Why'd you do a stupid thing like that?"

"Seemed like the thing to do."

Shaking his head in wonder, James examines the poem. "In the Pink?"

"It's about a soldier thinking about home before going up to the front line to die."

James squints at the cheap print and examines the three paragraph poem, lips moving silently as he reads. "I ain't no university man," he announces on conclusion, "but this looks like the sort of writin' that can get a bloke court-martialed."

"He's just saying what's on his mind," replies Mallory defensively. "We all think it. Why should it be a crime to write it?"

James hands the pamphlet back to Mallory. "Good thing most of our officers ain't bright enough to understand poetry, otherwise, someone would get shot for writing this sort of thing. Best stick to readin' King and Country," he advises.

"Where's the crew?" asks Mallory, seizing an opportunity to change the subject.

"Wilson's got 'em on a detail. I told 'im you and me got things to do to get Mother ready for the trials."

"Thanks," replies Mallory gratefully. "How goes construction on the proving ground?"

"Dunno, ain't been over there in a while."

"Let's go for a drive, then," suggests Mallory.

"Okay, why not?"

They climb aboard Mother through the left sponson, the door clanging shut behind them. "Go ahead and give her the spark, I'll crank," offers Mallory.

James climbs into the driver's seat. "Contact."

Mallory cranks the lever three times and the engine catches. The engine idling evenly, he climbs into the commander's seat and shoves the brakes forward. Mother lurches headlong and edges off the road; they cruise slowly cross country.

"You – er – not goin' barmy on me are ya?" asks James.

"What? No!" blurts Mallory. "Just because I think about how war affects our humanity doesn't make me some sort of pacifist."

"A what?"

"Pacifist…"

"I meant the *poetry*," laughs James. "If you're gonna grow your hair and start spoutin' a bunch 'a rhyming jibberish, we'll have to drag you along behind this bloody thing."

"You arse," chuckles Mallory. "Hey, turn right here, James. The test site's just beyond those trees."

Mother grinds right and ascends a gentle slope. As they top the rise, Mallory calls, "Clutch!" and jerks the brakes rearward. "Let's take a look," he announces eagerly and slides from his seat. They emerge overlooking a mock battlefield.

"Blimey," groans Mallory.

Across the open glen stretches a "steeplechase" course consisting of several nine foot wide trenches with parapets as high as six and a half feet. In front of mock defenses stretch hundreds of yards of barbed wire entanglements and defensive coils. Ammonite has been used to create realistic-looking shell craters and battle damage.

"Looks just like bloody Flanders," observes James.

Mallory wanders partway down the hill and halts, peering through the mist.

James arrives beside him. "What?"

"Not sure," replies Mallory. "It sort 'a reminds me of the end of the world. The trenches, the craters, the barbed wire - but no humans. It's like everyone's already been killed and there's nothing left but a vacant battlefield."

After an extended pause, James breaks the silence. "Well, we're still here. So if everyone else is dead, the pub is empty and we can have all the beer we want."

"You haven't a philosophical bone in your body, have you?"

"My people are farmers, Jack. Philosophy's for you blokes with upbringin'."

"Maxims don't care about upbringing, James. We're all equals under the gun."

"God, what's that smell?" asks Mallory as he recoils from the hatch.

James leans-in and takes a sniff. "Who the hell left Stinking Bishop in the tank over night?"

"Sorry, Sergeant," replies Devers sheepishly. "Me mum sent a package a few days ago. The lads won't let me open cheese in the barracks."

"So you left it *in the tank?*"

"I didn't want no one to steal it," explains Devers.

"Well, if they wouldn't let you eat it around 'em, why the hell would they steal it from you?"

"To drop on the bloody Hun," announces Gault.

As the laughter fades, they spot Swinton stalking briskly toward them.

"Lieutenant Wilson is indisposed," he announces. "You'll command today's demonstration, Sergeant."

"*Me?*" blurts Mallory.

"Who else? Wilson says you're ready."

"But I... yes sir."

"All set then?" asks Swinton anxiously, his eyes quickly sweeping the fresh-shaved men in clean overalls.

"Sah!" reports Mallory with a wink at James. "She's uh... ripe... for today's trial."

Swinton glances over his shoulder. "Well, she better be. Here they come." He straightens and adjusts his necktie. Clearing his throat, he tugs nervously on the hem of his uniform jacket and stalks to the side of the road to meet the several limousines approaching in the mist.

First to emerge is David Lloyd George, the Minister for Munitions, in his shabby suit and thick graying mustache overflowing his top lip. Arriving in the same car is the diminutive, balding Reginald McKenna, Chancellor of the Exchequer.

The two men greet Swinton jovially, Lloyd George eagerly surveying the test area. "Well? Well? Where is it?" he asks in a brash, Welsh accent.

"Soon enough, Minister. Soon enough," comes the casually superior reply from Secretary of War Lord Kitchener, who emerges from the second car with Chief of the Imperial General Staff, General William "Wully" Robertson.

The four men gather around Swinton, who explains the tests they are about to witness. As he concludes his briefing, a third car arrives to deposit First Lord of the Admiralty Arthur Balfour beside the group. Traveling with him is a tall, lanky army colonel who exits the car with a noticeable limp.

"Have I missed anything?" asks Balfour eagerly.

"Just preparing to introduce the crew, Minister," replies Swinton.

"Hullo, Hugh," announces Swinton and shakes hands briefly with the officer. "Come to spy for General Haig, have you?"

"Certainly not," replies Colonel Hugh Elles. "Despite what you may believe, Ernest, the General has high hopes for your new weapon."

"Well, that's rather good to know," responds Swinton tersely. He leads the dignitaries over to Mallory and his crew. The six men snap to attention as one.

Mallory salutes. "The demonstration crew is ready to receive your orders!"

Kitchener returns the salute. "So where is this *wonder weapon?*" he asks dryly.

The crew members glance nervously at one another. "Um, behind those trees, Sir," responds Mallory.

"You realize what this means, gentlemen?" blurts Lloyd George. "This weapon could break the stalemate on the Western Front. If what you show us here today can be reproduced, you may save thousands, nay, millions of lives!"

Kitchener and Robertson glance at each other and smirk.

"Yes, well. We'll see," replies Robertson. "Why don't you chaps run along and bring the thing 'round for us to take a peek."

"Detail! Fall-out!" barks Mallory in a shrill, cracking voice. The men take one step backward, turn and break into a run toward the woods. As they round the trees, Mallory discovers a frail, pale Wilson standing beside the tank. "Come on, come on," he urges as the crew lines-up on either side of Mother and squeeze through the hatches.

"Are you taking command, Sir?" asks Mallory.

"Heavens, no," groans Wilson. "I feel like walking death. I just didn't want to miss the show!"

Mallory climbs aboard last and settles into the commander's seat. He receives a "ready" from each crewman then turns to James. "Here we go," he breathes. "God help us."

He releases the brakes and James slips her into gear. Mother lurches forward, tracks churning the earth as she claws her way across the wet grass. The few minutes it takes to drive the quarter mile to where the dignitaries stand seems an eternity.

As they near, Mallory misjudges the distance and steers close to the observers. All scramble away, except Arthur Balfour, who is so entranced he stands fast, mouth agape as Mother churns to within a few feet and jerks to a stop.

Mallory opens his "pigeon hole" and peers out at the dignitaries. Deafened by the purr of the idling engine, he watches Swinton speak, arms waving enthusiastically as he explains what the dignitaries are about to witness.

"How's it going out there?" asks James, peering over Mallory's shoulder.

"He's got the civilians' attention," reports Mallory. "But it looks like Kitchener and Robertson are going to be a tough sell. Can't tell about the other officer."

"Damned fools! They still think the cavalry will carry the day," snorts James.

Concluding his speech, Swinton turns to the tank and nods curtly. Mallory nudges James, who revs the engine and releases the clutch. Fresh grass churning beneath its tracks, Mother jolts past the observers and angles toward the first of the obstacles, a field of barbed wire forty feet deep.

Mother grinds through the tangle-foot and waist-high wire, the scrape of metal on her armor grating like a child's fingernails on a chalkboard. Pushing effortlessly through the wire, Mother approaches a nine-foot wide trench. Climbing the sandbags, her hull extends across the gap before lurching nose-down toward the bottom of the ditch. Stern exposed in mid-air, she sticks fast, treads slipping in the glassy mud.

"Shit!" curses James.

"Down-shift!' orders Mallory. "Get some torque!"

Forgetting to clutch, James grinds the tank into low gear and depresses the throttle. The engine roars, exhaust billowing from the pipes as Mother trembles, gains a toehold on the opposite slope and begins to claw up the wall.

The crew cheers as Mother rears-up and regains level ground on the opposite side of the trench.

At the next obstacle, James down-shifts at the base of the parapet and applies the increased torque to drag the machine up a thirty degree incline. As she reaches the top, the parapet begins to crumble and Mother noses over.

"Bloody hell!" curses Mallory. "We're not perpendicular to the trench." He braces himself against the instrument panel as Mother slides with a crash to the bottom of the ditch, one tread stabbing into the wall, the other turning uselessly in the air.

"Gearsmen! Drop us into low gear. We need more torque."

Struggling to maintain positions at the rear of the tilting tank, the gearsmen downshift and return confirming thumbs-up. James slowly releases the clutch and gooses the throttle. Mallory tugs the right brake and Mother rights herself, both tracks biting into the walls.

"Now! Go! *Go!*" yells Mallory.

Uttering an impressive string of curses beneath his breath, James leans into the throttle. Shuddering violently, Mother claws her way up the opposite side of the trench.

"This is goin' to be ugly," insists James.

"Raise the wheels!" orders Mallory. One of the gearsman slaps a hydraulic control. With a moan, the piston slowly raises the "rudder", allowing Mother's stern to sink into the trench, her nose reaching skyward. Engine bellowing, she crawls up the opposite side of the trench, reaches center and noses over forward with a crash.

As they top the trench, a loud "clank" echoes through the interior and the vehicle slips sideways, the broken track spewing into a heap ahead of the machine.

"Shit!" curses Mallory to the general moans of despair within the confines of the tank. "We've thrown a track!!"

"Back to the bloody PBI," mutters James. He twists open the pigeonhole and peers out at the dignitaries.

The ministers race to the disabled Mother's side, hats waving and cheering like cricket fans. Kitchener and Robertson hold back, Kitchener's inscrutable face a mask of indifference. Robertson appears somewhat more impressed.

Leaving Mother idling, Mallory climbs down from the cockpit and works his way out the left side sponson. As he drops to the ground, Balfour grasps his hand and pumps it enthusiastically. "My God! That was magnificent!"

Lloyd George winks slyly and slaps Mallory on the back. "Good show! Bloody good show!"

"But the track, Sir?"

"Mechanical device," snorts Balfour. "There are bound to be glitches."

"Lieutenant Wilson has some ideas to redesign the tracks, Sir," Swinton informs Balfour. "I believe we can overcome the current 'difficulties'."

"None-the-less, that was the most extraordinary performance I've ever witnessed," announces McKenna. He turns to Swinton. "How much does one of these cost?"

"Who cares!" snorts Lloyd George. "Think of the lives it'll save!"

Robertson steps forward and offers his hand to Swinton. "Colonel, I'm not completely convinced, but you may be onto something here."

"Thank you, Sir."

"Yes, well," snorts Lord Kitchener. "It's a pretty mechanical toy, but wars are not won by machines."

"No, Sir," responds Swinton. "The tank is merely a tool. But I think we've demonstrated here today, in the right hands, a mighty tool she'll be!"

Kitchener tugs his mustache, a playful twinkle in his normally stern eyes. "We'll see…."

"Toss me a spanner," calls James. "I think I found what caused the track to break."

Mallory reaches into the toolbox and hands James the tool. "I'd have bet we were all-done once we threw the track," he sighs.

"Nah, everyone wants to be a believer," replies James. "See here? The idler spring was too loose; allowed something to get between the track and drive sprocket."

"What are we goin' to do about the 'rudder?'" asks Mallory.

James glances at the crew unbolting the twisted steering device. "If it was up to me, I'd get rid of it once and for all. Don't serve no purpose."

"I'll have a talk with Wilson again," replies Mallory.

A staff car roars over the hill and skids to a stop. Swinton leaps from the driver's seat and breathlessly announces, "The King is on his way!"

Mallory chokes. "The *King?*"

"His Royal Highness himself. Looks like Lloyd George and Balfour overrode Lord Kitchener's objections. His Majesty wishes to see Mother and decide for himself. With his support, Parliament would dare not deny funding!"

"How long do we have to prepare?"

Swinton consults his pocket watch. "Twenty minutes too much time?"

"Dear God!" blurts Mallory. He springs to his feet. "James," he snaps. "Send Devers to tell Gault and Michaels to get their arses over here on the double!"

At the appointed hour, the crew is in formation, lined up before Mother.

The King's Rolls Royce splashes to a halt a dozen feet away.

"Detail! Atten-shun!" barks Wilson; the five crewmen snap to attention in perfect cadence. From the corner of his eye, Mallory sees the bearded King emerge from his car dressed in a naval officer's uniform, a simple two rows of ribbons representing awards earned while serving as a young officer in the Royal Navy.

Swinton and other staff officers salute, bowing as His Royal Highness shakes hands and trades pleasantries.

"Here he comes," whispers Mallory from the corner of his mouth. At the King's approach, Devers begins to wobble dangerously. "Knees!" hisses Mallory. Flexing his legs, Devers shakes-off the nausea and resumes the position of attention.

Standing before the tiny formation, Wilson snaps a crisp salute. Mallory hears the King speak to Wilson, but can't make out what was being said.

Wilson responds with a delighted chuckle then, with a sweep of his arm, introduces the crew. "Your Majesty," he announces proudly. "This is your demonstration crew - finest soldiers in His Majesty's Army."

The King smiles broadly and steps before Mallory. "Good morning young man. How are you today?"

Mallory snaps a nervous salute. "Sah!"

"Don't be nervous son, I remember what it was like as a Midshipman. All those dignitaries prowling about my ship made me nervous as hell, too. Try and think of me as a kindly uncle, eh?"

"Yes, sir... I mean, Your Majesty."

"You're young to be a sergeant," observes The King as his eyes inspect Mallory's uniform. He spots the wound stripe. "Where were you wounded?"

"The chest, Your Majesty!"

Smiling tolerantly, the King corrects himself. "I'm sorry, I was imprecise. I meant, in what battle were you wounded?"

Face reddening, Mallory responds. "Loos, Your Majesty!"

"Ah, Loos. Came close to pulling it off, didn't we?"

Opening his mouth to speak, Mallory hesitates.

"It's all right Sergeant," encourages Wilson. "Tell His Majesty what you think."

Mallory takes a deep breath and announces, "Pardon my French, Your Majesty, but it was a bloody fiasco."

The King raises a surprised eyebrow.

"*Sergeant!*" blurts Wilson.

"It's all right Lieutenant," chuckles The King. "I've heard worse language aboard ship." Returning his attention to Mallory, he continues. "So what – in your estimation – went wrong at Loos?"

"I... I'm really not qualified..."

"Poppycock!" snorts The King. "That DSM and wound stripe say otherwise. Tell me."

"Machineguns everywhere, Your Majesty. Barbed wire intact. The gas blew back over us."

"You had protection, I assume."

"Of a sort, Your Highness. The hoods keep the gas out, but you can't see through them and it's nearly impossible to breathe."

"Yes, damned Hun gas. Must be awfully frightening."

"Yes, sir."

"And the machineguns?"

"Endless. One every few yards. Walking into them is like... like standing as wheat before a scythe."

"Eloquent," admits the King thoughtfully. "So, are we wasting lives in Flanders?"

"I... I can't say, Your Highness. But I do think we're fighting the last war using outdated tactics against modern weapons."

"So what about your steel contraption? This... this..."

"Tank, Your Highness."

"Yes, this Tank. Will it save soldiers' lives? Perhaps bring an end to the war?"

Mallory hesitates. He glances over his shoulder at the gray hulk. His eyes return to the King. "Yes, Your Highness. I think it will."

Bowing his head, Swinton stifles a relieved smile.

"Well, then," announces The King. "Show me what she can do!"

CHAPTER 5
Tank Proving Ground, Hertfordshire, England
March 1916

"To Mother!" shouts James and hoists his beer.

"To Mother!"

"Cheers!"

"A beau'iful bitch, she ish!" slurs James.

Crew members raise their mugs. The pub echoes to the clink of glass-on-glass.

"See here!" snorts a lieutenant at the next table. "I realize you're blotto, but that comment was really beyond the pale!"

James turns in his chair and raises his hands in mock surrender. "Don' get me wrong, Left'enant. I love Mother," he explains in all apparent sincerity. "I can't wait to get inside 'er and drive 'er home me self. But there's seven other blokes in line ahead 'o' me!"

The crude insinuation catches Mallory unprepared. He chokes, spewing a mouthful of ale across the table. Devers leaps out of the way and falls from his chair. Gault remains silent, passed-out with his head buried in his arms, drool on his sleeve.

"Now, *really!*" blurts the officer, face reddening as he rises angrily to his feet.

"He's just jokin', Left'enant," snickers Freddy, unable to control his laughter. "Ish an inside joke. Don't be takin' offence."

"I don't care! This is a public establishment…"

James rolls his eyes in exasperation. "Oh, bugger-off you sanctimonious sack of shit," he snorts.

The officer's face goes scarlet. "*WHAT!?!?*"

"I apologize for him, Sir," replies Mallory. "We're celebratin' a momentous occasion and he's a bit tipsy."

"What occasion?"

"The end o' the war, of course!" snorts James.

"The war's not … over," replies the officer uncertainly. "Is it?"

"Well, not *yet!*" guffaws James. "But once the beastly Hun meet Mother, they're gonna throw down their guns and yell 'Hoch, hoch, mein Gott!' Then we'll hang Kaiser Bill and be done with the lot o' 'em."

The crew lapses back into laughter.

"Sergeant! Get control of your men of I'll have you all on a fizzer!"

"Right, sir. Right...," gasps Mallory and relapses into uncontrolled giggling.

"That's *it!*" snaps the lieutenant as he rips a notebook from his pocket and gropes for a pencil.

"Detail! A-ten-SHUN!" barks a familiar, booming voice.

Chairs topple over backwards, beer spilling across the table as crew members stagger to their feet. Swinton stands in the doorway, fists balled on his hips, a scowl beneath his mustache.

Mallory glances down and notices Gault, still fast asleep with his head buried in his arms. He grasps the sleeping man's hair and lifts his head upright while he remains teetering at the position of attention.

"What's going on here?" asks Swinton.

"Jus' 'avin' a drink, Sir," slurs Mallory. "Or two."

"Sir!" snaps the lieutenant. "These men are drunk and disorderly. They've been rude, crude and insubordinate!"

"Rude and crude, I understand. But insubordinate?"

"Yes, Sir! Him," the officer announces, pointing at James. "He... he called me a... *a name*, Sir."

"A name?"

"I called 'im a 'sanctimonious sack 'o shit'... Sir," belches James.

"I see," replies Swinton sternly. "In your condition, I'm surprised you could even *pronounce* 'sanctimonious'. And what do you have to say, Lieutenant?"

"I wish to prefer charges, Sir! For drunkenness, for insubordination, for..."

"What if I told you these men are involved in a mission absolutely critical to the war effort?"

"It may be, sir. But they need to learn their place."

"Then he's right. You are a 'sanctimonious sack of shit'."

"*Sir?*" stammers the lieutenant. "I object to this maltreatment!"

"And I object to your presence," snorts Swinton. "You're dismissed, Lieutenant."

The red-faced officer snaps obediently to attention, turns on his heel, and marches from the pub. After watching the lieutenant depart, Swinton turns to Mallory and his crew. "He's probably a better soldier than any of you. But you're the ones I'm stuck with. At ease. Take a pew."

Mildly sobered by their commander's presence, the crew members right their chairs and regain their seats. "So we're going ahead with production, Sir?" asks Mallory eagerly.

"I've been instructed to leave Lieutenant Wilson of the Royal Navy – soon to be *Major* Wilson of the British Army – to oversee production of the first hundred tanks. He'll work with William Foster and Company to build the first twenty-five while the other manufacturer, Metropolitan Carriage, Wagon and Finance gears-up to produce the remainder. For my part, they've seen fit to elevate me to organize a Tank Detachment to take to France under the guise of 'Heavy Section of the Machine Gun Corps'."

"Blimey," breathes James.

"While you're establishing the training area at Bisley," continues Swinton. "I need to start recruiting heavily. Mallory, Sergeant James informs me you attended Oxford."

Mallory shoots James a nasty glance. "I didn't complete my studies, sir. I dropped out and enlisted after Mons."

"But you were in the OTC?"

"I began officer training, but again…"

"Well, that settles that. I'm nominating you for a commission."

"No thanks."

"You went to Oxford – at least for several years. You have a DCM, combat experience and my recommendation. If you apply, I assure you your commission will be approved."

Mallory shakes his head firmly.

"Why on earth not?"

"My family situation might prove an embarrassment. Officers are from the privileged class and I'm not so privileged."

His declaration meets with silence. Glancing up, Mallory realizes the colonel is staring at him. It's a stare colder than he ever could have imagined.

"What?"

"You coward!"

"I'm no coward…"

"Oh, yes you are! So you have some skeletons in your cupboard! Don't we all. Lieutenant Chilcott was one of those officers – his only 'privilege' was to die in Flanders leading you ungrateful types!"

"What do I have to be grateful for? He led us to slaughter."

"You went willingly enough!"

"I didn't realize what I was getting into."

"And neither did he! So now you know what war is like, you're going to let those young boys continue marching to their deaths?"

"I can't prevent that!"

"Yes, you can!" snaps Swinton. "You told the King you thought the tank could save men's lives, perhaps end the war sooner. Did you *lie* to His Majesty?"

Mallory's shoulders sag. "I don't know," he replies despairingly.

"You're a coward," repeats Swinton.

"Stop saying that!"

"Then why won't you lead? Are you afraid of personal responsibility? Or are you content just to stay home and let other men die while you play 'wounded war veteran'?"

"That's not fair! I watched my best friend die…"

"Good God!" snaps Swinton. "I've lost dozens of friends and I'm going to lose a hell of a lot more before this bloody war's over! You've got a choice they didn't have. You can make a difference! But more importantly, you owe it to them!"

CHAPTER 6
Battle of the Somme, Bray-sur-Somme, France
September 1916

"Those bloody, bloody, fools!" swears Swinton. "If they'll employ the damned things properly, the tank will change the face of the war! But by throwing them into the Somme battle to try and salvage a flawed plan, the General is pissing away a great opportunity!"

"Yes, I know old boy," replies Colonel Elles, "but the Somme is not going well and if we are to prove the value of the tank, the time to do it is *now*."

"*Hugh!* We've discussed this before. The tank must be kept secret until we have enough to make a real difference! If we let the General scatter them around in penny-packs to support local infantry action, we'll have squandered the breakthrough potential."

"The decision is made, Ernest. If we don't use what we have now, we may never have another chance. General Haig has ordered me to act as observer. If report a positive result – any positive result – the Heavy Section may become an independent tank corps."

"And if this premature use becomes a fiasco, then what?"

"I can't deal with 'if', Earnest. Now are you going to tell me how many serviceable tanks you have?"

"Two Companies; Forty-nine vehicles, in all."

"Then get them to the front line and distribute them between XIV, XV and III Corps immediately. Jump-off is at 0600 on the 15th."

"But *Hugh…*,"

The thud of boots on the wooden floor intrudes on the argument. Both colonels turn in annoyance. Swinton suddenly recognizes the new lieutenant. "Hello! Congratulations on your Commission, old chap!"

"Thank you, Sir."

"Where are you attached?"

"D Battalion, First Company Sir. I'm taking command of the Second Section."

"Where's Captain Steele?"

"I haven't met him yet. I was hoping to find him here, Sir."

"Hugh, you remember former Sergeant Mallory. He's the one who commanded Mother during the tank trials."

"Looks like good sense has prevailed, Lieutenant," responds Colonel Elles. "Nice to know the Army still values merit."

"I didn't mean to interrupt your meeting, sir."

"Nonsense! We were just discussing the Somme. They're breaking up the battalion, Mallory," explains Swinton. "Scattering you around like seedlings. What do you think of that?"

Noting the frown on Colonel Elles' face, Mallory realizes he's on thin ice. "Better if we're all together," he responds evasively.

Swinton slaps his thigh and howls. "See, Hugh! Even the new lieutenant can see we're making a mistake!"

Striding along the duckboard path between bell-shaped squad tents, Mallory peers inside each as he passes. Empty, all of them. Rain lashes him as he stands in the deserted billeting area, cap removed, fingers wringing the water from his short brown hair.

"Where the hell...?" he mutters.

Suddenly, he spots Private Sydney, the company clerk, dart between tents and disappear into the orderly room. Stalking to the tar paper shed, Mallory jerks open the door. The young man stands shivering in a sopping wool uniform, toweling his hair dry.

"Sydney?" asks Mallory with a hint of suspicion in his voice. "Where is the Section?"

Dropping the towel, Sydney turns pale. "Sir?"

"The Section, Sydney. Second Section, to be precise. My Section. Where are they?"

"Um, aren't they here?"

"No, Sydney. They're not. That's why I'm asking."

The young soldier's eyes dart around the room as if searching for a quick exit. Finding none, he stammers, "We thought you was in Abbeville until tomorrow, sir."

"Clearly. So, they're where?"

"Bray, Sir."

"Are they on a detail?"

"Not quite, sir."

"*Explain!*"

"Well, sir. Sergeant James went into town to get some supplies for the mess and discovered a ...uh... *establishment*, sir."

"You mean he went into town to get alcohol and discovered an *estaminet?*"

"Um, no sir. An *establishment*."

"What kind of establishment?"

"A brothel," admits Sydney.

"*A brothel?*"

"They call 'em 'maisons de tolérance'. He... uh... spent some time there and came back with... well... *stories*, sir."

"On which basis the entire section *deserted?*"

"I wouldn't say they deserted, sir. They just drifted away in twos and threes. You know, one bloke wandered off, then another, then another..."

"Where is this place?"

"There's a diff'rent one for officers, sir."

"*I'm not going to partake of the services, Private!*" sputters Mallory. "I'm going to locate my section! Everyone is supposed to be restricted to camp."

Sydney shrinks beneath Mallory's angry glare. "Number twelve Rue Pasteur, sir. A two-storey house half-way down the street. There's a blue lamp at the front."

Mallory fixes his cap firmly on his head and turns to leave.

"Ask for Elise," adds Sydney helpfully. "She's the madame."

Catching a passing French army lorry, Mallory rides into the tiny village of Bray-sur-Somme, its cafes swollen with passing soldiers and convoys moving north. Relieved the driver speaks no English, he pretends he speaks no French and is thus spared the humiliation of explaining the purpose of his trip.

As the truck rumbles across the bridge into town, he spots Rue Pasteur on the right. "Aarrêtez-vous ici."

"On trouve Les maisons de tolérance pour lses officiers de l'autre côté de la ville, Monsieur," explains the driver with a nod further ahead.

Mallory blushes deeply, realizing the driver realizes exactly where he is headed. Nonetheless, he points insistently at the corner bakery. "Je cherche seulement le pain frais."

"Pardon monsieur," responds the driver with a wry smile as Mallory slips from the truck.

Turning down Rue Pasteur, it suddenly dawns on him he can hardly enter the other ranks' brothel in an officer's uniform. Pondering his dilemma, he continues down the curved avenue until he spots a line of French poilus snaking around the corner. Smoking and chatting, they appear to be awaiting entry to Madame Elise's establishment. Mallory crosses the street and leans against the wall, watching the line feed slowly into the brothel as patrons appear from a side door, a look of rushed ecstasy on their faces.

He lights a Woodbine and agonizes over how to proceed. The side door opens and out steps a young British soldier, face flushed as he finishes buttoning his tunic.

"Private!"

The soldier freezes, eyes wide at the sight of the officer striding toward him. "I... I didn't do nuffin', sir. Honestly. I was just lookin' for a...a... friend."

"And I'm sure you found one," replies Mallory drolly. "How many of our people are inside?"

"I...uh. I dunno, Sir."

"Look here, young man. I don't intend to put you on a charge, but I want you to do me a favour."

"What, Sir?"

"Go back inside and call-out as loudly as you can that there is British officer outside and he's annoyed as hell. And make sure they hear you. Do you have that?"

"Sir!"

"Well, go on then!"

With a fleeting salute, the soldier turns and darts back through the door. The Poilu howl in protest, but the panicked Tommy pushes past the line and disappears inside.

Within seconds, Tommies begin to emerge through open windows, climbing half-naked into the alley, jackets tucked beneath arms with field boots in-hand. Several panicked men drop perilously from second-storey windows, landing with a clatter on the wet cobblestones and limping away dispiritedly. The poilu laugh and applaud as the queue becomes suddenly shorter. Within less than a minute, the exodus slows to a trickle then stops completely.

Mission accomplished, Mallory dashes his cigarette to the wet cobblestones and turns to leave. Abruptly, the door to the brothel swings open and the young soldier reappears, pursued by a petite woman in a worn, gray dress and high-heeled button-up boots.

"Où est cet officier?" she demands.

The soldier points at Mallory, who stiffens as the woman stomps toward him.

"*Why* – Englishman – are you interfering with my business?"

Shocked at her brazenness, Mallory stutters a reply. "This... this... is no place for a proper British soldier!"

"You are apparently the only 'proper British soldier' around, because my house was full of them until a moment ago!"

Staring into her liquid brown eyes, he is momentarily captivated by her porcelain face framed by a short bob that comes to points alongside an elegant jawline. Wearing no makeup, she is none-the-less stunning. Regaining his composure, he responds. "Yes, well. Such things might be acceptable in your society, but back home..."

"They are *not* 'back home,' as you call it. They are 'ere to fight les allemandes and tomorrow they may be dead! You would deny them the last chance for feminine company?"

Mallory's face flushes. "*Prostitutes?*"

"Oh, pardon *moi*, monsieur! You would have them impose their manly urges on the girls from the Parish?"

"Certainly not! But look here. It is my duty to return these boys home worthy of their families."

Madame Elise's face darkens. "And what of *our* families, monsieur? You think we do this for pleasure?" Motioning toward the brothel, she explains. "My girls have families to support. Children! Mothers and fathers!"

"And your families approve of your… work?"

"They are 'ungry, monsieur. They do not ask where the money comes from. They don't *want* to know."

"What of your husbands? Surely…"

"*Don't*, monsieur," she warns, eyes blazing as she thrusts a finger threateningly in his face. "You have no idea of what you speak. You are ignorant. *Arrogant!*"

Shocked and somewhat chastened, Mallory deflates. "I'm no such thing," he protests lamely. "I simply don't think it is right to corrupt young men's morals."

Elise shakes her head sadly. "You speak of morals?" She points to the wound stripe on his sleeve. "You 'ave seen war. Tell *me* of morality, monsieur."

"People use the immorality of the war to excuse all manner of behavior, Mademoiselle…"

"Madame," she corrects, turning her hand so he can see her wedding ring.

"Ah," Mallory snorts, his sense of moral superiority returning.

Her jaw drops in shock. Before he sees it coming, her right hand collides with his cheek, knocking the cap from his head.

Tears fill her eyes. "*Bâtard arrogante!* I hope you die as miserably as you've lived!" She stamps her foot angrily, turns on her heel and stalks back to the shabby house, leaving him standing dumbly in the middle of the street.

Thirty minutes later, Mallory returns to the orderly room. "Get Sergeant James in here. Now!"

"He's sleepin', sir."

"You mean sleepin' it off. Well, I don't care if he's bloody-well dead! Wake the bastard and tell him to report to me immediately!"

Sydney darts from the room, the wooden plank door slamming behind him.

Moments later, James appears in the orderly room, uniform mussed, head drenched with water in an apparent attempt to sober-up. He reeks of alcohol.

"Sergeant James reporting, sah!" he shouts and stomps his foot on the wooden floor. The noise makes him wince.

"Sergeant, do you recall the order of the day?"

James shifts uncomfortably. "Uh, yes sir!"

Mallory pinches the bridge of his nose in an attempt to forestall an impending headache. "Please repeat it."

"Military operations are imminent... uh... something about mending equipment and drawing iron rations...uh..." His voice trails-off.

"...And all personnel are restricted to the Company area," concludes Mallory. "Would you like to tell me why you disregarded my orders?"

"Well, uh, Sir. You wasn't supposed to be back for a couple 'a days..."

"*So my orders have no effect unless I'm here to enforce them?*"

Shrinking beneath Mallory's angry glare, James reconsiders his response. "No Sir. Of course they do."

"Then why in heaven's name...?"

"No excuse, Sir," declares James in classic military response. "Unless o' course you seen Elise's place," he adds hopefully.

Mallory sighs. "If we weren't moving out immediately, I swear I'd place you under arrest."

"Moving out?"

"That's why I returned early. We're joining the Somme battle. We stage between Flers and Courcelette tomorrow tonight."

James' face breaks into a toothy grin. "We finally going into action, then?"

"If it won't interfere with your social life, yes."

"I like fightin' almost as much as I like shaggin'... sir."

Mallory stares threateningly at James then, unable to retain his bearing, begins to chuckle. "All right, you horny bastard. Come over here." He spreads a map on the table and traces the route from Bray-sur-Somme to Delville Wood, their staging area seven miles northwest.

"What about rail transport?"

"'Fraid not. It's being used for ammunition and infantry. We'll have to get up there on our own."

James stares at the map. "Across open country, sir? We'll lose half the bloody tanks before we even get there!"

Mallory scoops up the map and begins to fold it into this bag. "Then we'd better get started. I'm heading over to Battalion to coordinate with the movements officer. You get the men kitted-out and over to the tanks, James. I want the section ready to move-out as soon as I return."

"Sah!"

"Oh, and by-the-by," Mallory adds with a wicked smirk. "Now that I'm your C.O., I'm privy to your personnel records."

"So…?

Mallory leans across the desk. "You ever go on a pisser like this again and I'll announce what I know to the whole bloody battalion."

"Announce what, sir?" James asks warily.

Mallory raises the brown cardboard file and glances at the first page. "Gaylord."

"What?"

"Your first name… Sergeant James… is Gaylord."

James pales. "Sir, you wouldn't dare!"

CHAPTER 7
Battle of the Somme, South of Mametz, France
14 September 1916

Deployment takes a full day and half, with most movement occurring under the cover of darkness. By the evening of the 14th, the tanks shimmer with a glaze of sleet as they trickle, one-by-one into the staging area.

Having lost several tanks to mechanical malfunction – and one irretrievably embedded in a bog – Mallory arrives, cold and wet with twelve of the seventeen tanks with which he started.

James dismounts the Section's command tank, "Mother II" and hands Mallory a cup of tea.

"Th-thanks James," replies Mallory through chattering teeth.

James brushes the frost from Mallory's wet tunic. "You should've ridden inside, it was plenty warm." He nods at the cup of steaming tea. "Heated that up on the engine manifold."

Mallory shakes his head. "After we lost Number 3 in the bog, I realized our vision is too limited to travel at night without a ground guide."

James peers around at their surroundings. "So this is Delville Wood," he scoffs. "Not much 'wood' to it."

Mallory surveys the partially-moonlit landscape. Around them, a half-dozen tanks rest at odd angles on the reverse slope of the hill. They're parked between shell holes and shattered trees rising from the ground like fingers reaching-out from a grave.

"I'm afraid the ground in front of the Hun line isn't going to be any better," he announces. "We'll have to do our best to avoid ditching along the way."

"I wish we had time to make a proper reconnaissance, sir," replies James. "We're steppin' off into the unknown tomorrow."

Mallory nods. "Maybe there'll be a delay and we can get a better look in the morning."

"You think so?"

He hands the empty cup back to James. "Here's my chance to find out. I've got to report to Captain Steele and see where he wants us deployed. Maybe he has good news. Either way, you survey the section and make certain we're ready for tomorrow."

"Right."

"And send a working party to see if we can salvage any of the tanks we lost along the way. Cannibalize if you must."

"What about the one we lost in the bog?"

"No. It'll take hours to dig her out and I want the crews to get as much rest as possible."

"You don't really think anyone's goin' to sleep tonight, do you, sir?"

Mallory shrugs. "I doubt it, but see to 'em anyway."

Making his way through the darkness, Mallory encounters one of the Company's other section leaders, Second Lieutenant Harold Leeds.

"So what's the word Jack?"

"Dunno Harry. I just heard Captain Steele wants to see us. Got a gasper?"

Leeds fishes through his tunic and shakes a Woodbine from its pack. Mallory clamps it between his chattering teeth and pats his pocket in search of a match. Harry produces his own and lights Mallory's cigarette, the glow illuminating Mallory's dark eyes.

"You scared, Jack?" asks Harry.

"Bloody right, I'm scared, old boy" Mallory replies before inhaling deeply and expelling the smoke into the frosty air. "Aren't you?"

"I should be, I suppose."

"You've never been to 'the show' before, have you Harry?"

"No," admits Harry abashedly.

"It's all right to be nervous," replies Mallory. "But it's unforgiveable to be callous."

"I just want to do well."

"Take care of your crew," advises Mallory. "Everything else will follow. And for God's sake, keep your Section together during the attack."

As they reach the command tent, Mallory pulls aside the flap end allows Leeds to enter first.

"Ah, there you are Leeds, Mallory," grunts Captain Steele. The two other Section leaders already present nod silent greetings.

"We had several break downs and ditched one in a bog, I'm afraid," replies Mallory.

"Total machines available?"

"Between Leeds and me, twelve. The crews are trying to effect repairs on the rest."

"Any chance they'll be ready in time for the show?"

"I doubt it."

"Hmph," snorts the Captain. "Well, come over here and I'll show you the start line."

The four officers lean over the map and examine the phase lines and timetables allotted to each segment.

"Noise from the artillery will mask movement until you're in-place," explains Steele. "The sappers have laid engineering tape to help guide you to your jump-off points. You're to be in-position at least half an hour before dawn. The plan is to move-out ahead of the infantry. They'll leave the trenches ten minutes later."

"What about artillery?"

"Artillery will concentrate on the enemy's second line. The goal is to get across no man's land and be into the Hun lines before their artillery can reply."

"Is that possible?" asks Mallory hopefully.

"We've been pounding their front lines for a couple 'a days," responds Steele flatly. "Hopefully they're too numb to respond."

"Hopefully?"

"I don't control these things, Mallory."

"Of course not."

"Mallory, Leeds, your two sections will support XV Corps' attack toward Fleurs. Dorrien, your section will support the attack on Gueudecourt," explains Steele as he hands out aerial photos of the terrain before them. "Study those. You won't get to see the ground until the attack begins and we're short of maps. Questions?"

Having none, the four lieutenants nod and turn to leave the tent.

"Stand fast Mallory," calls Steele. As the tent flap closes, Steele addresses him in a more fatherly manner. "Jack, you're the only one of the Section leaders with combat experience. You know as well as I what it's like when the bullets and wiz-bangs are flying."

"Yes, Sir. I do."

"So I want your Section out front. Show the other leaders you're not afraid of what's coming. They'll need your inspiration out there today."

"Okay."

"Best of luck out there tomorrow."

Mallory salutes and departs the tent feeling queasy. His mind reels with memories of Miller's limp corpse laying riddled on the battlefield. He can still picture Chilcott collapsing before a hail of Maxim fire and Adkins' brains oozing from his smoke helmet.

"Inspiration…," he mutters.

Nearing the scattered tanks, he notices Leeds waiting for him.

"Good luck to you today, Harry."

"Good luck to us all…" replies Harry. Then after some hesitation, completes his thought. "Look, Jack. If something happens to me…" he extends a sealed envelope addressed to a woman.

Mallory pushes it away. "You know better, Harry. Give it to the chaplain. If something happens to you, I'll be in it myself."

"But…"

"Leave it with someone more likely to survive," insists Mallory. "This is what Chaplains *do*."

"All right," nods Leeds and tucks the note back inside his tunic.

"Sir!" shouts James from atop 'Mother II' and raises a tin tea cup.

"Take care, Harry," concludes Mallory then walks over to James to accept the proffered cup. He takes a sip and winces. "What the hell?"

"A tot of rum for yer troubles," toasts James with raised cup.

"That's more than a 'tot'," observes Mallory.

"Yeah, well. A ration party got buggered by a Minnie, but the grey hen survived. I didn't want the rum ration to go to waste."

"I didn't realize you were so sentimental."

"'Spose, I am."

In the distance, the initial strains of "It's a long way to Tipperary" loft across the glen. James takes another gulp of rum and joins-in with a fine tenor voice. Several others join the chorus.

"That's the wrong way to tickle Mary,
That's the wrong way to kiss!
Don't you know that over here, lad,
They like it best like this!
Hooray pour le Francais!
Farewell, Angleterre!
We didn't know the way to tickle Mary,
But we learned how, over here!"

"Truly disturbing, Sergeant James," announces Mallory.

"Tommy's contribution to the arts, sir," responds James with a grin.

"How's the Section? Are we ready for tomorrow?"

"Yes sir. Fueled and ready to go. Three Hundred Forty-Four rounds for the 6 pounders and 3,000 for each of the Hotchkiss'."

"What about the Females?"

"Full load, Sir. But we've been having problems with the Vickers' overheatin'."

Mallory nods soberly. His Section has six tanks, three "Male" and three "Female". The Section's three "Male" tanks carry two 6-pounder naval cannons and two Hotchkiss medium machineguns. Unfortunately the Hotchkiss guns are fed from twenty-four-round strips and require constant reloading – they also tend to jam during the jarring ride across the battlefield and need to be cleared regularly. The Section's three 'Female" tanks, armed with four Vickers water-cooled machineguns instead of cannons, tend to overheat due to the suffocating armor affixed to protect the cooling jackets.

"Remind the gunners to fire in short bursts and only on-order," advises Mallory. "We'll be the first across and I don't want to flounder unarmed in front of the Hun trenches like some sort of beached whale."

After briefing the remaining five tank commanders in his section, Mallory follows along behind a sapper, leading his section slowly toward the sound of the artillery bursting over the German lines. In his hand is a lit cigarette, held carefully behind his back to hide the faint glow from enemy snipers to his front.

The drivers fixate on the burning ember as their commander leads them between shell holes and across the filled-in trenches to starting positions out in no man's land.

Assured each tank is properly situated, Mallory returns to Mother II and squeezes past the starboard gunner with an encouraging pat on the shoulder.

"Ready Devers?" he asks and receives a nervous grin and trembling thumbs-up.

He hefts himself into the commander's position and smiles weakly at James, who is slumped in his driver's seat, half-asleep.

The relentless rumble of artillery shakes the ground, deafening both the Germans facing the tanks across no man's land and the crew sweating in the heat and stifling fumes generated by the tank's engine.

Each crewman wears a bowl-shaped, riveted leather helmet with slotted goggles and a chain-mail mask to protect his face from any metal ricocheting inside the tank. Nearly blind beneath their equipment and perspiring like galley-slaves, the crew fidgets nervously at their positions.

Mallory checks his watch and nudges James. "The artillery should lift within the minute, James."

James nods irritably and grips the gearbox handles, his sweaty hands encased by heavy leather gloves.

As dawn begins to break over the horizon, the artillery suddenly goes silent.

"Off we go!" yells Mallory and releases the brakes. Mother II lurches forward across the British barbed wire, effortlessly snapping the wooden stakes holding the wire upright and dragging the remnants along behind. Blinded by the orb resting on the horizon, Mallory shields his eyes and squints out across the mangled terrain of tree stumps and churned earth. Shell-holes pepper the landscape, interconnecting to form arrays of water-filled bogs.

As Mother II moves across the battlefield, Mallory catches the reflection of the morning sun in a water-filled hole. "Hard right!" He grabs the right brake and jerks it to the rear.

Frustrated by his limited vision, James casts aside his goggles. "Where?"

Mallory points.

"Well... shit." The tank churns right as James downshifts and twists the wheel.

"No good!" he shouts as the steering wheels dragging behind the tank slide uselessly in the slime. Mother II tilts precariously toward the flooded hole as James feeds full power to the left track. Slowly, the track catches hold and turns them away from a watery pit.

"What the hell now?"

Mallory raises the large driving port and surveys the landscape before them. Interlocking mud-filled shell craters leave tiny islands of firm earth dotted across the landscape. "We've got to get out of this mud!" he shouts. He spots a flat area in the distance. "There!" Mother II turns her broadside to the Germans and trudges across no-man's land toward level-ground.

As they near the open field, Mallory realizes to his horror the area is littered with unburied British dead from the earlier Somme attacks. "God forgive me," he begs and guides his tank over his comrades' mangled remains.

Whoosh! Signal rockets whistle into the air from behind the German front lines. *Whoosh! Whoosh!* Within seconds, pre-registered German artillery responds by firing blindly at the advancing British.

"Are the others following?" calls Mallory over his shoulder.

Gault peers through the rear porthole. "No sir! Looks like Number Two's ditched and Number Four is pouring black smoke!"

"Was Number Four hit?"

"Can't tell, Sir. But I see the crew is abandoning her!"

Steel fragments ricochet around the inside of the tank as German machineguns rake the exposed flank, knocking loose rivets and melted flakes of armor. The left side gunner and loader drop to the floor, arms covering their faces as ricocheting molten steel burns holes through their sleeves.

Mallory jerks the brake. Mother II spins left and straightens, the enemy guns now directed head-on against the heavier frontal armor. He slams the outer porthole and squints through the narrow slit remaining.

"Devers, get a shot at that Maxim!"

Devers drags himself from the floor and swings his 6-pounder around to the front, its barrel parallel to the tank's movement. "Loader!"

Flynn grabs a shell from the rack and heaves it into the chamber, jerking the handle to close the breach block.

"Round up!"

Devers leans into the gun's rubberized sight and locates the telltale flash of the Maxim. "All right, you bastard," he mumbles and slowly squeezes the trigger. The cannon roars as Mother II suddenly plunges into a shallow, causing the round to plow into the earth a dozen yards ahead. Dirt and debris shower the tank.

"Keep 'er steady, sir! I can't aim while we're bumpin' 'round!"

"Got to keep moving!" yells Mallory as they emerge from the fold. "Try again!"

A fresh round in the breach, Devers reacquires the German machinegun and fires a second time, the tank rocking as the round leaves the barrel. As if in slow motion, Mallory sees the 57 millimeter projectile plow into the berm before of the machinegun and explode in a flash of fire and mud.

"Good show!" Mallory calls-out in congratulation.

The cannon on right side suddenly roars.

"What the hell are you firing at?"

"Hun!" yells Freddy. "They're all over the damned place!"

As they roll through the German wire, Mallory spots gray uniforms fleeing in panic down crowded communications trenches. Dozens of terrified soldiers bolt from the confines of the trench and risk their lives fleeing above ground.

"They're running!" shrieks James. "The bastards are running!"

Clearing the enemy wire, Mother II claws her way up the berm at the first trench. "Hold on!" calls Mallory. The tank reaches center and tips forward, its nose crashing through lumber revetments.

As the tracks gain a toe-hold on the opposite side, there comes a loud *CLANG!* The tank slides back into the trench.

"Shit!" swears Mallory. "We've thrown a track!"

The crippled tank slews awkwardly, like a wounded animal dragging a broken limb.

"Keep firing!" orders Mallory. "If they realize we're ditched before the infantry arrive, we're buggered!"

The guns fire. *CRACK!* Mother II rocks violently, her bulk descending deeper into the trench with each round fired.

"We're sinking!" yells James.

"Can't be helped," replies Mallory. "We've got to keep firing until the infantry arrive."

CRACK! The tank rocks and slides deeper, nose-down.

After several more shots, Devers lowers the breech of his gun nearly to the floor in order to gain elevation. "I can't fire over the parados!"

"Can you fire into it?"

"Not without blowing us to Kingdom come! We're too close."

James peers through the front visor. "Oh, shit! They're not running anymore. I think they figured-out we're in trouble!"

Mallory glances through his driving slit. The initial rout has turned to a cautious halt and slow advance back toward the crippled tank. "Michaels!" he yells to the rear gearsman. "How far away is our infantry?"

"Can't see nuffin' sir! Looks like we're on our own!"

Dammit! Mallory heaves his helmet to the floor and glances despairingly at the anxious crew. They peer back, eyes wide with fear as they await their commander's order.

"Bugger all!" curses Mallory. "We've still got one track and plenty of ammo. Drop 'er a gear Gault!" he calls to the rear gearsman. `

James grabs Mallory's sleeve. "What the hell are you doing, sir?"

"Making a stand. What's it look like?"

After several seconds, James realizes what Mallory plans to do. "Ballsy," he admits. "Stupid, but ballsy."

Billy drops the left track into low gear. "Ready!" he announces.

Mallory releases the left brake as James revs the engine to full power. Mother II shudders, the good track tearing up the trench wall as it goads the tank slowly around, presenting her left broadside to the approaching Germans.

Mallory locks the brake. "Kill the engine!" he orders. "Flynn, bring your Hotchkiss over here. We need your firepower on the flank!"

The right side loader jerks the machinegun from its mount, crawls to the left side of the tank and slides his Hotchkiss through a firing slit.

Tops of helmets bob along the edge of the perpendicular communications trench as the Germans move cautiously toward the crippled tank.

"Wait for my command," orders Mallory. "Let's make it count."

A pale face appears at the trench junction and peers at the stranded tank. Mallory shoves the barrel of his pistol through the pigeon hole.

"FIRE!"

The cannon erupts; the intersection disintegrates along with a half-dozen Germans. Like some grotesque Vaudeville act, the remaining attackers turn and retreat back down the trench, tripping and falling as they stumble over each other to get away from the wounded beast. The cannon roars again as Hotchkiss guns rattle, raking the top of the trench and showering the retreating Germans with lead and dirt.

"Cease fire! Cease fire!" screams Mallory over the noise. "Save your ammunition. They'll be back. Keep your eyes open!"

The stranded crew waits in silence, the only sound the unsettling echo of doomed men breathing.

James leans-in to Mallory. "Sir, why don't we escape out the other side and try to reach our advancing infantry?"

"It's too late. We hold-out, surrender, or die."

Mopping his brow, James shrugs. "Well as you put it that way…"

A series of blasts rock the tank, knocking the entire crew to a heap on the deck.

"Shit!" curses Mallory and pushes James off of him. "What the...?"

"Grenades," responds James. "Will our armor resist grenades?"

"Not for long."

Another series of explosions and the berm beneath them disintegrates. Grappling for hand-holds, crew members hold steady as Mother II slides onto her side and comes to rest in the floor of the trench. Her one, functional 6-pounder is buried in the mud as water from the trench sloshes through the useless gun's port; the remaining gun points uselessly skyward. The crew struggles to its feet, limbs broken and bleeding. Engine oil and coolant pour from the engine, slashing the crew with hot fluid.

"Shit! What now?" asks James.

"Son of a ..."

There comes a tap on the door at the rear of the sponson.

"Tommy, are you home?" asks a German-accented voice. The barrel of a Luger appears through the slit. "Come out, Tommy," calls the German gleefully.

The crew turns to Mallory as one.

"My responsibility chaps," he sighs. "Dreadfully sorry."

"We're coming out!" he calls to the German. As he reaches for the hatch's release, another explosion jars the tank.

"Oy!"

Gunfire erupts around them, screams of pain and terror echo through the trench as a confused melee ensues outside. Mallory and the crew flatten themselves against the interior of the crippled vehicle and await their fate.

Slowly the shooting tapers-off; the yelling ceases. There comes the slosh of men wading through the mud. Hobnailed boots clang against the upturned side of the crippled tank.

There comes another knock at the sponson's rear door.

"Hey mates, you all right in there?"

CHAPTER 8
Resting and Refitting, Albert, France
December 1916

Mallory rides atop the recovered – if not entirely repaired – Mother II as she clanks down the road towing the burnt-out hulk of a destroyed Mark I. As they round a bend, the hulk slips into a roadside ditch, acting as an anchor. Mother II shudders to a stop. Mallory drops exhaustedly from atop the roof and knocks on the sponson.

"Shovels!" he calls. The engine idles and crew emerges, grumbling.

"Shit," swears James as he and the crew begin hacking at the mud into which the hulk in mired. "Are you sure this one's worth salvaging?"

"No spare parts are arriving from Blighty for a while, so we'll have to cannibalize," explains Mallory.

As he watches the crew struggle to free the hulk, a group of civilians round the bend in the road. At the head of the group, a woman struggles to pull a small two-wheeled Ox cart carrying an old man draped in rugs and lying on a bed of straw. Two dusty young girls skip carelessly alongside the cart as a sweating teenaged boy pushes from behind.

Unable to pass the tank blocking the road, the woman lowers the traces to the ground and leans exhaustedly against the open front of the cart. She draws a cup of water from the clay pot lashed to the side and gulps lustily before pouring the remainder over her head and wiping her face on a dusty apron. She refills the cup and passes it to a petite girl with a tangle of black hair.

Mallory approaches the family. "I'm terribly sorry," he apologizes. "We'll have the road cleared shortly."

"Merci, Monsieur," the woman responds as she looks up at him with liquid brown eyes, her porcelain face framed by a short bob and comes to points beneath an elegant jawline.

Mallory knows the face, those eyes. "Madame Elise?" he asks.

She casts a panicked glance over her shoulder. The children stop playing and stare at the British officer as the old man in the cart continues to groan softly.

"Pardon, Monsieur. Je suis Madame Fousard," she announces with more dignity than her present circumstances seem to warrant.

"Pardon, Madame," apologizes Mallory. "I thought we had met before."

"I don't believe so, Lieutenant," she responds and shakes her head slightly, her eyes begging him to say no more.

Suddenly the old man erupts in a fit of coughing, blood spattering from his lips as his head bobbles drunkenly from side to side.

"Papa!" gasps Elise and climbs into the cart. Off balance, the traces began to rise and the cart tips backward. Elise stumbles across her father. Mallory grabs the traces and offsets the weight, returning the cart level.

Elise regains her balance and withdraws a rag from her apron pocket. She gently cradles the old man's head and wipes the blood from around his mouth. "Tout va bien, papa. Nous serons bientôt à Albert."

"Why are you going to Albert?" asks Mallory.

"There is a hospital," she announces and peers lovingly down at the old man. "My father is ill. They will care for him there."

A gurgle escapes her father's throat. Mallory reaches across and places an index finger gently on the old man's wrist. The pulse is weak. He places his ear against the man's chest and detects a deep rattle.

"How far away is the hospital?" asks Mallory.

"From 'ere? Perhaps five Kilometers."

"Sergeant James! Cut that scrap loose and turn Mother 'round! We're heading to Albert!"

He returns his attention to Elise. "Madame, you are right. Your father is extremely ill. We must get him to the hospital immediately. With your permission, I'll have my men load him aboard the tank."

"No, monsieur," she insists. "My children and I ..."

"There isn't time!" announces Mallory. "His lungs are filling with fluid. He's suffocating. *Please.* My vehicle moves much faster than yours."

Elise peers warily at the tank.

Mallory chuckles. "Yes, it looks like the devil's work, but I assure you it is safe."

"Tres bien, Lieutenant," she responds finally. "But I must come also."

"I'm afraid we have no room for your children."

"My nephew will see my daughters back to our home."

"Right," sighs Mallory with relief. "Sergeant James, bring some men and a blanket. We're taking-aboard passengers."

Elise calls the elder boy to her side and whispers instructions in his ear. The young man nods in hesitant agreement. "Oui, tante Elise."

In a haze of gray exhaust, Mother II pivots 180-degrees while James and three other crew members arrive beside the cart with the blanket. "What have we got 'ere?" asks James.

"Load the old man on top," orders Mallory. "Madame Fousard will come with us."

James glances at Elise and does a double-take.

"*Now*, Sergeant!"

"Sah!"

They shuffle the old man over to the tank and hand him up to the roof. Mallory climbs atop the tank and reaches back to help Elise, who springs aboard with the agility of a veteran crew member. She settles next to her father, holding his hand. Mallory takes a seat beside her and raps on the steel roof for the tank to proceed.

Within the hour, they arrive in the town of Albert. The local civilian hospital is overflowing with ailing refugees and wounded Tommies. As yet unaccustomed to the presence of tanks on the battlefield, bystanders stare in mute awe as Mother II clanks into sight and lurches to a stop before the entrance of the building.

"Wait here," Mallory murmurs to Elise. He drops to the cobblestone street and disappears inside to return moments later with a pair of stretcher bearers. The crew passes the old man down to the medics as Mallory takes Elise's hand and helps her from the roof of the tank.

"Get him inside," Mallory orders the bearers then turns to James. "Wait here. I'll be right back."

The hospital is a sad depiction of Hell. Bloody, wounded men sag pitifully against the walls or lay groaning in the corridors, some mumbling senselessly as fever from infected wounds leaves them delirious and dying. Scattered amid the wounded are elderly, ailing French refugees. Some are malnourished, some ill from drinking from stagnant, contaminated puddles, while others are simply dying from a far more malicious disease called hopelessness.

The once sterile, whitewashed walls and tiled floors are stained brown with dried blood and human waste. The coppery smell of fresh blood intermingles with the pungent odor of over-ripe cheese suggesting gangrenous wounds. Nuns in stained aprons pick cautiously between the sick and wounded, feeling for pulses and performing discreet triage to determine which patients will see the doctor and which will be left to pass away untreated but for a kind word and a cigarette.

An elderly nun meets them in the foyer and feels the old man's forehead before taking his pulse. She pulls open his tattered shirt and places her stethoscope against his pale, skinny chest. Shaking her head sadly, she announces, "I'm afraid this man is in the final stages of Consumption. There is nothing to be done."

Elise sags against Mallory and buries her face in his shoulder.

"How much longer does he have?" asks Mallory.

The nun shrugs. "It is impossible to tell. But the end is quite near." She places her hand gently on Elise's shoulder. "I'm sorry, my child."

Elise raises her head and wipes her eyes. "Is there something you can give him to make it... easier? Morphia, perhaps?"

"I'm sorry, but the Morphine is reserved for les soldats britanniques. You must understand it is only for the seriously injured."

"Oui," sighs Elise. "May he at least stay here until...?"

"Of course, my child," the nun replies. She catches the arm of a passing orderly. "S'il vous plait, trouver un endroit paisible pour notre frère."

"Bien sûr."

"The orderly will find a quiet place for you."

As the orderlies carry her father away, Elise turns to Mallory. "Thank you, Lieutenant. You 'ave been more than understanding. I am truly sorry I called you a bâtard arrogante."

"No need to apologize," mumbles Mallory self-consciously. "I... I didn't understand. Please forgive my appalling manners. I suppose I have much to learn about life."

Placing her hand affectionately on his cheek, she peers into his eyes. "You are a good man Lieutenant. Merci." She kisses him on the cheek then turns to follow the orderlies down the darkened hallway to spend the last few hours with her father.

Mallory wanders into the sunlight and stares up into the clearing sky. He smiles and immediately feels ashamed. Surrounded by death, he has no right to feel euphoria from Elise's simple, grateful kiss.

But he does.

The roar of Mother II's awakening engine shakes him back to reality.

"Ready, sir?" asks James and tosses him a helmet. Mallory removes his cap and starts to exchange it with his helmet. He hesitates.

"James? Do you still have whiskey?"

"Couple 'a bottles. Why?"

"May I... liberate... one from you?"

"Uh, sure, sir."

"Thank you." Mallory stands, expectantly.

"What, you mean *now*?"

"Please."

James shuffles over to the tank, reaches into the roof and rummages through his kit. He returns with a bottle of Jameson Irish Whiskey. "You goin' to drink that now?"

Mallory examines the bottle. "It's not for me," he explains. "It's for Elise's father. He's dying, poor chap. Probably won't survive the night".

"And you're goin to stay and 'comfort' Elise?" asks James with a mischievous grin.

"No. I... What?" Mallory heaves the helmet at his friend. "Sergeant James! Get your mind out of the latrine!"

James retrieves the helmet and straightens. "Sah!"

"Recover the damaged tank and get Mother back to The Loop," snaps Mallory. "I'll make my way back shortly."

"Right," replies James with a smirk and turns back to the crew. "Mount up, you bastards!"

As Mother II clanks away in a cloud of dust, Mallory wanders back inside the hospital. Locating the nun, he obtains directions to a back closet where Elise's father has been taken.

Elise gazes up in surprise as he enters the cramped space.

"Did you forget something, Lieutenant?"

Mallory dashes his cap from his head. "No madam," he blurts. "That is... I thought this might help make your father more comfortable." He hands her the bottle. She examines it with the learned eyes of a connoisseur.

"You are a man of many gifts, lieutenant."

"Not really," he replies self-consciously.

Reaching into her cloth bag, she withdraws a battered tin cup. She places it on the stool and opens the bottle. Spilling a few ounces into the cup, she slides her hand behind her father's head and lifts him slightly.

"Whiskey, Papa."

She places the cup to his parched lips and he slurps loudly. As she withdraws the empty cup, he licks his lips with the tip of his tongue. A faint smile creeps across his haggard face. "*Plus*," he croaks. She refills the cup and provides him another sip. He lays back and closes his eyes.

Elise refills the cup and offers it to Mallory, who waves it away. She shrugs and swallows the contents in a single gulp. Mallory's eyebrows shoot upward. She laughs delightedly at his response.

"You don't approve of women drinking?" she teases.

"Oh, no! Not at all," blurts Mallory. "I just, well. I didn't know they *did.*"

She refills the cup and leans against the wall. "My, you *are* innocent," she purrs as she sips the whiskey.

"Please don't say that," murmurs Mallory.

"Why? It is not a criticism."

"It feels like one."

She sighs. "Innocence is a gift, Lieutenant. Do not be ashamed of your gifts."

"Pass me a drink," he demands.

With a smile, she refills the cup and hands it to him. He sniffs the smoky liquid and nods approvingly. "Well, cheers," he announces and swallows the contents in a single gulp, only to burst-out coughing. "My God!" he gasps. "That's... shattering!"

Elise retrieves the cup from his hand and refills it. "No, it's lovely. Perhaps it is an acquired taste, certainly best when sipped. You will enjoy it longer. Like a good woman, n'est-ce pas?"

"You're making fun of me again," sighs Mallory.

"No. Please. I'm not. You did a beautiful thing bringing us 'ere. I want to thank you, not embarrass you."

"I'm pleased I could help," he replies as he overturns an empty mop bucked and takes a seat. "I suppose I have a lot to learn about life."

She places her hand on his. "You 'ave seen enough for your young life," she replies tenderly.

"I'm not so young."

"Oh, you are what? Twenty-two? Twenty-three?"

"Twenty-one," he murmurs.

She smiles faintly.

For more than an hour, they say nothing, just sitting together in silence as the old man's breathing becomes increasingly ragged. Mallory watches Elise silently stroke her father's hand, her glassy eyes unfocused toward a distant horizon.

As evening falls, light from outside the half-open door filters into the room. A soft, yellow glow cuts across Elise's profile, casting her in an angelic light.

Mallory feels suddenly ashamed. James is right. He's not here for her father, but for her. When they met in Bray before the battle, she was angry, a prostitute defending her turf. But as she sits beside her dying father, he begins to see her as a woman, a mother, a daughter, a fragile human being struggling against the rushing tide of war.

A tap on the door breaks the splendid trance. Mallory springs to his feet. Elise turns to the opening door. The nun appears with a doctor at her side.

"How is he?" she asks quietly.

Elise looks down at her father. "Resting," she reports.

"May I examine him?" asks the doctor.

"Oui," replies Elise. "Nous attendonsre à l'extérieur." She motions for Mallory to follow her and leads him into the courtyard.

"Thank you for staying with me… with us," she sighs as they stroll slowly through the trampled, blood-stained grass. "I knew he was ill, but still… one hopes…"

"Will life be… difficult without him?"

"Difficult? I don't know what the word means anymore," she replies darkly. "But he was a kind and affectionate father and I will miss our long conversations. The children won't understand, of course. They have suffered so much. They need a man's influence."

"But surely your husband…"

"… is dead," she announces.

"I'm sorry."

Elise dabs her eyes with a sleeve. Fidgeting with the simple gold band on her finger, she explains. "Henri was a captain of the Armée de Terre. He was killed at Mulhouse during the first few weeks of the war."

"My God. What did you do?"

"Our home is in Cambrai behind the Boche lines, so my children and I moved to my father's farm. He was already quite old and the war finally broke his health. So I tended to the few cows that are left while he watched the children."

"But you're a war widow. Surely there's a pension…"

She smiles weakly. "Eight hundred Francs par année cannot support a family, Lieutenant. It is why I run a brothel."

"What will you do now? Now that he's…"

"What do you mean?"

"Without your father. I mean…the children."

"Survive," she replies with a shrug. "I cannot keep them. Not doing… what I do. So I will send them to live with my sister Louise in Amiens. I can send her money to support them."

"By working as a…a?" He can't bring himself to use the word.

"Lieutenant, what I do, I do for my children."

"Of course."

Explosions erupt around them, anti-aircraft fire filling the night sky. Mallory pulls Elise to the ground.

"Air raid!" he hisses and struggles to shelter her beneath his trembling body.

Elise rolls him aside and stares up at the flashes. "Non, mon ami. C'est la nouvelle année."

She peers into his frightened eyes, gently places her hand on his cheek and kisses him tenderly.

"Happy New Year, Lieutenant."

CHAPTER 9
Heavy Branch Machinegun Corps, Headquarters Bermicourt, France
January 1917

"You know what we did wrong on the Somme, of course?" asks the diminutive, balding officer in a high, nasal voice.

"I know our tanks were *misused* on the Somme, Boney," responds Swinton. "What I need from you is armored doctrine I can take to Field Marshal Haig to convince him the tank can change the course of the war."

Lieutenant Colonel Fuller does not like being referred to by his nickname, "Boney", but it describes him well. "Is that all?" he asks with a twinkle in his eye. Reaching into his desk drawer, he retrieves a half-inch thick sheaf of papers bound with string and slaps it on the desktop.

"What's this?"

"Your new field manual, of course."

"What, already?"

"Certainly. Been thinking about how to properly employ the tank since I saw the demonstration in France a few months ago. Your after action report from Flers-Coucelette merely confirms what I already suspected."

"Which is?"

"Misuse!" blurts Fuller as he springs to his feet and begins to pace frantically. "We need sharp, fast penetrating attacks to break the deadlock. This dashing our heads against the wall is getting us nowhere!" He halts before a map of the Western Front, his long, thin finger tracing the front line from the North Sea to the Swiss border. "After the bash-up at Gallipoli, the Royal Navy is even less interested in conducting an amphibious assault on Germany's Baltic coast. But otherwise, there are no flanks to turn."

Swinton shudders at the thought of another amphibious landing. "I cannot imagine such folly."

"Yes, well. As a strategic concept, it's sound enough. But war is changing, old boy. It's not just a gentlemen's game anymore. Whole industrialized societies are mobilized against each other." He faces Swinton, one narrow shoulder dropping and he cocks his head like a bird listening for a worm beneath the soil.

"Industrialization brought about this stalemate and it has now provided the means to break it! When I saw your tank, heavy, solid and manoeuverable; this, I *knew*, could, for the first time in this bloody war return mass and manoeuvre to the battlefield!"

Swinton smiles broadly. Despite Fuller's reputation as a "Red Tab" staff officer who is "too smart by half", he is nonetheless a man of vision.

Fuller's face falls. "But those damnable boffins…". He shakes his head and stares silently at the floor.

Swinton clears his throat. "Eh, what about them?"

"What? Oh, sorry old boy. Just thinking about the most recent production reports. We're not going to have enough of the new Mark IVs to create a mass of manoeuvre before the end of the year."

"Yes, I know," replies Swinton sourly. "But Field Marshal Haig wants us to support his operations at Arras next month as part of a combined assault with General Nivelle's southern offensive."

Fuller collapses into a squeaky desk chair and gnaws on the end of his Swan fountain pen. "The French," he mumbles. He glances up at Swinton. "Do you know where I heard about Nivelle's vaunted offensive? In a café in Paris! This bally operation will come-off about as secret as Christmas Day!"

"And it will waste what Mark IVs we have," adds Swinton.

Fuller thrusts the pen between his teeth and resumes chewing. Finally, he slaps the pen on the desk. "Well, Haig can't have 'em! "

"And, you're going to tell the C in C?"

"Putting over the truth is rather like giving a puppy a pill, it has got to be wrapped in something the little bugger likes. I am afraid I am not good at sugaring pills."

"Well, we can't just say, no."

"No, I guess not. Can we?" admits Fuller. "I suppose we can scrape together enough Marks I and II to make a decent show…"

"Boney, that's not going to work! We already know the current models simply don't have the horsepower or armour to lead an attack against a prepared enemy."

Fuller nods thoughtfully. "All right," he concludes. "We'll offer them for mopping-up operations then."

"Dear God! That flies in the face of everything you've been preaching to me about! What about mass? What about manoeuvre?"

Ignoring Swinton's jibe, Fuller rises again to his feet and approaches the map. "We're going to have to develop two plans, Earnest," he announces. "One to keep Haig happy…"

"It's *Field Marshal* Haig, Boney…"

"Yes, well. We'll provide one for the upcoming offensive at Arras using the older models and, well, once he's shot his bolt, we'll have another plan ready for the real test - once we have enough Mark IVs."

"Over shelled ground, those older versions are going to be sitting ducks."

"Not if we can convince Haig…"

"*Field Marshal* Haig!"

"… to use his artillery for counter-battery fire instead of mucking-up the ground in front of the Jerry trenches. That way, our tanks can get across no-man's land and support the infantry as they mop-up Hun positions."

"I'll be damned if I'm going to tell the infantry they have to clear the way for the tanks." snaps Swinton. "Mallory would be appalled!"

"Hm? What? Who's this Mallory chap?"

Swinton shakes his head as if to clear a distressing image. "He *was* an infantryman, but now he's one of my best tank officers. If I tell him he'll be following the infantry instead of breaking the line for them, he'll go bloody berserk."

Fuller shrugs indifferently. "Yes, well. His is not to reason why, his is but to do or…"

"Goddamn it, Boney! These are British soldiers, not some desktop diorama for your damned war games!"

"I say, steady old man. You're taking this all too personally. I'm just saying, if we want to make a real show of it, we have to play the game."

"That's what it is to you, isn't it? A game!"

Fuller waves a dismissive hand. "Don't be so dramatic, Ernest. Of course I care about those boys. So does Hugh Elles."

"You've spoken with Colonel Elles about this already?"

"The Heavy Section is now Hugh's command, Earnest. You've got to let it go."

"So I have no say?"

"In whether we're successful? Certainly! You can have your chaps scour every training depot and motor pool in England and get us enough Mark I and IIs to make a go of it at Arras. In the meantime, kick the manufacturers in the arse and get us as many Mark IVs as possible. I'm talking about three or four hundred machines – with trained crews – ready for the real test!"

"Which will be when?"

Fuller flips open a report and scans the production numbers. "Six, seven months from now," he concludes. "The Generals still don't trust the tank. We're going to have to pull-off something spectacular to prove we're worthy."

"More auditions? Can't they see we are offering them a means for a break-through that could end the war? The more we waste our tanks 'proving' the concept, the longer the Germans will have to develop counter-measures."

"Look, here. No one agrees with you more than I, but this is the hand we've been dealt," admits Fuller. "Besides, if we're going to break the stalemate eventually, we've got to create kinks in the line allowing us to take the enemy in his flank. As you've so often said, we can't just keep butting our heads against the ramparts, hoping the castle will fall."

"So Arras will be a waste of our older tanks – and experienced crews – until the Mark IVs can be brought in for a proper audition?"

"Ernest, may I say, with all due respect to your accomplishments, you are too close to the tanks and their crews. It's one of the reasons Elles was given command in France."

"Why, because I care?"

"Just a bit too much, I imagine. There's concern at the War Office you will be too 'conservative' and the experiment will fail."

Swinton curses under his breath.

"For your information, Hugh Elles resisted taking command because of his respect for you. But you know he's a solid, effective combat leader and has Haig's ear."

"*Field Marshal* Haig…" corrects Swinton lamely.

Fuller stares bird-like at his friend. "Go see Hugh," he advises finally. "Get this straight in your head and let's move-on."

CHAPTER 10
Resting and Refitting, Bray-sur-Somme, France
February 1917

A squeal erupts outside the door. The thump of heavy boots reverberates down the hall and terminates with a slamming door. The cheap glass chandelier dangling from the ceiling of the makeshift office rattles as the brass bed in the room above collides with the wall and begins creaking rhythmically. Intermixed French and English voices echo through the house and meld into a dozen unintelligible conversations.

Elise yawns as she pulls a wad of mixed British military scrip and French Francs from her garter and drops the cash on her desk. Thumbing through the stack, she counts-out the money and records the totals in precise script within a large green ledger.

There is a knock at the door.

"Un moment," she calls and shoves the cash into the safe beneath the desk. "Oui?"

"Madame," one of the girls calls through the closed door. "Un soldat britannique is here to see you."

"Send him in."

The door swings open and Adele, a tall, willowy red haired prostitute clad in a fading, black silk negligee and long strand of fake pearls ushers-in a British corporal.

"You will bring James to see me later, no?" she asks the corporal with a wink.

"Bien sur," he responds. Adele giggles and closes the door behind her, leaving him alone in the room with Elise.

"What can I do for you Corporal?" asks Elise.

The soldier removes his cap and stands awkwardly at attention.

"Lieutenant! What are you doing here? And in a corporal's uniform? Did I get you in trouble?"

Mallory laughs. "No. I borrowed it from the laundry. I wanted to see you and I could hardly come in here dressed as an officer."

Elise smiles mischievously. "You wanted to see me?" She rises and walks to him, hips swaying luridly. "I don't serve les soldats, Lieutenant. I am only the operatrice."

He blushes. "Ha ha. Very good. No. Actually I came to bring you some things."

"Things?"

"Yes!" he announces eagerly and opens the door. Reaching into the hallway, he retrieves a large wicker basket and places it on her desk.

She glances at the covered basket and back at Mallory. "What is this?"

He whips the checkered cloth off the basket to reveal a pile of tins. "Voila!"

"What is this?" she repeats suspiciously.

"Rations!"

"Ahhh, rations. So you have come for dinner?"

"No, no. They're for you!"

"You stole these from the army?"

"I... well. Yes. I suppose."

"And you want me to 'ave them?"

"Yes."

"I see," she sighs sadly, the smile sliding from her face.

"But, you see. They're for you and the children. I promise there won't be any trouble."

"Ah," she sighs as she reaches into the basket and retrieves a tin of jam, examining it disinterestedly. "Is the British army now handing out rations to war widows?"

"Of course not. Look, these are just from me to you."

"*Why?*" she snaps.

"I... I don't understand. Don't you want them?"

"I want to know why you feel it necessary to steal rations and give them to me!"

"Because I want to help..."

"Then go pay and 'ave sex with one of my girls. That will help me too!"

Mallory flings his cap angrily to the floor. "What the hell is wrong with you? I brought food for your family!"

"Ah! Food for my family?" she squeals in a voice ripe with sarcasm. Storming to her desk, she rips open the bottom drawer. Reaching inside, she grabs a glass jar and slams it onto the desktop. "Caviar!" she announces then reaches back into the drawer. Slamming another tin on the desktop she announces, "butter!" She reaches back into the drawer, retrieves a packet and slams it on the desktop. "Biscuits!"

Mallory stares in muted shock before finding his voice. "Wh-what? Army food isn't good enough for you?"

She heaves the tin of army jam at him.

"Get out!"

"See here, Elise! What the hell?"

"*Out!*"

He snatches his cap from the floor. "Oh, I see. You'd rather shag your way to prosperity than eat army nosh!"

"Yes!" she shrieks and lobs another tin at him.

He ducks the second tin, disappears through the door and rumbles down the stairs. Pulling his cap onto his head, he stomps through the foyer and into the cobblestone street.

James is waiting in the car when he emerges.

Mallory climbs onto the running board and collapses in the passenger seat, fuming. "Shit!"

"Went well, sir?" asks James.

"Bitch!" curses Mallory. "Bloody army rations aren't good enough for her!"

James shakes his head. "Women," he snorts with a smile.

"'Women?' Is that the extent of your wisdom?" scoffs Mallory.

"Tha's about it."

James grinds the Vauxall into gear and pulls into the alley between the houses. From an open second-storey window, a shower of tinned rations rain down on them.

"What the hell…?" curses Mallory as a tin of beans cracks him on the head and lands in his lap. "Shit! Stop the bloody car!"

James slams the brakes and the car skids to a stop. Mallory stands in the seat and flings the tin back through the open window.

"*Bitch!*"

Elise's tear-stained face appears over the sash. She hurls a jar of caviar at him. It misses and crashes into the dashboard where it shatters, splattering black fish roe across the windshield.

James stomps on the throttle and the car leaps forward, heaving Mallory into the rear seat. As the car reaches the corner and careens onto the main street, Mallory hauls himself up from the rear floorboard.

"Shit!"

James drags a thick finger through the caviar and sticks it in his mouth. "Mmm, the good stuff."

"What the hell was *that* about?"

"She likes you."

"Likes me? She almost *killed me!*"

Noticing the perplexed look on Mallory's face, James attempts to explain. "Sir, why did you take her that food?"

"I told you, for her family."

"Why *her* family?"

"Well… they just lost their grandfather, didn't they?"

"And you thought a couple 'a tins of bully beef would make-up for that?"

"What are you saying, James?"

"Admit it. You like her."

"Well, of course I like her."

"Tha's not what I mean and you know it. You *like* her. You know, in a conjugal sort 'a way."

"That's absurd!"

"Is it?"

Mallory broods in silence. "Look here, I don't sleep with prostitutes," he declares finally.

"Which is why you don't want her working there?"

Mallory shakes his head in disgust. "Shit! You're probably right. But I can't…"

"You mean you won't."

"Why wouldn't she just *take* the food?" he asks desperately.

"Because you insulted her," explains James.

"No I didn't. Well later… maybe. But not before she went barmy and bunged a tin at me!"

"You don't really understand women, do ya' sir?"

"Apparently not," responds Mallory.

"Listen, you marchin' in there and handing her food says to her, 'I like you, but you're not good enough for me'," explains James. "If she was just another prostitute, she'd 'a taken the food and you'd be feelin' pretty good about yerself wouldn't ya?"

"So, rather than accepting my gift, attacking me was her way of telling me she likes me?"

"Well, yeah."

Rain falls heavily upon the tiled roof. The drum of thunder reverberates down the alley. A damp, musty breeze caresses lace curtains. Elise lies across her bed, brass headboard draped with recently washed undergarments left to dry as best they can in the persistent humidity.

There comes a knock at the door.

"Elise, un soldat britannique to see you," calls Adele.

Elise rolls onto her stomach. "No!" she snaps. "Pas plus de soldats britanniques!"

Despite her protests, the door opens and a man steps inside.

"Je suis juste un soldat solitaire en quête d'amour," he announces.

"Looking for love?" snorts Elise. "Amour is not free, lieutenant. You 'ave come to the wrong place."

"I'm prepared to pay," mumbles Mallory.

She peers up at him. "Why?"

He swallows before speaking. "I can't stop thinking about you."

"Ah, très romantique," she replies dismissively. "But you will not be happy until you rescue me from this 'orrible fate, no?"

"No. I'm beyond caring. We're being redeployed north in a few days. I've been resisting it all week, but I couldn't bear to leave without seeing you."

"So? You 'ave seen me. Au revoir."

"Why do you make everything so damned difficult?"

"If you think you will sleep with me and I'll fall madly in love, you are badly mistaken."

"I don't believe that, Elise. I'll take you however you will have me."

"Even as a client?"

"Yes," he admits hoarsely.

She examines him, standing, cap in-hand, his eyes pleading, afraid.

"You 'ave never been to such an 'establishment'," she observes.

"Certainly not!"

She climbs languidly from the bed and stands alluringly beside it. Untying the string at the base of her neck, she lets her dress slip down over her shoulders, left hand holding the soft fabric against her breast.

"I thought you said you don't see customers."

"I see whomever I wish. It is my prerogative."

He gulps.

"'Ave you been with a woman before?"

Reeling as if shoved by an invisible hand, he stutters. "Well... I say... I... I... mean *that* certainly is an inappropriate question!"

She laughs delightedly. "Lieutenant, there is nothing... absolutely nothing... inappropriate here. Now, tell me the truth."

"Not really," he mumbles.

"Not really?"

"Not at all."

"'Ave you been with a man?"

"Of course not!"

"Don't be such a prude, lieutenant. Many of your public school chums learned their way around a woman through the rear of their fellows."

"Well, not I!"

"So you are a virgin," she concludes. "Très bien. Then you will need some instruction."

Her hand drops to her side and the dress slides to the floor. Beneath she is wearing a heavily boned black satin corset accentuating her breasts and hips while squeezing her middle into an impossibly narrow waist. Garters extending from the corset connect with worn fishnet stockings. Her toned legs are encased in tall, button-up boots.

Jaw dropping, Mallory suddenly understands how he lost his entire Section to Elise's establishment.

Her footsteps echo through the room as she walks up to him and begins to unbutton his jacket. His hands reach for her and she slaps them away.

"No," she scolds in a smoky voice. "You do not touch me without permission." She continues to undress him, removing his belt, tossing his field blouse onto the back of a chair, pulling the undershirt over his head and discarding it on the floor.

Discovering the scars on his shoulder, she runs her fingers lightly over the glassy flesh. "Where did you get these?"

"Loos, last year," he replies hoarsely.

"Then you are my hero," she sighs and gently kisses the scar.

Fingers crawling down his body, she discovers him aroused. "Ah, I see you have already mastered the basics," she chuckles.

CHAPTER 11
Battle of Arras, France
April 1917

Drip, drip, drip…

The gunner drags a rag across the floor with the sole of his boot to sop-up the puddle forming inside Mother II's belly. "Bloody rain!" curses Private Harris, the new port side gunner.

"Flanders, mate. Ain't nothin' else 'ere but mud and rain," replies James. "The only time you'll find solid ground is in the winter when the mud freezes."

"So, what? We sit here until winter returns?"

"We'll jump-off soon enough. Don't get yer knickers in a wad."

Harris swears again and wrings-out the soggy rag through the firing slit above his gun. He peers into the blinding fog. "Where's the lieutenant?"

James shifts in his driver's seat and adjusts the cap covering his tired eyes. "Got called up to HQ. Probably gettin' the orders for the attack you're so bloody anxious about."

Moments later there's a rap on the right sponson. Harris looks to James, who raises the brim of his cap. "Well don't be rude. Answer the bloody door."

Harris pushes open the hatch. "Hullo?"

A young private is standing in the rain, poncho draped over his slope-shouldered frame, puttees caked with mud nearly to his knees. "Cap'n wants Sergeant James at the command post," he shouts over the rumble of thunder.

"What for?" calls James.

"How the hell do I know?"

"Shit," mumbles James. "Back out in the pissin' rain." He tugs the poncho over his head and squeezes past Harris. "If the lieutenant shows up, tell him I'm at the CP," he instructs as he steps through the hatch.

He trudges through the gooey mud and arrives at the sagging, bell-shaped tent serving as the Company command post. Pulling aside the flap, he enters the tent to find it crowded with officers.

"Ah, Sergeant James, thanks for joining us," announces Mallory. "We've had a change of plans since yesterday. Right-off, I should inform you Captain Steele has been promoted up to Brigade staff. As of now, I assume command of the Company," proclaims Mallory, though he fails to mention the third 'pip' on his shoulder indicating his promotion to captain.

"Good news!" Mallory declares. "The Americans have declared war..." A spontaneous cheer interrupts his pronouncement. As the cheering fades, he continues. "Of course it won't have any immediate effect because they apparently have not much of an army."

"So what the hell does it mean?" grunts James.

"It means, Sergeant James, we've got to hold the Germans until the Americans arrive in sufficient strength to tip the balance."

"Can't they at least send an expeditionary force?"

"Believe it or not, their army isn't even as large as the BEF at the beginning of the war."

"Dear God," groans one of lieutenants. "What have they been doing since 1914?"

"Not planning to join the war, apparently," scoffs James.

"I thought President Wilson said Americans were 'too proud to fight'," recalls an officer.

"Seems the German Foreign Minister sent a telegram to the German Ambassador in Mexico offering to award a portion of American territory to Mexico if it would declare war on the U.S.," explains Mallory. "That's enough to put a bee in the most ardent pacifist's bonnet. Besides, American merchant ships supplying Blighty are being attacked and sunk by Hun submarines daily. Seems the Yanks have had all they're going to take."

"About damned time," mutters James.

"Be that as it may, we have more immediate matters. First, it seems the Canuks took Vimy Ridge yesterday." There's a murmur of approval around the table. "Yes, yes. I know. We'll never hear the end of it - particularly because our tanks contributed *absolutely nothing* to the fight. All eight ditched before they were even in sight of the German lines." He surveys the room in momentary silence.

"*That*, my friends, is unacceptable," he continues. "Good infantry are dying on those ridges and *we* are supposed to be the instrument of maneuver. So tomorrow, we're going to try something new."

He leans over the map and makes eleven tick-marks with his pencil. "Gentlemen, *these* are your starting points. We're going to deploy our tanks at 80-yard intervals and attack simultaneously *without* artillery preparation."

"*What?*" gasps an officer.

"No, wait. It's good. Isn't it?" asks another.

"Will it work?" asks yet another.

"I ran the idea past Colonel Fuller earlier today and he thinks it's worth a try. Most of our assaults launched in the past two days floundered in the mud churned-up by preparatory fires. We've lost more tanks from ditching in our own shell holes than from enemy fire."

The officers trade knowing glances and nod grimly.

"Colonel Fuller believes – and I agree – that without artillery to announce our attack and muck-up the battlefield, we should be able to slice through the Hindenburg Line and arrive in the enemy rear-area before you can say 'Bob's your uncle'."

Mallory circles groups of 'tick' marks and sketches arrows indicating each group's routes of advance.

"Ben," he announces to the nearest lieutenant. "Once we're through the Hun line, I want your Section to wheel west and support the British 62nd and Australian 4th Divisions' attacks on Bullecourt."

Lieutenant Ben Grossman leans in and examines the terrain map. Noting the approximate distances and directions in his notebook, he nods curtly. "Will do," he replies firmly.

"Harry," Mallory continues to the second Section Leader. "I need you to chop two tanks to Ben and have 'em work their way along the line northwest of Bullecourt to clear-out any remaining machineguns along the Hun front line. You and Bert divide the remainder of your Sections and advance on Reincourt and Hendecourt."

The three lieutenants squeeze-in closer to the table for a better look at their objectives, their collective shadow obscuring the map.

"Harry," continues Mallory. "Sergeant James and I in Mother II will join your Section for the attacks on Reincourt and Hendecourt."

"Delighted," announces Lieutenant Harry Compton with a smile.

"I wouldn't bet on it," snorts Mallory then resumes making assignments.

"Bert," he instructs the third Section Leader. "With Harry's permission, I want you and your number two on either side of Mother. Your Mark IIs are untested in combat. So I'll take the lead and you lag in support."

Lieutenant Bert Solomon sighs with relief. "Thank you, sir."

"If there are no questions...," Mallory pauses to glance at his wrist watch. "We'll move out at precisely half past five tomorrow morning."

As with all well-laid plans, the attack is delayed for twenty-four hours. The crew continues preparing for battle amid intermittent April showers. James and the crew have just finished erecting the 'grenade screen' over mother's roof when Mallory returns from Battalion HQ. As he approaches, the crew withdraws into the tank. Mallory enters behind them and slams the hatch. Heaving himself into his seat, he flings his helmet angrily onto the dashboard.

"Uh, oh," groans James. "Something's wrong..."

"Several battalions of West Yorkshires didn't get word of the delay and attacked the Hun lines yesterday with heavy casualties."

"Damn!"

"Poor staff work," murmurs Mallory with an irritated wave of his hand. "Can't be helped now. But it means the Hun's alerted in our sector. So when we jump off this morning, they'll be expecting us."

"At least it ain't rainin' anymore," observes James.

Mallory glances at his watch then peers through the driver's slit into the graying light. "I'd hoped the weather would clear so I'd be able to monitor Solomon's tanks."

"Why are you so concerned about Solomon?" asks James over the hum of the idling engine.

"His Mark IIs are training vehicles. They never should have left England. Word from Colonel Swinton is the main armour on some of them may be just boilerplate. We don't know how it'll react to Maxims."

"My, God! Does Solomon know?"

"Yes, but the crews don't. Until the Mark IVs arrive, we've been told to 'make-do' with what we have."

"*Make do?*" explodes James. "We always *make do!* Do those bloody Red Tabs have any idea what that means *out here!*"

"Damn it, James!" erupts Mallory. "We set-off in five minutes. It doesn't matter *now!* We've convinced them to give us the open field we wanted, now it's up to us to get out there and *kill some Hun!*"

James stares at Mallory in shock. "Blimey, Sir. Sounds a bit blood-thirsty for you. Where's my weepy poet?"

"I'm not getting bloodthirsty," responds Mallory in exasperation. "I just want to get on with it! It's like waiting in the bottom of a trench for the signal to go over the top. I need to be *out there* where I can at least have some control over my destiny." He wipes the sweat from his brow. "I feel like I'm in a bloody coffin here!"

James sits in silence for a few minutes. "Yeah, well. If we survive this," he announces. "I'm goin' back to Bray and blow every bit 'o my pay at Elise's place."

Mallory's face flushes in the darkness. He sighs and closes his eyes, his mind filling with images of Elise lying beside him in her bed, a protective thigh drawn-up over his hip as she sleeps. He can almost smell her lilac shampoo; feel her warm breath on his neck as she stirs against him.

Only James knows Mallory has been seeing Elise regularly since his first, virginal romp. But he hasn't told his friend he's been spending the entire night and departing without her request for payment – clearly their relationship has somehow changed.

James revs the engine, jarring Mallory's mind back to the present. Elise evaporates from his imagination as he glances down at his watch. Oh-five-thirty-two. *Shit!*

"Let's go!" he blurts and shoves both brakes forward. James slips the clutch and with a shudder and growl, Mother II claws her way up the embankment and churns forward, following the white lanes of engineers' tape strung-out the previous evening. The makeshift path leads them the 800 yards across filled-in sections reserve and support trenches to the front line where they crash through the barbed wire entanglements and roll out onto flat, open ground beyond.

Mallory peers through the pigeonhole on the left side of his cupola into the thinning fog. "I see one of Solomon's tanks!" he shouts to James. "Anything on the right?"

As James opens his driver's port, bullets ricochet off the front armor. James slams the visor and curses. "Can't bleedin' look right now!"

A series of rockets whistle into the air from the German front line trenches, the red fireballs leaving lazy pink trails in their wake.

"Shit! There goes the call for artillery!"

As they are halfway across no man's land, artillery rounds begin dropping around them, the ground shuddering as a string of projectiles land in rapid succession, one impacting a dozen yards ahead.

"Hard right!" Mallory shouts as he jerks the brake and Mother II lurches to avoid the muddy hole yawning before them. As the tank veers, he catches a glimpse of Solomon's tank overtaking them on the right.

"Damn it! He's supposed to hold back!"

"He's trying to outrun the artillery!" replies James.

"*But...*"

Mallory's reply is cut-short when a German howitzer projectile drops through the roof of Solomon's Mark II, erupting among more than 300 rounds of stored ammunition. The tank disintegrates in a vicious flash, its left-side 6-pounder dislodging and tumbling end-over-end as it plows a furrow across the battlefield before exhausting itself a hundred feet away. Jagged chunks of armor rise into the air amid a cloud of black smoke before arching lazily back to earth. Flames lick what remains of the shattered hull. The crew is obliterated in a flash.

"Dear *God!*" breathes Mallory.

"Those poor bastards!" curses James.

Harris retches and vomits onto the deck beside his gun.

"Easy, Harris!" yells Mallory. "We'll see worse before this is over!"

Harris expels a plaintive sob.

"Concentrate on the flashes!" orders Mallory. "Pick out one of those bunkers and put a round up its arse! That's what we're here for!"

Mallory jerks the brake levers and pivots to resume the advance on the German lines.

Struggling to gain footing on the vomit-slick floor, Harris presses his eye into the rubberized sight. Leaning into the push-bar, he swivels the gun and picks-out a target.

Mallory doesn't hear Harris' gun fire, but he feels the tank shudder and spots a flash and shower of dirt erupt at the German line.

"Hit 'em again, Harris! *Again!*"

Glancing over his shoulder, he notes Harris has recovered his composure and is pumping 6-pounder rounds methodically into the German bunkers. On the left side, his veteran gunner, Devers, repeatedly hammers-away at the German line, the loader heaving shells into the breach and leaping aside to grab another round even before Devers fires.

Mother's crew has melded into a well-oiled killing machine.

Guns blazing, they churn effortlessly through the tangle of uncut German wire. As at Flers, panic ripples through the enemy line, sending gray-clad Germans fleeing as twenty-eight tonnes of steel emerges over the top of the trench and noses downward with a crash.

"Come-on, Mother!" Mallory yells. "Come on you lovely bitch!"

James down-shifts and slowly releases the clutch while goosing the throttle. Mother II shudders and gains traction against the rear of the trench. Agonizingly, she claws up the other side and heaves herself across the ditch to emerge almost miraculously on the opposite side.

Bullets clang against the hull with the sound of a dozen ball-peen hammers striking in rapid succession.

As they lurch across the undulating ground between successive trench lines, small groups of Germans fire off a few rounds before abandoning their positions to retreat in surprisingly good order.

After two more successive – largely unopposed – trench crossings, Mother II breaks into the open countryside beyond the shattered remnants of German artillery scattered like broken toys by counter-battery fire.

"Clutch!" yells Mallory and tugs the brakes. Mother II stutters to a halt.

"We've done it, lads! We've done it!" shouts James. Pandemonium erupts inside the tank as the crew cheers its first successful trench crossing under fire.

"Yes, *we* made it," confirms Mallory. "But did anyone else?"

The cheering fades as fear of isolation sets-in.

"Everyone! See if you can spot any of our tanks or infantry."

The crew peers anxiously through the firing slits.

"There's a tank on our left!" reports one.

"And infantry coming up behind!" reports another.

"*Our* infantry?" asks Mallory.

"I see Brody helmets! They're our blokes all right."

"Right! Open the hatches and get this stinking thing aired out," orders Mallory. He pulls off his helmet and snatches his cap from the dashboard. "Come on, James. Let's go greet the PBI.".

Emerging from the tank, he spots a line of Australian infantry advancing toward them waving helmets in the air and cheering uproariously. The Aussies swarm around the tank, slapping Mallory and James' backs and smiling deliriously.

"Bloody amazing!" blurts an infantry sergeant.

"High praise, indeed, Sergeant," admits Mallory. "But you've got to keep pressing or Jerry will turn on you."

"You ain't stoppin' 'ere, are you?" asks the sergeant.

"Hell, no. But I've got to coordinate with my command before we move along. Make sure you remain tied-in with the rest of your battalion. We'll catch up shortly and support your assault on Reincourt."

"Yes, sir," responds the sergeant with a toothy grin. "Come-on Diggers, let's chase 'em to back to Berlin!"

The platoon raises a final cheer and resumes its ragged slog eastward.

Returning to Mother II, Mallory spots Lieutenant Compton walking toward him.

"How many did we lose?" asks Mallory.

"Looks like Lieutenant Solomon's and two others, sir."

"Destroyed?"

"No sir. Just Solomon's. Two others ditched. No reports from Ben's Section at Bullecourt yet."

"How's your crew?"

"Two slightly injured – we were lucky." Compton presents a deformed blob of lead embedded with a steel penetrator. "We took a couple of these through one of the sponsons. Looks like some sort of armour piercing bullet."

Mallory retrieves the bullet and examined it closely. He sighs. "How many hits?"

"About a half-dozen, sir. Fortunately they deplete most of their energy on impact, so the ones making it through aren't moving fast enough to do much but create a bit of spall."

"That's not going to last," responds Mallory thoughtfully. "Do you mind if I keep this and send it back to Colonel Swinton?"

"I was kind of hopin' you would," replies Compton with a grin.

Mallory drops the bullet into his pocket. "Our orders are to continue on with the infantry. Why don't you take Mitchell and his Mark II to Hendecourt. We'll remain with the Aussies and help 'em take Reincourt."

"Right."

"How are you on fuel?"

"Probably enough to get to Hendecourt, but not much further."

"God, I wish we could exploit this breakthrough... if that's what this is." Mallory stares out over the eerily empty battlefield. "Head on to Hendecourt. I'm going to drop a note to Battalion."

"The flag's up, sir. The Aussies have marked our crossing location."

"That's not what concerns me. There were too few Germans holding this position. They retreated too readily and in good order. It's almost as if..."

"What?"

"As if they were luring us into a trap."

"Maybe they had to thin the line to reinforce elsewhere," suggests Compton.

"Or they've altered their tactics," Mallory replies warily. "Oh, well, on your way. I'm probably just being paranoid."

"Let's hope," murmurs Compton. He tosses a casual salute and returns to his tank. Mallory watches Compton's tank roar away.

"Devers," calls Mallory. "Bring me a carrier. We need to check-in with HQ."

Devers emerges from inside Mother II. "Sorry sir, looks like the exhaust fumes killed 'em all." He dangles a small wooden cage containing several dead birds.

"Shit," swears Mallory. "All right, load up and let's get moving. We'll go as far as we can on what petrol we've got. Maybe the Aussies can get a message back for us."

Amid good-natured grumbling, the crew remounts and cranks-up Mother II's engine. As they roll cross-country past shattered woods and abandoned trenches, distant sniper fire 'pings' harmlessly off the hull. Nearing Reincourt, an Australian corporal appears alongside and raps on the armor.

"Sir! We've got company!" calls Harris and Mallory brings Mother II to a halt. He drops from his seat and opens the hatch. James peers over his shoulder.

The corporal salutes. "Sir, Major Taylor sends his compliments. He asks if you can attack up the Rue de Clichy Road in about fifteen minutes."

Mallory surveys his surroundings. "In support of *what*? I don't see any infantry."

"Your attack will be a diversion, sir. The Major figures the Germans will be too focused on you coming up the road to see us sneakin' 'round the left flank."

"Into the valley of death rode the six hundred...," quotes James.

"Would you shut the hell up?" Mallory snaps to James then returns his attention to the corporal. "My compliments to Major Taylor. Please tell him we'll gladly provide the diversion he requires."

"Very good, sir. I'll inform the Major."

Ignoring James' disbelieving stare, Mallory returns to his seat and adjusts his helmet. "Would you rather be blasting our way across the trenches?" he asks finally.

"No. I'd rather be among a dozen other tanks. We don't know what we're gonna find inside the bleedin' village."

"No we don't."

"Shit!" curses James. "I wish we were female."

"Why Sergeant James, I'd have never guessed it with you…".

"Wha…? No! Bugger all! I meant this would be the right situation to be in a female *tank*. You know, with machineguns instead of cannons. Vickers are a hell of a lot better for clearing streets."

"What a relief. I was afraid I was going to have to tell Adele you'd gone over to the enemy…"

"You arse," chuckles James.

Precisely on schedule, Mother II starts down the road toward Reincourt. Through his port, Mallory spots Germans scurrying between the buildings as the tank approaches the outskirts of town.

"Looks like they're planning a welcoming committee," comments James.

As they enter the town, the tank is met by a hail of gunfire from the roofs of shops lining the street. A grenade dropped from the balcony over a shop clangs against Mother II's roof and skips off the grenade screen to explode harmlessly in the street.

Like a roused tiger, Mother II swivels and slashes at the building, shattering the front window and collapsing the overhead balcony. The grenadier falls off the balcony, lands atop the tank and rolls-off to make a miraculous escape.

As they enter the town square, German infantry emerges from the surrounding buildings and swarms the tank like locusts, attempting to shove grenades and rifle barrels through firing ports. The loaders frantically work their side-mounted Hotchkisses, but firing radius is limited and the Germans are assaulting from all directions.

"You're right, James - this was a bad idea!" yells Mallory as he and James veer the tank wildly in an attempt to crush the attacking Germans.

"Can I fire, sir?" calls Devers over the commotion.`

"No cannons! We don't know where the Aussies are!"

"Well, they better get here soon or it ain't gonna matter!"

The acrid smell of burnt cordite and pent-up engine exhaust slowly intoxicates the crew. Their shouted remarks become increasingly hysterical and obscene as they shove pistol barrels through pigeon holes and fire wildly at the throng of attacking Germans.

Suddenly, the throaty cough of Lewis Machineguns rises above the cries of surprised and dismayed Germans. Fixated on the tank, they're late to detect to the Australian approach through the eastern alleys.

Caught between Mother II's guns and the advancing Australians, the Germans have no choice but to retreat, abandoning their wounded and weapons in a rush for the exit. As Australian infantry fans-out across the square, a few final shots from the German rear-guard announce Reincourt belongs to the Australian 4th Division.

Night finds Mother II parked at the east end of the village, her guns directed northeastward in preparation for the inevitable German counterattack. The Australians' dixies arrive and there's plenty of leftover food to share, so the crew is at least grateful they don't have to break-out their own Iron Rations.

Mallory fills two mess tins and wanders across the tiny village through the darkness. Nearing Mother, he detects the faint scrape of a metal on metal.

"James?"

The sawing pauses. "Sir?"

"I brought you some food. What the hell are you doing up there?"

"Fixing the exhaust. Looks like it got crushed when we knocked down the balcony. All them engine fumes was being directed back inside. If the Aussies hadn't showed-up, we'd 'a suffocated."

"Good Lord!"

"Yeah, well. She's as good as new now," announces James as he drops to the ground and exchanges a piece of crushed exhaust pipe for the proffered mess tin.

As they dine in silence, James finally admits aloud what both have been silently thinking.

"You know, sir. We're nearly out of petrol. If things don't go well tomorrow, we'll have to abandon her."

Mallory nods. "Yeah, I know. It'd be a bloody shame." He affectionately pats Mother II's battle-scarred hull. "She's been good to us."

"Yeah, she has," admits James.

"The Aussies have assigned billets for the crew right over there," announces Mallory with a nod toward a small cobbler's shop. "Get 'em bedded down. I'll take the watch here with Mother."

"Want some company?"

"Naw. I've got memories of Elise to keep me warm."

"Yeah, well. Don't let Fritz catch you jerkin' off."

"I'll keep that in mind," chuckles Mallory. "But, seriously, if you hear gunfire, come at the double. Otherwise, I'll wake you all for morning stand-to."

James scoops the remnants of the nights' rations from his tin, licks his spoon and stands to leave. "Can I bring you somethin' – other than Elise?"

"Blanket would be nice," Mallory shrugs. "It's surprising how cold it gets by the end of a hot day."

"*Screeeee... BOOM!*"

"What the...?" Mallory bolts upright.

There's a rattle of machinegun fire on his left. He's fallen asleep at his post. Cursing his own carelessness, he kicks open the hatch in time to see James and the crew dashing toward the tank.

"Is this the counter-attack?" yells James.

"I dunno. Can't see anything yet," admits Mallory. As the crew enters the tank, he slaps each on his shoulder. "Mornin' Devers. Freddy, did you sleep well?"

"Lousy way to wake-up!"

"Yeah, I know. I'll speak with Innkeeper about the neighbors." He stops the gearsmen. "Gault. Michaels. You two come with me. Mother's not going anywhere and the Aussies are going to need all the help they can get. We're infantry today."

"Damned Army," responds Gault. "I want a word with my recruiter."

"Well, he's right over there. Follow me!"

As the three of them trot across the town square, Mallory stoops and grabs a Mauser and bandolier from a bloating German corpse. "Gault!" he shouts, tossing him the rifle and ammunition. "Find another for Michaels. Meet me at the command post at the Boulangerie."

"Right, sir!"

Mallory continues at a sprint across the square and enters the bakery to find Major Taylor frantically cranking a field phone. "Hullo? Hullo?" Taylor shouts into the handset. Receiving no response, he heaves the useless equipment across the table. "Bloody wires are cut!"

"Sir, Captain Mallory at your service! My tank is on the north side of town. We're low on petrol, but we can still use the guns to provide fire support!"

"Ah, yes. Mallory. Show me!"

Mallory leads him to the door just as German artillery begins dropping on the town. Through the smoke, he points-out Mother parked across the square beneath hastily strung camouflage net.

"We received no reinforcements last night and scouts report our right flank is in the air," announces Taylor. "If they get 'round on our right, we'll have to withdraw to keep our lines in-contact."

"I've probably got enough petrol to move my tank to reinforce the flank, if you think it might help."

Taylor grabs Mallory's shoulder. "Good on-ya mate!"

"Right!"

As Mallory bolts out the door, Gault and Michaels dart out from behind cover and follow him into the square. Half-way across, the wind is knocked from his lungs. He stumbles forward and lands on his face. Head swimming, he rises to his knees and tries unsuccessfully to stand. Blood drips onto the pavement beneath him. Wiping his face with a greasy hand, he discovers blood oozing from his nose, more dripping from his ears. His back burns as if salt has been rubbed into a hundred tiny incisions.

Gathering his strength, he staggers to his feet and turns back toward the center of the square. The cratered cobblestone is splattered with blood. Gault's upper torso lay several feet from his abdomen and legs, entrails still quivering as the body drains of life. His eyes stare blankly into the sky, his mouth open as if about to speak.

All that remains of Michaels are the fragments of a broken Mauser rifle and a boot from which extends part of a shattered leg. The rest of his body has disintegrated.

"*Oh, God!*" Mallory gasps and stumbles toward the blurry image of Mother II. He raps desperately on the rear door which Harris opens immediately. At the sight of his blood-splattered commander, the gunner's face falls. "My God! What *happened?*"

Ignoring the question, Mallory pushes past Harris and grasps James's arm. "We've got to get to the east side of town, NOW! The Aussies are about to be outflanked!"

James immediately begins flipping switches. "Where the hell are Michaels and Gault?"

"Dead," Mallory croaks as he pulls himself drunkenly into the commander's seat.

"*Dead?*"

"YES, dead! Bloody Hun artillery. Now let's move this damned thing or we'll be joining 'em!"

The assistant gunners work the crank and Mother II coughs reluctantly to life, her engine sputtering from a dearth of petrol. Mallory jerks the right brake as James guns the engine and Mother II pivots. Reincourt rapidly dissolves beneath the hail of incoming heavy artillery as Mother II makes her way toward the east side of town, climbing over piles of rubble that earlier in the day were the facades of quaint cafes and boutiques.

As they turn down the alley near the edge of town, several dozen Aussies dash past running the opposite direction.

"That don't look promising," snorts James.

As they near the end of the alley, a limping, blood-splattered lieutenant rounds the corner coming toward them assisted by two similarly wounded soldiers.

"STOP!" yells Mallory and Mother II skids to a halt. He raises the driver's port and presses his face through the opening. "What's happening?"

"We're overrun!"

"Where are they?"

"About a hundred yards behind us."

"Keep going! We'll cover you!" calls Mallory and waves them past.

"If we tangle with infantry and run out of petrol, we're buggered," advises James.

"I know, I know! We're not going to stand and fight, but we can at least scatter the bastards and give the Aussies a chance to evacuate their wounded."

"Noble bastard," swears James and spurs Mother II forward. Emerging from the alley, they spin left. Hundreds of gray uniforms dart between the piles of rubble a mere fifty yards away.

"Gunners, FIRE!" screams Mallory. Cannons roar, shattering piles of debris and bringing building frontages down atop the advancing Germans. After several salvos, the German attack stalls and begins to ebb.

Taking advantage of the reprieve, Mallory grasps James' shoulder and shoves him from his seat.

"Go! Take the crew with you! Head south. I'll catch up."

"I ain't leaving you here!"

"It's all right, the Huns' got his wind up for the moment. But I'm not turning Mother over to them." He displays two Mills Bombs. "A couple of these in the ammo locker and she'll be scrap."

James stares at him, incredulous. "You're barmy!"

Mallory glances through the driver's port. "And you're wasting time! They're regrouping; now *go* before they resume their attack!"

"Everyone out, NOW!" roars James. The crew departs through the hatch one-by-one and dash down the alley.

Before following, James thrusts a threatening finger in Mallory's face. "I'll be waiting for you at Bray. And if you don't make it, I'm gonna shag Elise myself!"

"Piss-off, you big ape. She only likes officers. Now *MOVE!*"

As the echo of boots on cobblestones fades, Mallory returns to the commander's seat. Unlocking both brake levers, he shoves the throttle forward and Mother II lurches toward the Germans.

Retreating to the hatch, he jerks the pins from both grenades, releases the arming levers and flips them inside Mother II. Timing his leap, he springs from the hatch and stumbles through the blasted door of a roofless church.

"Arrggghhh," he groans as he struggles to his feet.

"*Hande hoch!*"

He glances up to see a frightened German soldier pointing a rifle, its butcher blade bayonet inches from his face.

He raises his hands resignedly. "Bloody Hun," he swears.

Mother's engine sputters and dies.

"Shit." He smiles at the self-satisfied German. "Looks like you win, mate."

The German grins warily.

Mother suddenly erupts, the explosion rattling the beams and raining dust down upon them. A fraction of a second later, the stored ammunition explodes, the ground trembles and the remainder of the roof begins to collapse overhead.

The German glances up, open-mouthed. Seizing the moment, Mallory grasps the German's rifle and drives it into the stunned man's face. The German staggers backward several drunken steps and sinks to his knees. Mallory wrenches the rifle from his hands and brings it down on to top of the German's helmet. A loud clang of wood on steel and the German collapses onto his face.

Mallory flings aside the rifle and darts through the church, communion wafers crunching beneath his boots as he emerges into an alley and begins working his way south toward Entente' lines.

CHAPTER 12
Resting and Refitting, Bray-sur-Somme, France
May 1917

After an hour and a half bumping over dilapidated dirt roads, the steel-wheeled French Renault troop carrier arrives in Bray-sur-Somme.

"Nous sommes arrivés," calls the driver. Mallory drops from the canvas-covered cargo compartment along with a dozen exhausted French Poilu.

"Merci, Sergeant!" Mallory calls to the driver and struggles down the street, kit in-hand, to the gray stone building beside the alley. Unconcerned he is clad in an officer's uniform – which has in fact come to closely resemble that of the other ranks over time – he pushes past the Poilu and clomps exhaustedly up the stairs to Elise's bedroom. Without knocking, he pushes open the door and steps inside.

Startled, Elise looks up from beside her bed to see him standing crookedly, his right arm in a sling.

"So, this is how you come back to me?" she asks.

"I'm not much the worse for wear." replies Mallory as he drops his kit on the bed and begins to shrug-off his tunic, careful to avoid tearing lose the bandages plastering his back. "Just a bit of shrapnel. At least it earned me a bit of leave."

Elise sinks onto the edge of the mattress. "Why are you here?" She asks finally.

"Where else would I go on leave?"

"I never expected to see you again," she murmurs.

"Are you disappointed?"

She peers up at him with liquid brown eyes. "No, of course not … just… reconciled."

"Reconciled?"

"To the idea I'd never see you again," she replies with a shrug.

Kneeling beside her bed, he takes her hand. "I told you I'd come back. Why wouldn't I?"

"Isn't it obvious?"

"Of course, I could be killed…"

"Don't be naïve!" she snaps. "*Of course* you will be killed. We will all be killed before la guerre est terminée!" Her face is drawn and tired, seemingly ten years older than the month before.

"I seem to have come out of it pretty well so far," he insists gallantly.

"Oui, you have been wounded twice and fallen in love with a prostitute. *Très impressionnant!*"

"I'm content," responds Mallory with a tentative grin. "Besides, if you are right and we are all doomed, isn't it all the more reason to live while we can?"

Rising suddenly, she rips her hand from his grasp. She takes several steps then spins to face him. "What do you see happening between us?"

"I just want to be with you," Mallory replies as he rises to his feet. "I thought that was obvious."

"Jack, I'm not romantique… I cannot 'be with you' the way you mean it."

"Who said anything about romance?"

"Don't pretend with me, Jack. Do you really believe, if we somehow survive this hell, you will take me home to meet your parents?"

"I have no such illusions."

"Ah ha! Because you would be ashamed!"

"Not ashamed of you. Ashamed of my family."

"Pourquoi pas? You hated your parents?"

"No. Just my father."

"And your mother?"

"She's dead."

"I am sorry. But it does not change anything…"

"My father was a Sir Reginald McKenzie," Mallory announces. "Have you heard of him?"

She shakes her head silently.

"He was a politician of some note a few years ago," Mallory explains. "Good family, landed, fox hunting and all. My mum was a school teacher at a prominent girl's school where Sir Reginald's daughters studied.

"You mean, your sisters…"

"No. His daughters."

"Ah," Elise gasps in realization.

"She was his mistress, Elise. So you see, I really *am* a bâtard, as you said before."

Her hand covers a startled gasp. "I… I would never 'ave said it if I'd known."

A fleeting smile creases his lips. "Yes you would. Lord knows you go for the throat. My point is, I'm not the innocent you imagine me to be."

"No," she concedes. "Not any more. But still, one day you will be angry with me about something - or perhaps about nothing. That word will come out."

"What 'word'?"

"Whore".

"No!" snaps Mallory.

"*Whore!*" she repeats, louder.

"*Shut up!*"

"You see how easily it provokes you? Whore…"

"*Please,*" pleads Mallory. "Don't do this!"

"Why? You must know what it would be like. A person's past follows her forever…"

"It doesn't matter to me," he pleads and reaches out for her.

She shrinks from his grasp.

He lowers his arms and stands pathetically in the middle of the room, alone, like an abandoned child. "Sir Reginald murdered my mother."

Staring at her defiantly, he awaits her response.

For once, she seems speechless, as if a ghostly hand had reached down her throat and ripped the words from within. She steps before him, places her hand on his cheek and wipes the single tear trickling from his eye.

"Mon pauvre cheri," she whispers.

"He was drunk; he'd learned my mother was going to leave him. I was only ten years old at the time," croaks Mallory. "I witnessed the whole thing. All I could think of was that word, my father kept screaming over and over as he beat her to death: 'whore', 'filthy whore'..."

Tears streaming down his face, he collapses exhaustedly onto her vanity chair. She takes a seat gingerly on the edge of the bed across from him, as if too sudden a movement might break the spell.

"I was so young," he rasps. "I didn't even know what it meant, that word. But he was so *angry*. I just knew it meant she had done something *awful*, something that meant she deserved the beating..." His voice cracks. He buries his face in his hands and sobs quietly.

Elise slides from the bed and kneels at his feet. Drawing his hands from his face she gently pulls him into her shoulder, lightly stroking his hair.

"What happened to your father?"

He wipes his tears and looks down at her. "Nothing. He had friends in high places so the murder was found to be the result of an attempted rape by a passing merchant seaman."

"But your testimony?"

"I never told anyone what I saw," he croaks.

"*Mon Dieu!*"

His words are so cold she shivers at the blank, emotionless flatness of his voice. After a few minutes, he clears his throat, wipes his eyes and peers down into her angelic face.

"I fell in love with you the first day we met," he admits. "You were so defiant, so unrepentant. And I couldn't help thinking, *that's* how my mother should have been. But she wasn't. She *didn't lift a finger* to defend herself. I hated her."

Tears began to flow again. "I didn't realize all she was doing was trying to protect her children. Instead I blamed *her*. *Why?*"

Elise takes his hand and holds it to her cheek. "Because she left you," she whispers hoarsely.

"We're hit!" shrieks Mallory as the tank shudders to a stop. Choking smoke billows through the interior. "Everyone out, OUT!"

No one moves.

"James, *let's go!*" He shoves his friend who topples limply from his seat and lands, lifeless, in a pool of blood on the deck. Behind him, the gunners are dead, their skeletal bodies slump over rusting guns. The remainder of the crew lay in heaps of bleached bones and tattered uniforms.

Climbing over the corpses, Mallory grasps the hatch release. Glowing cherry-red, the handle sears the flesh. He screams and pulls away, a layer of skin clinging to the bare metal. From outside, an eerie "*hiss-whoosh*" announces a flamethrower.

"Sie sterben, Tommy!" screams a German. "*You die!*"

Liquid fire oozes through the firing ports and licks at his uniform.

"Stop! STOP!" screams Mallory. "I surrender!"

Hysterical laugher from outside offers no hope of mercy.

He's going to die.

"Nooooo!" he screams, flailing wildly as his flesh blisters and begins to char...

"Jack! Réveilles-toi mon amour! Wake up!" demands Elise, shaking him violently. He springs upright, sweat-soaked linen sheet sliding to the floor as he sits naked on the edge of the bed. Burying his face in his hands, he trembles violently. "My God! *My God!*"

"It is only a nightmare, my love. Just a nightmare," explains Elise as she wraps her arms around him, her bare breasts pressing against his back, her chin resting on his shoulder. "You 'ave had many nights like this. But I think you do not always remember..."

He sighs heavily. "God, it's so real..."

"C'est la guerre," she purrs. "It makes us all insane."

His breathing becomes regular, his heartbeat returning to normal. Elise's nude flesh, usually so soft, so cool, seems suddenly sticky; her embrace, confining. Wresting himself from her grip, he rises from bed and opens the window to stare into the cool, damp night. Rain patters heavily on the roof. He leans through the window and allows the cold spring rain to flow over his head. Gradually the nightmare images fade, leaving only a faint echo of horror.

Elise sits silently, cross-legged on the bed and watches as he retreats from the window to retrieve his tunic from the back of a chair and fish out a pack of Woodbines and trench lighter. With trembling fingers, he places the cigarette between his lips and lights it. Inhaling deeply, he holds the smoke in his lungs then slowly exhales through his nostrils. After several rejuvenating puffs, he again feels her presence.

He turns to speak; a flash of lightning illuminates her like a strobe, her petite, pale frame caught in the moment as if by a camera. As the room fades to black, he imagines he can still detect her ghostly silhouette.

"Would you like a cigarette?"

"Oui, pourquoi pas?" she responds. As he lights the second cigarette, she slides from the bed and steps beside him at the window. He passes the cigarette to her and they stand silently, listening to the rumble of thunder in the distance.

"When do you leave?" she asks finally.

"Not sure. A couple of days, I suppose. Colonel Fuller is waiting to debrief me about Arras."

"Must you?"

"Must I what?"

"Leave."

"Of course," he chuckles.

She slips her arms around his waist and snuggles against his chest. "Why do you say, 'of course'?"

He strokes her silken black hair. "I'm a soldier, Elise. An officer. I have no choice."

"You could refuse to return?"

"I'd be absent without leave. That would be a court-martial offense. It might even amount to desertion."

"But some have successfully 'disappeared' during the war. They've gone on to establish new lives."

He grunts. "As if I could."

"I know people in the black market…"

"Don't!" he warns, realizing she's serious. "I won't hear of it. Desertion is a death-penalty offence."

"But you 'ave done so much; sacrificed so much…"

"So far it's just been flesh. You would rather I sacrifice my life?"

She draws him to her, fingers gently brushing the scars peppering his back. "I am offering you a chance at life."

"Please don't talk such rubbish."

"Why rubbish?"

"A wise friend once told me, 'if you run away now, you'll be running the rest of your life'."

"But we could be together," she offers.

"You told me before the word 'whore' would always be on my lips. Well, the word 'coward' would be no less on yours – and mine." He shakes his head to clear the nicotine-induced rush. "No. Unthinkable."

"Damn you," she whispers.

"What?"

"I said *damn you!*" She shoves him away and stalks to her vanity.

"Why do you say that?"

"Because you come here and you hurt me and you ask me to endure even more pain," she hisses. "You are just like your father!"

"My...? *Good Lord, Elise!* I love you. I could never hurt you. How the hell can you say something like that?"

"You make me love you, then you go back to your *guerre detestable* and you break my heart!"

Her voice is shrill and demanding, like a petulant child.

"I won't break your heart, Elise," he replies. "You are always with me. Knowing you're here is what keeps me alive."

"But I *won't be.*"

"You 'won't be' what?"

"I won't be here when – *if* – you return."

He stares at her in disbelief. "What are you saying?"

"I will go away. I will find a place where you will never find me!"

"To avoid being loved?"

She grinds balled fists into her forehead. "Love is just pain différée! *Don't you see?*"

"No, I don't." He turns away and stares out the window.

"This damned war has cost me my husband, my father and it will rob me of you, too," she announces in a trembling voice. "*No!* I will not remain 'ere aching for your return. *It isn't fair!*"

He suddenly understands. "No. I guess it isn't. I can't imagine how you've suffered. But pain no longer bothers me. Maybe I've grown to embrace it – thanks to you."

"If that is true, then you are already dead!"

"Perhaps…"

"Then go!" She grabs his uniform from the back of the chair and heaves it at him.

"What? Now? It's the middle of the night!"

"Yes, now! I cannot stand to look at you!"

"It's raining."

"I don't care!" She glances frantically around the room and, locating his boots, retrieves them from beneath the bed and slings them at his feet. "Put on your toy soldier's costume and go play war with your friends. *Die with them!*" Hands shaking, she shrugs-on a sheer robe and stomps from the room, slamming the door behind her.

Cursing beneath his breath, he snatches his tunic from the floor and slips it over his head. He sits heavily on the edge of the bed, pulls-on his trousers and laces up his boots before winding his puttees from ankle to calf. Then he rolls his kit and tucks it beneath his arm. After one last glance around the bedroom, a final breath of her lingering perfume, he steps into the hallway and pulls the door closed behind him.

Descending the stairs, he passes through the main parlor where he hears Elise crying softly in the darkened room.

Grasping the door handle, he hesitates momentarily, places his cap on his head, pulls open the door and disappears into the pouring rain.

CHAPTER 13
Tank Corps Headquarters, Bermicourt, France
June 1917

Traveling from Arras to Headquarters to the newly assigned Tank Corps' headquarters, the gently rocking train and clack of steel wheels over jointed tracks lulls him into a deep, restful sleep.

As the train heaves to a stop he awakes groggily. The coachman raps gently on the door. "Pardon, Monsieur. C'est Bermicourt."

"Merci," replies Mallory with a yawn. He stretches exhaustedly and retrieves his valise from the overhead luggage rack, dismounting the carriage with no idea where the encampment might be.

"Captain Mallory?" asks a tall, thin bespectacled man in a neatly brushed uniform of a staff clerk.

"Yes?"

"Sergeant Alty at your service, sir. I'm Colonel Fuller's batman, here to fetch you." He sticks his head inside the compartment and peers around expectantly. "Er, where's your luggage, sir?"

Mallory smiles faintly and glances down at the valise in his hand. "This is it. Thank you Sergeant."

"May I, sir?"

"If you must," replies Mallory, feeling a bit foolish as he hands over the bag.

Alty leads him to a staff car that carries him along dry, rutted roads past recently plowed fields and small wooded copses. As the car tops a rise, he begins to detect the unmistakable signs of tank activity. The rolling hills and gently sloping valleys are marred by crisscrossing scars and gouges an experienced tanker would recognize as being formed by swarming tanks.

The next crest reveals a valley filled with row upon row of Nissen Huts and several large wooden barns, the camp surrounded by a barbed wire fence. Several dozen impeccably scrubbed, yet well-worn, Mark I and II tanks are lined-up in neat rows across a barren parade field. Scattered around the barns are a half-dozen disassembled steel carcasses cannibalized to provide parts for the remaining training tanks.

As the car passes through the gate and rounds the command Nissen, Mallory spots several officers inspecting a new, dark green tank; one is a familiar officer leaning on a gnarled cane.

"Wait!" blurts Mallory. "Where the hell are you going?"

"I'm to drop you at your quarters...."

"No. Stop here."

The car skids to a halt and Mallory leaps out before the orderly can dismount to open the door for him. "Drop my bag at my billet," he calls over his shoulder and stalks toward the tank.

The two officers notice Mallory closing rapidly upon them and turn expectantly. Mallory closes to within six feet, snaps to attention and renders a sharp, flat handed salute. "Sir! Captain Mallory reporting as ordered!"

The Tank Corps' newly-promoted commander, Brigadier General Hugh Elles, flips a casual return salute. "Ah, Mallory. Good to see you again. Heard a lot of good things about what you've been doing. You're a bit early, eh? Thought you had a few more days' convalescence?"

"Well... sir," stammers Mallory. "We've a... got a lot of ground to cover. I just didn't want to be swinging the lead when there's work to do."

"Splendid!" chimes-in Colonel Fuller. "Just the kind of attitude we need around here."

Mallory smiles, his gaze flowing to the tank. "So this is the Mark IV?"

"Yes," replies Elles. "Want to take a look?"

"Absolutely," murmurs Mallory as he clasps his hands behind his back and strolls eagerly around the olive green monster. "The guns are shorter," he observes.

"Mmm," replies Fuller with a nod. "Yes, new design. We had to shorten them so we can remove a few bolts and fold the sponsons inside so they don't have to be removed for rail transport. Shorter barrels have little effect on accuracy."

"Excellent! That'll speed-up embarkation."

"And save a few crushed fingers, too, I expect" agrees Fuller. He slaps a panel beneath the sponson. "Put a couple of extra doors on her too. You know, just in case. Also, another hatch up on top for the commander and driver."

"Much appreciated, sir."

"Don't thank me. Those letters you've been sending to Ernest have had an enormous impact on production. Of course he drives the boffins mad changing requirements. Not sure what it is about engineers. They seem to value predictability more than innovation."

"No doubt," chuckles Mallory. He reaches up and pats the barrel of one of the machineguns. "We've replaced the Hotchkiss guns, I see," comments Mallory.

"That's the Yank Lewis Gun. Feeds from a 96-round drum," explains Fuller. He nods toward the front of the tank. "Ernest had 'em slap extra ones front and rear, also. So now the commander and gearsmen can join the fight too. It provides the crew 360-degree firepower."

"That'll be important now that the Hun has lost his fear of the tank," admits Mallory.

Fuller casts a fleeting glance to see if Elles notes the comment. "Yes, well. Since the Somme, the Hun is expecting to see tanks on the battlefield," comments Fuller wryly.

Elles rolls his eyes. "What's done is done, Boney. Time to move-on."

"Sir!" replies Mallory, startled. "I wasn't criticizing…"

"It's all right, son," replies Elles. "When you introduce new technology onto the battlefield, there are always 'teething problems'."

"Of course, sir."

"You'll also notice we've jettisoned the absurd 'rudder' system," explains Elles. "After action reports indicate it wasn't effective and most were damaged crossing trenches."

"Yes, sir. Sergeant James insisted I mention it in my account. He hated those things."

"James?" asks Elles. "I say Boney, isn't he the chap cited in the report?"

"Yes, sir. And Major Taylor corroborated."

"I'm sorry...?" asks Mallory.

"Nothing, nothing," replies Elles hastily then continues. "We've also fitted it with an efficient muffler so we can get closer to the enemy without him hearing us coming."

"Muffler?"

"New contraption they're using on motorcars. It's a tube with a series of baffles to help silence the exhaust. We also did as you recommended and extended the exhaust to the rear of the tank away from the crew and installed fans to draw the fumes from inside. Should make for an all-around better environment for the crew, don't you think?"

"Absolutely! Any idea when we'll have enough of them to mass an attack?"

"Strange you should ask," replies Elles. "We've got a rather special opportunity to prove the Mark IV's value - thought you might like to help us out."

Inside the command Nissen hut, Fuller approaches a wall map of assembled aerial photographs pieced together to provide a picture of German positions around Ypres.

"I needn't tell you, Captain, Arras was a bit of a hash. We've been letting the ground commanders parse our tanks based on their own requirements," he admits. "Well, that's going to stop!"

Elles nods in agreement.

"The command staff will define the objective, as usual. But from now on, General Elles will decide how best to allot our forces to support the attack." He passes the pointer to Elles.

"Right," Elles rises stiffly to his feet, steadying himself with his cane he takes over the discussion. "You won't be surprised to find the after action reports all support the criticisms in your letters to Colonel Swinton."

"Sir, as I said, those are just my personal opinions. I didn't expect them to become public knowledge."

Elles waves a dismissive hand. "Not to worry, young man. No one is accusing you of going outside normal channels. Colonel Swinton has been sharing your 'personal observations' with me for quite some time. However I'd hardly call them 'public knowledge'.

Colonel Fuller and I have found them quite articulate and to the point."

"Thank you, sir."

"Truth is, it has become clear our tanks must remain concentrated within their regular sections and companies, with each force allotted a clear, achievable objective," explains Elles. "I understand you and your crew led the attack on Reincourt by yourselves and nearly got swamped by German infantry."

"Yes, sir."

"Well, from now on, we work in regular teams providing mutual support and firepower. And we jump off nearer the front so we don't lose so many to ditching before we can join the fight. We can't waste what few we have."

Mallory looks up in surprise. "Few, sir? I thought we'd have hundreds by now."

Elles glances at Fuller. "Boney?"

"We've got a show outside Ypres coming up," replies Fuller. "We'll test out the new tactics there."

"Using?"

"Two Battalions," announces Elles. "A total of 76 Mark IVs with 12 Mark I supply tanks to bring up fuel and ammunition."

"So it's still not the mass we've been hoping for?"

"No, but it'll be a suitable test for the new tactics," replies Fuller sternly. "Don't discount tactics," he warns. "All the tanks in the world swarming aimlessly over the battlefield won't get us anywhere."

"Yes, sir. But my crews need a rest…"

"And they'll have it," interjects Elles. "Second Brigade's going to crack this nut. It's only you who will be inconvenienced."

"Me?"

"I want you to go to Ypres as an observer."

"To observe what, exactly?"

"Second Brigade is going to support attacks on two objectives, Messines Ridge and rolling-up the Oostraverne Line. I need someone with tank combat experience to assess the new tactics."

"Sir, I'm just a captain."

"Good point," admits Elles. "So we'll draw you a new uniform, slap some red tabs on it and make you a member of my staff."

"Like hell!"

"*Captain!*" exclaims Fuller.

"Pardon me, sir. I don't mean to be rude, but I'm not staff material," protests Mallory. "Besides, if I show up as a staff officer, they'll sit me in a corner with a cup of tea and I won't be allowed to 'observe' anything."

Elles bristles with annoyance. "Well, you just made Captain. So the best I could do is brevet you Major."

"Sir, if I go as a line officer with a letter of introduction from you stating my role, I could probably get close enough to the battle to observe."

"What do you think, Boney?"

Rubbing his balding pate absently, Fuller seems annoyed. "I think there are two things our young captain needs to understand. First, without 'staff', those damned tanks aren't going anywhere."

"Sir, I didn't mean…."

"Don't interrupt me, captain!" barks the diminutive Fuller, who seems to grow taller in his anger. "If we are going to be a *Tank Corps* we are going to need experts in logistics, tactics, intelligence, and operations. Those are staff roles and if you want us to win this war, you'd better *bloody well* learn to perform them!"

Mallory gulps. "Yes, sir."

"And another thing," explains Fuller in a more relaxed tone. "You may not wish to admit it, but the prescience of your after action reports and observations to General Swinton mark you as excellent staff officer material – despite what you may think of us."

"I suppose it's just that I prefer to stay with my men."

Elles places a fatherly hand on Mallory's shoulder. "Perfectly understandable," he replies. "But I remind you, they're not 'your' men – or mine, really. They belong to His Majesty. And he expects his officers will serve where they're needed. Now, there's a graduation ceremony for our new crews tomorrow at oh-eight hundred. Get some rest. I expect you to fall-in with my staff at morning parade."

"Yes, sir."

After locating his billet and unpacking his gear, Mallory wanders through the compound toward the warbling sound of a

Victrola record player scratching out tunes inside a nearby hut. Above the door dangles a wooden silhouette of a Mark I tank with the words "Canteen" painted across it.

As he pulls open the door, the raucous sounds of drunken officers strike him like an invisible force. After a moment's hesitation, he enters and closes the door behind him. Several dozen boozy officers take scant notice of the veteran captain in their midst.

He sidles up to the bar and signals the bartender, a burly sergeant who looks as if he was in the same trade before the war.

"Scotch," he calls over the crowd.

"Scotch?" one of the lieutenants scoffs without looking at him. "That's a good one."

"Choices here are Vin Blanc, Vin Rouge and Beer," growls the bartender.

"What do you recommend," asks Mallory.

"Not a bleedin' thing. It all tastes like watered-down piss."

"Fine. I'll have 'Piss Blanc'."

The bartender winks and retrieves a bottle from the shelf. He removes the cork with his teeth, pours the locally made French wine into a tumbler and slides it across the bar before re-corking the bottle.

"Thanks very much," replies Mallory and drops a tattered red and white One Franc note on the bar.

"For a Franc, you get the bottle, sir," announces the Sergeant with a craggy-toothed smile. He slams the bottle on the bar and sweeps-up the note.

Mallory carries the bottle and glass to an unoccupied table in the corner of the room and takes a seat amid the stench of Woodbines and engine grease, sweat and cologne, spilt beer and vomit.

The recently commissioned second lieutenants give the grizzled captain a wide berth, several casting furtive glances his direction. Clearly he is invading their sanctuary.

"To hell with 'em," he snorts and tosses-back the contents of the glass. The pale liquid burns his parched throat, but soon a warm sensation crawls through his chest and makes its way down to his stomach where it settles with an amiable glow.

He refills the glass and sips slowly, contrasting in his imagination the watery consistency of the wine with the bottle of fine scotch he'd shared with Elise. Perhaps scotch isn't so great, he decides. Maybe what matters is the drinking companion.

"Elise," he mutters. "What the hell?" He downs the contents and immediately refills his glass. Leaning his chair back on two legs, he locks his heels on the edge of the table, closes his eyes and imagines she is somehow there with him. A faint smile crosses his face as he takes another sip, the warm sensation of the second drink giving way to the light-headedness of the third.

"Vin blanc? Nasty piss," snorts a disembodied voice. A bottle settles on the table. "You need a man's drink."

Elise's image evaporates. Irritated at the interruption, Mallory slides his feet off the table and lets his chair tip forward onto all fours. "Look here…" he begins.

"Oh, my God!"

"Not quite," a familiar voice replies. A glass of Scotch slides across the table.

"Father Hall? What the hell are *you* doing here?"

Fr. Hall spreads his arms and leans back in his chair to reveal a set of khakis adorned with a clerical collar. "Army Chaplain Department," he explains with a smile. "Thought I'd be better use over here with you boys than puttering around the Parish feeling sorry for myself."

"Jesus, Father," replies Mallory as he stares in disbelief at the white haired priest with the waxed mustache. "You shouldn't be here."

Fr. Hall raises his glass. Mallory responds in-kind. "May we get what we want, but never what we deserve," Fr. Hall toasts and throws-back the contents in a single gulp before slamming the empty glass down on the table.

Mallory downs the contents of his glass and repeats, "I'm serious Padre. You shouldn't be here. Victoria Cross or not, you're too old for this."

"Bollocks! I'm not a combatant."

"My God, you must be…"

"Fifty-three," announces Fr. Hall. "Got a waiver from Ernest."

Noting the distress on Mallory's face, Fr. Hall continues. "Oh, come on. This isn't my first show."

"This isn't the Transvaal, Padre. It's a bloody slaughter."

"I know, old boy. That's why I'm here. I've met some of the new chaplains and frankly, I'm alarmed."

"At what?"

Fr. Hall shrugs. "They think we're here on some sort of Holy Crusade. But you and I both know it isn't any such thing, don't we? The Department is telling them to minister from behind the lines and buck-up morale about fighting for King and Country. How do you think it will be received by the troops?"

"They'll be laughing stocks," admits Mallory.

"Right! Well I'm not willing to lose an entire generation of good Christians because the C of E doesn't realize a chaplain's job is to get into combat and bring succor to the living and comfort to the dying."

"True."

"So here I am," he declares.

"And what happened to the tripe about being a 'non-combatant'?"

"I won't be armed," replies Fr. Hall innocently.

"That's even more outrageous," snorts Mallory. "I know you, Padre. You'll go up there and get your arse shot-off!"

"Not while I have my bodyguard with me."

"Your what?"

"Bodyguard. You," replies Fr. Hall and leans back in the chair to light his pipe. The tobacco in the bowl flares as he inhales deeply.

"Sorry?"

"I'm going to Ypres with you. Word is there are mines under the Hun lines we're going to explode simultaneously. Don't want to miss *that!*"

"Why, so you can minister to the troops?" asks Mallory wryly.

"No. So I can see what happens when your tanks go into action."

"How's that translate into God's work?"

"People *will* die, won't they?"

"Yes. Yes, they will."

"Then I'm here to serve."

"You're nuts."

"Probably. But I'm not under your authority, so piss off."

"You're too obstinate to argue with."

"That's what Ernest said."

"How'd you arrange to get to the Ypres front, anyway?"

"Same way I got my commission – through General Swinton," he explains and takes another sip of whiskey. "By the way, he responded to my request for overseas service the same as you. But after I reminded him of a certain battle in 1902, he threw in the towel and arranged I be appointed Tank Corps chaplain."

Mallory smiles and shakes his head in admiration at the older man's persistence. "It's really great to see you, Padre. Or do I call you Chaplain?"

"Padre will do, son. Or, should I call you, Captain?"

"I always kind of preferred, 'Son'," admits Mallory.

"Thank you, my son," replies Fr. Hall. He reaches for the bottle of scotch and refills both glasses.

"But for tonight, it's just good old Mike and Jack, eh?"

Mallory awakens face-down on his cot, his mouth feeling as if stuffed with cotton, head pounding. The light is too bright by half. Dragging himself upright, he slumps gloomily on the edge of his bed. On a rickety folding table beside his bunk he discovers a glass of water, two pills and note reading, "These are aspirin. Take them. You'll feel better. See you on Parade."

"Parade?" He glances at his watch. "Bugger!" He rises unsteadily to his feet and examines his uniform. One puttee is half-unraveled and his tunic is a wrinkled mess. He tugs at the hem and hastily tucks the errant strip back into the puttee. Outside, the bugle calls the parade to attention.

He opens the door to his room and staggers through the empty barracks. The morning light is like an explosion at close-quarters - a bright flash followed by blindness. His cap feels like a vice, but seems to be the only thing clamping the throbbing mass together.

As the individual training companies provide the morning report, he surreptitiously slides into the staff formation. Several staff officers peer at him askance as he tugs self-consciously at his uniform and readjusts his cap.

Daily orders are read to the assembled training companies. The Sergeant Major snaps to attention and performs a precise about turn.

"Sah! The parade is ready!" he barks to Elles, who is standing only a few feet away.

"Very good, Sergeant Major. Post."

The Sergeant Major presents a perfect backhand salute and holds it until returned by Elles then performs an about-turn and marches away smartly, leaving the General alone in front of the formation.

"Captain Mallory, *come forward!*" bellows Elles in his best parade ground manner.

Hearing nothing, Mallory remains at attention, praying the parade will end before the contents of his stomach boil to the surface.

"Sir," rasps a lieutenant of the staff. "The commander is calling you to report!"

Bugger! One day here and I'm already in trouble.

Mallory performs a right-turn and marches briskly to the front of the formation, his left puttee unraveling behind him. His face burns with embarrassment.

Ignoring his failing uniform, Mallory steps before General Elles and salutes. "Sir!" he shouts and holds his salute until Elles returns it.

"About, turn!" snaps Elles and Mallory turns on his heel to face the formation.

Damn it all! Not in front of everyone!

"Lieutenant," Elles announces. "Read the citation."

The general's ADC raises a parchment scroll and reads aloud at the top of his voice:

"Attention to orders! On April 22, 1917, Captain John Kean Mallory, Commander, First Company, 'D' Battalion, First Brigade, Heavy Section, Machinegun Corps, lead a successful assault on enemy frontline positions near Arras. He deployed his tanks in such a manner as to support His Majesty's Forces' attacks upon three separate objectives, accepting personal responsibility for the attack on Reincourt. There, advancing with a single tank, Captain Mallory and his crew diverted enemy attention away from the main assault by entering the town ahead of the infantry and killing a number of the enemy. Thereafter, he positioned his tank such as to help hold the town throughout the evening and into the next day, during which he received wounds resulting in a second wound stripe. Despite his wounds, upon learning the town was being flanked in great strength by enemy forces, Captain Mallory directed his tank to the flank and held-off several waves of enemy attackers, permitting Empire forces to successfully withdraw from the town with its wounded. After dismissing his crew, Captain Mallory rigged his tank to explode and directed it into the advancing enemy before abandoning the vehicle. The tank subsequently exploded, killing numerous enemy personnel and buying time for the infantry to redeploy south of the city.

For his actions, His Majesty, King George V, hereby awards to Captain John Kean Mallory the Victoria Cross!"

Mallory's knees begin to wobble. He straightens in time to see Elles appear before him, Fr. Hall alongside, his own Victoria Cross signified by the crimson ribbon emblazoned with a bronze cross pattée.

"Good show, Captain. Bloody good show," announces Elles as he affixes the medal to Mallory's tunic. "I wasn't entirely sure you'd arrive this morning fit for the presentation. Should've known better than to leave you two alone with a bottle of scotch."

"Y-yes, sir," stammers Mallory.

Elles offers his hand. "You'll be presented to His Majesty at a later ceremony. But for now, I'd like you and Chaplain Hall to join me in my private quarters tonight – unless you have plans," he offers with a wink.

"No, sir. I'd be honoured," replies Mallory, his head swimming as sweat beads on his forehead.

Elles steps aside and Fr. Hall takes his place before Mallory. "Well, well. You've come a long way since Loos," he murmurs as they shake hands.

"You knew about this last night, didn't you, you silly bugger?" mumbles Mallory through a forced smile.

"I haven't the faintest idea what you're talking about..."

CHAPTER 14
Battle of Messines, Ypres, France
June 1917

"Out of the trench and onto your stomachs!" calls a voice from the darkness. Ulstermen of the Royal Irish Rifles emerge from the trenches into no man's land, their way lit solely by the periodic flashes of shells bursting over the German trenches.

"What the hell are we doing?" asks Fr. Hall.

"Just find yourself a comfortable plot of ground, cover your ears, and open your mouth, Padre. Trust me."

Despite the rumble of artillery, Mallory can still hear Fr. Hall's anxious breathing beside him. He cups his hand over his watch and squints at the luminescent dial. They lay in relative silence, the artillery impacting on German lines echoing like distant thunder. Finally, it's 3.10.

It begins on the left, from the direction of Spanbroek Mill - a tremble, a vibration really. Then the ground heaves, lifting Mallory and the Ulstermen several feet before dropping from beneath them and allowing them to plummet back to earth. Like an enormous exploding volcano, muffled, beneath the surface, the blast erupts into the open with an expanding roar sending a shock wave across the prone soldiers as they cling to the quaking earth.

While the first eruption still echoes across no man's land, a second and third mine explode on the right from the direction of Kruisstraat Farm. Like the first, the eruptions lift the Ulstermen and drop them like rag dolls back to earth, the ground shaking as the explosions slowly spend themselves. As Ulstermen lay waiting for the whistle signaling the advance, debris and clods of sodden earth fall among them.

A rock ricochets off Mallory's helmet.

"My God!" shouts Fr. Hall and he and Mallory burst into laughter - not a humorous outburst, but the insane, nervous laughter of men who have just witnessed a life-altering event.

Finally, whistles shrill and Ulstermen struggle to their feet beneath heavy packs, bayonets fixed, rifles poised at the ready as they slowly move across no man's land toward the German lines.

As the troops move past, Mallory and the padre rise to their feet and glance back toward the starting line. The roar of engines announces the departure of the Second Brigade's tanks beneath the growl of low flying aircraft sent to mask the sounds of the tanks' approach. The Mark IVs pass between the infantry and spread out in small groups toward their objectives.

"Come on, Padre. We're not going to see anything from here."

Fr. Hall's teeth flash in a smile beneath his silver mustache. He lifts himself from the damp earth and picks up a rifle.

"Non-combatant, eh?" chides Mallory.

"Well, the Hun doesn't know that. He'd just as soon shoot me as you."

"True enough," agrees Mallory. He withdraws the Webley from its holster and leads Fr. Hall forward with the attacking Ulstermen. As they clear the assembly trenches, a halfhearted enemy counter-barrage begins falling on the abandoned positions.

Ahead, the creeping barrage has done its work. Within a half hour, the Ulstermen advance to the German first line with few casualties. By the time Mallory and the Padre arrive, there's only desultory mopping up among pill boxes bypassed by the spearhead 107th Brigade. Tanks rumble parallel alongside the trenches, machine gunning and blasting the German hold-outs. As a tank passes, Fr. Hall walks to edge of the trench and peers down at the mutilated remains of several dozen dead Germans.

He shakes his head sadly. "What a waste," he mumbles.

"Better them than us," scoffs Mallory.

Fr. Hall glances down the dead. "But I say to you, Love your enemies, bless them that curse you, do good to them that hate you, and pray for them which spitefully use you and persecute you."

Mallory shakes his head in wonder, "Jesus…"

"His words exactly," replies Fr. Hall with a smile.

They continue across the battlefield toward the sound of fighting, treading carefully between the occasional corpse and shattered remnants of fortifications strewn across the battlefield.

Fr. Hall breaks the silence. "So are you going to tell me about Elise?"

Mallory stiffens. "What about her?"

"I don't know. After a couple of shots of whiskey the other night, you seemed pretty besotted."

"What did I say?"

"Not much. That's why I'm concerned."

"It's just a local girl," sighs Mallory. "It's pretty much over between us."

"Why?"

"She doesn't want to get involved with a soldier."

"Wise girl," admits Fr. Hall. "So where did you meet her?"

"Does it matter? I said it's over."

"Well, it's certainly not over for you."

"Look, Padre. It's... complicated."

"Most wartime romances are. Do her parents object?"

"Her parents are dead."

"So what's the problem?"

"Other than the fact she's a prostitute, nothing."

Fr. Hall halts so abruptly that Mallory is several steps ahead before he realizes the chaplain is no longer beside him.

Mallory glances back. "Does that shock you?"

"Not really," replies Fr. Hall with a chuckle. "It's just that I can't help being amazed at the parallels in our lives."

"What do you mean?"

Fr. Hall sighs. "Alas, I was once young, too."

You fell in love with a prostitute?"

"I say, steady old boy. I wasn't always a man of God."

"Do tell."

"Truth be told, it was a beautiful thing. I was a young lieutenant in South Africa. She ran a brothel in Johannesburg catering to British officers," he sighs, a faint gleam in his eye. "Inge. Gorgeous young lady. Tall. Blond. Good German stock. On more than one occasion I was late paying my subscription to the Officer's Mess because of her."

"My God! I can't believe you."

"I was young and randy in my day, too," replies Fr. Hall defensively.

"No. It's just.... well... you've taken such a wildly different path – you know, being a man of the cloth and all."

"Not really. After all, Jesus ministered to prostitutes..."

"And you were 'ministering' to Inge?"

Fr. Hall glances wryly at Mallory. "Ah, no. I wouldn't call it that. But I did tithe quite a bit of my pay..."

Mallory laughs in amazement. "So what happened?"

"We talked about getting married after the war, even made plans to buy a farm in Swaziland. But as with the best laid plans, things fell apart."

Mallory nods sagely. "Couldn't get over her being a prostitute, eh?"

"Oh, no dear boy! I was smitten. I'd have married her no matter what she did for a living!"

"Well then, *what happened?*"

"She was arrested as a bloody Boer spy."

Mallory halts again. "You bastard! If you're just making this up..."

"Certainly not!" replies Fr. Hall sternly. "I was a witness at the hanging. Went down fighting, Inge did. Kicked the hangman right in the..."

"Stop it! Stop it!" gasps Mallory through his laughter. "You're just saying this because you don't want me to feel bad about Elise, aren't you?"

"God's honest truth," replies Fr. Hall.

Wiping the tears from his eyes, Mallory resumes walking. "So you don't think there's anything... immoral... about me seeing Elise?"

"Oh, well. I wouldn't say that. You are living in sin after all."

"So you disapprove," replies Mallory.

"Officially, yes. But unofficially, not so much..."

"Well, thanks, Padre. But it doesn't matter anymore. She's chucked me out."

"Hmph."

"Hmpf, what?"

"So you give her the last word? I guess she really is just a whore to you."

Mallory grasps Fr. Hall's sleeve and spins him around. "Damn your righteous pretensions! You have no right to speak poorly of her! I'd have thought..." He suddenly notices the smirk on Fr. Hall's face.

"So, she *is* worth fighting for, eh?" Fr. Hall asks.

"You bastard," swears Mallory.

"I'm just saying, if she's the one you want, you'd better be willing to fight for her."

They continue forward as the fighting shifts east. Near the top of the ridge, they spot a Mark IV in a shell hole, half submerged in muddy water. Mallory pokes his head through the hatch and discovers the crew gone.

"What happened?" asks Fr. Hall.

"Abandoned. Looks like they ditched."

"Ditched?"

"Stuck in the mud," explains Mallory. He walks around the stranded vehicle inspecting its predicament. "That shouldn't be," he declares finally. Glancing around, he spots several railroad ties used to reinforce what was once a German machinegun post. "Padre, come here and give me a hand."

Fr. Hall rests his rifle against a shattered tree stump and helps Mallory drag the tie over to the tank. After several minutes of cursing and sweating, they finally work the timber in-place beneath the partially submerged tracks. They take a rest on the rim of the crater and pass canteen of water between them.

"Horses are easier," observes Fr. Hall sourly.

"Yes, but horses aren't bullet-poof." Mallory takes a final gulp and hands the canteen back.

"Okay. Let's get aboard and see what we can do."

He climbs in through the sponson followed by Fr. Hall.

"Wait here. I'm gonna flip the ignition and we'll see if we can get her started."

Mallory reaches for the dashboard and flips the contact. Then he slips the gearshift into neutral and returns to Fr. Hall.

"Do like this," he explains, grasping the starting crank. "On three, we give her a couple quick turns." Fr. Hall grasps the handle and awaits Mallory's count. On three, they crank several times and the engine catches, roughly at first, before smoothing-out to a steady rumble.

"Bloody good! Now what?" Fr. Hall calls over the smooth hum of the idling engine.

"Now, you become a charter member of the Tank Corps." Mallory slaps the back of the commander's seat. "Take a pew. We're gonna see if we can get this thing out of the mud."

"What do you want *me* to do?"

Mallory drags himself into the driver's seat. "Once we're in gear, you take hold of the brake levers and alternate shoving them forward and back. That'll get the tank rocking and maybe we can work her out of this mess."

He slips the tank into gear and slowly releases the clutch while applying the throttle. The tank leans forward hopefully then slides dejectedly backward, its tracks slipping in the pasty mud. He jerks the shift into reverse and the tank slithers rearward a few more feet. As it retreats, he feels the railroad tie slide beneath the tracks. Thrusting it into first gear, he shouts, "Now!"

Fr. Hall squeezes the brake releases and begins alternating the levers rapidly. Little by little, the tracks gain purchase on the railroad tie; the tank jerks forward in small bounds, inches at a time. The engine bellows as Mallory applies full throttle, tracks gnawing at the wooden tie with a deafening clatter, the steel links acting as teeth on a saw. Little-by-little the tank claws its way from the half-filled crater and emerges in a sopping heap onto the flat ground above.

"Yes!" hisses Mallory. "Welcome to the Tank Corps, Padre!"

"Now what?"

"Keep going. You're getting the hang of it."

Cresting the ridge, they begin down the eastern slope as dawn breaks over the horizon revealing a glorious, blinding sunrise making Mallory forget for the moment he's in the midst of battle.

"Halt beneath the crest, we need to locate the other tanks." The machine rolls another fifty feet and jerks to a halt. Mallory raises the hatch above the commander's seat and peers out cautiously. He spots the battle taking place in the distance. Retrieving binoculars, he stands in his seat to survey the battlefield. The panoramic view is striking.

Fr. Hall appears in the commander's hatch. "So how are we doing?"

A mile ahead to the left is the town of Wytschaete. Partially obscured by smoke and fog, its church tower rises above the mist like a beacon for the attacking infantry. Across the plain are scattered clumps of Ulstermen, some advancing in good order, others pinned down on the outskirts of the town. Beneath plumes of exhaust are scattered groups of tanks moving in twos and threes. Packs scurry about the battlefield converging on German strongpoints. An occasional blast from a cannon announces the tanks' contribution to the attack.

As he watches, a German 15.6 Centimeter howitzer projectile crashes through the top of an attacking Mark IV, splitting it open like an overripe melon. The tracks spew from the drive sprockets like entrails spilling from a torn belly. Flames lick the paint. Greasy black smoke engulfs the wreck. No one emerges from the stricken beast.

Mallory slaps Fr. Hall on the shoulder. "Let's get down there and see what we can do to help out."

Fr. Hall drops inside and locks the left track. The tank turns slowly and resumes its march toward the shell-scarred village. Approaching the town, they begin to encounter stretcher-bearers stumbling through the mud dragging their charges back toward the aid station. Among them stagger the walking-wounded, arms and legs swathed in bloody, mud-splattered bandages.

"Dear God," breathes Fr. Hall.

"That's what 'victory' looks like," explains Mallory.

"How on earth do you tell the difference?"

"Numbers… If we'd lost, there would be a hell of a lot more of them."

"I…," begins Fr. Hall, only to be interrupted by a loud clanking against the side of the tank. Mallory crushes the clutch. "Brake!" he calls and Fr. Hall jerks the levers.

"One of ours?" he asks.

Mallory pulls his pistol from its holster and approaches the right sponson. "We'll see." He leans against the hatch.

"Identify yourself!"

"Jock McPherson! Now open the hatch or I'll reach in and drag you out of there through the firin' port!"

Mallory glances at the padre with raised eyebrow. He pushes open the hatch to reveal a grimy tank officer in grease-smeared overalls, his left arm wrapped in a makeshift splint constructed of two German trench bayonets and suspended from a gauze sling.

"You're not Lieutenant Smith!" blurts the officer.

"Clearly," chuckles Mallory.

"Where is the silly bugger?"

"No idea. We found the tank abandoned in a shell hole on the west side of the slope."

McPherson swears under his breath. "Ach, well. That's no surprise."

"What do you mean?" asks Mallory as he holsters his pistol.

"Pardon me, sir. But Smith is a little piss-ant. He got the wind-up and told me he was going to ditch the first chance he got. Said he couldn't face no more shellin'."

"You're telling me you think he ditched this tank on purpose?"

"Aye, sir."

"Where's your tank?"

"Over there," he replies and points off toward the edge of town. "Took a Hun 77 through the right side. Killed me driver and one 'o me gunners. Two others wounded. Plus myself."

"Is your arm broken?"

"Ay, a piece of the armour broke loose when we were hit and smashed it up a bit."

Mallory lifts the gauze and examines the wound. Bone protrudes from the torn flesh.

"You need to get back to the aid station."

McPherson adjusts his sling and pulls the gauze back over the wound. "All in good time, sir. We still got a battle goin' on 'ere. It'd be bad form to retire early."

Mallory immediately takes a liking to the plucky Scot. "Look here, we're a scratch crew," explains Mallory, "There are only two of us manning this thing. Are any of your crew up to lending a hand?"

"Yes, sir!" replies McPherson. "Beats the hell out of walkin' w' the PBI. My crew is bedded down in a ditch beside the road."

"Show me," shouts Mallory over the crash of renewed German artillery fire.

They meet the survivors of McPherson's crew in a drainage ditch alongside the Wulverghem-Wytschaete Road. Mallory leans out the door.

"I need a couple 'a gunners and someone to help load!"

Three crewmen climb aboard and take over the vacant positions. To Mallory's surprise, Lieutenant McPherson scrambles aboard and pulls the hatch closed behind him.

"Jock, you know better. Go get your wound checked-out."

"My crew, my tank," replies McPherson stubbornly.

"All right, Jock," sighs Mallory. "Where to?"

"When we got hit, we were headed to 'Fanny's Farm' to clear out the snipers and machinegun nests holdin' up the infantry."

"Let's go," orders Mallory. He turns to Fr. Hall. "You want me to replace you with one of Jock's crew?"

"No. I think I'm rather getting the hang of it."

"Then go straight ahead," shouts Jock. "You'll see our boys up against the Hun stronghold."

As the tank rumbles up the road, an officer sprints out of the ditch and hammers the right sponson's rear hatch with the butt of his pistol. The tank continues rolling as Jock pushes open the door and leans out.

"Where's the action, mate?" he shouts.

"Maxim on the left side of the road about a quarter-mile ahead," the officer announces. "There's also a sniper and artillery observer in the bell tower!"

Jock nods and slams the hatch. Arriving between the commander's and driver's seats, he shouts. "Just ahead on the left! Do ya see it?"

Mallory partially lifts the armored driving slit. Bullets splatter against the front of the hull.

"*Shit!* Yes, I see it! A little left, Padre. We need a clear shot."

As the tank veers to the left shoulder of the road, the gunner leans into the rubberized gun sight and calls out, "ready! Steady! *Now!*"

"CRACK!" The 6-pounder launches its projectile into the machinegun emplacement. The Maxim flips up on-end. As the smoke clears, Mallory spots limp, blood-soaked bodies lying in grotesque positions among shredded sandbags.

"Scratch one Hun machinegun!" he shouts.

The tank continues grimly down the road toward town. As they near the still-smoldering position, Mallory spots two Germans scramble to the destroyed machinegun nest and attempt to right the gun.

"Don't do it," he mutters. *"Don't do it!"*

The Germans swing the Maxim around and fire point-blank, the gun's armor piercing bullets punching through the left sponson. The tank's gunner drops to the floor and buries his face beneath his arms.

"Hard left!" shouts Mallory as bullets ricochet around the interior. He hears a cry as a bullet strikes home. One of Jock's crewmen drops to the floor, blood streaming from a wound to the face.

Fr. Hall jerks the left brake and shoves the right handle forward. The tank spins left, crashes down the embankment into the midst of the machinegun nest, and comes to a temporary rest.

Garbled voices scream from beneath the tank.

"Our Father...," prays Fr. Hall over the cries.

Mallory downshifts and guns the engine.

"... who art in heaven."

The tank lurches forward, its stern plunging from the embankment to land with a crash atop the struggling Germans.

The screams cease.

"Hallowed be thy name..."

Leaving the crushed gunners behind, the tank emerges, animal like, into the open field and emerges among the retreating Germans. Panicked soldiers discard their rifles and scatter like a covey of disturbed quail.

Jock lurches for control of the forward Lewis Gun and rakes the retreating Germans. They fall in pathetic clumps.

"... thy Kingdom come, thy will be done..."

The cannon roars, rocking the tank back on its springs. Amid of the blast, a half-dozen Germans stumble forward onto their faces, rifles spinning through the air and landing in the mud with a splash.

"Veer right, Padre!"

A steeple emerges from the fog a hundred yards ahead.

"… on earth as it is in heaven…"

Bullets clang off the armor.

"Gunners! Get those bloody snipers!"

Both guns fire simultaneously, the collective recoil halting momentarily the tank's forward movement. The upper third of the steeple disintegrates in a shower of splintered wood and ancient stones, the church bell peeling a death knell as it tumbles to the ground.

"…Give us this day our daily bread…"

The tank continues over a field of German dead and wounded. As it nears the church, the remainder of the damaged steeple keels over and plows into the centuries-old church yard cemetery.

"…and forgive us our trespasses, as we forgive those who trespass against us…"

Germans pour from the collapsing church dragging wounded comrades. Pale white faces flash beneath the rims of steel-gray helmets as they glance back in panic.

The tank claws over the rubble and emerges into the village, guns blazing.

"… and lead us not into temptation, but deliver us from evil…"

As the town's defenses collapse, a wave of Ulstermen flow around the tank and spread like grappling fingers down the alleys in pursuit of fleeing Germans.

"…For thine is the kingdom…"

A group of Germans fleeing across the village square stop and turn to fight; charging Ulstermen fall upon them with slashing bayonets.

"…The power…"

"Stop!" yells Mallory. Fr. Hall jerks both brakes rearward and the tank jolts to a halt.

"…and the glory, for ever and ever."

The Germans routed, an eerie calm settles over the village. Flames lick the surrounding structures, smoke rising over the fallen village as the firing stutters to a stop.

"Amen."

"Amen indeed," sighs Mallory.

Beside him Fr. Hall sits sweating and pale, his fingers white around the steering levers.

"Padre?"

The chaplain's face turns to him, bottom lip trembling as tears stream down his pallid face. His mouth moves dumbly. Finally he utters, "What have I done?"

Mallory pulls his friend's head against his shoulder and embraces him. He feels the unspent adrenaline surge through Fr. Hall's body. Tears dampen Mallory's shoulder.

"It's okay, Padre," he whispers reassuringly. "It had to be done."

Fr. Hall doesn't respond. Mallory draws away and grasps him by his shoulders. "Time to get hold of yourself, Padre."

Fr. Hall looks up at him with tragic, red-rimmed eyes.

"I know it was horrible…" begins Mallory.

"That's not it," gasps Fr. Hall.

"Sorry?"

"I liked it."

CHAPTER 15
Tank Corps Headquarters, Bermicourt, France
July 1917

"What the *hell* were you thinking?" demands Elles.

"He said he had your permission, sir," replies Mallory from the position of attention.

"To go to Ypres, yes! But not to partake in combat! He's a chaplain, for God's sake!"

"Yes, sir."

"Yes Sir', what?"

"I agree, sir. He shouldn't have been out there. But…"

"But what?"

"He was bloody marvellous, sir!"

"Really? You know he's asked to be relieved of his duties, don't you?"

"I don't understand, sir."

Elles deflates as if a heavy burden has suddenly been placed on his shoulders. He motions for Mallory to sit and drops into a seat behind his own desk. "Something about that action made him question his ability to minister, Jack."

"He told me he 'liked it', Sir."

"Yes. He told me, too. Silly thing to say, actually."

"Is it really, Sir?"

"No, I suppose not. But, damn it all! I thought he'd put the Transvaal behind him. That was fifteen years ago, for God's sake."

"Some experiences stay with us forever."

"Well, I can't have him running around the battlefield killing Germans when his job is to minister to the troops!"

"No. I suppose not."

"So I've asked he be posted back to Blighty. He's an old war horse and I couldn't bear to relieve him completely. He can still be of use to the Service. But…"

"That's probably best, sir."

"Yes, I suppose so."

They sit in silence for several minutes. Finally Mallory speaks. "Have you had the opportunity to read my report, sir?"

Elles smiles faintly. "Yes, as a matter of fact. Well done recovering the tank. We're putting some of our chaps at Bovington on it to work out how to best un-ditch a tank under fire. The railroad tie seems to have worked for you, but you can hardly have the crew playing Coolie while the Hun takes pot-shots at them."

"So did they find the lieutenant who ditched?"

"Yes, poor chap. An artillery section found him cowering in a barn a few miles behind the line. Pathetic sight, I understand."

"What about the crew?"

"Seems they thought the ditching was legitimate. Most of them joined up with the Infantry and continued the advance. I understand the driver was killed outside Wytschaete."

"What will come of the lieutenant?"

"I'm not sure. Field Marshal Haig is awaiting my recommendation." He peers inquiringly at Mallory. "What would *you* do?"

Mallory shakes his head sadly. "I don't know. A year ago I would have said 'let the poor sod go home'..."

"And now?"

"I can't blame a man for being afraid."

"But?"

"If word gets out cowardice – no matter how justified – is a ticket back to Blighty, discipline will collapse."

"Do you really think the British army is so brittle?"

"Certainly not! Most stick it because they don't want to let down their mates. But still, if word gets out cowards get a free boat home..."

"So, what do you recommend? Shoot him?"

"I don't know."

"Confinement?"

"It'd have to be confinement at hard labour. Otherwise there's always some poor slob who would gladly swap the danger of the trenches for the safety of the brig."

Elles nods thoughtfully. "I think you're right. I'll recommend confinement and hard labour."

"Probably best for all concerned, sir."

"In the end, it's the Field Marshal's decision, thank God."

"The privilege of command," sighs Mallory.

"Yes, well…," mumbles Elles.

"I suppose the question now is what's next for the Brigade."

"You know what's next," replies Elles darkly. He leans across the desk and pushes aside stacks of paper to reveal a map. "Phase II," he announces and thumps his index finger on a spot northeast of Ypres. "End of the month. Lloyd George is resisting the plan – wants to wait until the Yanks are here in-force before going on the offensive. But that will be some time."

"So who has the final say?"

"Parliament holds the purse strings, but Field Marshal Haig could give the government a black eye if he let it be known the prime minister was withholding men and supplies."

"Who wins *that* argument?"

"My money is on Haig. I tend to agree with him - we can't just wait for the Americans. They're building an army largely from scratch and it's going to take some time before they arrive in sufficient numbers to have any real effect. If we sit and wait, our force will atrophy while we provide the Germans time to prepare for a major offensive to end the war before the Yanks arrive."

"Then we attack."

"Yes, but I'm not comfortable with the battlefield."

Mallory leans over the map, squinting at the roads and contour lines playing across its folds. "What's the terrain like?"

"I'm afraid it's a bit marshy, but if the weather cooperates, the ground seems firm enough to support our tanks. I've ordered First Brigade to be brought up by train. You'll be attached to XVIII Corps to help seize the Steenbeek River crossings at Mon du Rasta and Military Road."

"What's our objective?"

With his finger, Elles traces a line directly east of Ypres. "Here," he concludes. "Someplace called Passchendaele."

"Give way!" shouts Sergeant Alty. He bangs angrily on the horn. Dusty, exhausted Tommies and struggling mules ignore the west-bound staff car and continue flowing east. A team of snorting, frothing horses drawing steel-wheeled 60-pounder guns scrapes past, its hub ripping a gash in the side of the General's car.

"Bloody hell!" rages Alty. "No respect! No respect at all!"

Mallory chuckles quietly in the back seat.

After six hours swimming upstream against a flood of men and supplies, they finally arrive, dusty and exhausted, at First Brigade's staging area at Ouderdom, eleven miles west of Ypres. Nearly a hundred Mark IVs are dispursed in sections of four alongside clumps of bell-shaped tents and tar paper huts. Stripped to their waists, crews swarm the machines, hatches open, tools strewn on tarps, guns and breach blocks lying out in the sun glistening with oil.

The staff car rolls up beside a hut. A hand-painted sign reads "Headquarters, 'D' Battalion". Mallory emerges from the back seat and places his hands on his hips, stretches his lower back and readjusts his mussed uniform.

"Sergeant, please deposit my kit in the Orderly Room. I'll retrieve it later. And thanks for the ride."

Alty nods irritably as he stands surveying the large gash in the side of the staff car. "No respect," he mumbles. "No respect at all."

Mallory approaches the rear of the nearest tank. All the hatches are open and engine parts lie beside it on a tarp. From inside echoes the clank of a hammer on steel. The rhythmic "clank" suddenly changes to "thud".

"*Shit!*"

"Sorry Sergeant. It slipped."

"We'll try again, ya moron."

"Watch your language, you great bovine oaf!" shouts Mallory.

"What the...?"

A face appears in the door of a half-folded sponson. The red-faced scowl turns to a toothy grin. "Cap'n! 'Bout time you got your arse back here. Er, wait a sec. I'm com in' out."

James emerges from the tank, grease covered and sweating. "Welcome back!" he announces. "I thought maybe you'd become a red tab and wasn't comin' back."

"No such luck," responds Mallory with a broad, sincere smile. "I hear the food is better with the Tank Corps, anyway."

"My arse," snorts James as he wipes his hands on a greasy rag.

"Looks like you received the new Mark IVs. What do you think?"

"Great!" beams James. "More horsepower and a hell of a lot more hatches. Ya don't feel trapped inside. Also got rid of the damned 'rudder' finally. So how was Ypres?"

"Another bloody mash-up," snorts Mallory. "We took some ground, but many of the tanks ditched and the remainder got scattered in packets all over the battlefield. We've got to stay concentrated. But mostly we've got to get out of *this-damned-mud!*" His stern face falls into a shy smile. "Sorry. Just a bit frustrated."

"I understand," replies James.

"So… what were the boys up to while I was away?"

"Oh, you know. A bit o' this and a bit 'o that."

"And a bit more of one than the other?"

James glances around at the soldiers moving in small groups around them. "Let's get out of 'ere," he insists and takes Mallory's arm. They walk down a well-worn trail to some trees beside a small stream. James stoops and dips his hands into the cold water, rubbing fiercely to remove several layers of dirt.

"Me and the boys been up to Bray a few times," James announces.

"Still seeing Adele?"

"Yeah, she's my favorite. Half the time she doesn't even charge me."

"Careful there. It'll cost you one way or the other."

"Yes, it will," responds James with a wink. Then his face changes from a contented grin to a look of concern.

"What's wrong?" asks Mallory.

"Have you thought about goin' to see Elise?"

"Hmph! I was there on convalescence leave. She pitched me out in the rain."

"Yeah, well. That's neither here nor there. Adele says she's miserable."

"I can't help that," insists Mallory. "I've tried to be there for her, but she pushes me away."

"Look, sir. I ain't no expert in romance. But she loves you – and forgive me for sayin' – I think you love her too."

Mallory stares off into the trees. Larks sing in the branches, a chorus of high-pitched ascending notes with a characteristic down pitch ending in a flourish. He doesn't reply.

"Good God, Sir! She cries herself to sleep at night."

"She's a prostitute, James. I told her I don't care, but we agree it's not a basis for a long-term relationship. Besides, she can't stand the sight of me."

"That's just a woman's way of expressing her frustrations. It ain't true."

Mallory shrugs indifferently.

Hurling the towel to the ground, James thrusts a finger angrily in Mallory's face. "And ya know what else? I'm tired a' hearin' ya call 'er a prostitute! She was a proper lady before the war took 'er husband and chased her family from their land. The war made her a prostitute. It's what she does. It ain't what she is! And someday this war will be over!"

"And what? You imagine she can return to her former status after the war?"

"Ya know, you was a lot more fun before you became an officer," snorts James contemptuously.

"What do you mean?"

"When I met ya', you used to live for the day. Now you plan everythin'. Takes the spontaneity out 'a life."

"I'm just looking ahead," replies Mallory. "Isn't it prudent to know where one is headed before starting the trip?"

James scratches his head. "Sure. But if you're so fixated with stayin' on the path, you'll never see the opportunities growing alongside."

"Why, James! You're becoming a philosopher!"

"Sure, I'm not!"

"I don't have to know how the journey will end. I just need to know if I'm heading for a cliff."

The rumble of artillery echoes through the woods. Startled, the Larks take flight.

"What if the cliff is unavoidable?" asks James.

"Meaning?"

A bomb drops nearby. A pitiful scream rises in the distance.

"How many times can you tempt fate, sir?"

"You mean death?"

"Sure I mean death. How many times do you think you can take one of these tin coffins into battle and come back in one piece?"

"It does no good to think about it," scoffs Mallory.

"Exactly!" James announces triumphantly. "It does *no good* to think about it!"

"So?"

"Go see Elise!"

"Absolutely not!" blurts Major Croft. "We're on the verge of resuming the Somme battle and I can't have my officers away from the command!"

"Settle down, Ben," replies Elles. "Captain Mallory has done his bit to get his crews ready. The next few days will be Sergeant's time, getting the men squared away and the tanks to the railhead."

"But sir, this is highly unusual!"

Holding aloft a piece of note paper, Elles announces. "I have a communication from the Corps' Chaplain making a persuasive case for compassionate leave."

"But transport back to Blighty…"

"He's not going to Blighty," interrupts Elles. "He'll be taking his leave in France."

"Well, that's even more outrageous, Sir! What if he's out drinking and lets slip something about upcoming operation?"

"I shouldn't worry, Ben. It's his crews at risk. Besides, I trust his discretion."

"But surely it's the right of his Battalion Commander to make this decision…"

Elles places the Chaplain's letter gingerly on his desk and glances up at the battalion commander with a look of steel in his normally kindly eyes. "All right, Ben. The decision lies with you. But you don't know Mallory, do you?"

"Well I know about the DCM and the VC, if that's what you mean."

"There is a lot more to Captain Mallory than medals, Major. He is one of the original members of the Tank Corps and has a bright future ahead of him… if he isn't killed first."

"We all take the same risks, sir."

"No. Mallory takes rather more risks than others and a bit more than he should. But he does the right thing at the right time and I'm damned short of that kind of officer. So if he needs seventy-two hours compassionate leave, I believe he's entitled

"So you are overriding my judgment?"

"No. I'm telling you your judgment is flawed and I expect my officers will learn from their mistakes. Do you understand what I'm saying?"

Rising rapidly to his feet, Major Croft barks, "Yes, sir!" He snaps a salute and stalks, red-faced, out of the general's office.

Captain Smart, Elles' ADC, grins at the departing officer's back. "Seems a bit 'miffed', doesn't he?"

Elles rubs his tired eyes. "Some officers see their men as appendages of themselves rather than as individuals. They think that by exercising rigid control of their men, they can somehow *will* them to behave as desired."

"That's not true?"

"No. It isn't fear or discipline driving these lads 'over the top'."

"What is it, then?"

"Grim determination to get on with the job, I suspect. But there's also a fear of letting down their chums. You can't order a man to feel that way. And as an officer, you have to respect the men's' capacity to judge for themselves."

"So what makes Mallory different?"

Elles shrugs. "He 'gets it'. His crews will follow him through Hell because they don't want to let him down."

"So he will get a 72 hour pass?"

"Indeed." Elles retrieves Chaplain Hall's letter and scans the text. "Otherwise, the Chaplain might come back over here and do what he says here."

"Sir?"

"'Remove my genitals'."

"My God! The Chaplain said *that*?"

Folding the letter, Elles replies, "Not in those precise words. But his meaning is clear. Mallory is near the breaking point and I need him sharp."

CHAPTER 16
On Leave, Bray-sur-Somme, France
July 1917

In the darkness, the house seems older, more dilapidated than before. Mallory walks slowly through the torrential rain to the heavy Oak front door. Rain beats a tattoo heavily on his helmet and flows down his jacket to the cobblestone street.

He grasps the handle and shakes it. The door is locked. He lifts the ancient brass knocker and drops it heavily against the striker. There's no reply. He backs away and stares up at the three storey house. The windows are dark throughout.

"Where the hell is she?" mumbles Mallory. He walks around to the rear of the house and peers through the kitchen window. Inside, a woman sits quietly at the table, a sewing basket beside her as she squints in the dim candle light and draws a needle and thread through a piece of dark cloth.

He taps on the window. The woman glances up, startled.

He taps again.

"Allez-vous en! Nous sommes fermés pour la nuit," she shouts and returns to her work.

He taps again.

She shakes her head angrily.

He taps again.

With great flourish, she stands up and flings her sewing onto the table. Reaching for the hook, she retrieves a massive key, unlocks the door and opens it.

A flash of lighting illuminates them both for a fleeting moment. She sees from the silhouette he is a British soldier and switches to English. "We are closed for the night. Please come back tomorrow."

Despite the resuming darkness, he recognizes the shadowy wisp of a sheer black negligee, a long string of pearls wrapped several times around a long, elegant neckline.

"Adele?"

She squints into the darkness. "Who is it?"

"It's Jack."

She gasps and covers her mouth in surprise. "*Jack?* What are you doing out there? Les soldats sont tous confinés à la caserne!"

"I have a 3-day pass. Where's Elise?"

"Come. Come! Get in out of the rain."

He brushes past and she closes the door behind him. The kitchen is warm and inviting, the smell of bread baking is overwhelming. He removes his helmet and places it on the table. Adele rushes forward and embraces him, her body trembling as she spouts a torrent of unrecognizable French.

"Wait a minute. Wait a minute. What the hell are you saying?"

She releases him and motions to a chair. They take seats facing each other beside the grand kitchen table. There are tears in her almond-shaped eyes. He reaches over wipes away a drop trickling down her cheek.

"I knew you'd come back!" she gasps through her tears. "*I told her!*"

"Yes, yes. I'm back. But where is she?"

"She went to Amiens to see the children."

"Damn!"

"No! It's all right. When we heard there was a battle coming, she knew les soldats would be restricted to camp. So she sent everyone to see their families for a few days." Adele glances at the clock on the mantle above the massive hearth. "She will return in a few hours. She will be so glad to see you!"

"Will she?"

"But of course! She has been a terror since you left - out of her mind with worry."

"Adele, when I was here last, she told me she didn't care if I died. In fact she ordered me to leave and never return."

Adele wipes away another tear. "You English really don't understand les femmes françaises, do you?"

"Why do people keep telling me that?"

"Because you're an idiot," Adele laughs delightedly.

"I don't know, Adele. She was quite… persuasive."

"Oui, that is another caractéristique of French women. We are extremely passionate and sometimes say 'orrible things when we are in pain. But it is only to express how much we care."

"Well, how the hell is one to know?"

"The eyes, Jack. They do not lie."

"The eyes? Really?"

"Oui. A French woman can never hide her true passion," she replies coyly.

"So what would you say if I asked if you are in love with Sergeant James?" he asks as he peers intently into her eyes.

Squealing, she throws back her head and laughs. "*James?* Of course I am in love with him! The eyes reveal no secrets there!"

"But, what does that mean?" stumbles Mallory. "I... I mean, will you marry after the war?"

Adele squeals again. "You are so funny. I 'ave no idea what will come of our love. Isn't it enough that we care for each other?"

"No. Well, yes. Oh, hell. I don't know."

"Ahh, you believe in fairytales. I don't understand why English nurses fill their charges' heads with such foolishness. You actually think you will find the love of your life, marry and live 'appily ever after, no?"

"Isn't that what we're *supposed* to do?"

"*Supposed to do?* Says who?"

He throws-up his hands in exasperation. "Well... Isn't it the *way* of things?"

She places her hand tenderly on his cheek, her eyes searching his for understanding before suddenly filling with sadness. "You really don't know, do you?"

"Apparently not."

"Jack," she asks seriously. "Do you love Elise?"

"I... I think so, yes."

"What does this mean, 'I think so'? Do you love her or not?" she demands.

"Yes. Of course I do."

"Then why do you want to ruin her?"

"I don't, my God. I don't!"

"You tell her you love her then raise the impossibility of the relationship at the same time? What is that?"

"I'm just being... realistic..."

"Ah," she snorts and waves a dismissive hand. "I don't see why French women fall in love with Englishmen. You are all so *ennuyeux*."

"All right. You say you love Sergeant James..."

"Oui..."

"...yet you continue to 'work'."

"Oui," she replies and waits expectantly, as if he has left something unsaid.

"I mean, you still work... as a prostitute."

"It's my job."

"But what about fidelity? Loyalty?"

"I am absolutely loyal to James!"

"But... what about your customers?" he whispers insistently.

"I do not love them," she shrugs. "James knows this."

"You've *discussed it* with him?"

"Non, mon cheri. That is what love is about. It's about accepting without judgment, understanding without speaking." She raises a threatening finger to his face. "Now, don't you start forcing your quaint sense of morality on my James!"

"No. No. Of course not!"

"He doesn't care what I do for a living. I could be a church secretary or a fish-monger. It would make no difference. What else would he 'ave me do, live off his Sergeant's pay? Then he couldn't afford to get drunk every night."

"It doesn't bother you?"

"Of course not! It's who he is. I would no more ask him to change than he would ask me."

"But... what about *other men?*"

She covers her mouth in shock. "He's seeing *other men?*"

"No! Of course he's not!" Mallory blurts. "I mean... you! You see other men all the time!"

"But I don't love them," she explains patiently. "Besides, what matter is it to you? I am speaking of James and myself, not of you and Elise. She is the Madame. She does not see customers."

"*What?* She told me she sees whomever she wishes!"

"Oui, which is nobody."

"*Ever?*"

"Once or twice when she first came 'ere," concedes Adele. "But we could see how much it hurt her to betray her dead husband's memory. So, we dismissed the former Madame and placed Elise in charge."

"You fired the boss?"

"No. Le manager. We are a collective 'ere."

"You're Bolsheviks?"

"Some of us, yes. We are... what do you call it? Ah! We are like a business partnership. Is that capitalist enough for you?"

"But your line of business..."

"Jack, Elise is a product of the middle class. Honestly, I think she believes in the same fairy tales as you. If she didn't need to feed her family, she would not dare consort with us. But, being from the middle class, she realizes she can never go back after what she has done. You torment her by reminding her of that."

His head sags. "Damn it all! Why did she lie to me?"

"To give you a reason to hate her," shrugs Adele as if the answer is obvious.

"But, that's absurd!"

"Is it?" she asks in surprise.

"I... shit," he swears. "So what do I do?"

"Just love her, Jack. And stop acting as if you're embarrassed."

He nods morosely.

"Besides, if you don't reconcile, she will 'ave to move-on," adds Adele slyly. "Is that what you want? To drive her into another man's arms?"

"You're a devil."

"Oui, my spécialité."

A flash of lightning awakens him. He shifts uncomfortably in the worn burgundy arm chair and squints at his watch. It's after seven. The sunrise is blotted by rain clouds. An anemic gray light of dawn struggles between parted curtains.

A key rattles in the lock. The door creaks open on rusty hinges and a soft, flickering yellow light appears in the foyer. From the darkened parlour, he spots a gloved hand holding aloft a small lantern. The arm raising it fades into darkness. The lantern lowers to the ground and he can make out the silhouette of a cloaked woman setting basket on the cold stone floor. She unfastens the cape and shakes the water from it before hanging it on a coat hook.

It's Elise.

She retrieves the basket and starts toward the stairs. The light from the stairwell catches her face in profile, illuminating her tall forehead, upturned nose, pouting lips and elegant jawline. A slash of black hair cuts across her cheek.

He sighs at the simple elegance of her beauty.

She halts and turns toward the darkened parlor.

"Adele, c'este?"

He rises slowly from the chair. "Non, c'est moi."

She cocks her head and squints at the shadowy figure across the room. "Jack?"

"Oui."

She lowers the basket to the floor and walks hesitantly into the parlor. "Why are you here?"

"I don't know."

"Is James all right?"

"Yes."

"Then… why have you come?"

He steps toward her. She halts and retreats several steps.

"I can't explain it, Elise. I'm drawn to you like a moth toward the flame."

"I am the flame?"

"Yes."

"Dangerous?"

"No. Illuminating."

They stand in tense silence.

"Do you want me to leave?" he asks.

She licks her lips nervously. "No."

He steps toward her, places his fingers beneath her chin and raises it. Without speaking, he kisses her lightly. Her lips are full and inviting. The effect is stunning. As their lips part, she leans into him and wraps her arms around his neck. Weakening, his hands seek her hips and draw her against him as if steadying himself to prevent falling into the abyss.

His damp uniform has long-since dried in the warmth of the room. Her clothes remain clammy; she shivers in his embrace.

"Elise…"

"No. Say nothing," she pants. Taking his hand, she leads him across the room. As they move up the creaking stairs and down the darkened hallway, he hears a door crack open. A giggle escapes the room and the door slams.

They enter Elise's damp, musty room, closed while she was away at Amiens. She releases his hand and strikes a match to light the lantern resting atop the dresser. In the flare, her face alights with a warm, inviting glow.

"Open the window," she urges.

He throws open the window and a damp breeze invades the room.

She shivers.

"I'm sorry. Too much?"

"Non, mon cheri. It is invigorating." She lets her peasant skirt slide to the floor and unbuttons the blouse to reveal her naked body beneath, pale skin taut against the chilly air. She stoops to remove her boots and tosses them aside. She looks up at him with a look of utter innocence. Her liquid brown eyes are framed by dark circles. She's tired, but aroused.

"Come here," he insists and she walks languidly over to him.

He reaches into the bed and pulls back the covers, then lifts her gently lowers her onto the sheets. Pulling the blankets over her, he leans down and kisses her.

"Now you," she purrs as she draws the blankets beneath her chin and stares up at him alluringly.

Undressing clumsily, he leaves a trail of discarded clothes across the floor, finally pulling his undershirt over his head to reveal a spidery scar on his left shoulder and a back peppered with small, shiny white scars.

"Oh, shit its damp in here!" He rips back the covers, jumps into bed, and pulls the blankets over him.

Snuggling against him, her body is warm and inviting. He kisses her neck; she squeals delightedly.

He awakes beside her, their bodies tangled like the vines covering the ancient house. The rain has ceased; the sun struggles to break through clouds holding desperately to their position, like Germans defending a trench against attack.

Elise lies on her stomach, breathing lightly, her head on his chest, his arm wrapped around her shoulders. The blanket has fallen to the floor, the sheet is pulled taut across her pert, round behind. A smooth white leg emerges from the tangle of sheets and lies protectively across his thigh.

His stomach growls.

Her eyes blink open. "You are awake?"

"Yes."

"How long?"

"I don't know. Quite some time."

"Why did you not wake me?"

He shakes his head slightly. "I didn't want to. I just wanted to look at you."

"And what do you see?"

"Everything I ever wanted or needed."

"But…"

"No, 'but'," he scolds. "I'm as content as any man alive."

She snuggles against him. "So what shall we do?" she asks playfully.

He rolls to his side and peers down at her. "I thought we might go into town and have lunch."

"Into town? Together?"

"Sure. If you don't mind being seen in public with me."

Her eyes begin to well with tears. "Well, I don't know. You English have a reputation…"

"I'll be on my best behaviour," he promises.

Fifteen minutes later, they emerge from her bedroom like the royal couple. He, resplendent in his Captain's uniform. She, in a layered blue silk dress belted around her tiny waist and topped with a wide-brimmed hat to shade her pale skin from the admittedly anemic sunshine.

As they emerge, they discover several of the girls from the house lounging in the parlor. Conversations cease, tea cups remain suspended mid-sip as they peer up at the couple descending the stairs.

Adele squeals – her seeming reaction to everything – and hurries to meet them.

"Mon Dieu! What a handsome couple you make!"

Elise kisses her on both cheeks.

"We are going to lunch," she announces proudly.

Adele's eyes fill with tears.

Mallory takes her hands. "Now, we've had quite enough emotion for the moment. Just keep the place quiet and don't draw the interest of the Provost."

"Oui, Jack," agrees Adele. "But what of the officers?"

"Nonsense," he scoffs. "An officer wouldn't be caught dead in here." He winks at her.

"Shall we?" he asks Elise and escorts her out the door.

As they cross the square, he glances back over his shoulder. The girls crowd the doorway, waving.

Adele is crying.

He and Elise stroll down the street, arm-in-arm – an officer and his lady.

CHAPTER 17
Battle of Passchendaele, Bertincourt, France
July 1917

Entering the tar paper hut, Mallory is amused to see the newly-promoted orderly, Corporal Sydney, scrambling around the room exchanging buckets to catch rain water dripping through the leaking roof.

Mallory glances up at the growing leak and shakes his head. "You're wasting your time, Syd," he calls over the continuous rumble of distant artillery.

"Sir?" shouts Sydney.

Mallory points to a growing blot in the ceiling. "That whole section of roof is about to give way!"

Sydney glances up at the ceiling, eyes wide. "Cor' Blimey," he groans and frantically clears maps and orders from the desktop.

"Where's Major Croft?"

"Up on the line, sir! There's been a change to the order of battle and he's trying to straighten it out!"

"Show me where he went," shouts Mallory. "I'm going up!"

Sydney withdraws a salvaged map from beneath his arm and unrolls it. "Here," he shouts. "North of Ypres in XVIII Corps' area."

Mallory traces the roads with his finger and locates one closest to where Battalion headquarters is located. "What's the change of plan?"

"I don't know, sir! A courier brought a message a few hours ago. He cursed and left in a hurry."

"All right. I'm heading up to Battalion now."

"May I go with you, sir?" Sydney blurts.

Mallory hesitates. "Why on earth would you want to do that?"

"I gotta get into the war, sir!"

"You are in the war, Syd."

"No, sir. I mean really *in it!*"

Mallory glances up at the ceiling. "When that thing collapses, you'll be in it up to your arse."

Sydney stares back at him, uncomprehendingly.

"Syd," Mallory sighs. "This *is* the war. It's rain and mud and constant misery punctuated only by occasional death on a grand scale. What you do here keeps this battalion together; all of those bloody requisitions and reports you send-up make our lives at the front a little better."

"*But* I can't go home without a medal or wound stripe or somethin'," he insists. "I got to make me parents proud..."

"There's no 'pride' in war, Syd. There's only life and death. Choose life while you've still got a choice. I'm sure your parents would rather have you home safely than have some bloody decoration to place over the hearth."

Sydney nods miserably. "Yes, sir."

As Mallory exits the orderly hut, he hears Sydney scream as the roof collapses.

"Damned rain," curses Jack as he mounts the duckboards and walks down to the vehicle-jammed road. He waves-down a passing ammunition lorry.

"Can you give me a lift to 'D' Battalion H.Q.?"

A Corporal leans out the window and nods. "Yes, sir. But you'll have to ride in the back!"

Mallory waves his assent and climbs over the tailgate. Beneath the tarp-covered truck bed, he restacks the ammo boxes to create a makeshift seat and pulls a rain poncho around his shoulders. Despite the July heat, the dampness penetrates his bones, making him shiver.

It's nearly nightfall when the truck lurches to a stop and the driver knocks on the rear of the cab. "'D' Battalion Headquarters," he announces.

"Thanks," grunts Mallory and drops off the tailgate into the Flanders muck. Struggling through the mud sucking at his boots, he finally arrives at a small, partially destroyed house serving as the battalion command post.

Pulling back the tarp covering the door, he encounters chaos. Major Croft stands before a map snapping-off orders as he erases battalion boundaries and sketches new routes of advance. Phones clang loudly as staff officers stride from the message center to the map, providing updated information.

Mallory approaches the map board and comes to attention. At a break in the commotion, he announces, "Captain Mallory returning from leave, Sir!"

Croft casts him a brief glance and returns his attention to the flimsy in his hand. "Davies!" he shouts. "Didn't you bother to read this before handing it to me? It's bloody gibberish!" He flings the note back to the clerk. "Confirm that message!"

Mallory remains standing at attention. Finally the battalion commander acknowledges him.

"All right. All right. Stand at ease!" snaps Croft. "As you see, we've got a mess on our hands. Damned rain for the past two days and the preparatory barrage has destroyed the drainage system. It's a swamp out there!"

"Is the attack postponed?"

"Like hell!"

"Have the conditions been communicated to Corps?"

"It's raining there, too, Captain."

"But the tanks, sir! Do they understand the effect on our operations?"

"I assume so! That's why they've decided to launch the attack before the weather gets any worse. If it comes down to it, we'll just have to stick to the roads."

"Enemy artillery will have already registered on the roads, sir," cautions Mallory.

"Well then, we'll have to hope counter-battery fire and aerial bombardment take care of the Hun guns."

"Hope? Hope isn't a plan, sir," replies Mallory. "And aircraft can't fly in this weather."

"We have our orders, *Captain!*"

Realizing there is no point in further argument, Mallory retreats. "Do you have any instructions for the Company, sir?"

"I've posted them to the acting commander."

"Acting commander? What acting commander?"

"Captain Nettles assumed command in your absence."

"Nettles?" blurts Mallory. "You're joking!"

"He's my executive officer, Captain," warns Croft.

"I...," Mallory begins before realizing the futility of further comment. "Right, any updates before I return to the Company, sir?"

"'D' Battalion is supporting the attack on St. Julien. Your company is leading. Captain Nettles has the details. Speak with him. Dismissed!"

Mallory salutes and turns before Croft can share any further bad news.

Panic. It stinks like a decaying body. His battalion commander is a cavalry officer from outside the Tank Corps. The short-course on commanding tanks in battle little prepares him for the realities of armored operations.

And Captain Nettles?

Mallory tromps through the rain, the mire slowing him as he trudges the half-mile to Company headquarters. Nearing the H.Q., he notices the tanks parked in neat clumps.

He arrives wet, angry and frustrated, emerging like a storm inside the command tent. Captain Nettles glances up, eyes wide as if seeing a ghost.

"Mallory? What the hell are you doing here?"

"Resuming command," announces Mallory as he drops his helmet on the map desk. "Major Croft wants you back at Battalion."

"See here, Mallory. I'm in command here."

"You were acting commander in my absence. Well, I'm no longer absent, am I? So move along."

"Do you have that in writing?"

"My conversation with Major Croft wasn't that formal. You've done your bit. Now you're dismissed."

"The Company has been fine without your legendary 'expertise'," challenges Nettles.

"Really? Are you the one who ordered the tanks laagered like that?" He motions toward the tanks parked outside.

"Yes, of course. For ease of communication..."

"So they can be targeted by Hun artillery?"

"You might have noticed there is no Hun artillery."

"At the moment! They should be dispursed. It's SOP, if you'd read Colonel Fuller's guidance. I'd think, after your *sterling* performance at Messines, you'd be a bit more wary of Hun artillery."

Nettles pales. "That was not my fault! The Hun artillery had us bracketed!"

"Not until you led them into it!"

"I had no choice!"

"There's always a choice. Have you never had an original thought in your life?"

"But... orders!"

"Sod orders! Adapt to the situation! You're an officer, that's what they pay you for. But *you*..." His voice trails off as the loathing robs him of the ability to continue.

Unnerved, Nettles retrieves his helmet from the coat hook and struggles into his jacket. "I'm reporting your behavior to the Major..."

"Good. Send him my regards..."

Nettles departs in a huff.

Mallory hovers over the map outlining their route of advance. "This can't be right," he mumbles. He pokes his head outside the tent and shouts to a passing Sergeant. "Sergeant Bova, have the Section Leaders report to me immediately!"

"Sah!" replies the sergeant and starts off at a trot. Within fifteen minutes, the Section Leaders crowd into the tent, a look of collective relief on their faces as they realize Mallory has resumed command.

"We're receiving conflicting orders, so I want to` clear-up a couple of points. Despite what you may have been told, you are not to enter the defile leading toward Poelcappelle. It's a low area that'll be flooded by the time we get there and it's most certainly pre-registered by Hun artillery. There's higher ground to the north, so keep to the railway on your left and for God's sake, stay off the roads."

"We're still going forward in this pissing rain?" asks a lieutenant.

"Unless I hear otherwise," confirms Mallory. "We jump-off at oh-three-forty-five tomorrow morning. It's going to be difficult to maintain formations in this fog and rain, not to mention the bog. Just do your best to stay with the infantry and clear the way.

"Supply tanks will be following along behind us," he continues. "So when you get to the rally point, find cover, disperse and await resupply. The Germans will have to counterattack before dark or they'll never regain the initiative. Be prepared to stand your ground or all of this will have been a waste. "

He surveys the room before continuing. "I'll be leading in… What's my new tank number?"

"F-Five, Sir."

"Right. Tank F5," confirms Mallory. "We'll be supporting the 39th and 51st Divisions. Our first phase line is at the Steenbeek River where we'll help secure the crossings. It's not much of a river, but it'll be marshy down near the banks, so keep well back until we are ready to push across. Any questions?"

Hearing none, Mallory continues.

"I want your tanks dispersed tonight. If the Hun gets wind of what we're up to, he'll rain hell down on us. We don't need to take any casualties before this thing even gets started."

A chorus of agreement echoes through the tent.

"Good luck, then. I'll see you on the Steenbeek."

The officers filter from the tent, bundling up inside rain jackets as they disburse to their Sections. "Harry," Mallory calls to the last lieutenant. "Can you show me where my tank is?"

"Pleasure," replies Lieutenant Harry Compton, one of his veteran officers. They trudge through the darkness to a group of tanks parked side-by-side.

"There you go," announces Compton.

"Which one?"

Compton lights his torch. "There," he replies with a grin. Across the front side of the tank, painted beneath the "F5", is the name "Elise."

From inside the tank comes a booming, "Turn off that torch, you damned fool!"

"Well open the bloody door then, you great bovine oaf!"

"Captain!" announces James gleefully and the door creaks open. "I thought you were gonna sit this one out!"

Mallory folds himself through the door and pulls it shut behind him. "Welcome back, sir. How was Bray?" he asks with a wink.

"Given what you've named the new tank, I gather you've already guessed that answer."

"Seemed fittin' and proper. She is a female tank, after all!"

"Right," responds Mallory as he notices the array of Lewis guns. "Excellent! But how did you know I'd get things straightened-out with Elise?"

"I know women," beams James. "Speakin' 'o which. How's my Adele?"

"In rare form. You'll have your hands full with that one.'"

"Ah, she's a good girl, Cap'n."

"Yes, yes. She is a 'keeper'. Now, who do we have here?" asks Mallory, surveying the strangers among crew.

"Major Croft broke up the veteran crews and sprinkled 'em among the new Sections. Said we needed to 'season' the pot."

"When did he do that?"

"Last week."

"A week ago!" sputters Mallory. "Have you trained together?"

"Not live-fire," James admits. "But we've been doin' crew drills and they seem to be coming along fine."

"Well… that sounds… acceptable," replies Mallory unenthusiastically.

James proceeds with the introductions. "This is Grimes and Davies, yer machine gunners, and Philpot and Schmidt, yer new loaders."

Mallory nods encouragingly to each. "Gentlemen, welcome aboard. I hope Sergeant James hasn't been filling your heads with any disturbing bedtime stories."

"Certainly not," replies James. "I just told the truth."

It's clear from the expressions of awe on the crew's faces James has been telling tales of the crew's exploits.

"Where are the brakemen?" asks Mallory.

"They went to get the grub," replies James. "I told 'em to bring enough for the whole crew – including Captain Nettles. You can 'ave his bit. Have you run across him yet?"

"Yes," replies Mallory with a smile. "We've discussed the change of command and he's agreed it is best to return to his natural habitat."

"Thank God!"

"Oh, I almost forgot." Reaching into his satchel, Mallory retrieves a package. "Adele sends her love. She says you're to share it with the crew."

Judging the heft of the package, James quickly surmises the contents. He unrolls the cloth to discover two bottles.

"Ah, vin blanc anglais," he announces reverently.

"That ain't wine," blurts one of the new gunners.

"Course it ain't, ya silly bugger," grumbles James. "It's good English whiskey – too good for the likes 'o you."

"But the Cap'n says you gotta share. Ain't that right, sir?"

"Adele's orders, I'm afraid" acknowledges Mallory.

"I say, who's Adele?"

"Mind your own business and hand me your cups," grouses James.

The crewmen scramble for their packs, each retrieving a tin cup from his mess kit. James breaks the seal on the bottle, lustily inhales the fumes, and pours the amber contents into the cups vying for his attention.

Mallory offers a toast. "To our wives and sweethearts."

"May they never meet," concludes James.

The crewmen chuckle.

Mallory takes a sip, a smile creasing his face as the contents slide down his throat to warm his belly.

Gunner Grimes swallows his ration in one great gulp and bursts-out coughing.

"Sip it next time, Grimes," chuckles Mallory. "This isn't your daily rum ration."

Still choking, Grimes nods exaggeratedly and extends his cup for a refill.

James looks to Mallory. "What about it, sir? Another round for medicinal purposes?"

"Why not," replies Mallory with raised cup. "But save some for the gearsmen."

The crew relaxes and sips the whiskey, savoring the musky liquor in silence as rain patters on the steel roof.

There comes a knock on the sponson.

"Sorry, we're closed for cleanin'," shouts James.

"Aw, come on! It's raining out 'ere!"

James pushes open the door and the two gearsmen climb aboard. Each carries four metal cups filled with watery stew and two loaves of bread.

"Plumley, Green. Meet the Cap'n."

They each hand out the cups of stew and pass the loaves to the gunners. Mallory greets them.

"Go ahead and eat up. May as well finish it before it gets any colder. Sergeant James has a special pudding once you've finished."

"Thank 'ee, Sir," they mumble as they tear-off chunks of bread, dip them into the stew and eat ravenously.

While the crew dines, Mallory catches James' eye and motions toward the front of the tank. They climb into the respective driver's and commander's seats. Part of the crew, lubricated by two cups of whiskey, break into a chorus,

"Mademoiselle from Armentières
Par ley voo,
Mademoiselle from Armentières
Par ley voo,
Mademoiselle from Armentières,
She hasn't been kissed for forty years,
Hinky, Dinky Par ley voo..."

"Look, this isn't a battlefield for tanks," explains Mallory quietly over the noise of increasingly risqué second and third versus. "It's too muddy and shot to hell. Now, I don't want to say it in front of the crew, but the only way we'll get out of this alive is to move carefully, keep to the high ground, and try to make it to the river without ditching. This battle is not worth anyone's lives."

"Is any battle worth it?"

"Yeah. The final one. But this sure as Hell isn't it."

Approaching jump-off time, Mallory raises the hatch and stands in his seat. Fog distorts the impact of artillery landing amid the German defenses. The eastern horizon lights-up with dull flashes dissipated by the haze. He drops back inside.

"Can't see a damned thing out there!"

"Well, how the hell are we supposed to traverse the battlefield?" asks James.

Mallory scratches his head irritably. "I'm going to have to act as ground guide."

"*What?* You can't just walk across no-man's land in the middle of an attack!"

"The infantry does it all the time. I don't see as I have a choice. We've not going to get 50 yards without ditching unless someone gets out there and leads."

James throws off his seatbelt and begins to climb from his seat.

"Not you," cautions Mallory. "I need a driver."

"And we need a commander!"

Ignoring James' plea, Mallory twists in his seat. "Have any of you had any driver training?"

"I did, sir," announces Private Schmidt, one of the loaders.

"Then get up here and take my seat," orders Mallory as he climbs down from his position.

"I ain't a commander, sir!"

"And you're not going to be. I just need someone to help Sergeant James steer."

"Where will you be?"

Mallory points through the driver's slit. "Out there. You and James just keep your eyes on my movements and follow along behind."

"Tha's barmy, sir."

"Maybe. On the other hand, we may be able to take advantage of this fog. If the Germans can't see the tanks, they can't see me, either."

"A bullet don't need to see you to find you, sir."

Mallory glances at James. "He's a smart one," he admits with a wink. "I'll be fine, private. Now watch for me when I light the cigarette."

He retrieves his Brody helmet from the dashboard and exits the tank. The rain has stopped, but a cool dampness lingers. He buttons his rain coat beneath his chin and straps on his helmet. Walking to a point about twenty feet ahead, he turns back toward the tank. The trench lighter flares, illuminating his face as he lights the cigarette and inhales. The burning ember glows brightly.

"Got it?" he shouts.

"Got it!" replies James.

Mallory glances at his watch. "Five minutes!"

Suddenly, the artillery tenor changes. The barrage is lifting. A whistle blares.

"Or not!"

He turns toward the German trenches and clasps his hands behind his back, cigarette between his knuckles. Taking a deep breath, he steps forward. The tanks rumble, following along behind like faithful dogs as he picks his way around defensive barbed wire and strolls into the broken ground and discarded waste of no-man's land.

Light from distant flares and impacting artillery reflect erratically off water-filled shell holes, illuminating a treacherous path toward the German lines. He leads the tanks between likely ditching hazards. In some places, there is no option but to wade through knee-deep water in hope of reaching firmer ground beyond.

He hears several tanks struggling, down-shifting gears as engines fight against the vacuum caused by the sucking mud. Elise still follows.

Nearing the first German line, Mallory dodges through barbed wire cut by British shrapnel. Detecting the roar of engines, Maxims open fire, blindly engaging the tanks rumbling toward their positions. Bullets appear through the fog and snap overhead.

An alert rocket "whooshes" from its launcher behind the German lines leaving a lazy glowing trail of red in its wake. Artillery immediately begins to fall, the blasts illuminating the battlefield around him.

The attacking tanks return fire, raking the German lines with cannon and machinegun fire. Bullets *whiz-snap* past him.

Shit! Bullets dash in all directions. He flings the cigarette to the ground and turns back toward Elise. A bullet ricochets off the back of his helmet, knocking him to his knees.

Elise continues toward him, the roar coming ever nearer as he struggles in the mud, half-blind with concussion. Head splitting, vision blurred, he falls drunkenly onto his stomach.

A shadow appears over him. He rolls to his left, Elise missing him by inches as she continues forward.

Searching for his pistol, Mallory grapples at the lanyard around his neck and reels-in the mud-caked Webley. Gripping the barrel, he hammers desperately on Elise's steel flank. The tank lurches to a stop and the door on the back of the sponson creaks open.

"Captain?"

"Down here!" croaks Mallory.

Strong hands reach down and drag him inside the tank.

"You damned fool!" curses James.

Sitting dejectedly on the deck, Mallory slides-off his helmet and examines a fist-sized dent.

"Blimey, sir," sighs the gunner. "You almost bought it."

"Almost," replies Mallory as he gently touches the growing lump on the back of his head.

"Not nearly enough," growls James. "Now are you gonna listen to me and stay inside the bloody tank?"

"Oh, hell yes," replies Mallory. "Schmidt! I'm taking over!"

Private Schmidt slides eagerly from the commander's seat and Mallory climbs up in his place.

James grasps Mallory's arm. "You sure you're up for this?"

"Just a bash on the head. Besides, I'm a terrible passenger," laughs Mallory.

"Bloody fool…"

"I'm fine! Let's go," interrupts Mallory irritably and shoves the brake handles forward. Elise continues forward through the barbed wire, the wooden support stakes cracking beneath her treads. Bullets ping off the steel hull.

"Gunners, there's your invitation!"

The tank fills immediately with the *"thut-thut-thut"* of Lewis guns raking the trench line ahead. After a few desultory attempts at return fire, Germans defending the first line break contact and scurry down the communications trenches toward their next belt of defensive positions.

The open trench yawns before Elise as she emerges into the German line. "Here we go!" shouts Mallory and the crew grapples for the nearest handhold. Elise plunges nose-down into the trench, engine straining as she seizes the wall opposite and claws up the revetment, timbers cracking beneath her tracks. As she crosses, her stern dips toward the bottom of the trench before being dragged toward the surface beyond. She emerges with a rocking crash on the opposite side of the ditch, the suddenness of the arrival flinging crew members to the deck.

"Clutch! Low gear!" screams Mallory over the roar.

The gearsman drops the lever and Mallory immediately jerks the brake. "Power!" James guns the engine and Elise churns left, parallel to the trench. Panicked Germans stare-up at the invader, eyes wide in terror.

"Gunners! Clear that trench!"

As the gunners pour fire into the trench, bullets strike Elise's hull from the opposite side. Chips of armor break loose inside and shower the crew with metal splinters.

"Action right!" yells Mallory.

The right-side gunners shift fire toward a hidden machinegun nest. Oil evaporates from overheating Lewis Guns as brass shell casings spew from ejection ports to litter the floor beneath the gunners' feet.

The Maxim crew takes cover from the enfilading fire.

Click!

"Shit!" A gunner rips loose an empty ammo pan and crams it into the ammo rack. As he reloads, the Maxim resumes firing. Amid the rattle of impacting bullets, the gunner grabs a loaded pan and slaps it atop the gun, working it in-place to assure it's secure. Maxim bullets slap the sponson. Molten steel flakes knocked loose by the impact shower the gunner, searing his face and knuckles. He ignores the pain. Swinging the gun toward the enemy, he rips the charging handle to the rear and resumes firing.

Thut-thut-thut-thut!

Elise makes her way along the trench as Germans pour from a dugout hurling grenades. A grenadier emerging from the middle of the pack is struck in the face by a bullet and drops his armed grenade. His comrades scream and scatter. The unwary are caught in the explosion. The gunner squints through the dust and smoke, spotting survivors crawling away down the blood-filled trench. He raises his weapon, unwilling to massacre the wounded.

This fight is over.

Dawn breaks over the horizon. Mallory spots a tank half-buried in a shell hole, a track unraveled from its drive sprocket. The crew has taken cover behind the tank. German artillery impacts all around them. Mallory flips-open his hatch and pokes his head through the opening

"Get away from the tank!" he yells.

The lieutenant raises a hand to his ear and shakes his head. Amid the artillery and roar of engines, he can't hear what Mallory is saying. Mallory waves for the crew to get away from the tank, but they remain stubbornly immobile. Finally, a howitzer round lands atop the tank. It belches, steel plates rising amid black smoke and falling lazily to earth. The survivors crawl away from the burning hulk.

"Bear right!" shouts Mallory as he drops back inside and jerks the brake lever. Elise comes-round and returns to the advance as Germans continue to retire. Elise dodges between water-filled craters and crosses the second defensive line. All around them, British and Canadian troops clear dugouts using grenades and bayonets. Groups in gray uniforms warily raise their hands, begging to be taken prisoner. The lucky ones are driven at bayonet-point back toward British lines; the remainders perish where they stand.

Crossing the third line, the Steenbeek River appears before them, identifiable at a distance only by what remains of the trees lining its course. Once green and majestic, the trees are now bare, shattered by artillery fire, charred and arising along the bank like burnt match sticks. The river, once clear and flowing eastward toward the sea has been violated by shellfire. Its banks pockmarked with craters; the rain-swollen river regurgitates its once life-sustaining water into a surrounding marsh.

Across the river, the Germans regroup in hastily dug firing pits to resist the inevitable British attempt to cross. German artillery continues to fall on the west side of the river. For once, the rain is a blessing. Spotters can't locate the new British positions and observation balloons remain grounded by the pitiful weather.

Yet, still, the artillery fires.

Mallory draws Elise beside a destroyed farmhouse and jerks to a stop. "James, have the crew sweep-up these shell casings and restock the magazines. I'm going to see who's in charge". He straps-on his dented helmet and slogs over to the dilapidated shack. Inside, he finds a makeshift aid station and small command post.

Filthy, sweaty and bleeding, he approaches the officer in-charge. "Sir."

The major gives him a quick glance. "Over there, captain…" he replies with a nod toward the aid post.

"I'm not wounded sir, I command the tank company sent to help seize the bridge."

The major takes a closer look. "Sorry, Captain. Most of the men coming in here looking like you rather tend to be wounded."

"It's just a ruse, sir. I put it on to attract sympathy."

The major smiles and offers him a Woodbine. "Have you seen the bridge yet?"

"No sir."

The major passes him a pair of binoculars and nods over his shoulder as he lights his own cigarette. "Straight east, about a hundred yards away. Mind the snipers."

Peering cautiously out the window, Mallory follows the course of the rutted road until he spots a rickety bridge about fifty feet long. "Not much of a bridge," he snorts. "How do you plan to seize it?"

"I'd rather hoped your tanks could take the lead. I lost a dozen men trying to rush it about an hour ago. Maxims are strewn across the river and there's no cover from here to the bridge."

Mallory sweeps the river with the glasses. Shell fire has damaged the banks allowing water to flow into the adjoining craters. What should have been firm bank up to the bridge is now a muddy swamp. "Damned artillery," he mumbles. "The only way we're going to be able to cover your advance is to get up on the road and lead you across."

"Will the bridge support your tanks?"

"Well, now. There's the question," admits Mallory. He backs away from the window and collapses tiredly atop an ammo crate. "But unless your men can swim in full kit under fire, we're going to have to give it a go."

"Thank you," replies the major with obvious relief.

Mallory hears another tank from his platoon meandering around the battlefield avoiding water-filled shell holes and looking for Germans to kill. He peers out the door and discovers the hull number, F2, Lieutenant Simon's tank.

He scribbles a memo in his notebook and tears loose the page. "May I borrow your runner?"

"Yes, of course." The major signals a corporal, who rises, secures his helmet, and grabs his rifle.

Mallory hands the paper to the runner. "Take this note to the tank over there. And for God's sake, be careful as you approach. Visibility is poor so they might mistake you for a Hun."

"Oh, blimey," groans the corporal.

"Once you've made contact, tell the commander to find two more tanks and have them assemble here," explains Mallory.

"The more the merrier, eh?" quips the major.

"Let's just say that 'misery loves company'."

CHAPTER 18
Battle of Passchendaele, Belgium
August 1917

Within the hour, Mallory assembles four of the Company's tanks behind the crumpled barn near the house. The tank commanders kneel in the mud encircling him while the infantry major stands to one side, observing. Using a bayonet as a pointer, Mallory sketches-out the river, the road and the bridge.

"Parisher, since you and Clive have the male tanks, I want you to take positions as near the bank as possible on either side of the road this side of the river. Simon and I will attack in-column up the road. I'll lead. When you see the Hun Maxims open-up, hit them with your six-pounders. Once we cross the bridge, Simon and I will split-up and sweep-up the Huns along the banks."

The lieutenants nod in unison.

"Once we're across, get your arses over the bridge immediately and keep pressing east. After we clear the banks, we'll catch-up. Got it?"

"Got it!"

"Right."

Mallory looks up to the major. "Anything to add, sir?"

The major flicks the ashes off his cigarette butt. "No, Captain. Looks like you've covered it all. As your last two tanks start to move, we'll close-up behind and cross the bridge."

Thirty minutes later, the two "male" tanks rumble from behind the barn and secure positions on either side of the road, an interval of fifty yards between them.

The Germans don't respond.

"Maybe they withdrew," offers James, hopefully.

"I doubt it. The river's a good defensive line. They're just holding fire until we try to cross."

James sighs and crosses himself. "All right, let's go."

Mallory eyes him with amusement. "You're not Catholic," he laughs. "Come to think of it, as far as I know you're not *anything*."

"Yeah, well. Adele's Catholic and she says I need all the help I can get. So today, I'm a bloody left-footer."

Mallory nods sympathetically. "Drop a good word for me while you're at it."

"A sinner like you?" snorts James. "Best go to Confession first…"

"Don't want to shock the priest. Poor bastard would never be the same."

"Tha's true," admits James with an approving nod. "How 'bout we just pray the ruddy bridge holds?"

"Indeed."

Elise lurches into gear and makes her way through porridge-like mud onto the rutted road. Simon's tank follows cautiously 50 yards back. They pass between the covering male tanks and approach the bridge. From across the river, the Maxims finally reveal themselves.

In response, the male tanks' guns roar several times and the Maxims stutter to silence, the gunners either dead or too frightened to reply.

At the abutment, James downshifts. "You don't suppose they've mined the bridge, do you?"

"No. They'll need it for their counterattack," replies Mallory, before adding under his breath, "probably."

Elise starts across the rickety span amid growing resistance from the defending infantry. Through his porthole, Mallory spots Germans dashing from shell hole to shell hole as they vie for positions near the tank. A baled charge flies through the air and clangs against Elise's hull. It bounces off the armor, rolls into the water and explodes beside the bridge sending a shower of water fifty feet into the air.

Mallory glances over his shoulder at the crew. Peering through their firing slits, they watch, mouths agape as the tank rumbles, alone, across the bridge.

"Any time, gents!" he shouts testily.

Awakened from their trances, the Lewis gunners man their weapons and open fire.

As they're halfway across, the bridge begins to sway, timbers cracking like rifle shots beneath the tracks.

"Come-on, baby," coaxes James. "Just a few more feet."

Elise emerges safely on the muddy east bank, tracks sliding in the muck as Mallory jerks the brake as she trundles slowly to the left. Germans manning water-logged shell holes half-heartedly toss a few grenades before abandoning their positions in the tank's path.

"Is Simon following?" calls Mallory.

"Yes, sir," responds the gunner. "He's just reaching the bridge now..."

There is a pause.

"Oh, shit!" swears the gunner. "The bridge is collapsing!"

"Goddammit!" swears James.

"So much for religion," grunts Mallory. "Did he make it across?"

"No, sir! Looks like he's stuck in the river!"

"We're alone on the wrong side of the damned river!" James growls. "What now?"

"We find a defensible position and hold on until the infantry get across," replies Mallory.

"*What?*"

"We've only got three options," he insists. "Defend, continue the attack alone, or surrender."

"Or we can abandon Elise and try to make our way back across the river!" suggests James.

As if in response, bullets slap the armored hull.

"You want to try abandoning her out in the open? In daylight? Under fire?"

James curses.

"I thought not," replies Mallory. He cautiously raises the hatch over his seat and spots a small, partially damaged embankment erected in more peaceful times to contain the river during flood. He drops back inside and jerks the right brake.

"What the hell are you doing?" demands James.

"On the right, there's an embankment. We're going to use it for cover."

"You're barmy!"

"Am I?" The tank churns to the base of the dyke and jerks to a stop. Mallory turns to the crew. "Dismount and take your Lewis guns! We're establishing a perimeter!"

James stares at Mallory in shock. "*Dismount?*"

"We've got defensible positions here," explains Mallory. "But the tank's going to draw fire. If we disburse the Lewis guns on the rim of the embankment, we can hold the Hun all day long. If we stay in here, the artillery is going to find us and blow us to hell."

James' eyes fall. Mallory surveys the crew. Each member turns away.

"If any of you have a better idea, I'm willing to listen," announces Mallory. Awaiting a response, he glances out the driver's visor. "They've stopped retreating," he reports. "If we're going to have any chance at all, we need to seize our positions now."

James snorts in resigned disgust. "*Right!*" He flings-off his seat belt and begins struggling to dismount the forward Lewis gun. He glares at the apprehensive crew. "You heard the Captain. *Dismount!*"

The crew springs to life, recovering Lewis guns and gathering ammunition. Laden with guns and burlap bags full of drums of ammo, the crew takes positions inside the doors at the rear of the two sponsons.

"Move fast and seize good positions!" orders Mallory. "This'll be home for the next 12 hours or so."

The crew members nod nervously.

"Ready? Steady. *Go!*"

The doors spring open simultaneously and the gunners drop to the ground, slipping and sliding in the mud as they fan-out toward the curving levee. The last one out of the tank, Mallory draws his pistol and follows James at a dash toward the levee fifty feet away.

A German appears over the top of the rise. James drops to one knee and shoulders the Lewis gun. *Thut-thut- thut!* The man tumbles forward and slides down the berm. James dashes the few remaining yards, throws himself against the soft earth and flings the gun's barrel onto the berm's ledge. On the other side, several Germans glance up, startled, and die before they can unsling their rifles.

Mallory arrives moments later and dumps several magazine pans of ammunition onto the ground beside James. He casts a glance at the dead German. "You girls okay on your own for a few minutes? I need to emplace the rest of the guns."

James nods irritably. "We're fine," he snorts. "Just get your arse back here soon. Fritz ain't much for conversation."

"Right!" replies Mallory with a nervous grin. He spots the other two crews, dashes off at a crouch, and throws himself down alongside the nearest team.

"Good afternoon, Gentlemen. Lovely weather!"

They gape at him.

"Oh, come-on. It's not all so bad."

He peers carefully over the ledge and drops back down.

"The nearest Hun position is two hundred yards away," he explains. "Pass me the gun." Retrieving the Lewis Gun from the gunner, he pushes it up onto the edge of the berm. "All right, man your weapon."

The gunner slips cautiously behind the gun and tucks the machinegun's butt into his shoulder.

Mallory points over the berm. "See the group of tree stumps, the ones that look like fingers telling you to fuck off?"

"Yes, sir," chuckles the gunner nervously.

"That's your left boundary." He points off to the right. "Now, see the destroyed hay cart?"

"Yes, sir."

"That is your right boundary. Between the two is your field of fire. Kill anything approaching from between those markers. Ignore all else. The other gunners will cover the remainder of the field. Got it?"

"Yes, sir."

Mallory turns to the assistant gunner. "How much ammunition have you?"

The boy fumbles with several ammo pans, examining the 96-round magazines. "A couple of hundred rounds, sir."

"Fine. But you're going to need to reload those empty pans as quickly as he empties them. Can you do that? Can you keep him loaded?"

"I think so, sir," replies the boy. His face is pale, eyes wide with fear.

"We're not alone," explains Mallory reassuringly. "The tanks and troops across the river will cover us."

"Y-Yes, sir."

Mallory locates the third crew and dashes across the open field toward their position, drawing fire from several alert German snipers. He collapses against the muddy berm, breathing heavily. The gunners listen carefully as he describes their field of fire.

Crack! Bullets snap overhead. Across the river, the 6-pounders respond, projectiles striking among the German positions.

"How long will we have to hold, sir?" asks the gunner.

Mallory peers back toward the river. Simon's tank is sunk in the shallows, muddy water rising halfway up its hull. The remainder of the bridge dangles from its abutments. Simon's crew lines the edge of the east bank, dismounted Lewis guns peering over the ledge. Simon spots Mallory and waves.

Thut-thut-thut! James' gun opens fire. A 6-pounder across the river lends its support.

"I've got an idea," announces Mallory. "Cover me while I make contact with Lieutenant Simon."

"Yes, sir."

Skirting the levee's inner perimeter, Mallory works his way to within a dozen meters of the river's edge.

"Simon!" he shouts. "Have your men salvage some lumber and see if they can construct a bridge between the riverbank and the roof of your tank. After dark, the major can move his men across the river."

Simon acknowledges with a wave.

The rain, already falling steadily, becomes torrential. Mallory trudges back to the abandoned tank, soaked to the skin with mud caking his puttees to his knees. Climbing inside, he gathers the remaining machinegun ammo into a haversack. The engine has gone cold, but the rain pattering on the steel roof reminds him that Elise is inviting and dry. Shaking off his lethargy, he heads reluctantly back out into the rain and distributes the ammo to the crews around the perimeter. His last stop is beside Sergeant James.

Reaching into the haversack, he presents a ground sheet. "Want some cover?"

"Naw, won't do no good. I'm soaked to me skivvies already. Why don't you cover Fritz 'ere? He's startin' to annoy me. You can stick the ammo under there with 'im and keep it dry."

Mallory covers the dead German and slips the ammo pans beneath the groundsheet. He peers out over the muddy, pockmarked field. The interconnected craters brim with water. "Well, at least we know the Hun is as miserable as we."

"Yeah, but you know where I'd rather be," James grins.

"You and I, both," sighs Mallory.

"Hey, fantasize about your own lass," chuckles James.

They lay, side-by-side in the rain, silent but for the rumble of distant guns – or is it thunder?

"What do you think you'll do after the war?" asks Mallory, more to break the silence than because he cares.

"*After* the war?" snorts James. "You think we'll make it that long?"

"Someone has to? Why not us?"

"Never pegged you as an optimist," chuckles James.

"Fine. *If* you survive the war…" insists Mallory.

"*If* we survive, I'll probably stay over here and try to make a go of it with Adele."

"You think you'll marry her?"

"I dunno. She ain't really the marryin' type. But I love 'er and I'm gonna have to do somethin' after the war, so why not stick-it-out?"

It's Mallory's turn to chuckle. "Now who's the optimist?"

James' eyes shine beneath the brim of his helmet. "Th' war's changed everythin', hasn't it? Th' old order is collapsin' all around us. Life won't be the same as it was. There's a new day comin'."

Mallory nods thoughtfully. "Yes, I suppose. But the old order won't go quietly…."

James rolls onto his side. "Already has. Look 'ere, what's the likelihood you and me would have been mates before the war, what with you at university and me workin' the fields?"

"Unlikely, I suppose," concedes Mallory.

"So, what are you gonna do when you see me on the street after this shit's over, ignore me?"

"Heavens no! After what we've been through together?"

"Society relies on class distinction," insists James. "But now we've shared this lot, ain't much distinction left, is there?"

"You say the damnedest things," admits Mallory.

"Well, ain't I right?"

"Damned if you're not."

"Well, there ya go," replies James with an air of self-satisfaction. "Pals to the end."

German artillery begins dropping outside the perimeter and slowly walks toward them. James rolls onto his stomach and shoulders the Lewis gun. "Speakin' o' the end, 'ere it comes now."

"They'll try to advance behind the artillery," observes Mallory. "Keep your eyes open. I'm going to check the rest of the crew. I'll be right back."

"Keep yer bloody head down," grunts James.

Unable to spot the remaining crews in the pouring rain, Mallory gropes his way along the inside of the levee until he stumbles upon the second position. The gunners lie beneath a ground cloth, the gun's muzzle protruding across the dyke.

He slaps a helmet beneath the tarp. "Oy! Stay awake!"

The gun jerks and the assistant tosses back a corner of the sheet. "Blimey, sir! You scared the shit out of me!"

"The Hun won't be coming from behind, son. They'll be coming from out there," he shouts over the closing artillery.

"Shouldn't we dig in?"

Mallory glances up at the sky. "Would you rather drown or be blown-up?"

The boy's forehead furls in concentration. "Blown-up would be quicker," he decides.

"Well, there's your answer."

He slaps the boy on the back and starts for the third gun position. As he nears Elise, a howitzer round lands atop the tank. The heat sears his face and flings him violently into the mud.

"Shit!"

He gropes for his helmet and sits upright. Elise is aflame, fuel feeding the raging fire as she burns steadily like a gas-lamp illuminating their tiny perimeter.

Deafened by the blast, he spots muzzle flashes as the third crew fires across the levee. Clearly they remain alive and alert.

Gunfire erupts around him. A final glance at Elise and Mallory scrambles back to James' side. "What's up?"

"Fritz is probin' the perimeter," reports James. "Lookin' for a weak spot. Don't think he found none."

Mallory glances at his watch and realizes it's nearly too dark to read the time. "It'll be night soon," he shouts to James. "The infantry will be on their way."

James raises a hand for silence. He rotates his head side to side, listening for something in the distance. "Hear that?"

"All I hear is this damned rain."

James raises a cautionary finger. "Listen. That *clinkin'* sound: Fritz is emplacin' a trench mortar out there somewhere."

"How the hell can you tell from just the sound?"

"Heard it before, on the Somme. That's when Fritz first started usin' mortars – the *clank clank* noise they make when they're diggin' 'em in."

"If he gets it into action, we're buggered," swears Mallory.

"Well and truly."

Mallory raises his head over the berm and peers into the darkness. "Can't see a bloody thing. What do we do, wait until we see the muzzle flash?"

"Don't have to," replies James. "I was watchin' a couple of shell holes out past those tree stumps before it got dark. Someone got anxious and started stringin' a groundsheet between some 'o those branches."

"Really? What do you propose?"

"I says we slide over there and give 'em a knock."

"What, just the two of us? We haven't even got any Mills bombs."

"Oh, I wouldn't worry 'bout that." James reaches inside his jacket and displays a German 'potato masher' grenade.

"Where'd you get that?"

He nods toward the body beneath the tarp. "Fritz had it tucked inside his boot." He motions toward the group of dead Germans across the berm. "My guess is his friends over there got a few more."

Mallory makes the rounds between the Lewis gun positions and explains to the crews what he and James are about to do. When he returns to the perimeter, he brings along one of the assistant gunners and places him behind James' Lewis gun.

"We're going straight north from here about a hundred yards," he explains to the gunner. "If something happens to us, kill the bastards. Otherwise, don't fire while we're out there. Got it?"

"Y-yes, sir," mumbles the private.

Mallory and James strip off all their non-essential gear. Leaving helmets behind, they slither over the top of the levee and slide down the mound toward the Germans James shot earlier in the day.

"Keep watch," whispers Mallory. "I'll search the bodies."

Mallory's hands sweep down an officer's tangled corpse, feeling for anything that may be a weapon. At the belt, he discovers a leather holster. Withdrawing a Luger, he nudges James. "Take this."

James feels the cold steel in his hand; a set of white teeth return a smile.

Finding no grenades on the officer, Mallory crawls to another corpse. Stung in a sack around the man's neck, he discovers another stick grenade.

"Got it," he rasps.

"That'll do. Follow me," instructs James and starts off at a low crawl toward the German positions.

Raindrops slap the water-filled shell holes around them like bullets striking armor plate, the noise masking their descent into no man's land.

It's slow-going as their advance is repeatedly blocked by unfordable bogs, they struggle to work around obstacles. Disoriented by the constant changes in direction, Mallory glances periodically over his shoulder to get a fix on the burning tank still glowing inside the makeshift perimeter.

His muddy uniform waterlogged, muscles aching, he clenches his teeth to prevent them clattering as he shivers in the cold July rain.

Clank! The unmistakable scraping of metal-on-metal beacons like a claxon.

Mallory tugs James' foot. A hand reaches down and pulls at his uniform. Mallory slithers forward and finds himself beside James.

"'Bout twenty feet over there," whispers James. "After ya arm your grenade, hold it for four seconds before you throw. Otherwise they'll have a chance to toss it back at us."

"How do I arm it?" whispers Mallory.

"Oh, for God's sake …," swears James. He retrieves the grenade from Mallory's hand and unscrews the cap on the bottom of the handle. A small porcelain ball tied to a string dangles from the opening. "Pull the string and count four. Got it?"

"Yes."

From the German position come murmurs. The clanking has stopped. A wooden box splinters and hasty instructions are provided. There is a scrape of metal on metal.

"They're preparin' to fire," hisses James and gropes for his grenade.

"Bereit? *Feuer!*" From the German position comes the scrape of a mortar round sliding down the tube. It strikes the firing pin and erupts from the tube with an earsplitting *WHUMP!* The glowing round arches toward the perimeter and buries itself in the mud before erupting in a muffled *WHOMP!*

Mallory smiles in gratitude for that one, merciful glitch.

James nudges him and rolls onto his back. He unscrews the end cap on the grenade's handle and lets the pull cord dangle. Mallory does the same.

James grasps the pull cord and jerks. The grenade begins to hiss. Mallory does the same.

After several seconds, James rasps, "*now!*" and pitches the grenade end-over-end into the mortar pit. Mallory follows-up with his grenade, which strikes the tarp and slides into the hole.

"Was ist das?" a voice yells. "Finden! *Finden!*"

CRUMP! CRUMP!

The grenades explode in rapid succession, the blasts setting-off a chain reaction among the ammunition stacked beside the mortar.

Mallory and James bury their faces in the mud, covering their heads as the heat of explosion boils over them, singeing their hair as the fireball expands and ascends, pieces of glowing shrapnel arching in all directions and falling gracefully to the ground.

As the blast recedes, Mallory tugs James' ankle and yells, "Let's get the hell out of here!"

Ignoring the low crawl, they jump to their feet and scramble back toward their perimeter a hundred yards away. As they near the levee, rounds begin snapping over their heads from inside the perimeter.

"Damn it, man! It's Sergeant James and I!" yells Mallory as he throws himself flat on his stomach.

"Sorry, sir!" comes the reply. "Come on in!"

Mallory and James rise to their feet and dash the last 20 yards, stumbling and sliding in the churned earth. Diving over the levee, they find themselves face-to-face with a dozen Tommies, bayonets fixed, staring down at the mud-covered intruders.

"Well, don't look at us!" snarls James as he gingerly pushes aside the nearest blade. "Fritz is out there! Go get him!"

CHAPTER 19
Tank Corps Headquarters, Bermicourt, France
September 1917

"What's the matter, Sir? You look troubled," announces Colonel Henry Tudor, 9th Division's artillery commander.

"Hello, Henry" replies General Elles. "What brings you up here?"

Tudor retrieves a chair from the next table, draws it up across from Elles and takes a seat. He places his swagger stick and cap on the table and signals the waiter.

"Oui, Monsieur?"

"Whiskey, neat," replies Tudor. "Can I get you something Hugh?"

"Sure. How about a wide-open battlefield and a few thousand tanks?" snorts Elles.

"Nice enough if you can get them," chuckles Tudor.

"Sorry, Henry. I'm just feeling sorry for myself at the moment. Yes," he replies to the waiter. "I'll take a Whiskey, neat, also. Merci."

The waiter nods and returns to the bar.

"So, old boy," continues Tudor. "What's got you down? I hear your tanks are performing splendidly!"

'Yes, well. As far as it goes," snorts Elles. "This Passchendaele battle is buggering me senseless! It's not a suitable battlefield for tanks and we're contributing damned little to the fight! All we're doing is wasting tanks. I feel like we're marching backwards."

Tudor nods thoughtfully. "Yes, bad show all around. Ghastly weather."

"It's not just that, Henry. It's the terrain and - if you'll pardon me - the damned artillery. My tanks are made to cross trenches, not swim across a churned-up battlefield."

"Well, then. You're in luck, Hugh." Tudor reaches into his pocket, withdraws a cone-shaped metal object and places it on the table.

"What's this?"

"You know damned well what it is - it's an artillery fuse. But a special one."

Elles picks up the fuse and examines it with a critical eye. "Special, how?"

"It's the latest thing: a Number 106. We call it a 'direct action' fuse – it explodes immediately on contact."

"That's what we were told about the graze fuse," shrugs Elles. "But it still buries itself in the ground and makes a hell of a crater."

"Ah, but this is different! Look here," insists Tudor. "When it fires, this collar pops-off in flight leaving the hammer extended." Holding the fuse in his right hand, he arches it through the air like an incoming artillery projectile and dashes it against the palm of his left. *Click!*

"Immediate detonation!"

Elles retrieves the fuse and examines it with renewed interest. "Does it really work?"

"Tested it myself! It's bloody marvellous!"

"All right. So why are you showing it to me?"

Tudor glances around the room to ensure they're out of ear-shot of others. He leans-in conspiratorially. "See here, I've got an idea for an attack in the IV Corps sector using sound ranging and silent registration. It'll allow us to lay our guns and be prepared to fire without ranging rounds. When the attack begins, the Germans will be taken completely by surprise."

"And with the new fuse…"

"There won't be craters all over the place!"

Elles leans forward and gently places the fuse on the table. "Sounds like you could use some tanks to provide a breakthrough."

"Precisely what I was thinking," admits Tudor.

"And I have your battlefield," Elles announces, slapping his hand on the table. "Do you know 'Boney' Fuller?"

The limo draws up to Tank Corps Headquarters at Bermicourt chateau. As Mallory steps from the car, Elles emerges from the front door and offers his hand.

"Mallory, my boy!"

"Sir!" replies Mallory and snaps a flat, back-handed salute.

Elles returns the salute casually, takes hold of Mallory's sleeve and tugs him inside. "Good timing! The briefing is about to begin and I wanted you here for it." They move briskly down the marble hallway toward the sound of voices and emerge into a large, baroque ball room, ornately carved French Renaissance chairs lined up in neat rows.

"Take a seat," directs Elles. "We'll begin directly."

Bewildered, Mallory finds a seat near the back of the room, self-conscious in his faded field uniform and mud-spattered puttees. Spit polished staff officers mill around the room in small clusters talking excitedly. Mallory spots Colonel Fuller standing alone beside a large tarp-shrouded map board erected on an easel. As officers scurry around him, he remains intensely focused on the papers in-hand.

"*Staff, atten-shun!*" shouts the Headquarters Sergeant Major. The officers snap to attention, except for Fuller who continues thumbing through his papers.

"At ease. At ease. Take your seats," orders Elles as he stalks to the front of the room and assumes a position beside the map board.

"Good morning, gentlemen!" he announces. "Those of you who've been with us since the beginning have heard Colonel Fuller repeatedly insist for tanks to be effective, they must attack en-masse and surprise the hell out of the Germans. Well," he announces with dramatic pause, "here is our opportunity!"

He grasps the edge of the tarp and tugs; the cloth crumples to the floor to reveal a large map of the Nord-Pas-de-Calais. Fuller's head snaps-up as he realizes the briefing has begun. He slinks away.

"The target, gentlemen, is Cambrai!"

Voices murmur enthusiastically, the room vibrating with excitement.

"Code named 'Operation GY', this is to be a raid," explains Elles. "We'll advance, hit, and retire before the enemy can react.

Rather than supporting the infantry attack, the infantry and artillery will support the tank attack. *That* means coordination. Infantry will train with the tanks for the next few months in order to develop teams for each phase of the operation.

"To achieve surprise, there will be only a short creeping barrage to chase the Hun into his dugouts. No effort will be made by the artillery to cut the wire or destroy machineguns. That will be the responsibility of the tanks. When the second and third echelons attack, the artillery will restrict itself to counter-battery work and shelling enemy lines of communication to delay counter attacks."

He raises in his hand the artillery fuse Colonel Tudor has provided him. "I'm assured our new fuse will ensure minimal cratering and the tanks can pass-through shelled areas without ditching."

Mallory raises his hand tentatively.

"Yes, Captain Mallory?" asks Elles.

"Sir, forgive me, but counter-battery work takes some time. As soon as we start the attack, the Hun's going to pound us with artillery. How quickly can we respond with just sound-ranging to locate the enemy guns?"

"Good question!" Elles points to a Major in the front row. "Care to answer, Johnny?"

The tall, willowy officer with the wings and tell-tale scarf of a flying officer rises slowly to his feet and turns to the assembled crowd. "The RFC will provide close air support and attack the Hun artillery as the battle commences." He nods to Mallory, "But of course our bombs make a bit of a mess, so you'll pardon the occasional crater."

The assembled staff officers chuckle in unison.

"So long as you hit your targets," replies Mallory gamely, "you'll hear no complaints from the Tank Corps."

More laughter.

"More than four hundred tanks in nine battalions - the bulk of the Tank Corps — are committed to the operation," explains Elles. "Supporting forces include the Third, Fourth and Seventh Corps totalling ten infantry divisions in the attack with five in reserve, plus a cavalry corps of three divisions, and a thousand guns."

"What about follow-on forces?" asks Mallory.

"I stress this is a raid, not a general offensive. But if a breakthrough occurs, the First, Second and Fifth Cavalry Divisions will exploit the breach and our reserves will follow-on."

A renewed clamor of excitement surges through the room.

"This is our opportunity, gentlemen," announces Elles. "Preparation, training and execution are the keys. But in the end, it is the judgment and pluck of our commanders and crews that will decide this battle. And in them, I have full confidence!"

A clamor arises through the room. An officer begins a cheer and the rest of the staff join-in: *'For he's a jolly good fell-ow, for he's a jolly good fell-ow, for he's a jolly good fell-ooow, and so say all of us...'*

"That's all for now, gentlemen," announces Elles over the cheer's dying strains. "I'd like the artillery and RFC liaison officers to remain behind for a few minutes and meet with my staff to receive your training and deployment schedules. The rest of you I'll see on the training grounds."

"Staff, atten-shun!" barks the sergeant major. Chairs scrape on the hardwood floors, some falling over backwards as the staff members bolt to their feet.

Elles strides down the aisle and disappears through the elegantly carved doors. Following Elles, his red-tabbed ADC hesitates beside Mallory.

"Captain Mallory, the general would like to see you in his dining room."

"Um, sure," stammers Mallory. He stoops, retrieves his cap and follows the ADC out of the ballroom and down the hall. The captain stops at a door and knocks gently.

"Enter!"

He and Mallory enter the baroque room to find Brigadier General Elles hanging his tunic and cane on a coat hook. "Ah, Jack. Thanks for dropping by. Why don't we take a spot of lunch while we talk, eh?"

Mallory places his cap on a hook and warily takes a seat opposite Elles at an ornately carved table.

"Don't look so suspicious, Jack. I'm not going to try and make you a staff officer or anything so devious."

Mallory relaxes. "Well, what a relief sir."

A side door creaks open and an orderly enters the room with a tray of cold cuts, cheese and loaf of bread. He places the tray on the table and turns to retrieve a cut-glass decanter from the sideboard. Placing two wine glasses before them, he fills each.

"Will there be anything else, sir?"

"No, Perkins. Thank you."

Elles notes the look of renewed discomfort on Mallory's face.

"Now, see here, Jack. I don't like this mumbo-jumbo either, but it allows me to work through the day without breaking for meals."

"I didn't say anything sir," grins Mallory.

"Yes, well. I know what the troops think about generals and their chateaus..."

"Not at all, sir."

Trying to decide if Mallory's being sarcastic, Elles eyes him suspiciously. "Well, then," he announces finally. "Grab yourself a bite to eat and let's talk about the Brigade."

In silence, both men prepare sandwiches, each passing the condiments between them. Sandwiches made, Elles retrieves his glass of Cabernet and leans back in his chair.

"So how do you find the Brigade after this Passchendaele mess?" he asks.

Mallory retrieves his glass and examines it with interest. "As you'd expect, sir. The tanks are scattered from Ypres to Lens to Bermicourt and are badly in need of repair and overhaul." He takes a sip and nods approvingly. "Mmm, that's good."

"What about the command?" asks Elles.

Mallory toys with the glass in his hand, studying the way the liquid clings to the glass before sliding back to its source. "Sir, I'm really not qualified to evaluate the command..."

"Of course you are," replies Elles. "What about battalion commanders? Is everyone up to snuff?"

Mallory shifts uncomfortably in his seat. "I haven't had much opportunity to evaluate the battalion commanders," he replies cautiously.

"But you're well-connected with the crews," insists Elles. "You know how the men feel. Are there any complaints about the command?"

"Soldiers complain all the time sir. It's their lot in life."

"So are any of the complaints justified?"

"Some, probably," he concedes.

"Fine," snorts Elles and places his glass back on the table. "You won't throw anyone under the cart and I respect that. So here's what I'm hearing. Word is Major Croft has built a cadre of lackeys collectively unqualified to pour piss from a boot."

Mallory nods without smiling. "He's a cavalryman," he replies. "He doesn't like mechanical things and he doesn't understand them. And he likes people that agree with him."

"That's what I suspected," replies Elles, appearing agitated. "Cambrai will be the most important operation we've ever undertaken and I need my best officers commanding."

"I agree, sir."

"Good!" declares Elles. "Then you'll take over the battalion."

"Sorry... *WHAT?*"

"You're being gazetted Major. You'll take 'D' Battalion."

Having declared his intention, Elles retrieves his glass and takes a sip. "Now, let's finish-up this lunch. We've got a lot of work to do."

"What's *that* mean?" asks James warily.

"It means someone else will be taking the Company," replies Mallory.

"And what about the crew?"

"They'll get a new commander, obviously."

James stares at him hard. "That's *it*, then? 'Thanks for a wonderful war, now I'm passin' you off to some new lieutenant that don't know his arse from a hole in the ground'?"

"Look, James. It's not that way..."

"Course it is!" snorts James. "I never would 'a thought *you*..."

"Now, see here," interrupts Mallory. "Orders are orders. I tried to talk him out of it, but the truth is if I don't do it, who will? Do you want Major Croft to remain in command? Besides, I'm still with the battalion, so it's not like I'm leaving!"

Deflated, James concedes Mallory's point. "Naw, I know you're the right bloke for the job. It's just ... well..."

"We've been together for a long time," concludes Mallory.

"Yeah, we 'ave."

A look of misery crosses Mallory's face as he sits scratching his stubbled chin. Suddenly, he breaks into a grin. "Wait a minute, why don't you come over to Battalion as my Sergeant Major?"

"Sar' Major? *Me?*" guffaws James. "That dent in your helmet must've gone to yer head!"

"Why the hell not?"

"We're short of NCOs and the crews need sergeants with battle experience. Besides, you're the only officer I can stand the sight of. Hangin' around all those red tabs would give me the vapours."

"Now you're just looking for excuses."

"No, I'm really not," protests James. "I ain't no regular soldier. I'm just 'ere for the duration. A battalion needs a real Sar Major; one that looks and acts the part. No, I ain't sar major material."

"Blast! I felt fairly good about myself before I spoke with you."

James rises to his feet. "Well, I'll bless your new command if ya do two things for me." He retrieves his cap from the major's desk. "First, gimme' your best replacement lieutenant..."

"Of course. And?"

"Give me namin' rights on Elise's replacement tank."

"Adele?"

"Adele."

"Perhaps you can have Adele bless it herself," replies Mallory. "The entire Tank Corps is going to back to The Loop at Bray-sur-Somme. We'll deploy from there."

CHAPTER 20
On Pass, Bray-sur-Somme, France
October 1917

"D Battalion!" the Transport Officer calls-out to the assembled officers and NCOs awaiting the order of departure for deploying units.

"Here!" yells Mallory over the din.

The Transport Officer defers to his French transport liaison. The Frenchman checks his clipboard.

"Train zéro six à onze. Commencez chargement 23rd Octobre à 3,00," he announces.

"Hah!" laughs James, rubbing his hands together with delight. "Three days away!" he turns to Mallory. "So?" he asks excitedly.

The Frenchman passes a bundled set of date-stamped orders to Mallory over the heads of the other battalions' officers. "Merci," shouts Mallory. He tucks the orders beneath his arm and turns to James. "I'll give you a pass, but you've got to be back well before 3.00 on the 23rd. I need you to oversee the loading. We've got a lot of new crews that know how to load flatcars in-principle, but don't have any practical experience."

"What about you?"

"I don't think I'm going to be able to get away."

James' face falls. "Shit! I can't go see Adele without you," he whines. "Elise will have my guts for garters!"

"Don't be so dramatic. Elise will be glad to see you and Adele will be absolutely delirious."

"Elise won't understand why I came and you didn't," cautions James.

"She's the widow of an army officer," replies Mallory. "She'll understand as well as anyone."

James stands defiantly. "Well, I don't care. If you ain't goin', neither am I."

"Don't be daft. You've been looking forward to this ever since Passchendaele."

"Don't matter!"

"Look," reasons Mallory. "I can't have you abusing yourself every night. Go see Adele and get your fill of her. There's no telling when we'll make it back here again."

James deflates like a whipped puppy, his brown eyes begging for a favorable response.

"Don't do that," mumbles Mallory. "I can't have your misery on my conscience."

"Then *come with me*," begs James. "We can pick up some vin blanc anglais, take the girls out on the town, and spend a couple 'a nights soilin' the sheets."

"Soiling the...?" snorts Mallory. "Where the hell do you find these colloquialisms?'

"Where do I find... what?"

"Oh, never mind," laughs Mallory. "All right. We'll take a few days with the ladies."

When they arrive in the village, Bray is crowded with Tommies from General Byng's Third Army. Red-capped Military Police patrol the cobblestone streets keeping order, checking to ensure groups of soldiers are properly attired and validating passes.

As Mallory and James stroll down Rue Pasteur toward the gray two-storey house, they find the block surrounding Elise's establishment cordoned-off. Soldiers being turned-away shuffle dejectedly up the block toward them, faces drooping as if denied Last Rites.

"Oh, those damned red caps!" seethes James.

"They must be restricting access to public places for security reasons," decides Mallory.

"How is Adele a risk to security?"

"She's not, of course. But we're trying to prevent the Germans from getting wind of the operation, so it makes sense."

"Well it don't make sense to me and it sure as hell ain't gonna make sense to Adele."

"No, it won't, will it?"

Mallory suddenly realizes how badly he wants to see Elise.

"All right. Just shut your mouth and follow my lead," announces Mallory. As they approach the nearest guard, Mallory reaches into his pocket and withdraws his pay book. Handing it to the guard he preempts the impending protest. "Major Jack Mallory, Third Army Intelligence," he snaps authoritatively. "This is my bodyguard Sergeant James."

"Sir?" asks the confused red cap.

"We're here to interrogate the subjects," insists Mallory.

"Subjects, sir?"

"The girls, man. Don't you know why this building is cordoned-off?"

"Public establishments are off limits, sir."

"Oh, for God's sake," scoffs Mallory. "This house has been quarantined at the direction of Army Intelligence. We believe there may be a leak emanating from this establishment. Some of these girls may have been pumping our young men for information and supplying it to the Hun! Sergeant James and I are here to probe the key personnel."

James snorts in an attempt to cover his laughter.

The sentry examines Mallory's pay book. "Says here you're Tank Corps."

"Attached to G2," explains Mallory irritably. "You don't think the Tank Corps requires intelligence, corporal?"

"No, of course not sir. I mean…, of course, sir." Flustered, the sentry returns Mallory's pay book without further examination.

"Stand aside and whatever you do, don't let any uncleared personnel inside this perimeter," orders Mallory.

"Sah!" replies the sentry and steps aside to let them pass.

Mallory marches smartly past the barrier, James snickering at his heels as they proceed to the heavy oak front door.

"Shhh," hisses Mallory as he attempts to restrain his own laughter.

He lifts the heavy bronze knocker and hammers the door insistently. A curtain beside the door parts and a pair of eyes examine them briefly. With a rattle, the door cracks open and Mallory shoves his pay book through the opening.

"Major Mallory, Military Intelligence," he barks loudly. "We're here to search the premise and interrogate your key employees. Now stand aside or I shall have to resort to stern measures!"

"Stern measures?" purrs Adele. "How titillating!"

"Just open the bloody door and let us inside," whispers Mallory, urgently.

She opens the door and Mallory and James stride into the foyer. As the door closes, Adele lets-out a squeal and throws her arms around James' neck, kissing him feverishly as tears flow down her tanned cheeks. "Mon cheri, je savais que tu reviendrais!"

"Same 'ere, Adele. Same 'ere." They stare longingly into each other's eyes with an expression Mallory imagines must be true love. After a few awkward moments, he clears his throat.

Adele gasps. "Mon Dieu! Je suis désolée!" Releasing James, she runs to the foot of the stairs. "Elise! Elise!"

A chair scrapes on the floor above. Urgent footsteps patter across the floor. A door swings open, the handle slamming into the wall. "Qu'est-ce...?" Elise hesitates as she spots Mallory staring up at her from the bottom of the stairs. "Mon Dieu!" she breathes and descends the stairs into his arms.

"How did you get in here? La police militaire are blocking the street."

"Low friends in high places," laughs Mallory. "Seems, besides being a den of iniquity, your establishment may also be a nest of spies. James and I are here to investigate."

"Oh, my," she gasps. "Will the interrogation be thorough?"

"Absolutely! Why, I can't imagine it taking less than three days."

"Seems excessive," she chides.

"Oh, I intend to be thorough," murmurs Mallory lustily. He glances around the nearly empty house. "Where is everyone?"

"I sent them home. The police militaire placed public establishments off-limits. I believe it is a precaution because of 'Operation GY'."

"What do you know about Operation GY?" asks Mallory suddenly, his face becoming stern.

"Nothing," shrugs Elise. "It's just something I heard."

"Well forget you ever heard that," scolds Mallory. "If the Provost thought you knew anything about it, they'd take you into custody."

"Well, who am *I* going to tell?"

"It doesn't matter. Security…"

"Ah, sécurité," she scoffs. "There is no such thing as security in a brothel. Men will spill their guts to impress a beautiful woman, you know that."

"Well, even so. A few days ago, your government executed an exotic dancer on allegations of espionage…"

"Mata Hari," replies Elise.

"Yes. Mata Hari. I don't know what the evidence was against her, but just knowing things that are supposed to be classified can get one killed these days."

"Oh, well. I don't know anything anyway. I'm just a travailleuse du sexe trying to make a living."

"Speakin' 'o which," James chimes-in eagerly. Adele squeals and the two of them ascend the stairs in a flurry of groping hands and discarded clothes.

The door slams and Elise turns to Mallory. "So," she purrs and drapes her arms around his neck. "Since we are now a respectable couple, what shall we do?" He pulls her close, her thigh pressing between his legs.

"Ah, I think I feel an idea coming-on," she laughs.

"*What?*" gasps Mallory as he jerks upright in bed. Elise grasps his arm. The morning light breaks through parted curtains.

There's hammering at the bedroom door.

"You awake in there?" shouts James.

Mallory glances at Elise's partially exposed nude body and tosses the sheet over her. She giggles and draws it down to her chin.

"We're awake now," growls Mallory irritably. "What the hell do you want?"

The door bursts open. James and Adele stumble into the room, his arm is wrapped around her shoulders, her arm locked around his waist. He's wearing her pink silk dressing gown. She's dressed in a sheer negligee through which the light easily passes. There's a bottle of Champaign in James' grip.

"Adele and me got an announcement to make!"

"We're out of vin blanc anglais?" asks Mallory sarcastically.

"Nah!" booms James. "We're gettin' married!"

Adele giggles hysterically.

"You're *what?*" blurts Mallory.

"Gettin' married! We just decided."

"You're *drunk*," snorts Mallory.

James raises the bottle. "Nope! Still corked!"

Mallory groans and collapses back onto his pillow.

Elise nudges him playfully. "Tres agreeable."

"It's not *sweet*, it's *absurd*," declares Mallory.

"Qu'est-ce que signifie 'absurde'?" asks Adele.

"It means… It means… Well, you… you can't get *married!*" stammers Mallory.

"Sure we can," insists James. "The conseiller municipal is a friend 'o the family, so to speak. Adele says he'll do us up proper."

"You mean, he's a customer," grunts Mallory.

"O' Course."

"Look here, you've got to get permission from the army," explains Mallory. "You can't just '*do it*'."

"Army Regs says I can get married with the permission of my commanding officer," insists James. "Tha's you. So, are you gonna deny the happy couple the blessin' of marital bliss?"

Mallory sits up again. "My God! You're *serious*, aren't you?"

"Serious as death," announces James.

Elise rolls onto her side, a hand holding the sheet against her bosom. "Why *not?*" she asks. "They are in love. There's a war on. I don't see why they shouldn't."

"Well… *because* there's a war on," insists Mallory. "I mean… what if something *happens?* You know, to James."

"People die. Life goes on, mon cheri," sighs Elise.

"Yes, yes, of course," replies Mallory. "I'm sorry darling. I forgot who I was speaking with." He gently kisses her bare shoulder.

"Then you'll approve it?" asks James eagerly.

"I suppose I will."

"*Hurrah!*" James yells and lifts Adele, spinning in circles around the tiny room. "You won't regret it, sir!"

"Yeah, well, you might!"

James places Adele gently back on her feet.

"When do you want to do this?" asks Mallory.

"Huh? Oh, today!"

"*Today?*"

"Sure, why not? Waitin' ain't gonna change anythin'."

"I should remind you we're in a house surrounded by the provost's minions," replies Mallory. "I hadn't actually considered how we're going to get out of here. We're supposedly interrogating suspects."

"Blimey, I hadn't thought about *that.*"

Adele lets out another sudden squeal. "Un moment!" She ducks beneath James' arm and disappears down the hallway. Giggles echo through the hall as she returns to the room with a pair of handcuffs. A finger hooked through the chain, she dangles them before James and winks playfully.

"Where *on earth* did you get those?" asks Mallory.

She shrugs shyly.

Elise grooms Mallory's uniform with a stiff brush, fussily assuring the wool combs the same direction to form a consistent green tinge. Mallory shrugs her away. "Stop it," he chuckles. "It's nearly threadbare already."

"Well, you must look handsome for the arrest," she replies with a warm smile.

"You look lovely for a suspect," he chides. "Chiffon suits you."

Elise examines herself in the mirror, her layered ivory-colored chiffon dress swaying around her bare ankles, a matching string of Adele's pearls wind several times around her elegant neck.

"You don't think it's too formal for autumn?"

"I think the military police downstairs will never believe I'm taking you into custody."

"I'll wear a coat over it," she pouts. "I want to look good for James and Adele's wedding. This is a special day for them and I want everything to be right."

Mallory appears in the reflection over her shoulder. He places his hands on her shoulders and kisses the back of her neck lightly. "Do you want to make it a double wedding?" he asks.

She places her hand on his and strokes it tenderly. "Thank you for asking, Jack. But, no. I've had my time. It was wonderful, but it is not something I can do again."

"You know I love you," he reminds her.

"Yes," she sighs. "And I love you."

There's a knock. "You two 'bout ready?" James calls through the door.

"Yes, yes. We're ready," Mallory replies impatiently. The door swings open and James strolls into the room dressed not in his uniform, but in top-hat and tails of a pre-war fashion. Adele enters with him, dressed in a slightly risqué version of what she supposes to be formal attire.

Elise takes one glance at James and bursts into laughter. Mallory's jaw drops. "You can't go out dressed like that!"

"It's my weddin' day," announces James defiantly. "I ain't getting married in my khakis."

"But… you're out of uniform! If you're caught, you'll end up in the brig!"

"Don't care…"

"Well, I think he looks tres chic," announces Elise.

James doffs his hat and bows formally. "Merci Mademoiselle."

"Madame," Mallory corrects. "And where the hell did you find the get-up?"

"A German businessman named Baron von Prittwitz left it 'ere back in August 1914," explains Adele. "When the war started, he departed one-step ahead of the Gendarme." Then she examines James admiringly. "I think it makes him look très sophistiqué."

"He's going to be 'très arrêté' if he's caught in civilian clothes. Now, how the hell am I supposed to get you past the provost?"

James places the hat jauntily on his head. "I don't look like a soldier, so why would they suspect anything?"

"No, you look like a character out of Punch," snorts Mallory. "They'd sooner expect you're this Baron von whatshisname."

Adele squeals. "Magnifique!"

"He can be the German spy you were looking for!" Elise chimes-in.

"*What?*"

James straightens and raises his chin arrogantly. "Ich bin ein…" He pauses and turns to Adele. "How do you say German spy, love?"

"Espion allemande."

"Right. Ich bin ein elpsilon allyman!"

Mallory buries his face in his hands. "Dear God, lousy French and even worse German. You're going to get us all arrested."

"Well, I ain't changin'."

"All right. Adele," decides Mallory. "Get the cuffs. I'm taking von dumbass into custody." He turns to James. "But you're a bloody Frenchman, not a Hun. And if I hear one word of *any* language out of you, I'll damned well shoot you myself."

"Oui, mon commandant!"

With a twinkle in her eye, Adele pulls James' wrists behind his back and starts to cuff him. "Monsieur, I arrest you au nom de l'amour."

"No, no!" rasps Mallory. "Cuff them in front. If this plan goes tits-up, we may have to fight our way out of this."

"If I must," she replies with disappointment.

James winks at Mallory.

"Later, love," he whispers to Adele. "Later."

The ceremony doesn't take long, the embarrassed civil official stumbling his way through the rites as you'd expect of a man that is intimate with the bride and fearful of both the British authorities and the man she is marrying.

"Aavez-vous l'anneau de mariage?" he asks.

"Mon Dieu," Adele gasps. "I almost forgot."

Elise slides off her wedding ring and slips into James hand.

"But Elise," James gasps.

"La vie est pour les vivants," she whispers hoarsely. "Life is for the living…"

Mallory stares down at the deep red indentation left on her ring finger. His calloused hand closes around hers.

"… therefore in the name of the Civil Authority of the French Republic, I announce you husband and wife."

Adele squeals – not quite unexpectedly – as James lifts her. The kiss is longer and bit less decent than is typical at such solemn events, but…

"What now?" asks Mallory as they emerge beneath an overcast sky.

"Well, we got to celebrate, don't we?" announces James.

"I know a quiet estaminet where we can get a good meal and Champagne to toast the happy couple," announces Elise.

"Unless you two would prefer to consummate the marriage first," jibes Mallory.

Adele slips her hand through James massive paw and snuggles against him. "I want to dance," she announces. "I want to dance all night."

"Then we dance," agrees James.

"Lead-on, darling," Mallory encourages Elise.

The two couples amble down the street, arm-in-arm, as passing British soldiers stare agog at the strange assemblage of martial pomp and decadent reverie strolling past. Rounding into an alley, they approach a small estaminet from which music drifts like a lark on a warm summer breeze. Adele enters first, the patrons glancing up in surprise at the well-known prostitute. James enters behind her and the room falls silent. Elise and Mallory enter and close the door behind them. The locals stare at the mixed couples suspiciously.

"What's 'a matter?" blurts James. "You ain't never seen a weddin' party before?"

"Qu'est-ce qu'un 'wedding party'?" asks a burly French patron.

"Fête de marriage," Elise translates.

The brute steps forward and glares at James. "A 'wedding party,' eh?"

Sensing an imminent fight, Mallory quietly presses Elise back toward the door and plants his feet.

Unexpectedly, the brute grasps James hand. "Félicitations!" He jerks James forward and kisses him on either cheek.

A cheer erupts inside the room and locals flow around the happy couple, slapping James on the back and kissing Adele's cheeks. They then make their way to Mallory and Elise with similar expressions of congratulations.

"Oh, no. We're not…" protests Mallory, but Elise tugs at his sleeve and shakes her head. Clearly she enjoys basking in the glow of James and Adele's moment.

Mallory peers down at her as she watches the happy couple move to an area between the tables and begin shuffling to the music scratching-out on a crackling Victrola. Her eyes are moist with memories of another day, another marriage. Mallory suddenly sees her in a different light, a time before the war when she was innocent - the young, virgin newlywed wife of an officer in the French army.

And he suddenly feels inadequate, like an interloper in the midst of someone else's dream. His uniform seems strangely out of place, his presence wicked, as if he is the specter at a celebratory feast.

As he stands watching James and Adele dance, he slowly becomes aware Elise is watching him, a look of pity on her beautiful face.

"What?" he asks.

She reaches up and wipes away the tears streaming down his cheeks.

CHAPTER 21
Staging Area, Bertincourt, France
November 1917

"What the *hell* is he doin' to Adele?" squeaks James.

"Installing something devised by Major Johnson over at Central Workshops," replies Mallory. "It's for the unditching beam."

"Unditchin' beam?" asks James uncertainly.

Mallory points out a ten-foot oak beam with metal end caps and chains dangling near either end. The beam leans against the tree as crews from the Central Workshop drill and rivet parallel rails along the roof of James' Mark IV tank, "Adele."

"How's fixin' rails over the top of her goin to get 'er outta the mud?"

"Not sure, actually," admits Mallory. "But there's a demonstration in a few minutes that should enlighten us. Thought you might like to come-along."

"Yeah, all right." James wipes his hands on his overalls and retrieves his grease-stained cap. The two men stroll across the workshop yard strewn with tanks under repair and cross a small footbridge over a stream.

"How's Adele?"

"According to Elise, she's bloody useless," replies James with a grin. "Seems she's lost interest in her work."

"I hear marriage will do that to a girl," laughs Mallory.

"Well, it could get serious! If she can't earn her keep, Elise will have to fire her."

"Like hell!" blurts Mallory. "They're best friends. Besides, Elise is not so committed to the business."

"Think so?"

"Yes, I do," laughs Mallory.

"You know," observes James. "You have been a lot jollier since you and Elise patched things up."

Mallory nods. "Yes, I suppose so."

"So?"

"So, what? Elise doesn't want to marry again. She's content with things the way they are and so am I."

"Well, tha's good enough."

"Indeed it is."

The path leads through the woods and opens into a field of Mark IV tanks draped lazily with camouflage nets. Most have the rails already installed; others sit idly while work crews install the remaining rail systems. The sound of hydraulic hammers echoes through the woods.

They approach an NCO standing before a parked tank. As they near, they hear him talking a crew through use of the new contraption. Several crews are watching the demonstration with interest.

"No, no! Don't try and lift the bally thing!" yells the sergeant. "It's more than a' thousand pounds. Hook the chains through the tracks and let the tank do the work!"

The crew follows the instructor's directions and affixes the long beam to the front of the tracks, a meter of slack chain connecting the beam and tank. The sergeant directs the driver into the tank and orders him to reverse the monster, slowly. As the engine roars, the tank inches backward, lifting the beam and drawing it up over the front of the vehicle. The wood strikes the tracks with a screech and is dragged up over the roof along the rails.

"Stop!" the sergeant calls. The engine coughs and dies. The driver exits the tank and joins the crew staring up at the beam riding crookedly atop the rails.

"I'm going to show you how to stow it first then demonstrate how it works." The sergeant directs the crew to mount the roof of the tank and climbs atop the driver's cupola from which he continues to instruct. "Disconnect the chains from the tracks and wrap 'em around the rails," he directs and the crew complies, jostling the beam toward the rear of the rails. After several failed attempts, the crew finally secures the beam in-place.

The sergeant peers down from the tank and addresses the crowd gathering in the breezy field. "This is the transport position.

When you go into combat, it'll be out of the way at the rear of the vehicle. Now," he continues as he addresses the crew. "Reattach the chain to the tracks. Come-on! Come-on! We haven't got all day."

Crew members slide the chains through the clevises and reattach them loosely to the tracks as before. "Now we'll demonstrate how it gets you out of the mud!" At the instructor's direction, the driver returns inside the machine. "Move forward slowly!" calls the sergeant and the tank proceeds, its tracks dragging the chains that draw the beam forward along the rails. As it reaches the front of the tank just above the driver's cupola, the beam clangs loudly off the rails and dangles before the tracks. As the vehicle continues forward, the beam slips neatly beneath both tracks and the tank rolls over it.

The sergeant stalks slowly alongside the vehicle pointing to the progress of the beam passing beneath the tracks. "Note how the beam provides additional traction," he explains. "This'll free the tank from most any bog you're likely to encounter. And as she reaches the end of her trip...," he pauses. The beam is dragged up the rear of the tank and back over the roof to slide along the rails and repeat the process. "She starts all over again."

He slaps the armor and the tank lurches to a stop.

"Questions?"

James steps forward. "How long can she go on with it thing scrapin' over the top?"

"It's an imperfect solution," admits the sergeant. "It's made to get you out of a ditching situation, not to cross the entire battlefield. So I'd say it lasts as long as the beam remains intact."

James eyebrows shoot upward. "You mean the crew is hookin' this thing up under fire after they're already ditched?"

"Of course," replies the sergeant.

"Cor, blimey," James sighs. "Someone's gonna have to have balls 'o steel!"

The group laughs.

Mallory steps before the group. "It's still better than sitting in a flooded shell hole waiting for the Hun artillery to blast you to bits," he announces. "Now, Sergeant Davies will be working with the battalion for the next week. I want each of the crews to practice attaching and storing the beam until you're confident you can do it under the worst circumstances."

The crews nod.

"Keeping your tank in the fight is as important as gunnery or tactics," he concludes.

As the instruction ends and the crews begin to disperse, Mallory spots a staff car bouncing across the field coming toward them. Red cap and arm bands identify the passengers as staff officers. As the car nears, Mallory recognizes the grim-faced Colonel in the back seat.

"Uh, oh," mumbles Mallory. "Colonel Fuller looks well and truly pissed. This can't be good."

"Well," sighs James. "This don't look like sergeants' business, so with your permission…" He salutes and turns to depart.

"You're not afraid of Colonel Fuller, are you?" asks Mallory with a chuckle.

"Eh, no sir. He just sorta rubs me the wrong way. I think it's the way he stares at people like he's studyin' 'em for a lab experiment. Gives me the creeps."

Mallory laughs. "All right, then. Off with you." He returns James' salute and James scurries away. The car draws-up beside Mallory and skids to a stop on the wet grass. Mallory salutes, holding it only long enough to realize the distracted Fuller is unlikely to return it.

"Major Mallory," announces Fuller. "Seems we've run into bit of a sticky wicket." He leans forward in his seat and passes Mallory a stack of aerial photographs. Mallory glances at them and turns back to Fuller, a question on his face.

"Those were taken over Havrincourt two days ago," explains Fuller. "See anything unusual?"

Mallory takes a second look at the photos, sorting through them as he examines images of the jagged German trench lines with their cut-backs and traverses. "The defence looks pretty extensive," he replies. "What's the problem? Are they being reinforced?"

"Don't be thick, Major," scoffs Fuller as he retrieves the photos and sorts through the packet. He locates the photo he's seeking and presents it to Mallory. "Does that look like a standard Hun trench to you?"

Mallory squints and changes the angle of the glossy black and white photo to reduce the glare. Recognizing the anomaly, he looks-up sharply. "Are they all like this?"

"The first few lines, yes," replies Fuller.

"How wide are they?"

"Our photo interpreters believe the Hun trenches in this sector are as wide as twelve feet."

"Shit," mumbles Mallory. "We can't cross anything *that* wide!"

"Don't I know it!" replies Fuller. "Clearly the Hun knows it, too! He's widening his trenches to prevent our tanks crossing."

"Why the hell are we just now learning about this?"

"Weather, old boy. Too cloudy to get good photos until a few days ago. Good thing our chaps in intelligence caught it, though. Otherwise our battalions would have got stuck at the first Hun line and been cut to pieces by artillery fire."

Mallory passes the photo back to Fuller. "So what now? We can't just keep making our tanks longer."

"Working on that, actually," announces Fuller. "Something called a 'Tadpole' with a longer tread base. But it won't be ready for this battle."

"I assume you have a solution, then?"

"Fascines!" replies Fuller. "And a lot of them!"

"Sorry. What?"

"Fascines," repeats Fuller. "They go back to the time of the Romans. Been used to cross narrow gaps ever since." He hands Mallory a specification provided by the sappers.

Mallory examines the drawing. "Looks like a bundle of logs."

"Right! Four and a-half-by-ten foot bundles, to be specific. The chaps at Central Workshops are pulling them together. We've got Coolies chopping wood all over Flanders! You'll need to carry them on top of the tanks and dump them in the trenches so you can cross."

"Dear God! All my tanks need to carry these?"

"As many as possible," confirms Fuller. "Certainly the lead tanks and their back-ups."

Mallory examines the drawing. "How do you anticipate deploying these things once we reach the Hun positions?"

"Simple! Just pop the top hatch and shove the bloody thing into the trench!"

CHAPTER 22
Battle of Cambrai, France
19 November 1917

An officer hands Mallory a mimeographed sheet:

"Tomorrow the tank corps will have the chance for which it has been waiting for many months - to operate on good going in the van of battle. All that hard work and ingenuity can achieve has been done in the way of preparation. It remains for the unit commanders and for tank crews to complete the work by judgment and pluck in the battle itself. In light of past experience I leave the good name of the Corps with great confidence in their hands. I propose leading the attack for the centre division. – Hugh Elles, B.G. Commanding Tank Corps. November 19,1917."

"So the general's going to lead it himself," announces Mallory with an approving nod. He hands the paper to James who scans Elles' announcement.

"He don't belong in the front lines," protests James. "It ain't proper."

"I thought you once told me a new day is coming…"

"Not in the army! I meant the rest 'o society. Army's got traditions. Besides, he's a good bloke. Shouldn't risk gettin' himself killed."

Mallory snatches the paper from James' hand. "Well, *I'm* a pretty good *bloke* and you don't seem to mind me risking *my* life," he snorts with mock indignation.

James smiles broadly. "You're a silly bugger like the rest of us. After all this, we ain't fit for peacetime life. Why, as soon as you get off the boat back in Blighty, they'll lock you away and chuck the key in the Thames just to keep you away from the nice, church-goin' girls."

"Your vision for the future is truly remarkable, James. H.G. Wells' would be proud."

"Who's this Wells bloke? He in the battalion?"

"No, I rather doubt it," chuckles Mallory. "I appreciate General Elles letting me go in with the attack," he admits. "Usually the battalion commander gets stuck in the rear waiting for signals."

"Well, he can't hardly leave you in the rear if he's leading the attack, can he?"

"No, I suppose not," agrees Mallory. "I know Colonel Fuller wants the commanders up-front to make sure the tank-infantry assault teams stay together and get across the first three lines."

"So, you think this is goin' to work?" asks James.

"I don't see why not. We've got everything in our favor and the Hun doesn't seem to know what's coming."

"Well, at least it ain't rainin'."

Mallory glances at his watch. "I've been summoned to meet with General Elles. Do you need anything before I depart?"

"A three day pass…"

"Into Bray," laughs Mallory. "I know, I know…"

Mallory weaves between the amassed tanks sheltered on the reverse slope of the rise. Engines remain silent as crews complete final preparations.

He discovers Elles leaning against the hull of his personal tank, "Hilda", examining a large map board resting against the sloping front armor. Mallory salutes.

"Ah, Mallory. Good to see you."

"You also, sir." He glances up at Hilda and spots an unfamiliar tri-color flag of green, red and brown horizontal stripes.

"Um, what's that, sir?" he asks.

Elles glances up at the flag and smiles. "Something suggested by Colonel Fuller – the unofficial Tank Corps flag. 'From Mud, Through Blood to the Green Fields Beyond'. Thought it might make it easier for the crews to spot my tank in the heat of battle."

"Very Roman of you, sir," replies Mallory. "Are you also going to wear a red tunic so your men can't see you bleed?"

"Well, I'm wearing brown. We'll see what *that* may disguise…"

Elles' uncharacteristic bawdy humor catches Mallory off-guard. A spurt of laughter bursts forth.

"I say, steady, old man," whispers Elles with a wink. "The Hun is just over the rise."

"Sorry, sir," chuckles Mallory.

"I'll get right to the point," announces Elles seriously. "Major Carter has been taken to hospital with appendicitis, so I need you to take over 'E' Battalion."

"When?"

"Immediately," responds Elles.

"But, sir! What about 'D' Battalion?"

"Have Captain Simon take it. I need experience on my left with the 62nd Division. It's going to be the key to this battle and I need my strongest leaders alongside."

"But...," stammers Mallory.

"Now look here," Elles announces as he directs Mallory's attention to his map board. "'D' Battalion will be attacking Flesquieres with the 51st Division in-support. I need you and E Battalion on their left flank, supporting the 62nd Division attack toward Bourlon. You'll have 25 tanks. I want you to bypass Flesquieres and drive like hell to the northeast to flank Cambrai and clear the way for the cavalry."

"Yes, sir," replies Mallory less enthusiastically than he ought.

"Jack," Elles scolds. "It's not about the battalion, it's about the battle. I need you in-harness and chomping at the bit. Can I count on you?"

"Of course, sir," replies Mallory.

"And please congratulate Sergeant James on his nuptials. I'm sure they'll be very happy."

Mallory hesitates. "Yes, sir," he replies distractedly.

He wanders into the hazy evening and returns to D Battalion headquarters. Stuffing his binoculars and personal items into his satchel, he snaps irritably, "Get me Captain Simon!" A runner plops a helmet on his head and darts through the tent flaps in search of Simon.

Corporal Sydney hands him a mug of tea. "Here ya go, sir. A nice cuppa' is what you need."

"Thanks Syd," replies Mallory gratefully.

The boy's kind, innocent eyes are as welcoming as those of a loyal dog. Mallory feels a pang of guilt as he realizes his irritation comes from abandoning a family he has lived among for more than two years; a family closer than any he has ever known.

Bending over the map table, he examines the contour lines and terrain features over which D Battalion will attack Flesquieres. A gently sloping rise to a ridgeline topped with train tracks then undulating ground upward toward the town. *The town.* Mallory shudders as he remembers being swarmed by German infantry at Reincourt.

"Sir?" asks Simon, standing before him expectantly.

Mallory jerks upright. "Simon! Good to see you old boy," he responds awkwardly. "Look here, we've not got much time, so I'll get straight to the point. I need you to take command of the battalion."

"Me?" asks Simon.`

"Of course you. Why not you?" asks Mallory irritably. "You're the best company commander I've got and God knows you're the only one I trust with the battalion."

"Well… thank you sir," responds Simon with surprise. "But what about you?"

"Major Carter has been taken ill and General Elles has ordered me to take over E Battalion."

"Blimey, sir."

"As my Exec, you know the plan as well as I. The crews respect you and you know how to keep the units moving."

"Shall I inform Sergeant James?" asks Simon warily.

Mallory sighs. "No. I'll do it."

He stands and offers his hand. "Good luck today, Simon. Keep your formations tight and don't outrun your infantry."

"Will do, sir," responds Simon. "Er, shall I have your kit sent over the Battalion?"

"No. This is just temporary reassignment. I expect I'll be back once Major Carter returns."

"Of course you will, sir," replies Simon.

"It's all right, Simon," responds Mallory kindly. "You'll do fine. I trust you."

"Thank you," replies Simon gratefully.

Mallory leaves the command tent and wanders into the darkness. In the still of the night, he can almost believe there's no war. Artillery has not yet begun its preparatory bombardment; the ground is not yet rent with craters. The war seems a million miles away. A sinking feeling in the pit of is stomach reminds him the peaceful present will not last and the impending battle will pose unforeseen challenges. Like a parent sending his child off to school unescorted for the first time, a dizzying array of paranoid illusions haunt him.

As he nears the parked Adele, he detects James' telltale snoring. Stepping gingerly between the flea bags in which the crew is resting, he stoops beside his slumbering friend. In the moonlight, James sleeps restfully, a slight smile upon his hatchet-face. Eyebrows rising innocently, he looks like a friendly, sleeping bear – perhaps a character from a child's comic. Mallory reaches to shake his friend, but guilt seizes him by the throat. His hand hovers inches from James' shoulder. Fingers tremble as he hesitates.

Slowly, he draws his hand away.

"Good hunting tomorrow, my friend," he whispers softly. "We'll meet again in Bray-sur-Somme."

He rises slowly, eyes fixed on the great sleeping hulk.

One of the crew members stirs. "Sir, is that you?"

Mallory stoops beside the sleeping bag. "Yes, Schmidt. It's me."

"Is everything all right?" cracks the innocent voice.

"Of course," replies Mallory reassuringly. "I just wanted to wish you all the best for tomorrow."

"Thank 'ee sir. We trust you to get us through."

"Schmidt…"

"Sir?"

"Nothing. Just get a good sleep and I'll see you on the field tomorrow."

"We'll give 'em hell, sir."

"I know you will, son."

An hour later, Mallory enters E Battalion's headquarters. The staff is busy posting last-minute orders. There is an air of electricity in the tent. He dumps his helmet on the desk and the staff freezes in expectation.

"Good morning, gentlemen," announces Mallory as he runs a hand through his hair. "Major Craft has been taken ill and I've been posted to command the battalion."

The adjutant stands and offers his hand. "Aubrey, sir. We heard you'd be takin' over the battalion and we're pleased as hell."

"Good of you to say, Aubrey," Mallory replies. "Please have the company commanders and senior NCOs report to the command post. I'd like to discuss my views on our mission."

"Yes, sir," responds Aubrey. "Corporal," he snaps to one of the clerks. "Notify the officers and NCOs." The clerk quickly departs.

Mallory hovers over the map table and examines the proposed line of advance. If all goes as planned, his tanks will advance five thousand yards by 10.00 tomorrow morning. *Is that truly possible?* His finger traces the route between Flesquieres and Braincourt. They'll be attacking up hill, taking fire on both flanks from the strong points formed by the fortified towns.

Gradually, he becomes aware the staff and company commanders have assembled around him.

"Gentlemen," he begins. "I know Major Craft was a popular commander and I want you to know I've no intention of trying to replace him in your hearts. But I need you to accept I will be interim commander as we have a battle to fight tomorrow."

There are murmurs of approval.

He examines the fresh, young faces, many of which have not yet seen combat. "You have all been briefed on our mission." He thumps the map. "Bourlon Wood and the village beyond are our ultimate objectives. At best, I estimate we have three days before the Hun can move-in enough reinforcements to mount a counter-attack. So speed is essential. Avoid the cities. Stay in open country and drive like hell!"

"Hear, hear!"

"Jolly good!"

"This is the day for which we've been training for months and about which we old-hands have fantasized for years," continues Mallory. "We have a pristine battlefield and know exactly what we are getting into. We have the latest model Mark IVs with improved engines, drive trains and fuel systems. We have fascines to help us across the trenches and unditching gear to remove us from any bogs. The Germans don't know we're coming and we're not going to provide any warning. We'll be in their positions before they ever know what hit them. In short, all the advantages are ours. So, trust your equipment, work together, and for God's sake, stick with your infantry."

At 6.10, amid a heavy ground mist, Mallory orders E battalion forward. Twenty-five tanks divided into 3-tank clusters emerge from their laagers and crawl toward the Hindenburg line a thousand yards beyond. As they pass the British trenches, Tommies of the 62nd West Riding Division rise behind the tanks and spread out in skirmish lines to follow in their wake.

"Brakemen!" calls Mallory over the roar of the engine. "Keep the infantry in-sight! Let me know if they begin to fall behind. We'll adjust our speed accordingly."

"Right, sir!"

Despite limited visibility, there is little chance of ditching on the firm ground ahead, unspoiled by churning artillery fire.

"Is this the way it's supposed to be?" the driver asks Mallory as they roll across no man's land unmolested.

"I don't know. I've never been this way before," shouts Mallory over the roar of the engine.

Suddenly a sound like a tearing bed sheet rips overhead. Through the gray mist appear short, sharp flashes of exploding artillery rounds. Seconds later the sound breaks over them like a wave, shaking the ground and drowning-out the hum of the engines.

Mallory consults his watch. "Those are our guns. Right on time."

As they near the line of exploding shells, the barrage lifts, only to reappear 250 yards further-on. Beneath their tracks, lightly churned earth gives evidence the new artillery fuses work as advertised, exploding on contact to spread destruction outwards and upwards rather than creating impassable craters. As they reach the enemy line, the lead tank turns parallel to the trench, enfilading the Germans pouring in panic from within their dugouts to die feebly in the unprotected ditch.

Barbed wire screeches beneath Mallory's tracks, the iron posts groaning as his tank crushes the outer defenses and drags away the battlefield offal. Blinded by the mist, the hated German Maxims roar to life, bullets clawing in all directions, the occasional errant round singing off the steel hull. The first trench looms before them.

"Get ready to launch the fascine!" yells Mallory.

One of the brakemen climbs atop the engine housing and lifts the hatch to release the fascine. His knees buckle; he slides back inside and collapses in a heap on the bare deck.

"Jeeter's hit!" shouts one of the gunners and abandons his gun to check for a pulse. Blood and brain matter ooze from the shattered skull. "He's dead, sir!"

"Dammit!" curses Mallory. "Gunners! Clear that damned trench! I don't want a Goddamn Hun alive within 50 feet of this tank!" As the Lewis gunners spray the length of the trench, Mallory throws-off his seat belt and drops to the deck. He steps over the dead brakeman and emerges through the open hatch. Groping the release, he finally gains a handhold and jerks violently. The chain securing it to the rack pings loose and flies over the top of the fascine, which remains stubbornly in-place.

"Bugger!"

He ducks back inside, drops from the cowling and resumes his commander's seat.

"Reverse this bastard!"

The driver clutches and grinds the gears into reverse. Mallory slams both brakes forward. The tank lurches rearward as the massive bundle rolls lazily forward and bumps to a rest against the protruding front tracks, blocking the driver's view.

"Again!"

The tank heaves backward and the bundle tumbles over the front of the tracks and lands several feet in front of the trench.

"Shit," curses Mallory. "Put 'er back in-gear and let's push it into the trench!"

The tank crawls forward and nudges the bundle. It rolls into the ditch with a crash.

"Now, go! Go!" The tank rolls forward and noses over into the trench. The tracks make contact with the fascine, which compacts slowly beneath the weight of the tank, crackling as the vehicle moves across the makeshift bridge and emerges safely on the other side.

Mallory jerks the brakes rearward and the tank halts. "Marker!" he shouts.

One of the gunners rips the coiled flag from its rack and drops from rear door. He stabs it into the ground beside the fascine to identify the crossing point for the remaining tanks. A breeze catches the red and yellow banner as it pops in the wind. The trailing tanks spot the flash of color and converge on the marker. The gunner gives a victorious wave. Bullets slap the earth around him and he darts back inside the tank.

"Rough out there, is it?" Mallory calls over the roar.

"Bloody hell!" the gunner laughs hysterically.

On the left, a machinegun opens-fire, it's armor piercing bullets raking the side of the machine. Spall ricochets throughout the tank, the crew dropping to the deck in search of safety.

Mallory jerks the brake and the tank rumbles left. The German machine gunners flee their positions, scrambling and stumbling across the open field as the tank's gunners regain their positions and open fire. The bullets kick up dust around the retreating Germans like fingers reaching up from hell and dragging them to earth. As the tank closes, the wounded attempt to crawl clear while others stagger and fall before the continuing onslaught.

"Where's the infantry?" calls Mallory over the gunfire.

"Clearing trenches!" replies the gearsman.

Ahead, between the lines of trenches are scattered strongpoints, each containing a Maxim and small contingent of troops positioned to reinforce the line. Mallory steers the tank toward a mound of log-reinforced sandbags. "Gunners! There's your target!"

The Lewis gunners at the front of the sponsons replace their ammo pans and swing their guns forward. *Tut-tut-tut-tut!* Receiving no reply from the German position, Mallory jerks the tank right in search of new targets and proceeds toward a second mound.

Suddenly, the silent position erupts with fire, the gun crews having lain quietly while the tank sniffed and rejected their position.

"Bastards!" yells Mallory as armor-piercing bullets sweep the starboard side, molten steel and flakes of dislodged armor plate shower the crew. The gunners scream, flinging arms over their faces as if by doing they might deflect the lead and shrapnel tearing around the cabin. Two gunners collapse in bloody heaps, their guns falling silent and drooping forward in their mounts like heads hung in mourning. Mallory feels a sting across his back; blood immediately seeps between his shirt and the seat back.

"Keep going!" he yells to the driver as the strongpoint ahead begins firing point blank, the bullets deflected by the downward slope of the frontal armor. "Arrgggghhhh!" Mallory growls as the tank rears-up and tips forward atop the trapped Germans. "Die, you bastards! Die!" he screams. He locks the brakes. "Clutch!" The driver places the tank in neutral and Mallory kicks the left side wall. The port side gearsman drops the low gear into place and pounds the armor in response.

Mallory releases the right brake and yells, "Power!"

The tank pivots in-place atop the bunker, grinding it into the earth along with any survivors. Reaching a forty-five degree turn, Mallory shoves both brakes forward and the tank lurches down the mound toward the bypassed strongpoint. He grasps the forward Lewis gun's grip and pours fire into the position. The German occupiers scatter. Suddenly on his left, another tank looms into view. Mallory jerks the tank to a stop as the emerging male tank pumps two rounds from its 6-pounders into the position at close range.

The strongpoint erupts in smoke and flame, the Maxim and its tripod separating in mid-air and tumbling end-over-end to the ground. As the dirt and debris settle, a pair of arms emerge miraculously from the smoke. A lone German gunner rises, his uniform smoking, helmet askew, face blackened with soot. Beneath the helmet's rim, a pair of vacant eyes stare warily back at him. Mallory leans into his Lewis gun and fixes its sights on the lone survivor. He breathes heavily. The tank's engine idles in the background as man and machine face each other.

"Sir?" urges the driver. "He's surrenderin', Sir."

Mallory licks his chapped lips. His grip on the gun loosens.

A moan draws his attention to one of the wounded crewmen lying pitifully on the blood-slick deck. Mallory glances over his shoulder. A brakesman cradles a wounded gunner's head in his lap, wiping the sweating face with a greasy rag. Another crew member leans over the prostrate man, a blood-soaked bandage in his hands, pressing on the wounded gunner's chest. The wounded moans are haunting; the coppery smell of warm blood is nauseating.

Mallory's eyes cut back to the German. He readjusts his grip; finger tightening on the trigger.

The German turns slightly and drops to his knees, arms still raised as a group of advancing Tommies surround him at bayonet point.

Mallory lowers the gun. "Let's get out of here."

CHAPTER 23
Battle of Cambrai, Bourlon Wood, France
22 November 1917

After three days of relentless battle, the infantry are exhausted. Commanders, realizing the importance of fresh troops, relieve the drained 62nd with the unsullied 40th Division. No such consideration is given to the condition of the exhausted tank crews. Mallory sits atop his command tank watching the mauled troops trudge to the rear as fresh infantry occupies the hasty defenses thrown-up to protect against German counter-attack.

As the last of the 62nd trudges past Mallory's scarred, bullet-ridden tank, a departing battalion commander stops and calls up to him. "Major!"

Mallory shakes his head as if awaking from a trance. "Sir?" He slides off the sloping frontal armor and lands on his feet, staggering with exhaustion. The colonel offers a steadying hand.

"Good show, Major! Your crews certainly proved their mettle over the past few days."

Mallory nods tiredly. "But no breakthrough," he sighs.

"Not yet," admits the colonel. "But with reinforcements, Bourlon should be ours tomorrow."

"What I need is fresh crews, fresh tanks, more ammo…"

He's interrupted by the sound of an approaching tank, its engine geared-down and straining desperately. Around the edge of copse appears a gray, battle-scarred Mark I dragging several heavily-laden sledges. The bulging sponsons contain no armament, as indicated by the words "SUPPLY" stenciled across the front and sides of the obsolete vehicle. Several more Marks I supply tanks follow.

"Well, there you are," chirps the colonel. "The cavalry!"

"Not quite, sir. But it's a start."

"Good luck tomorrow, Major. Whatever comes of this battle, the Tank Corps contributions will be remembered as noteworthy."

"Noteworthy. Yes, sir."

"Cheer-up, son," replies the kindly colonel. "Word from back home is that church bells are ringing all over England because of our success here."

"Well, I guess that's something," admits Mallory with a sad nod. Oddly, victory doesn't feel much different than defeat. Soldiers are still dead and mangled. Villages are in ruin. *What have we won?*

As he watches the last of the infantry disappear over the rise, several tanks appear from the south. One flies a tattered green, red and brown flag.

Mallory wipes his greasy hands on his smudged overalls and approaches the tank, "Hilda". The tank rocks to a halt and General Elles appears from the commander's hatch.

"Mallory, my boy! Is that you?"

Mallory drags a sleeve across his gunpowder-blackened face and snaps a passable salute. "Sir!"

"How many tanks do you have left?"

"I'll have about ten serviceable for tomorrow if the parts I requested arrive with the supplies."

Elles' face falls. "Less than half your force?"

"With a few days to recover and repair the remainder, I can probably field fifteen."

"Well… wait a minute," replies Elles. "Let me get down there so we can have a proper chat." He climbs from the hatch and slides down the frontal armor. Dropping to the ground, he props himself on his cane and calls to his driver. "Hand me the map!" The crewmember passes the map through the front driver's port and Elles unfolds it against the gently sloping armor.

"Your battalion is here," he explains, thumping his finger on the map. "I believe that's Anneux," he announces with a nod toward the fire-lit town to the east.

"Yes," confirms Mallory. "We lost a couple of tanks and took about dozen wounded there. Lost count of the dead…"

Elles' eyes narrow. "I say, are you all right?"

Mallory wipes his weary eyes. "Yes, sir. Of course. Please continue."

"Good. I need you in top form."

"Close enough, sir," announces Mallory with a tired grin.

Elles places a finger on the map and glances off to the northwest. "Bourlon Wood is in front of you, right?"

"Yes, sir. I just scouted the line with the blokes from 40th Division."

"Well that's your objective for tomorrow. Any thoughts on how you'd like to tackle it?"

"The wood is pretty thick, so I don't see getting inside unless we can find some sort of logging trail," replies Mallory. "The Hun infantry are dug-in out front of and just inside the wood. I think our best plan is to act as cover for the infantry right up to the edge, then provide machinegun and 6-pounder support as deeply as possible while they fight their way through the woods."

Elles refers again to the map. "I'd like to provide flanking support on either side of the wood toward Bourlon and Fontaine."

"That's a lot of coverage for ten tanks," replies Mallory. "Any chance we can get some reinforcements? How about D Battalion?"

Elles hestitates. "I don't think it will be D Battalion," he replies darkly.

"Why not?"

"Things didn't go well for the battalion at Flesquires."

"What happened?"

"The fifty-first Division deviated from the original attack plan. D Battalion outran its infantry and was badly mauled by Hun artillery as it crested the ridge in front of the town."

"Do... do we have an estimate of casualties?" asks Mallory, trying to mask the dread in his voice.

"Not yet, Jack," responds Elles, placing a fatherly hand on Mallory's shoulder.

"Then, you don't know if..."

"No, I don't know if there were any casualties among Adele's crew."

Mallory remains mute for a few seconds, then clears his throat and straightens. "So, will you be with us tomorrow, sir?"

"I'll be in the area," replies Elles. "Infantry-tank coordination is starting to fall-apart. I want to see if I can pull-together some cooperation."

"I'm meeting with the 40th to coordinate tomorrow's attack, sir. We'll be ready."

"I know you will, Jack," replies Elles. "Keep your chin-up. We've more than proved Colonel Fuller's tactics here today. The future of the Tank Corps is assured."

"Very good, sir." Mallory steps back and salutes. "We'll see you on the morrow, sir."

Mallory descends into a west-facing German bunker converted to a command post by one of 40th Division's battalions. A communications unit is busy wiring phones into the lines laid at great risk by a group of muddy signalers. The battalion commander looks up with relief on his face as Mallory enters.

"Major!" he booms. "Glad to have you and your tanks with us for the attack. I saw your supplies coming-up. Are you all set for tomorrow?"

Mallory salutes. "Yes, sir. We're topping-off the petrol now. Racks are re-stocked with ammo. I've ordered my crews to get some rest."

"Good!" the colonel beams. "Major Marlowe here is our artillery liaison," he explains by way of introduction.

Marlowe offers his hand. "Yes, we've met. Good to see you again, Jack."

"Hullo Bill," Mallory replies with a warm smile. "Glad to have you coordinating for us."

"My pleasure."

Mallory steps up to the map pasted on the concrete wall. "Sir, with your permission, we'll advance behind the artillery in teams of three abreast a hundred yards apart with one tank in support," he explains to the infantry commander. "Keep your infantry behind my tanks and we'll escort them right up to the wood line."

"Excellent, major," replies the colonel. "How many tanks will you have?"

"Twenty-five, thanks to General Elles. He's scrounging some reserves from other battalions. That'll give us six attack groups jumping off at…?"

"Oh-six-thirty," announces Marlowe.

"Right," Mallory confirms. "We're only about 600 yards from the wood, so this first phase should move fairly quickly. Have your troops trained or worked with tanks before?"

"No, not really," admits the colonel. "We were scheduled to train with you, but the first-wave battalions took-up all our training time."

"Typical," snorts Mallory. "The key is for us all to move together. We should have a squadron of RFC Camels flying cover in the morning. They'll strafe any Hun reserves caught moving-up in the open. Bill's artillery will be peppering those woods pretty thoroughly. I saw a shelled wood back near Graincourt the other day. These new fuses explode at the first contact and splinter the trees horribly. The Hun infantry will find no refuge in the forest."

"Should my troops follow the tanks in-column?" asks the battalion commander.

"Better if they're dispersed," replies Mallory. "Our tanks' guns will suppress the Maxims, but if the Hun artillery catches your men bunched-up in the open, there'll be hell to pay. My section commanders are instructed to keep pace with the infantry," continues Mallory. "If they fall behind, we'll slow to give 'em time to catch-up. But the truth is, the faster move across the open area, the less time the Hun will have to bring his artillery into play. So please emphasize to your troops the need to advance rapidly with my tanks."

"Right," affirms the colonel confidently. "Stay close. Move fast."

"Now, about Bourlon," continues Mallory. "Once the woods are cleared, the infantry will need to re-form to continue the attack toward the village. How long do you think that'll take to organize?"

The grizzled battalion commander shakes his head uncertainly. "Hard to predict. Fighting in wooded areas plays hell on unit cohesion. By the time we're through, our troops will be scattered all over the place."

"If we don't renew the attack immediately, any retreating Germans will have taken-up positions to reinforce the village."

The battalion commander nods thoughtfully. "That's what we all fear," he admits.

"Cor blimey, look!" calls an infantry sergeant.

Overhead, a dozen Sopwith Camels roar across the treetops in a "V" formation, machineguns blazing at an enemy beyond the woods while another squadron circles protectively overhead looking for targets in the open.

"Must have caught the Hun trying to reinforce the wood!" Mallory shouts over the combined roar of tank and airplane engines. He checks his watch. "But they'd better break-off their strafing run unless they want to get caught in the artillery barrage!"

"When, sir?"

"About… now!" replies Mallory. He glances back toward the western horizon. Within a few seconds, he spots a series of ghostly flashes, the report of the cannons preceded by the sound of incoming projectiles traveling faster than the speed of sound. The edge of the wood erupts with smoke and flame.

"There's our cue," Mallory shouts and slaps the top of the cupola several times. The tank lurches forward with Mallory standing in the hatch. As the three tanks with his Section move forward across the un-churned earth at a steady four miles per hour, the infantry rises from its temporary defensive positions and advances confidently toward the tree line. Several hundred yards on either flank, he spots the remaining Sections roll forward in unison.

He drops inside and closes the hatch over him. "Watch the infantry," Mallory warns the crew. "We don't want to arrive at the dance without a date!"

"Yes, sir!" replies the driver.

As they advance, a mix of high explosive and smoke rounds wreak havoc on the edge of the wood. Treetops shatter like airbursts, showering the defenders with splinters of steel and wood.

"Slow down a bit!" orders Mallory as the artillery continues to pound the wood on their approach. They're fifty yards away when the artillery finally lifts. "Okay! Now, go! GO! Gunners! Watch for targets!"

From behind the smoke, bullets claw blindly at the attackers. Rounds ping off the armor and ricochet into the infantry following behind. Men drop in twos and threes but the remainder continue persistently forward, bayonets fixed as they dodge between dead and wounded comrades.

As the tanks close on the edge of the wood, Mallory spots the scars of freshly-dug earth bristling with machinegun and rifle barrels. Mallory's gunners rake the positions at close range, forcing the defenders to either duck below the earthworks or stand and fight in the face of certain death. At first, the Germans hold their ground then begin to abandon their positions in trickles of two or three, the flood steadily growing to dozens, then hundreds as the tanks near.

Seeing the German line collapse, the attacking Tommies let-out a roaring "*Hazza*", surging forward around the tanks, bayonets slashing as they drive the Germans deep inside the deceptive shelter of the beaconing woods.

"Cease fire! Cease fire!" Mallory shouts to the crew and brings the tank to a halt just outside the wood.

He cautiously pushes open the commander's hatch and stands in his seat. The tanks have all reached the edge of the wood and stopped, the impassable forest separating the lumbering tanks from the nimble infantry. Within the darkness of the woods, a fight rages to which the tanks cannot contribute. Other commanders emerge from hatches and peer around, temporarily spectators to the fight.

The driver appears in the hatch beside him. "This is frustratin'," he sighs. "Can't go inside and can't fire for hurtin' our own men."

"Well, we can't just sit here," growls Mallory. He retrieves his binoculars and scans the fields to the left and right. On the right a quarter mile away, he spots an anomaly in the waving grass. Dark forms move like turtles through the uncut wheat. Periodically, a human form leaps to its feet and dashes forward a few yards before dropping back into the grass.

He grabs the driver's sleeve. "Wait a minute. We've got a company pinned down in a wheat field over there." Lowering the glasses, he points off to the right. The driver squints.

"I think you're right, sir!"

"Hand me the Very pistol," snaps Mallory. The driver drops inside and reappears with the blunt, fat-barreled pistol. Mallory cocks the hammer and directs the muzzle skyward. A loud *POP!* and a flare climbs lazily into the clear sky. The tanks' crews follow the ascent of the flare back to its source and see Mallory waving and pointing. In near unison, three tanks pivot right and begin crawling toward Mallory's position.

"Here they come," announces Mallory and drops back inside. "Gearsman, pivot right!"

The driver mashes the clutch and the gearsman drops the left drive into low gear. Beneath of plume of white exhaust, the command tank churns right and halts to allow the gearsman to reset the drive. Once set, the tank proceeds south down the tree line toward the beleaguered infantry. As the tanks follow the tree line's eastward curve, the Germans spot the tanks closing on them. A line of tracer rounds arc across the open field, ignoring the infantry and angling instead toward the attacking tanks.

Maxim rounds ping off the tank's hull, either ricocheting in all directions or impacting with a flat slap against the armor. The Germans either are not using armor piercing rounds or they are firing from too far away to be effective. Either way, the Mark IV's armor continues to resist the incoming gunfire without penetration.

As they near, the defenses come into view, a series of shallow fighting positions scraped out of the rich Flanders dirt, the excess piled up to form a semi-circular berm around the machinegun positions. Peering through the small slit in the commander's port, Mallory grasps the Lewis gun's pistol grip and walks tracers toward the enemy positions.

"Gunners! There's your target!"

From either sponson, the forward-facing guns add fury to the offensive firepower pouring from the command tank's guns. The trailing Mark IVs concentrate fire into the edge of the wood line parallel to the advance at anyone daring to challenge the attacking tanks.

Flanked and outgunned, Germans rapidly abandon their fighting positions and disappear like their brethren into the presumed safety of the forest.

As the tanks arrive at the last abandoned defensive position, the British infantry rises from the wheat and jogs forward at the double. Ignoring the tanks, the first wave filters into the woods in pursuit of the retreating Germans. The following wave slows its advance to give an exhausted "hurrah!" to the tanks occupying the German positions, engines idling.

Sitting atop the command tank, Mallory leans inside and calls for a runner. A gearsman appears from the left sponson and peers up at Mallory. "Lookin' for a runner, sir?"

"I need you to notify the company commanders to gather at my tank in, say, half an hour."

"Sah!"

"And tell them to have their crews break-out their iron rations," Mallory adds as the runner starts-off. "It may be a few days before we're resupplied."

"Sah!"

Within the hour, the company commanders have huddled around Mallory's command tank. Dead Germans are scattered around the overrun positions, bodies swelling in the afternoon sun. Small fires continue to smolder, the black smoke wafting over the scarred command tank. Flies buzz around the assembled officers as Mallory sits on the sponson, legs dangling on either side of the powder-blackened barrel jacket of a protruding Lewis gun.

"Good work this morning," he announces. "We really gave the Hun a kick in the arse. But now, as they say, no good deed ever goes unpunished."

A good-natured groan arises among the commanders.

"We're rather like a dog chasing a motorcar," announces Mallory. "Now that we've caught the damned thing, we've got to work out what to do with it."

More laughter.

"By the end of the day, Bourlon Wood will be ours," he announces. "Now we need to help the 40th take the village." He points to the northeast. "See the rise over there just to the left of the wood? Well, Bourlon is on the other side. Presently, our infantry is scattered all through the woods, but they're regrouping and we're going to assemble what infantry the battalions can cobble together and take the town at a rush before the Hun can consolidate his defences."

"What about supplies?" asks an officer.

"We've sent word we need more fuel and ammunition, but I don't know what's coming-up or when it might arrive," replies Mallory. "This morning's show shouldn't have taxed our resources too much, so have your NCOs tally usage and cross-level the fuel and ammo across your units."

"Will we have air cover?"

"That's the plan," shrugs Mallory. "We'll also have artillery. So when we jump-off, I want everyone to hug that barrage. We can't go through the woods, so we'll have to come over the crest and we have no idea what the Hun may have by way of defenses. But the key is our tanks *will not* enter the town unless the infantry is with us."

"Hear, hear!"

Mallory grins. "I thought you'd like that. We've lost too many tanks getting-in among the Hun without infantry support. Now, any questions?"

"Did you hear about D Battalion?" asks one of the commanders.

The smile slides from Mallory's face. "Yes, I did," he replies frostily. "Any other questions?"

Hearing none, he dismisses the company commanders to return to their units.

As the officers disperse, Mallory overhears one say to another, "Cold bastard, isn't he?"

CHAPTER 24
Battle of Cambrai, Outside Bourlon, France
24 November 1917

"Where *were* they?" asks Mallory impatiently.

"Barely made it out of the woods," explains the infantry major. "The assault was disorganized. When the Maxims opened fire, too many of the units fell apart. We need time to regroup for a proper assault."

"Damn it!" curses Mallory and flings his helmet at the ground. "Hun artillery has this place registered! I lost five tanks just getting over the rise! I can't afford to waste tanks and crews!"

"The infantry suffered serious casualties, too," the major challenges.

"Yes, yes. Of course they did," sighs Mallory. "I'm sorry. I'm just short on fuel, armour and crews at the moment, so I'm a bit miffed."

"I understand, sir. Colonel Barclay sends his compliments and asks you disperse your tanks for a day or two while we regroup."

"The more time the Hun gets to reinforce the village, the more difficult it's going to be to dislodge him," warns Mallory.

"Yes, sir. But surely yesterday's disaster proves we need time to regroup for a proper attack."

"Major, you're getting daily reinforcements," explains Mallory. "I have the same crews I started-out with four days ago. What do you think it's like inside a bloody tank, hmmm? I've lost seventy-percent of my force and most of my crews. While you're gaining combat effectiveness daily, I'm losing it. Please impress that fact upon your colonel!"

The major nods grimly. "Of course I'll pass-on your recommendations, Jack," he replies. "In the meantime, rest your crews."

The major walks away, leaving Mallory sitting in the trench beside his camouflaged command tank.

A crewman – Mallory has avoided learning names as a form of emotional self-defense – hands him a cup of tea. "Thanks son," he mumbles to the crewman who couldn't be more than a year or two younger than he.

"Sir? The adjutant asked me to pass you this note."

"Thanks," Mallory replies and grabs the yellow flimsy. As he reads it, the crewman turns to leave. "Wait a moment," calls Mallory. He finishes reading the note. "Please inform the adjutant I've been summoned down to Flesquires to meet with General Elles. And see if you can find me a horse. I don't want to waste fuel taking a tank. We've damned little left."

"Sah!" barks the crewman and disappears into the woods. He returns twenty minutes later leading a magnificent Chestnut. "Compliments of Lieutenant Colonel Riser, sir. It's his personal mount. Name's Thunderbolt."

Mallory stands and inspects the horse. It's a fine animal of about 16 hands with a fine, even reddish coat and dark, nearly black, extremely kind eyes. He immediately takes a liking to the animal. As he strokes Thunderbolt's velvety muzzle, he has the crewman to retrieve the map from inside the command tank.

"I'll be back in a few hours," explains Mallory. "If the supply tanks arrive in my absence, have them report to Captain Aubry. He'll oversee distribution of supplies."

"Yes, sir."

Mallory mounts Thunderbolt and turns south toward Flesquires, his route taking him over the recent battlefield. The speed of the previous days' advance is evidenced by a lack of churned earth and abundance of enemy bodies strewn about the fields awaiting a burial that will never come. Anneaux smolders on his left and smoke still rises from Flesquires, two miles distant.

To avoid British convoys moving north along the rutted road toward Bourlon, he edges east of Braincourt and cuts across country, the horse walking at a natural gait. The air is crisp and cool with the fields on this side of the village barely touched by the effects of war. He passes an abandoned farm, its once rich fields fallow since 1914. Whole sections of the farm house have been stripped for firewood, the remainder being used to billet occupying German troops. He recalls Elise telling him her home was near

Cambrai and wonders suddenly if the farm might have once belonged to Elise and her husband. No, he realizes. Surely there are hundreds of similar farms throughout the valley. But the thought he may be near her home provides him a sense of well-being.

As he tops a hillock, the war returns with startling clarity.

On the descending slope, Flesquires burns in the late afternoon sky, smoke rising from a hundred small fires still alight in the heavily-shelled village. A dark hulk sulks nearby, its rhomboid shape deformed by an enemy shell. Mallory suddenly realizes it is probably one of D Battalion's tanks. He turns Thunderbolt toward the hulk and nudges the horse to a trot. As he nears, he recognizes the name, "Suzie", emblazoned across the hull – Lieutenant Compton's tank.

The hulk appears to have been split down the middle, its right side intact, a broken track emerging from the top of the bogie wheels like a cowlick from a small child's hair. The frontal and roof armor have been peeled-back like the top of a tin of sardines, leaving the trackless left side sagging pathetically without support. The cupboard-like hatches below the right sponson dangle open, a bloated corpse partially hanging from the opening.

To his horror, the body appears to be moving.

"My God!" he gasps and spurs the horse the remaining dozen feet to the tank. As he nears, he realizes the illusion of movement is provided by rats feasting on the dead crewman's flesh. Hand trembling with rage, he draws his pistol and empties all six rounds into the corpse, killing several rats. The remaining rodents slink away sullenly, casting furtive glances at the angry human that has robbed them of a fine meal. Furious at the rats' arrogant disdain, he breaks-open the pistol, reloads the cylinder and continues firing until the rodents break into a run and scatter into the tall grass. His anger spent, he shoves his pistol back into its holster and lets-out an anguished sob.

He knew some of Compton's crew. Davies, the driver from Reading, always cheerful, a persistent grin accented by an abnormally large gap between his two front teeth. The gunners, Peter and Terry – or Terrence, as Terry preferred to be called – were distant cousins reunited by the war. Peter was a textile worker from Manchester, while Terry was the son of a solicitor from

Lancashire. Inseparable, their difference in upbringing was overcome by genetic links that horrified their respective parents. The brakeman, Reggie – probably short for Reginald – was a farmer constantly lecturing the crew on the virtues of Norfolk-raised barley as the basis for superior brewing. The other brakeman and assistant gunners were new to the battalion and Mallory hadn't had the opportunity to meet them. His opportunity had now passed. The crew lived together, fought together and died together on a grassy slope history will soon forget.

He checks his watch. He's not due to report to General Elles for another hour and a half. Overcome with a sense of dread, he is both drawn and repelled by what he may find on the battlefield south of the city. Nervously licking his chapped lips, he spurs Thunderbolt down the slope toward the blackened hulks littering the pale green fields below.

The horse moves in a nearly reverent manner, its head bowed as if in silent prayer as Mallory moves like a ghost among the charred remains of a dozen destroyed and ditched tanks. "Terror", Lieutenant Sykes' tank, lies on its side in a ditch, the apparent victim of a hidden cut leading from the town downhill toward the railroad embankment. Clearly the ditched tank has been abandoned.

Fifty yards away, what appears from the front to be an intact tank turns out to be half a vehicle, the rear section ripped-away by a howitzer round that penetrated the roof. The engine and differential are strewn-out in the field like entrails dragged behind a dying animal. The name on the hull identifies it as Lieutenant Willis' D12 tank. The absence of corpses indicates at least part of the crew escaped with its dead and wounded.

He halts the horse and peers around. Off to the left, its front half-buried in a shell hole, protrudes the rear of a tank. He jerks the reins and the horse comes round to a trot. As the horse crests the slight rise, Mallory is struck by tightness in his chest, like an invisible belt constricting his ribcage and forcing the air from his lungs.

There is something familiar about the tank, or perhaps he's just being paranoid.

"Whoa, Thunderbolt," he murmurs and the horse slows to a stop. Gripping the reins in one hand, he slides from the saddle and leads the horse toward the burnt-out shell. Blackened streaks rise around the firing slits from the intense fire that burned within. Buried nose-down in a crater, the tank's stern protrudes high in the air, the rear armor plating blown-off by a blast and resting in the field twenty feet behind.

He walks around to the front of the tank and finds it buried up to the commander's cupola. There's a single, distorted five-inch hole through the mangled driver's port. Dropping to his knees, Mallory peers hesitantly through the opening, the soot-blackened interior lit by sunlight passing through the yawning gap in the rear of the tank. Inside he discovers a tangle of badly mangled bodies, flies crawling hungrily over the rotting flesh. The stench makes him retch. He backs away and vomits into the grass, his head pounding as his stomach empties and bile burns his parched throat.

Releasing the horse's reins, he crawls to the side of the tank and begins scratching at the earth, trying to scrape-away the dirt obscuring the name painted on the left side of the tank. The clods of earth are like concrete, tearing his fingernails until they bleed. Finally, he rips loose his helmet and plunges the rim into the remorseless earth, chipping and scratching dirt away from the steel hull. Finally, he discovers white paint, the outlines of a letter. Breathing heavily, he digs frantically, slamming the rim of his helmet into the dirt and clawing madly.

More letters appear, then more - until a single name emerges: Adele.

Mud-spattered and bleeding, Mallory approaches a pair of sentries guarding the gutted Crédit Commercial de France bank building in Flesquires. Rifles slapping, they bring their weapons to present arms. Mallory stares at them through hollow eyes. "I'm told this is Tank Corps HQ."

"Yes, sir!" snaps the guard.

Mallory nods and starts through the door.

"Er, may I see your papers, sir?" blurts the other guard. The first guard grasps the man's arm and shakes his head. "It's all right, mate. Let 'im be."

Mallory shuffles down the hall and follows a hand-lettered sign reading, "General Officer Commanding." He enters the outer office.

"Where the hell have you been?" snorts Captain Smart, General Elles' ADC. "And what do you mean coming in here dressed like that?"

"Where's the general?" Mallory asks hollowly.

"Inside, but he's with General Byng at the moment."

Before Smart can react, Mallory grasps the door handle and pushes into the room. Bounding from his chair, Smart bolts through the door in pursuit. The two officers arrive in the room with a clatter. Both generals look up, startled by the interruption.

"I'm sorry, sir!" blurts Smart. "I told him you were engaged."

Elles peers at Mallory and detects the slight insanity in his eyes, an insubordinate hint in his bearing.

"It's all right, Captain," he replies soothingly to his aide. "What can I do for you, Jack?"

"Where are the reinforcements?" croaks Mallory.

"The what?"

"The reinforcements!"

"I say," replies General Byng. "Is this one of your officers?"

"Yes, sir," replies Elles. "He commands E Battalion..."

"I command *D Battalion*," insists Mallory.

"Yes, of course," replies Elles. "Come on in and have a seat, Jack..."

"I don't want to have a bloody seat! I want *reinforcements!*"

General Byng rises slowly to his feet, piercing grey eyes overhung with a heavy brow. "Get hold of yourself, son," he insists with the quiet authority of a grandfather dealing with an errant child.

Mallory turns to him, startled, as if noticing him for the first time. Eyes wild, face smeared with gunpowder and grease, fingers bleeding, Mallory stands trembling. "Sir," he rasps. "We're attacking Bourlon tomorrow. I need more tanks, more crews..."

"Yes, we were just discussing that," replies Byng. "I think it might be time to bring this offensive to an end. The Germans are preparing a counterattack and we need to consolidate or we'll lose the gains we've made."`

Mallory directs a trembling finger eastward. "But the *breakthrough!* We've broken the Hun lines. Where is the cavalry?"

"There's not going to be any cavalry, Jack," replies Elles. "This was a raid, remember? It exceeded our wildest expectations, but now's not the time to get greedy."

Mallory turns to Elles. "Greedy? *Greedy?*" he shouts maniacally. "My battalion... *both my battalions*... are gone! There's no one left! There's *nothing left!* Now you tell the *goddamned cavalry* to get out there and *exploit that fucking breakthrough!*"

"It's not going to happen, Major," replies General Byng sternly. "Your battalions performed brilliantly, but this offensive is over."

"*You can't do that,*" hisses Mallory.

"I have an entire front to command," explains General Byng. "I can't risk the entire army for the sake of a minor local success."

"*Minor?*"

"Comparatively, yes."

"Jack, all he's saying..." begins Elles, but is interrupted when the door swings open and three military policemen burst into the room. They grab Mallory and twist his arms behind his back. Mallory drops to his knees, screaming.

"You bastards! *You bloody bastards!*"

The sergeant reaches into Mallory's holster and retrieves his pistol.

"Come-along Major," orders the sergeant. "You're under arrest..."

"No!" blurts Elles. "Get him over to the M.O. and stay with him until he's sedated. Tell them I want a full report on his condition tomorrow afternoon."

"Yes, sah!" barks the sergeant. "Pick him up," the sergeant snaps and the MPs comply.

They drag Mallory, struggling, from the room.

"*No! NO! NOOOOOO!*" he screams.

As the door slams behind them, General Byng turns to Elles whom he discovers visibly shaken. "I say, are you all right, Hugh?"

"No, sir. I don't think so."

"Shell-shock," replies Byng. "I've seen it before. Some men just can't take it."

"Not Mallory, sir," insists Elles. "He's been in every major battle since The Somme. But he just found out his best friend was killed two days ago in the fighting south of here. It seems to have pushed him over the edge."

"I dare say…"

CHAPTER 25
Malassises Hospital, Amiens, France
December 1917

Damned ping-pong.

Click, clop, click, clop...

The sound is maddening.

Whack! "Ah-ha! Gotcha!" shouts the victorious blue-robed lieutenant.

"For God's sake, give it a rest!" blurts Mallory.

Seated in an overstuffed leather chair in the library-cum-recreation room, he rustles the newspaper, thumbing irritably through the pages. "Oh, great. Ammunition worker's strike," he announces to no one in-particular. "They want more pay and shorter working hours. How about that?"

A half-blind captain with an eye patch replies. "Right! Think I'll tell Haig I want shorter fighting hours and more pay. Better rations, too! How'd you think that'd go?"

"They'd probably clap you into a lunatic asylum... oh, wait. You're already in one," Mallory laughs sarcastically.

"I say, steady, old boy," drawls the captain. "This is just a rest camp."

"With bars on the windows?"

"Well," replies the captain with a wink. "Enforced rest camp, then!"

An orderly enters the room pushing a small cart. As he approaches Mallory and the captain, Mallory drops the newspaper and begins groping at the empty chair before him. "Mother? Mother? Is it you, mother? Where have you been?"

"Very funny, major," snorts the orderly. He hands Mallory a paper cup containing several pills and fills another from a lacquered water pitcher.

"Warm milk?" Mallory asks innocently.

"Whiskey," replies the orderly.

Mallory dutifully swallows his pills and slaps the empty water cup upside down on the table. "So when will the trick cyclist be dropping-by? I need another chance to eat his notes."

"You keep doin' that and you'll never get out of here," scolds the orderly.

"Oh, I'm just keeping him entertained. He's so bloody certain I'm a lunatic I'd hate to disappoint him."

"Yeah, well. Won't be comin' by for a while. He's on-leave for a couple of weeks."

"Leave? What the hell for? He doesn't do a damned thing around here but push pills."

"Well, if you must know, his wife's havin' a baby, so the command surgeon took pity on 'im."

"Hmpf! Flimsy excuse..." scoffs Mallory. "So, now what? Can't someone else ask me, 'how does it *make you feel?*'"

"Stop makin' stuff up and maybe they'll believe you."

"I'm not making stuff up."

"You said you were related to Field Marshal Haig."

"Actually, I said I was his illegitimate son."

"But you're not."

"How the hell do you know?"

"Because you're still in here," insists the orderly. "If you were Haig's son – illegitimate or not – he'd have you out of here before you could say 'Bob's yer uncle'."

"Fair enough," Mallory concedes. "I'll come-up with something better."

"Why 'come-up' with anything? Just tell the truth."

"Dull! Boring! Old-hat!"

"Yeah, well. The truth will set you free."

"My arse," grumbles Mallory.

"Well, cheer-up," replies the orderly. "You've got a visitor."

Mallory sits upright and casts aside the paper. "A visitor? Who?"

"Dunno. The nurse just said to tell you there's a visitor waitin' for you in your room."

"A woman?"

"Didn't say."

Mallory springs from the armchair and bounds up the stairs to his room in the east ward. He hesitates outside the door and runs his fingers through his hair then adjusts his robe and re-ties the cloth belt. With a deep breath, he grasps the door handle and steps into the room.

Seated on the bed is Major General Swinton, a small wicker hamper on his lap.

"Sir!" Mallory blurts in surprise.

Swinton stands, sets aside the hamper and offers his hand.

"Jack, my boy. I can't tell you how glad I am to see you! When I heard you were in hospital, I naturally assumed... Well, you know."

"No such luck," replies Mallory with a mischievous grin. "Seems I unravelled in front of General Elles."

"And General Byng too," adds Swinton.

"Yes, him also," admits Mallory. "I suppose I owe them an apology."

"I don't believe any apology is required or expected. How are you feeling now?"

"Well enough," responds Mallory, evasively. "I still have some rough nights."

"Yes, I can imagine."

"You heard about Sergeant James?"

"Yes, I'm awfully sorry. Didn't I hear somewhere he'd just got married?"

"Yes, sir. A French girl named Adele."

"Has she been informed?"

"I doubt it. They didn't actually go through proper channels so I don't think the Army officially acknowledges the marriage."

"So, she won't be receiving a pension?"

"I don't think any pension is expected or required."

"Ah, so she's a woman of means?"

"I suppose you could say that, yes."

"Still, damnable business, eh?"

"Yes, sir. I'll go see her once I'm released from this 'enforced rest facility'."

"Well, that's why I'm here. You look fit to me. Anything to prevent you returning to work?"

"Work? If you mean the war, sure, I'm ready. What's the mission?"

"Whippets!"

"I thought flogging was outlawed in the British Army."

"Funny," replies Swinton dryly. "I'm talking about the new Whippet Medium tanks!"

"You finally got them into production?"

"Indeed. F Battalion has been receiving deliveries since October and they are finally complete."

"And you need a new battalion commander to take charge," Mallory concludes confidently.

Swinton hesitates. "Actually, I need someone to train the crews."

Mallory bows his head. "I see."

"It's important work!" insists Swinton.

"Yes, I'm sure." Mallory falls silent for a few seconds. "Still, I guess you can't call the GOC a 'damned bastard' and expect to remain in-command."

"It's not that way, Jack," insists Swinton. "General Elles thinks the world of you – as do I. But you need to pace yourself. You know, ease yourself back into the saddle."

"Right," replies Mallory with a nod. "I suppose it's better than a court-martial."

"There's the spirit!" Swinton retrieves his cap from the bed top. "Besides, Colonel Fuller has some rollicking-good ideas for using the Whippet in-place of cavalry!"

"So, you can get me out of here?"

Swinton nods toward the fresh uniform draped across the back of the chair. "Already arranged!"

"Bless you, sir," sighs Mallory. "It'll be good to get back to work. By the way, how did Cambrai work out?"

Swinton sighs. "We never took Bourlon…"

"No surprise there," scoffs Mallory.

"First and Second Brigades were withdrawn from action on the 27th."

"So that was it?"

"Ah, no. The Hun counterattacked on November 30th and drove Third Army back pretty much to its starting line."

"Shit!" swears Mallory. "So it was all for nothing?"

"No. I wouldn't put it that way," replies Swinton earnestly. "We took more than ten thousand yards of front in less than twelve hours, captured eight thousand Hun and a hundred guns at a cost of fewer than four-thousand casualties."

"You make it sound like a victory."

"It was. It was a victory for the Tank Corps. We proved the armoured concept and those damned cavalry generals will have to give us a major role when the Big Push comes!"

"Which will be when?"

Swinton shrugs. "Not sure. We're standing pat for now."

"Why?"

"Because our armies are exhausted," replies Swinton. "Back home, people are starting to raise questions about the conduct of the war. Word is Lloyd George is withholding troops because he doesn't want them wasted in Flanders. Of course, then there's the French…"

"What about the French?"

Swinton leans-in and whispers conspiratorially. "We have reliable information the French army mutinied over the summer."

"*What?*"

"Ever since the Nevelle offensive failed, half the French divisions have refused to leve their trenches."

"Dear God!"

"Nivelle was sacked and General Petain promised if the army will stand on the defensive, no offensive action will occur until the Americans arrive in-force."

"I didn't realize things were so tenuous."

"It's worse than tenuous. The Bolsheviks overthrew the Czar and are threatening to make peace with the Kaiser."

"They'll regret that!"

"Yes, well. There you have it. If the Russians surrender, the Kaiser will be able to shift hundreds of thousands of troops from the east to the Western front."

"So it's a race," replies Mallory.

"A race?"

"Between the Germans and the Americans," concludes Mallory. "Whoever gets here soonest with the largest force wins."

Swinton nods thoughtfully. "I suppose that's about that."

"Well, we'd better get moving then," Mallory concludes and strips-off his robe. "Got to keep the bloody Hun at bay until the Yanks show-up."

"True," agrees Swinton. "But first, I believe you have an appointment in Bray."

CHAPTER 26
On Pass, Bray-sur-Somme, France
December 1917

Mallory walks past the gray stone house several times, his trench coat collar upturned against the howling wind. A Christmas wreath adorns the huge oak front door. The traditional candles in the windows remain unlit for fear of lighting the way for German bombers. On his fourth pass, he halts in front of the house and stares up at Elise's window. The room is dark. Adele's room is around the back, so he walks to the rear of the building and peers up at the window, hoping to find it dark also. Light filters between the plush velvet curtains. Fingering the small gift-wrapped present in his pocket, he stands dejectedly in the alley, torn between the anticipation of seeing Elise and the dread of facing Adele.

"It's not fair," he mumbles. "It's so bloody unfair."

Summoning his courage, he knocks hesitantly at the back door. The elderly housekeeper shuffles to the kitchen door. "Oui Monsieur?"

"Claire. It's me, Jack."

The half-blind maid peers up at him inquiringly. Her lined, haggard face breaks into a gap-toothed smile. "Aaah, Capitaine! Joyeux noel!"

"Happy Christmas to you, also," he replies and kisses her on either cheek. "Is Elise here?"

"Non, Capitaine. She is at Mass with the others."

"Mass?"

"Church, stupide! À l'église de St Nicolas."

"Of, course," replies Mallory, it never having occurred to him someone in Elise's profession might attend Christmas Mass just like anyone else. "Where is the church?"

As if on cue, a bell tolls in the distance. Claire points toward the sky. "Ah, Dieu vous appelle!"

Mallory kisses her cheek and departs down the alley.

He strides briskly through the sleet toward the sound of the beckoning bell. Rounding a corner, he spots small groups of civilians dressed in their ragged best converging on the Church of St. Nicholas in the town center. It's a strange parade comprising the elderly and the very young, the widows and the widows yet-to-be. Several military-aged men limp along on crutches or are pushed in wheelchairs. A few Poilus fortunate enough to obtain Christmas leave stroll wearily alongside elderly mothers and fathers, a wife or girlfriend clinging possessively to a blue-sleeved arm.

Mallory hesitates at the door of the church and removes his helmet, the aroma of burning incense stinging his eyes. The organ roars abruptly to life and the altar boys lead the procession holding aloft lit candles, the light of soft flames glittering off the polished brass Crucifix preceding the robed Priest down the aisle toward the pulpit standing majestically before the ornate Tabernacle. The music is familiar, yet the words sound strange performed in another language.

> Les anges dans nos campagnes,
> Ont entonné l'hymne des cieux,
> Et l'écho de nos montagnes,
> Redit ce chant mélodieux,
> *Gloria in excelsis Déo!*

Surveying the sanctuary from the rear, all he detects among the crowd are balding pates, fidgeting children and lace shawls draped respectfully over ladies heads. He stands on tip-toe, searching for Elise among the crowd, but it's no use.

Recognizing Mallory's British uniform, an elderly usher with a massive white mustache approaches him. "Pardon, Commandante. May I 'elp you find a place to sit?"

"Merci."

The usher takes Mallory's elbow, leads him down the aisle and seats him beside a withered elderly woman. She raises herself agonizingly with her cane and scoots several inches to make room for him in the crowded pew.

At the front of the sanctuary, a priest mounts the curved mahogany staircase to an altar adorned with a trumpeting angel and begins the service. "Au nom du père et du fils et du saint esprit. Amen."

Mallory mimics the worshippers, making his own awkward Anglican-version of the Catholic sign of the cross.

As the priest begins the service, the elderly woman slips her hand within Mallory's grasp. Her gnarled, veined fingers gently squeeze his calloused hand. He turns to her and realises her eyes are fixed on the Tabernacle at the front of the Church. Slowly, a single tear slides down her cheek and drips off her jaw.

He gently squeezes her hand in-return and her face slants toward him, lovely, angelic, full of life. He wants to speak but finds himself speechless. Her kindly eyes seem to tell him, *I know*. The pain he feels is no less intense than the love he has known. Neither is greater than the other; both are the same. He cannot love, truly love, unless he embraces the pain that grips his heart and squeezes it such that he wishes it would stop beating. Death would be so much easier than life. It haunts him in the night, approaching him through dreams that make no sense and serve as a mockery to his mortality. He is already dying, he is sure. If not today, then tomorrow and every day thereafter on a hundred different battlefields. It would be a blessing, a relief.

But until then, he must survive, if for no other reason than that he owes it to those unfinished lives haunting his sleep.

Suddenly the elderly woman is standing, knobby left hand on the crook of her cane, right hand still one with his. He rises in response. Worshipers ahead of him file from the pews and shuffle down the aisle. Is the service over? No, it can't be, he realizes. He has been in a trance, but for how long? The woman draws him forward. At the front of the queue he spots a tall, robed priest gently placing small wafers on the outstretched tongues of parishioners too reverent to touch the host with bare hands.

"I... I can't" he whispers to the woman. "I'm not Catholic."

She smiles and continues urging him forward.

"Je ne suis pas Catholique!" he insists.

At the communion rail, she plants her cane firmly in the ancient rug and begins to stoop toward the kneeler. Mallory grasps her arm and lowers the frail, weightless figure to her knees. Her insistent hand urges him to kneel beside her and he reluctantly submits.

The priest works his way down the queue. The woman opens her mouth and extends her tongue to receive the bread. As she draws-in the wafer, her eyes close in ecstasy; as if she has received the gift of life itself. Her head bows and she crosses herself with a trembling hand.

Mallory glances up to see the priest standing expectantly before him.

"Je ne suis pas Catholique," he whispers.

The priest smiles, nods and traces the sign of the cross on Mallory's forehead. "God bless you and keep you safe, my son," he murmurs before moving-on to the young, black-clad widow to Mallory's right.

A sense of well-being settles upon him like a warm blanket on a chilly night. He smiles slightly, his heart momentarily at peace. He wishes he could remain kneeling here indefinitely. But the elderly woman struggles to stand and Mallory leaps to his feet, lifting her gently as creaking bones wobble beneath her. She pats his hand and turns to head up the aisle to return to her seat. As they shuffle back to their pew, she seems stronger now, both hands gripping his forearm, her cane abandoned at the front of the church.

"Madame…," he begins and motions back toward the rail. She shakes her head and continues up the aisle as if on a mission.

He halts abruptly. Kneeling in a front pew are Elise, Adele and several of the girls from the house. His eyes lock with Elise's then flow reluctantly to Adele. A lump arises in his throat. His mouth works dumbly, no words emerging as his lips tremble. He is frozen in-place. Tears form in his eyes.

Adele's hand moves to cover her gasp. Tears burst forth as she struggles to her feet and stumbles over the worshippers blocking access to the aisle. Elise watches her depart before turning to Mallory, eyes questioning. Realization dawns on her face and she, too, rises and pushes her way out of the pew to pursue Adele who has disappeared through the church's huge oaken door.

Mallory glances down at the elderly woman. She smiles and tugs him forward. He escorts her up the aisle and helps her to her seat. Lowering the kneeler for her, he whispers, "Que Dieu vous bénisse, grand-mère."

"Tout ira bien," the old lady whispers to him.

"No, my dear," Mallory replies sadly. "All will not be well." He lightly kisses her hand and makes his way to the rear of the church.

Bursting through the door into the bitter cold, he peers rabidly up and down the vacant street. Breaking into a run, he dashes toward the old gray mansion. As he nears the building, he spots Elise holding the door for Adele who slips inside, face buried in her hands.

"Elise!"

She sees him and raises her hand in warning. "No, Jack," she croaks. "Leave her alone."

She steps inside and closes the door. Mallory finds himself standing alone in the wet cobblestone street beneath a dimly-lit lamp post. Snowflakes swirl around him. He shoves his hands into his pockets and shuffles dejectedly up the street. At the end of the curve is a small brick estaminet crowded with British soldiers. Above the door is a painting of two comical Frenchmen tugging a double-handled mug of ale. Inside the bar, someone is pounding-away on an out-of-tune piano, the unidentifiable Christmas carol drowned-out by drunken voices and clattering glasses.

He grasps the door handle and pushes inside. Drunken soldiers sporting a dozen different regimental badges are packed four-deep around the bar, the tables crowded with others unable to stand or passed-out drunk. Mallory shoulders his way into the throng, careful not to jostle too many others as he makes his way to the bar.

"Vin blanc," he calls the bartender who shakes his head in denial and hands Mallory instead a tepid, watered-down beer. He sags exhaustedly against the ancient bar and takes a sip, the warmth settling in his empty stomach.

"Hullo, sir," comes a Cockney voice from behind him.

Mallory turns to see one of the D Battalion NCOs. "Good evening, Sergeant Crowley."

"Merry Christmas, Sir!"

Mallory purses his lips and nods.

"Why so glum?" Crowley asks. "It's Christmas!" He raises his beer in toast and takes a deep gulp. "Ahh, nasty piss," he grunts. Reaching into his tunic, he withdraws a flask and adds a tot of whiskey to his beer. He offers the flask to Mallory.

"Sure, why not," murmurs Mallory and the sergeant pours a generous splash into his beer.

"Cheer-up, Sir. I hate to see ya like this on holiday."

"Can't," Mallory croaks. "You heard about Sergeant James."

"Heard? Hell, sir. I carried the big tub o' lard back to the aid post. Must 'a been two miles and all he did was bitch the whole way!"

Stunned, Mallory closes his eyes and sets his mug on the bar. "You did *what?*"

"Well, when I say 'carried', I mean he used me as a crutch. He limped most 'o the way."

Mallory grabs Crowley's lapels and jerks him upright. "Are you telling me Sergeant James is *alive?*"

"Well, 'o course," Crowley chuckles nervously. "People don't die from getting' shot in the arse – 'less it goes septic."

"But I saw his tank outside Flesquires!" insists Mallory. "The whole crew was dead!"

"Well, yes sir. I'm afraid the crew was killed. But James wasn't one 'o 'em."

"How the hell is that possible? The tank took a seventy-seven right through the driver's cupola!"

"Lieutenant Clifton," replies Crowley with a shrug.

"*Who?*"

"The new tank commander, sir. He took a dislikin' to James. Said he was goin' to 'ave 'im busted for insubordination and sent him back to Battalion as a runner."

"So he wasn't *in* the tank during the attack on Flesquires?"

"No, sir. But he caught a piece of shrapnel in the arse while rescuin' a wounded crewman from another burnin' tank. He's a bally hero."

"*My God!* Where is he now?"

"Dunno. Dropped him at the aid station. He's probably recoverin' home in Blighty by now."

Mallory releases Crowley and shoves his way through the bar, knocking into people and causing a general row. He emerges into the frigid air, a half dozen drunken Tommies in-pursuit. A hand grasps his shoulder and spins him around, the man's fist barely missing his face.

"Damn it all, I'm an officer!" he shouts to the men.

"You spilled my beer," slurs one of the soldiers.

Sergeant Crowley appears at the doorway. "Are you all right, sir?"

Mallory tosses a wad of Francs at Crowley. "I'm more than all right! It's bloody Christmas! Drinks are on me!" he shouts and dashes off into the light snow blanketing the city.

He arrives at the bordello out of breath. Without knocking, he bursts through the door.

"Adele! *ADELE!*" he shouts maniacally and sprints up the stairs taking two at a time. As he bolts down the hallway, Elise's bedroom door swings open and she steps out pulling-on a robe.

"Jack! What are you doing?" asks Elise.

He grabs her around the waist and lifts her into the air. "He's alive! *He's alive!*"

"Who?"

"James!"

Adele appears at the door, mascara smeared, eyes red from crying. "What are you saying?"

Mallory returns Elise to her feet and takes Adele's hand. "I just learned James is not dead," he explains with tears in his eyes. "He was only wounded."

Adele gasps and sags to her knees. Burying her face in her hands, she begins to sob.

"By some twist of fate, he wasn't in the tank when it was destroyed," explains Mallory.

Elise takes his hand and holds it to her damp cheek. "It is more than fate, Jack. It is un miracle de Noël."

CHAPTER 27
Second Battle of the Somme (Michael Offensive), France
March 1918

"It's so quiet it almost seems as if the war is over," observes Elise as they stroll along the vine-covered path beside the Somme. "Les allemans have not been shelling. I think they are tiring of the war. Perhaps an armistice is coming after all."

Mallory walks contentedly beside her, his sleeves rolled-up, tunic slung over his shoulder. He draws a handkerchief from his pocket and mops the sweat from his face. "I thought I'd be glad when winter ended," he laughs. "But now that it's warmer, I rather think we'll be hearing from the Hun shortly."

Dressed in a light summer dress, Elise slips her arm through his and snuggles against his shoulder. "I think you have been at war so long you cannot imagine life without it."

"Oh, I can imagine it," replies Mallory. "I'm just afraid to hope for peace too soon."

"Too soon?" she asks sharply. "It cannot come too soon!"

"We have to defeat the Hun, darling. The war can't just 'end'. Nothing will be resolved."

She draws away from him as if he's uttered heresy. "So, you wish it to continue?"

"I don't wish it to, but it must," responds Mallory. "All things end in their own time. Not before."

"So, if les allemands don't attack us, we'll attack them?"

Mallory stops and turns to Elise. He grasps her hands tightly. "Do you want the Germans to continue to occupy French – and Belgian – soil? Don't you want to see your farm again?"

She peers desperately into his eyes. "Not if it means losing you."

"Well, now that I'm a Major, I don't see as much action any more. So, fear not."

"That's what my late husband said," replies Elise with a frown.

"Look, except for some local actions and trench raids, we're not going to pick a fight until more Yanks arrive. Tanks are offensive weapons. So unless the Hun breaks the line, we're just sitting safely in reserve for now."

"So you'll be in Garrison for the time being?" she asks.

"Yes. But most of the time we're training, training, training," sighs Mallory. "Now that James is back, we've received a shipment of the new Whippet tanks so he's been putting the crews through their paces."

"Adele says he walks with la canne d'un vieillard."

"The walking stick is only temporary, until he recovers fully from his wounds."

"Why did they send him back if he's not récupéré?"

"You know James," Jack grunts. "He probably made such a nuisance of himself that they deported him."

She stops and peers around, a mischievous smile on her face. "Take my hand," she whispers and leads him off the path into the woods.

"Where are we going?"

"Shhh. It's a secret."

A quarter mile into the woods they come upon a clearing where a small, crystal clear pond rests in seclusion.

"Beautiful," observes Mallory.

"Come," she insists. "Let's go for a swim."

"I haven't a bathing suit..."

"Neither have I," replies Elise. She brazenly pulls the light cotton dress over her head and discards it over a bush. Kicking off her sandals, she shrugs-off her brassiere and slips out of her petticoat.

"What if someone comes along?"

"They'll have to find their own swimming hole."

"But... in the buff?"

"Come on," she begs. "I'm hot."

"You certainly are," he observes.

She winks alluringly and wades into the water, her pale hourglass figure sinking slowly beneath the surface until she disappears up to her neck. Spreading her arms, she leans back and pushes off from the sandy bottom. Her small round breasts and taut stomach emerge on the surface, water flowing off her exposed body to leave a shimmering film. She draws her arms down alongside her body, propelling herself through the water as her hips appear, a tuft of black pubic hair framing the intersection of her quivering thighs as she paddles lazily across the surface of the pond on her back.

"Mmmmm," she purrs. "L'eau est très apaisant." She dives beneath the surface and reappears several seconds later nearer the grassy bank where he stands. Regaining her footing, she rises, standing naked in water up to her waist. She throws back her head and wrings the water from her hair, her shining face flushed with contentment. She holds out her arms to him. "Come."

He self-consciously undresses as she watches, amused at his discomfort. But the bemused expression fades from her face as each layer of discarded uniform exposes another scar, another burn, another discolored bruise. By the time he wades into the pond, her eyes are welling with tears.

"What's wrong?" he asks and gently takes her hands in his.

She runs her fingers lightly over one of his older scars; the one on his chest and shoulder.

"I know, they're ugly," he mumbles awkwardly.

Her liquid brown eyes turn up to meet his. "No," she sighs. "They are beautiful. But they remind me of your pain and it makes me sad."

"Only you could find beauty in such things," he chuckles softly and grasps her narrow hips, pulling her to him. He kisses her gently, the full softness of her lips as arousing as the image of her naked body. Her hand slides behind his neck and holds her lips to his, freezing the moment in time. Her tongue probes his lips for an opening and he responds, the intimacy of their kiss more visceral than any sexual encounter. After an eternity that could only have been a few moments, they part, each staring at the other with a sense of awe coming only with discovery.

"I love you so much," Mallory declares earnestly.

"And I love you," she responds.

"No. It's more," he corrects. "You told me once that English nurses fill their charges' heads with childish fantasies of one true love and life happily ever after. It's no fantasy."

She draws away in panic. He pulls her back to him and her resistance collapses.

"I want to marry you," he declares. "If not now, then once the war is over."

'But…"

"But, what? Do you love me or not?"

"Yes, but…"

"Marry me."

She seizes him and buries her cheek in his chest. He feels the wetness of her tears flowing down his bare flesh.

"I know it's a lot to ask," he admits. "Your daughters don't know me. The war continues. But give me a chance. Let me into your life and I promise I won't break your heart."

"I want to," she croaks. "I want to so badly."

"Then let's stop pretending this is a wartime romance," he insists.

A noise like a tearing cloth precedes the roaring blast that knocks Mallory from his cot. "What the…?" His question is interrupted by another blast and third in rapid succession. Reaching beneath his bunk, he retrieves his boots and slips them on over bare feet. He grabs his Sam Browne with holstered pistol, tosses it across his shoulder, slaps the helmet on his head and darts into the pre-dawn morning clad only in khaki undershirt and shorts.

Around him, trainees emerge from their tents, eyes blurry with sleep and squinting toward the nearly continuous flashes lighting the eastern sky from the direction of Cambrai.

"Oh, you bastards," curses Mallory. His operations officer dashes past in panic without noticing his commander.

"Spears!" shouts Mallory. "Get to the communications hut and find out what the hell is going on! This is no harassing fire. Someone's bloody serious!"

Spears snaps a hasty salute. "Sah!" He dashes off down mud-spattered duckboards toward the telegraph office.

James comes limping toward Mallory, partially dressed and carrying his Enfield. "What do you think, sir? Fritz coming out to play?"

"Dunno. I sent Spears for information." He glances down at his sorry state. "I'd better get dressed. We may be a training unit, but we're the only tanks in this sector. So I expect we'll be needed somewhere."

"I'll get the men ready for action," announces James.

"You won't do a damned thing. You're still on light duties until the M.O. releases you."

"Pardon my French, sir. But piss-off." He points toward the flashes in the distance. "Bray is right over there and there ain't much to stop 'em. And there isn't time to waste hanging around feeling sorry for myself."

"All right, you bastard, assemble the crews and have them fuel the tanks. Then get over to the depot and see what ammo we can scrounge. I want the detachment ready to move in five hours."

"Without orders, what do you intend to do?"

"Defend Bray."

"Because Elise is there?"

"No, because it's a major Somme crossing."

"Of course, right you are sir." James salutes and limps back toward the training area. Mallory returns to his billet.

He pulls on his uniform, feeds the shoulder strap through his epaulette and fastens the Sam Browne around his waist. Wearing cavalry boots rather than puttees, he adjusts the helmet on his head and glances into the mirror. He's thinner than before the war. Despite the excessive drinking, his body is lean, almost skinny. Cheeks hollow, skin alternately burned and pale, he appears ten years older than his mere twenty two years.

He departs his Nissen and stalks along the duckboards toward the communications hut. As he nears, Captain Spears bolts from the hut, flimsy in-hand. "Sir!' He shouts. "It's a rout!"

"Have the Hun broken the line?"

"Completely, sir! Storm troops cut through the lines and were into our trenches before the artillery ever opened fire."

"What do you mean?"

"Our lines have been penetrated in dozens of places. Fifth Army is in retreat and Third Army is bending back its right flank in order to stay in contact with the Fifth."

"Dammit!"

Mallory glances around frantically. His car comes bouncing down the road toward the command Nissen and skids to a stop. "Sah," shouts his orderly-turned-driver, Corporal Sydney. "Where to?"

Mallory hands the flimsy back to Captain Spears and withdraws a pad of paper from his pocket. He jots a note and passes it to Spears. "Send that to the Chief of Staff, Third Army and to Brigadier General Elles at Tank Corps Headquarters in Bermicourt. If I haven't heard anything back by Noon today, I'm moving my tanks east of Bray to defend the city."

"Without orders, sir?"

"Look, we're a training unit. We don't appear on anyone's order of battle. I've reminded Third Army and General Elles we're here for them to use as desired. But if they're too busy to respond, I'm not just going to sit here and wait to be overrun."

"Right, sir!" replies Spears and dashes off to the telegraph station.

"All right, Syd. You wanted to get into the war? Well here it bloody comes!" Mallory climbs into the rear seat without opening the smashed door. Unlike most staff cars, Mallory's beat-up Renault is a rolling armory containing Lee Enfield rifles, a French Chauchat light machinegun and several crates of ammunition. If not particularly comfortable, the vehicle is at least well-armed.

"Get me to the troop line!"

Twenty-two Whippet Medium tanks idle along the tree line east of the training area. The odd looking vehicles appear to be facing the wrong direction, with the engines in front, box-like three-member crew compartments in the rear, Hotchkiss machineguns emerging from ports on four sides. Unlike the heavy Mark IV, the Whippet's tracks protrude from its sides and do not encircle the entire frame, giving it greater speed, but less trench-crossing ability.

As Mallory arrives, he spots James limping among the parked tanks, shouting orders to young second lieutenants, the ink on whose commissions is barely dry.

"What's going on?" asks Mallory as his car draws up beside James.

"We got a Company of tanks, but we ain't got any platoon leaders or company commanders, sir! Just a bunch of wet-behind the ears…"

"I'll command," announces Mallory.

"But you're a battalion commander, sir! It ain't proper."

"Sergeant James, don't go Regular Army on me now. I need that insolent, unmilitary bastard to help me get these tanks to Bray."

"Well, as you put it that way."

Mallory spots a runner darting across the open field toward the tree line. He arrives out of breath and speechless. Gasping, he salutes and hands Mallory a flimsy. Mallory scans it quickly and wads up the paper. "Not Bray. Bapaume," he informs James. "59th Division is collapsing and needs our help. I'm going to head up there to scout positions," explains Mallory. "The roads are going to be crammed with refugees. So take the column and head for Bapaume. I'll send back a runner with any changes."

"Right," snaps James. "But what about the girls?"

"Look, they've probably already gone. Elise has a sister in Amiens so they'll likely head there. Besides, Third Army has to hold the Somme bridges, so Bray should remain secure for the present."

"I hope you're right, sir. It'll make me feel better if they ain't around to see this."

Mallory nods. "I'll see you in Bapaume!"

As predicted, the road is congested with troops marching east and refugees flowing west. Unlike the heartbreaking image of fleeing families at the beginning of the war, this collection of evacuees consists of the old and infirm, the owners and wait staff from the local estaminets, and farmers who'd attempted to reclaim their land amid the shattered remains of the old Somme battlefield. The resigned orderliness to their trek is both heartening and sad.

Passing through Albert, the flow of refugees slows to a trickle. It's not long before Mallory can make-out the outline of Bapaume. He enters the town to find it rife with panic. Red capped military police direct traffic through a crowded street, rounding up stragglers and placing them in assembly areas. The constant shrill of the police whistle is as annoying as the German guns firing on the outskirts of town. Mallory's car draws-up alongside a red cap.

"Who's in command here?" he calls over the roar of passing vehicles.

"In command? Why Colonel Whithers, sir. The Provost Marshal."

"I'm not looking for the constable, sergeant! I'm looking for the officer commanding this sector! Where is 59th Division's command post?"

"Haven't seen the commander, sir. But my men have rounded-up a right lot of stragglers from the 59th."

"Where are they?"

The sergeant points toward a field in which several hundred dejected-looking men sit scattered in small clumps. A dozen military police stand wary guard in a loose perimeter, one eye on the mutinous-looking stragglers, the other eye cast east in the direction of the German advance. They seem uncertain which threat is most imminent.

"Pull over, Syd," snorts Mallory disgustedly. I'm going to speak with those men." Sydney pulls off the road, Mallory hops over the closed door and trudges across the muddy field. Men cast their eyes downward at his approach – not a good sign. He spots a bloodied sergeant sitting in the grass smoking a cigarette and staring back at him insolently.

"What's your unit Sergeant?"

"Sixth Battalion, Sherwood Foresters."

"Stand-up when you address an officer!" snaps Mallory.

The sergeant rises defiantly to his feet. "All right, I'm standin' sir. But the answer's the same as when I was sittin'."

"Sherwood Foresters? That's part of the 59th Division isn't it?"

"For what it's worth… sir."

"Where's your headquarters section?"

"Dead, sir. Wiped out at Bullecourt."

"Dead? All of them?"

"Enough of 'em."

"Well… who's senior here, then?"

"I suppose I am," admits the sergeant.

"Look here, I'm bringing a company of tanks to help fill the gap in our line. We'll need infantry support to defend the high ground!"

Seeming interested, the sergeant straightens somewhat. "Tanks, sir? How many?"

"Twelve."

"Blimey. That's what I call reinforcements." He glances hopefully toward the road. "Where are they?"

"Well, at the moment they're tied-up in traffic. But they'll soon be here," explains Mallory. "I need to know if these men will help us stand fast here at Bapaume?"

The sergeant's face falls. "Some of 'em – maybe. Sir, you gotta understand, we've been shelled, gassed and overrun. Most of 'em are exhausted."

"What do you think is going to happen when the Hun arrive? Do you plan to just surrender?"

"We ain't got no weapons, sir," insists the sergeant. "These bloody red caps disarmed us when we was retreating."

"Fine. If I can get your weapons back, will these men fight?"

"Get our weapons back to us and show me tanks and, yeah. They'll fight."

"That's all I need to hear. Gather your men," orders Mallory. "I'll be right back!"

He darts across the congested dirt road and locates a military police lieutenant. The officer seems startled at Mallory's arrival. "Lieutenant! Where are these men's arms?"

The officer salutes smartly. "In the warehouse over there," he replies motioning toward a stone building absent roof and windows. Several burly MPs stand protectively at the door.

"I want the weapons returned immediately. Tanks are on the way and we're going to hold the high ground here on the edge of town."

The lieutenant wipes his nose with the back of a hand. Shaking his head, he replies, "Sir, I've got orders to disarm any stragglers and hold 'em 'til someone arrives to sort 'em out."

"Fine," replies Mallory testily. "I've arrived to sort them out. Now give them back their weapons!"

"I don't see any tanks, sir," replies the lieutenant as if Mallory has somehow failed to uphold his part of the bargain.

"What are you implying?"

"Nothin', sir. But the Colonel will have my arse if I re-arm these men and let 'em slip away."

"Well, I'll be buggered!" swears Mallory. "How about I put you under arrest for interfering with an officer performing official duties?" He reaches for his holster; several MPs unsling their rifles, uncertain whether to challenge the major.

"Sir, I...," begins the lieutenant but is interrupted by the roar of Whippets coming up the road. James waves cheerfully from the open hatch of the lead tank. Mallory signals him to spread the tanks across the field. James, in turn, swivels in his hatch and waves for the tanks to disburse and cut their engines. The tanks respond in best training ground manner, pivot neatly off the road to fan out across the open field.

"I believe you were asking about tanks," suggests Mallory. "Now, the weapons?"

"Sir, I can't just..."

"I've had enough of *this*," snaps Mallory. He sticks his thumb and middle finger between his lips and whistles shrilly. James glances up from the hatch. Mallory pumps his fist rapidly several times. James shouts down inside the turret. A puff of exhaust erupts from the ports on either side of the tank as it churns across the road toward them. The lieutenant's eyes widen at the Whippet's approach. It rocks to a stop beside Mallory and the lieutenant. James salutes smartly.

"You call for a taxi, sir?" asks James.

"Yes, Sergeant," replies Mallory loudly enough for the guards to overhear him. "Please relieve the guards and secure this building. We're going to distribute the weapons and defend this position!"

"Yes, sir!" replies James enthusiastically.

The lieutenant's face pales as the tank edges toward the dilapidated building; the two guards glance first at one another, then warily at the approaching tank. Ten feet from the door, the tank grinds to a halt. The forward-mounted machinegun swivels level with the guards who stand their ground uncertainly.

"Now, look 'ere boys," announces James cheerfully. "I've got this bloody big tank and a couple 'a machineguns to your pair 'a match sticks. In cards, we'd call that a pretty fair hand."

"Sir!" blurts the lieutenant. "This is highly irregular! You're threatening my men!"

"Not at all, Lieutenant," replies Mallory casually. "You and your men are welcome to join us. But the whole Hun army is about to come charging over the hill and you're leaving unarmed men to die. That'll amount to poor reading in your Regimental diary."

The lieutenant's mouth moves dumbly as he grapples for a response. Finding none, he snaps to attention. "Have your men draw their weapons, sir!"

As the MPs step aside, the Sherwood Foresters dash across the road and line-up in good order to await distribution of their weapons from the sergeant, who has now taken charge of the stragglers.

A soldier takes hold of a proffered rifle and checks the serial number. "Hey, this ain't my rifle!"

"You're as likely to be killed today anyway," grunts the sergeant. "*If* you survive, we can sort it out later. If not, who the hell cares?"

"Yeah, all right," replies the soldier with a shrug. He reaches into a pile of discarded cartridge belts and retrieves ammunition and a bayonet. As he moves along the rest of the stragglers follow suit, retrieving rifles and heading toward the crest east of town.

From atop the rise comes a shout. An MP dashes down the hill waving his arms and yelling. As he nears, Mallory finally hears the words.

"They're coming! They're coming!"

Mallory and the lieutenant run to meet him. "Who's coming?" asks the lieutenant.

"The whole bloody German Army!"

"How far away are they?" asks Mallory.

"In five minutes you can shake hands with 'em," replies the MP, breathlessly.

"Sergeant James! Get the tanks on-line and prepare to advance!" yells Mallory and jumps into the back seat of his staff car. "Sergeant! Get your troops onto the crest of that hill!"

"Sah!" shouts the sergeant. The Sherwood Foresters spread out and begin the long uphill dash.

"Come-on, Syd. Get me up there!" Mallory shouts to the driver. Dirt and gravel fly as Sydney stomps the gas pedal; the Renault bounces across the road and up the grassy slope. Nearing the crest, Mallory orders a stop, leaping from the car as it skids to a halt. He flings himself onto the ground and crawls the last few feet to the crest, where he quickly realizes he needs no binoculars.

"Syd!" he rasps. "Bring me the Chauchat, quickly!"

Sydney grabs the automatic rifle and a handful of curved ammunition magazines from the car and dashes up the hill. Throwing himself down alongside his commander, he gasps.

"Holy Mother of God!"

"Indeed," replies Mallory. He unfolds the bipod and inserts the magazine. Ripping back the charging handle, he shoulders the Chauchat and opens fire on German infantry advancing a mere hundred yards away. Over the slow, methodical slap of the firing mechanism, he hears tank engines rev as the Whippets progress up the hill.

From injury or instinct, Germans advancing directly in front collapse into the tall grass. Oblivious to the local action, hundreds of Germans stretched-out in skirmish lines dash forward on either flank. Mallory swivels the gun and tries to stem the advance by firing into the flanks of the advancing enemy. But there are too many.

Clank!

"Ammo!"

Sydney calmly passes him another magazine. Mallory slaps it in place and resumes firing.

The Sherwood Foresters reach the top of the hill and continue over the crest, bayonets fixed, a roar of angry defiance echoing across the valley. Stunned by the sudden appearance of British infantry rushing forward with fixed bayonets, the German advance stutters to a halt, Officers and NCOs react in confusion to the insane courage of the small British force descending into its ranks.

"Come-on, Syd!" shouts Mallory and joins the charge, machinegun at his hip, firing short bursts at small groups of clustered Germans caught in the counter attack.

"Sir!" shrieks Sydney. "On your right!"

As Mallory swings the gun right, the Chauchat suddenly runs dry. "Magazine!" he calls and thrusts his hand blindly in Sydney's direction.

Sydney shoves Mallory aside and draws his Webley, emptying his pistol at several Germans advancing from a few feet away. Two fall to the ground and the third collides with him and Mallory. Knocked to the ground, Mallory heaves the Chauchat aside and pounces on the German. Rolling him off Sydney, he leaps atop the attacker and pummels him with bloody knuckles. After several seconds of uncontrollable rage, he realizes the left side of the man's face is missing. He's already dead, caught by Sydney's gunfire.

At that moment, a dozen Whippets crest the hill, charge through the Sherwood Foresters' ranks and descend into the midst of the Germans. With no cover behind which to retreat, many of the attackers throw themselves to the ground in panic and are quickly crushed by the advancing tanks. The remaining attackers turn and dash rearward, panic in the center of the line rapidly spreading to the flanks as the tanks' machineguns rake the retreating mob.

The fight passes like a summer storm. Sounds of battle fading, Mallory lowers his weapon and stares out across the carnage strewn field. Wounded and dead German troops lie mangled and twisted in the mud. Victorious, blood-spattered Sherwood Foresters let out a shrill battle cry, waving their rifles and helmets in the air, heckling the retreating Germans. As the cry fades, the Sherwood Foresters spread-out and begin to dig-in along the crest, preparing for the inevitable German counter-attack.

Mallory turns back to the west and spots a medic bent over Sydney. He's whispering softly and pressing a large white compress against the boy's heaving chest. Mallory drops to his knees beside the pale-faced driver and grasps his hand. "Syd?" he asks softly.

The boy's kind, innocent face swivels toward him. "Looks like I finally earned that wound stripe," he breathes.

"Don't speak, son," begs Mallory. "We'll get you to a dressing station immediately!"

"But... who'll drive...?"

"I think I can make 'er run," replies Mallory through a nervous smile.

"It ain't proper, sir..." breathes Sydney. "Ain't proper at all..." The boy's face freezes, his voice halting mid-sentence, as if a switch has been pulled. His hand goes limp in Mallory's grasp.

"Sydney?"

The medic thumbs-back an eyelid. "He's gone, sir."

Mallory stares down at the youthful face, once so eager for action, now so peaceful in death. "I'll get you that medal, Syd," he promises. "Your parents will be proud..."

CHAPTER 28
Second Battle of the Somme (Michael Offensive), Amiens, France
April 1918

"How on earth do you know *that?*" asks General Rawlinson, Fourth Army commander

"It makes sense," replies Colonel Cranston. "They must attempt to take Villers-Bretonneux again. From the heights, Germans would be overlooking Amiens. They could shell us into rubble and force our withdrawal without a fight."

"Yes, but your source," scoffs Rawlinson. "He could be a Hun spy for all we know, sent to feed us disinformation!"

"I doubt it," replies Cranston. "He's just a boy."

"Exactly! So how would he know the Hun's intentions?"

"He says he's just a courier. Though he's the same one that brought us news the German drive was stalling because their troops were stopping to raid our stores."

"Yes, well. I find that difficult to believe," snorts Rawlinson. "I rather think they were delayed by the excellent fighting abilities of our troops."

"Of course, sir," concedes Cranston. "On the other hand, there was a rather surprising failure of the Hun to follow-up his success in our sector…"

"Well, maybe. But who is his source? A teenaged Frenchman would hardly have access to such information."

"He won't say. But he has risked crossing our lines twice to bring what amounts to surprisingly useful and precise intelligence. He keeps asking for a British officer. Says this officer can vouch for him."

"Have you found the officer?"

"No, sir. No such chap at headquarters, but we're looking."

Rawlinson slumps into his chair, pulling absently on his mustache as he considers the situation. "If I reinforce 8th Division at Villers-Bretonneux, instead of sending reinforcements south, the Germans may well drive a wedge between us and Debeny's French First Army."

"Sir," replies Cranston. "If the Germans drive us from Amiens and we have to retreat toward the ports, our entire line south of the city will be threatened and we'll be separated from the French anyway. I think the boy is telling the truth."

Rawlinson launches himself from the chair and approaches the map spread across the wall. He traces the line of German advance from Saint Quentin and Cambrai. "Get some observation aircraft up there to confirm German movement. Send two battalions to reinforce Villers-Bretonneux."

"Yes, Sir!" snaps Cranston and turns to leave.

"And get some tanks up there, for God's sake! We need all the help we can get..."

Mallory sits atop the track of one of his new battalion's Whippets, nicknamed "Demon". A map board across his lap, sleeves rolled-up in the spring heat, he hums tunelessly as he draws a grease pencil across the celluloid-covered map. His tunic hangs on the barrel of one of the tank's Hotchkiss guns, Sam Browne belt dangling over it. Beside him, his helmet rests upside-down in readiness for another German air attack.

From the west, a small dust cloud billows from the road announcing the approach of a fast-moving vehicle. Beyond the cloud, the heavily shelled remnants of Amiens stood like gravestones. Nearby, a dozen, battle-scarred Whippets and Mark IVs are parked along the gentle folds of rolling hills and beneath small copses of trees scattered across the countryside. Tank parts are strewn about the vehicles as crews sweat in the mid-day sun to repair recent combat damage.

The staff car bumps across the field and skids to a halt beside Mallory's tank.

"Any news, Sar' Major?" shouts Mallory.

"Good news and bad news," announces James as he descends stiffly from the running board.

"Do tell."

James hands him a flimsy. "Bray has fallen."

"*What?*" blurts Mallory. "That means the Hun has secured a crossing at the Somme!"

"And the girls are right in the thick of it," adds James.

"Maybe not," replies Mallory as if trying to convince himself. "Surely they fell back on Amiens."

"I just got back from Amiens. The Red Cross set-up a Refugee Center to help families locate each other. I got a peek at the roster and Elise and Adele ain't on it."

"Shit!" snorts Mallory. After a few seconds of silence, he clears his throat and announces. "There's nothing we can do for the girls until we stop the Hun attack."

"I know, sir. But..."

"I understand, James. Until we find out where they are, we'll just have to pray."

"And fight," adds James.

"Yes. And fight. Now, what's the good news?"

"I ain't through with the bad news yet."

Mallory sighs. "Come on, let me have it".

"Intelligence says the Germans have their own tanks now," announces James. He passes Mallory a photograph of a box-like vehicle sitting atop a set of tracks, cannon emerging from the nose of the beast and Maxims bristling from ports on either side.

"Do we know how many?"

"Here," replies James and provides Mallory another photograph. "This was taken from the air earlier today. It looks like at least three, maybe four of the damned things are headed this way."

"Is that all?"

"Dunno. That first photograph was taken at Bray a couple 'a days ago. Ugly bastard, ain't it?"

Mallory examines the photo closely. "Ugly, yes. But the way the tracks run beneath it, it doesn't look terribly mobile. It sure as hell isn't going to be able to cross trenches."

"Yeah, well. I don't see no trenches around here," replies James, surveying the rolling countryside. "Besides, intelligence says Fritz also has some captured Mark IVs. Take a look at this. You can see 'em in this aerial photo." James provides Mallory a glossy 8"x10". The photo, taken from a moving reconnaissance plane at

1,200 feet is slightly blurry, but the black and white image clearly shows several Mark IVs with large Maltese Crosses painted on their upper decks.

"Lovely," sighs Mallory. "I wonder what the first tank-on-tank battle will be like."

"We'll find out soon enough," replies James.

"What?"

James provides a packet containing maps and orders. "The good news is we're finally getting back into action. We got orders to support the Australians moving up to help the 8th Division retake Villers-Bretonneux."

"Retake it?" asks Mallory in surprise. Opening the packet and sorting through the documents, he reviews the order. He consults his watch. "Shit! We've got to get moving. The Aussies are planning a counterattack first thing in the morning!" Grabbing his tunic and belt, he leaps from the track and begins snapping-off orders as he dresses. "Get 'C' Company's Whippets on the road immediately!" He hands James the map. "If the road's open, run like hell toward Villers-Bretonneaux in-column. I'll bring along our remaining Mark IVs behind you."

"Pretty bloody dangerous, sir," warns James. "Its broad daylight and you'll be invitin' enemy air and artillery attack."

"I know, but if the Aussies run onto those Hun tanks without our support, it'll be a slaughter."

It's growing dark by the time Mallory's Mark IVs arrive outside Villers-Bretonneux. Military Police manning checkpoints along the road wave the tanks aside to make room for the advancing Australians. Mallory speeds ahead in his staff car and arrives at the Australian 15th Brigade's headquarters located in a damaged farmhouse just off the main road.

He enters the main room and discovers it surprisingly calm for a brigade headquarters preparing a major counterattack. Several staff officers glance up at his arrival. Mallory slips off his helmet and waits expectantly. A tall, gangly major breaks from the map board and offers his hand.

"Whatley," he announces. "Operations officer."

"Mallory. First Tank Battalion," replies Mallory and the two shake hands.

"Glad to see you," replies Whatley. "We're receiving reports of German tanks prowling around our positions. Anything you can do to help out?"

"What do you have in-mind."

"The general thought you might send some tanks to help secure our major lines of communication."

"We're better when massed for an assault," cautions Mallory.

"The assault will take place tomorrow night. Last time we worked with tanks, I got the impression night operations weren't your thing."

"True enough," replies Mallory. "Where do you want us?"

Whatley leads Mallory to a map on the wall and points-out several railroad junctions. "We need to secure the rail lines so the Hun doesn't prevent us bringing up reinforcements. We've got packets of infantry guarding the junctions, but they could really use some help."

"Can do," replies Mallory. "We'll get up there immediately. Seen any Hun tanks in the area?"

"No recent reports, but be careful. The battlefield is still fluid."

"*Fluid?* You mean buggered?"

"Why, yes," replies Whatley. "I think it sums it up nicely."

Inside a dimly-lit tent alongside the makeshift tank laager, Mallory briefs the section leaders on the new assignment. The lieutenants are unenthusiastic at the prospect of remaining on the defense while the Aussies conduct a night assault.

"We wouldn't be able to see where we're going, anyway," explains one of the section leaders.

"Couldn't the artillery fire flares so we can see where we're going?" asks someone.

"Ours or the Germans?" responds one of the veterans.

"What?... Our's, of course..."

"Lieutenant," sighs Mallory. "Has it occurred to you, if the artillery lights up the battlefield for us, they'll be doing the same for the Germans?"

"Oh!"

"Bloody wanker," snorts one of the others and the tent fills momentarily with laughter.

"All right, all right. Settle down," chuckles Mallory. "Mack, I want you to disburse your Section along the rail line here." He points to a line on the smudged, dog-eared map. "Work out your dispositions with the battalion in the area, but make sure you place your tanks so they don't draw Hun artillery fire. You're there to help defend the Aussies, not make them a target."

"Right, sir," responds Mack.

"Now, the plumb goes to you, Mitchell. Take your section to the Cachy switch line and lend a hand to the 1st Worcesters. We don't know if the Hun is going to press the attack toward Amiens. But if so, we'll need to retain the railroads so we can move troops rapidly."

"Just my three Mark IVs?" asks Mitchell.

"I'm going to create a mobile reserve using the Whippets," replies Mallory. "If things get too tense, fire up a blue flare and we'll come charging."

"Sir, my crews suffered casualties during the mustard bombardment," explains Mitchell. "I've only got four of my regular crew of eight. The other crews in the Section are missing two or three each."

"Well, you'll have to make do," replies Mallory with a shake of the head. "We're short on crews right now, so you'll have no replacements. Besides, you'll be in static defenses. You probably won't have to move, anyway."

"The old man's pretty confident," announces the Section Sergeant as he and Mitchell leave the tent to return to their tanks.

"The 'old man' - as you call him - is probably only about twenty years old," scoffs Mitchell.

"Awfully young for a Major," replies the sergeant.

"I rather think war ages a man into the rank, not the other way 'round."

As they near the Section's one male and two female tanks, the crews begin mounting their vehicles. Engines cough and sputter to life, the soft hum heard outside belaying the hellish roar within. Mitchell climbs up the front of the male tank and drops through the hatch, replacing his Brody helmet with a crewman's leather-clad bowler. Twisting in his hatch, Mitchell signals the two female tanks to follow his tank in-column. Receiving an acknowledging wave, he leans down and shouts for the advance to proceed.

Lurching forward, Mitchell's tank grinds toward Cachy. As night overtakes them, the trip becomes increasingly treacherous, beset by continuous stops and starts to clear obstacles and traverse impassable bogs nearly invisible in the darkness. As they near Cachy, a runner dashes forward and waves them down. Mitchell pops open his hatch and peers down at the muddy infantryman.

"Number One Section, A Company," shouts Mitchell. "Where do you want us?"

"Beggin' your pardon, sir. But the colonel says to spread out about a hundred yards ahead. I'll guide ya'."

"Lead-on," replies Mitchell and knocks on the roof of his tank. With a roar, the tank crawls forward slowly, its lozenge-shaped body jerking left and right as it threads past machineguns and mortars dug-in to the hastily-established defenses. Once in-position, he leans inside and shouts down to his driver. "Kill the engine!" The motor sputters to a stop. In the murky distance, he hears the Section's other tanks' engines also go silent.

The night is warm and humid. A thick ground mist settles over the tanks like a camouflage net. After several hours, dawn begins to appear in the east. As the sun continues to rise, the gray fog becomes infused with an eerie orange light seeming to glow around the tank rather than shining upon it. A meadowlark sings somewhere in the distance, its squeaky, undulating call reminding Mitchell of home.

Thunder rumbles lightly; Mitchell squints skyward through the mist. He can barely make-out the yellow orb rising in the east. He glances down at his driver who sits, half-asleep in the cupola beside him. "Is it supposed to rain today?" he asks.

The driver shifts tiredly and adjusts the cap over his eyes. "Don't think so," he mumbles. "Supposed to be hot and dry all week."

A rumble comes again - this time longer and more persistent. Mitchell leans back through the hatch. "Crank 'er up!" he shouts.

"Fritz is up to somethin' and we ain't gonna get caught with our pants down."

Upon hearing the lead tank start its engine, the two females follow suit. As the fog continues to thin, Mitchell is finally able to make-out the two female tanks on his right flank. A warm breeze brushes his ear as the fog continues to dissipate. Squinting across no man's land, he spots a large, square hulk several hundred yards away. He reaches inside the tank and retrieves his binoculars from the dashboard. Eyes focused on the hulk, he raises the glasses. The hulk moves. Lowering the glasses, he shakes his head before lifting them again and peering at the object. Again it moves, slowly pivoting left and crawling forward a few feet.

"My God!" he blurts. "It's a bloody Hun tank!"

He waves frantically to the two other tank commanders lounging atop their tanks. They acknowledge his signal and follow his frantic gesture toward the German lines. Peering at the dark object, both commanders are suddenly struck by realization. He signals frantically for them to button-up and follow. Without acknowledging his direction, they disappear inside their tanks.

Mitchell closes the hatch over him. "We're about to make history, chaps," he announces to the crew. "The order is... advance!"

German artillery begins to drop around them. Mitchell jerks the brake levers as the tank zig-zags across the open field toward the oncoming German. His other two tanks move toward the German behemoth, which spots the females first and opens fire on them.

"Fire!" screams Mitchell and both six-pounders erupt simultaneously. The rounds pass over the German and land harmlessly a hundred yards beyond. "Again!" he shouts.

Again they miss.

"Take your time and hit the bastard!"

"I can't bloody aim while we're moving!" replies the frustrated gunner.

A puff of white smoke blooms from the German tank's single cannon. To his right, a flash announces one of the females has been hit. But its machineguns continue firing, the crew remaining safe behind the twisted armor plate.

Mitchell's gunner fires again, missing.

The German has got the range of the female tanks, his long-barreled gun erupting repeatedly and peppering them with hot steel. Dented, mangled armored plates twist in all directions, exposing the wounded crews to continuing fire. Another hit! The female slews around to its right. Another round lands beside it, burying the defenseless tank with dirt.

"Keep firing!" shrieks Mitchell. He tries to distract the German from the females that are retreating as quickly as a speed of four miles per hour allows.

The German finally spots Mitchell's tank and opens fire with its Maxims while the main gun continues to engage the females. Molten steel spall ricochets around the interior as armor piercing rounds puncture the sponsons. A machine gunner screams and falls to the deck grasping his shins as blood oozes from between his fingers.

"Shit!" yells Mitchell. "Stop!"

The tank lurches to a halt.

"Now *hit the bastard!*"

The cannon roars, its round striking the ground in front of the German.

"You've got the range, now hit him!"

The next round strikes the German's flank, exploding against the armor and charring the paint. The tank shudders and begins to turn away.

"He's manoeuvering! Fire again!"

Three more rounds strike the boxy German before the tank slews into a trench and heaves onto its side, collapsing like an exhausted elephant. The skyward-facing side hatch swings open and the crew emerges. One-by-one they drop into the mud beside their stricken tank.

"They're abandoning her!" yells Mitchell and the crew cheers. He mans the Lewis gun and peppers the Germans with .303 caliber rounds. Steel jacketed bullets spark off the hardened armor and ricochet into the struggling crew. Several fall in sad heaps, crew members grasping their mates by the arms and attempting to drag away the wounded before giving up and abandoning them to their fate.

A blast erupts beside Mitchell's tank, the explosion ringing inside like a gong. Shoving open the commander's port, he peers out across the battlefield and spots more of the boxy German tanks emerging through the fog, infantry following in their wake.

"Two more headed this way!" he shouts to the crew.

"Bloody hell!" responds one of the gunners. "Do we have to do this all by ourselves?"

"Shit!" swears Mitchell as he recalls Mallory's instructions. He grabs the Very pistol and flings-open the hatch. Raising the gun overhead, he thumbs the hammer and fires. A loud *pop* and the glowing blue flare sails lazily into the sky leaving behind a smoky trail. "Help's on the way!" he shouts. "We gotta hold until they arrive!"

His gunners open fire on the advancing German tanks and, to the crews' surprise, both tanks halt and begin to turn away. "They're running! They're running!" announces Mitchell hysterically.

"Go, baby! GO!" shouts one of the gunners.

Mitchell squints through his commander's periscope. "Uh, oh! The infantry are still advancing! Reverse and get some distance before they swarm us. Then hit 'em with case-shot!"

The tank rumbles rearward as it opens fire on the advancing infantry. Steel shot rips through the ranks of advancing Germans, kicking-up a wall of dust as it shreds the unprotected men caught in the open.

German artillery retaliates with everything it's got, bracketing the tank with howitzer, gunfire and mortar rounds. Sweating profusely, Mitchell frantically works the brakes back and forth, zig-zagging to avoid the artillery as the tank's guns continue to fire on the attackers.

A massive explosion and the rear of the tank slips into a shell hole, hurling the crew to the deck. The engine sputters and dies.

"Jeezus...!" one of the gunners swears.

"Get back to your positions!" cries Mitchell, dabbing his sleeve across the gash in his forehead. "Get this thing, started!" he growls to the driver. "If they overrun us, there'll be hell to pay."

"The engine's not getting any petrol," announces the driver. "There must be a leak in the vacuum system." He flings-off his seatbelt and drops down into the hull. Steadying himself on the interior frame, he works his way alongside the engine tracing the fuel line. Near the rear of the tank he locates the torn vacuum hose. Wrapping the hose with a rag, he squeezes his hand around it and shouts, "Give her a couple 'a cranks!"

The machine gunners abandon their weapons and give the crank several sharp turns.

The engine coughs.

"Prime it, sir!"

Mitchell reaches across the seat and primes the throttle. "Go!"

The gunners crank again and the engine catches.

"I've got to hold the vacuum until we're level! Get us out of here, sir!" begs the driver.

Mitchell slides across the seat and slips the tank into gear. He pops the clutch, the tank lurches forward and noses over with a crash, tossing the crew about the interior like rag dolls. Amid a chorus of curses, the crew struggles back to their fighting positions as the driver comes forward.

German infantry surge toward the tank. "They're nearly on top of us!" yells Mitchell.

Suddenly, he spots a platoon of Whippets converging from the flank. Speeding along at eight miles per hour, they rapidly overtake the Mark IV and wade into the midst of the confused German battalion. Machineguns blazing, the Whippets overwhelm the attackers, shooting and crushing the disorganized mob as panicked infantry scatter in all directions.

The Whippets quickly disappear from view as they pursue the retreating Germans into the mist.

"What do you say?" Mitchell calls out to the crew. "Shall we join them?"

The crew cheers and Mitchell shoves the brake handles forward. The tank lurches into the fog, German artillery continuing to fall intermittently around them.

A fourth German tank emerges - or perhaps one they've seen previously.

"Target! A thousand yards!' shouts Mitchell.

The gunners slam rounds into their six-pounders and open fire without further orders. Punch-drunk and exhausted, their rounds impact all around the German that roars back in defiance, its single 57 millimeter gun erupting in response.

As the tanks trade fusillades, a mortar round arches gracefully from the German line and strikes Mitchell's front left track with an earsplitting, *CLANG!* The tank slews sideways, the damaged track spewing from its drive sprocket like a Cobra preparing to defend itself. Bereft of traction on one side, the tank drags itself in a circle.

Deafened by the impact and blinded with blood streaming from the cuts on his face, Mitchell jerks the brakes and the engine sputters to a halt. He wipes his eyes and peers back at the bruised and bloody crew.

"So much for a static defence!" he shouts and begins laughing hysterically. Eyes tearing, his laughter chokes into a sob as his face collapses into his hands and he begins to weep.

CHAPTER 29
Second Battle of the Somme (Michael Offensive)
Amiens, France
June 1918

"Withdrawn!" blurts Mallory. "Why?"

"My, God, Jack!" replies General Elles. "Look at your men. They're exhausted; you're exhausted. Besides, you don't have a single tank left not in need of a complete overhaul."

"Then give us new tanks, Sir," begs Mallory.

"The new Mark Vs have gone to Third Brigade. They're training with the Australians for an upcoming assault on Hamel," replies Elles as he places his cap back on his head and retrieves his walking stick, preparing to depart. "Your battalion and the rest of the Brigade are being sent east of Amiens to rest and refit with the new Mark Vs and V*. Now get with Sergeant Major James and work it out. We need you fresh for the upcoming general offensive in August."

"August? That far off?"

"Look here, Jack. I've always had the greatest admiration for your fighting abilities, but you've got to get some balance. It takes time to stage a battle, particularly as part of a larger offensive. Take a few days off. Go see your lady friend…"

Mallory's face falls.

"What's wrong?"

"I don't know where she is," replies Mallory. "She was in Bray when the Germans overran it. I don't know what happened to her."

Elles places a fatherly hand on Mallory's shoulder. "Awful business. I see now why you're so anxious to get on with it."

Mallory nods dejectedly.

"But you're not going to liberate Bray by yourself and the truth is you're not going to do anyone any good if you don't get some rest."

"I know, sir. But if I could just get some word about her…"

Elles pulls at his mustache, twisting it between his fingers as a thought enters his mind. "You know, I shouldn't do this, but there's a chap up at Fourth Army intelligence with a source inside Bray. Perhaps you should come back to Amiens with me and have a chat."

"Could I, sir?"

"Certainly, why not?"

Within the hour, Mallory and Elles arrive in Amiens. The half-destroyed city is alive with activity. Australian and Canadian infantry clog the streets as they depart the railheads and march eastward away from the city center. Estaminets and shops lining the roads are clogged with dominion troops buying souvenirs or having a last drink before heading up the line.

"Nice to see fresh troops for a change," observes Mallory as the tall, tanned, healthy-looking dominion troops stride confidently toward the haggard, exhausted Germans still holding the line east of Villers-Bretonneaux.

"How are the French holding-up?" asks Mallory.

"Quite well, actually," replies Elles. "The Americans have finally arrived in force and were able to stop the Hun on the Marne fifty miles from Paris. Marshal Foch is delighted."

"I feel better knowing we're getting fresh troops from America. Maybe the tide is turning."

"Yes, I think the Germans have shot their bolt. One more big push and I'm convinced the German army will collapse."

"Are we getting reinforcements from Blighty?"

"New crews are coming over daily," replies Elles. "In fact, we're expanding the Tank Corps."

"About damned time."

"Well, you know what *that* means."

"Sir?"

"Leadership. I need someone to take over the First Brigade. So you've been gazetted Lieutenant Colonel."

"What?" blurts Mallory, twisting in his seat and staring at Elles. "Sir… I'm not cut-out to be a Lieutenant Colonel! Hell, I'm barely qualified to be a Lieutenant!"

"Yes, well. There are those of us – Colonel Fuller and General Swinton included – that think you show promise. Either way, what's done is done. Oh, and tell James his promotion to Sergeant Major has been made permanent."

"Oh, he's not goin' to like that, sir," chuckles Mallory.

Elles sighs heavily. "See here! I really don't understand you New Army men. In the Old Army one would kill to be promoted as fast as you chaps, yet you all seem so bloody unimpressed!"

"We're not professionals, sir," replies Mallory with a shrug. "We just serve for the duration. Once this war's over, we expect to return to our civilian jobs and families."

"And what will you do?" asks Elles.

Mallory sits silent for a few moments. "I don't know, sir,' he responds finally. "I haven't really thought about it. Maybe return to university."

"And…?"

"Again, I really don't know, sir. I never expected to survive the war, but it's looking like I might. I'd like to marry Elise. But from there, I'm stumped."

"What if I told you there is a move in Parliament to offer admission to Sandhurst for some of our outstanding young officers that received battlefield commissions. Might you be interested?"

"*Sandhurst!*" gasps Mallory. "Me? A regular officer?"`

"Well, *why not?* We've got to capture some of this experience before the army demobilizes and it's all lost."

"I'll certainly think about it," replies Mallory.

"You do that."

The car draws-up before Fourth Army Headquarters. The entrance to the grand house is guarded by regular troops, the area around it patrolled by military police – the hated "Red Caps". With a slap of metal on wood, the guards bring their rifles to Present Arms as Elles dismounts and Mallory follows him into the foyer. At a desk inside the door sits an orderly who snaps to his feet at the general's approach.

"Good morning, Sergeant," drawls Elles. "Can you tell me where Colonel Cranston of Intelligence Branch resides?"

"Do you have an appointment, sir?"

"Does a general need an appointment to see a Colonel?" asks Swinton.

"Well, um. I really hadn't looked at it that way. That's just the usual manner, sir. He's on the second floor. Third office on the right."

"Right. Thanks so much."

Elles and Mallory ascend a battle-damaged marble staircase to the second floor. They find the Colonel's office door guarded.

"Step aside, son," orders Elles. "We're here to see Colonel Cranston."

"Sah!" barks the burly Sergeant. "I cannot allow anyone inside without authorization!"

"I say, you *do* see I'm a general?" asks Elles with obvious annoyance.

"Sah!" shouts the sergeant, but remains fixed before the door.

"We need to see Colonel Cranston," demands Elles.

"Not without prior authorization," replies the sergeant.

"By God, I'll have your stripes!"

The door behind the burly sergeant swings open. "What the hell is going on out here?"

"We're here to see Colonel Cranston – or apparently, God Almighty!" barks Elles.

"*We*, who?"

"General Elles and Lieutenant Colonel Mallory…"

"Lieutenant Colonel *who?*"

"Mallory," replies Elles.

"Let them in, sergeant," snaps the colonel.

The door swings open. Elles and Mallory enter a large, dusty room stacked with bundles of paper and staffed with a group of harried-looking intelligence officers and clerks. The walls are covered with pieced-together aerial photographs of the Amiens sector and the German lines east of the city. The desks are littered with folders and coversheets marked, "Eyes Only".

The colonel brushes past Elles and examines Mallory as if he's a science experiment. There's something about his eccentric manner that reminds Mallory of Colonel Fuller.

"So *you're* Mallory?"

"Yes," replies Mallory uncertainly. "Why?"

"Do you know François Durant?"

"*Who?*"

"*François Durant,*" repeats Cranston.

"Not that I know of," replies Mallory in confusion. "Why do you ask?"

"He's a French courier that's been bringing intelligence across the German lines," explains Cranston. "We've been trying to establish his bona fides for months. He says a 'Major Mallory' can identify him."

"Durant? The name isn't familiar," replies Mallory with a shrug. "Perhaps if I met him?"

"Sergeant! Go get Durant," snaps Cranston to the guard.

"Can you describe him?" asks Mallory.

"Teenaged boy, about fifteen. Tall. Gangly. Black hair."

"A teenager?" mumbles Mallory. "I don't know any French teenagers. Are you sure I'm the Mallory you're looking for?"

"I've located a Sergeant Mallory and a Lance Corporal within this command," replies Cranston. He looks Mallory up and down. "You've still got Major's pips. How long have you been a Lieutenant Colonel?"

"About an hour."

"Well, then. You are the only Major Mallory in Fourth Army I can find. Are you with the tanks?"

"Yes," replies Elles. "He's one of my battalion commanders."

Cranston peers queerly at Elles. "And, who are you again?"

"General Hugh Elles," he growls. "General Commanding, Tank Corps."

"Do you have another Major Mallory under your command?"

"Not that I'm aware of."

"Well then, this must be our man."

The door rattles open and the burly sergeant reappears, his paw wrapped around a boy's upper arm. There's something familiar about the young man, but Mallory can't place him.

"Do we know each other?" asks Mallory.

"Non," the boy replies. "But I know who you are."

"How?"

The boy lowers his head sheepishly. "You are Tante Elise's lover."

The color drains from Mallory's face. "Oh, my God!"

Both Elles and Cranston notice Mallory's shock. "What?" asks Elles.

"He's Elise's nephew," Mallory replies, stunned. "I remember him now. I saw him on the road to the hospital in Albert last year!"

"I say, who is this Elise woman?" asks Cranston sharply.

"She's a woman I know," replies Mallory evasively.

Cranston grasps the boy's arm and spins him around. "Is this 'Elise' your source?" he demands.

The boy doesn't respond.

"*Is she your source?*" repeats Cranston, shaking the boy.

Mallory grabs the young man's other arm and pulls him away from the haranguing colonel. "Leave him alone! You're scaring him," growls Mallory.

"Then *you* ask," snaps Cranston.

"Is Tante Elise the source of your information?"

"Oui."

"Where is she?"

"At home," he replies.

"In Amiens?"

"Non. Bray-sur-Somme."

Mallory's knees go weak; he slumps against a desk. "Yes," he sighs. "Elise is the source." He looks to Elles. "So she didn't evacuate Bray," he explains weakly. "She stayed there to spy on the Germans."

"Dear God," breathes Elles.

"So how would *this woman* gain access to classified German plans?" asks Cranston.

"Yes, how *would* she get access?" repeats Elles.

Mallory takes a deep breath – he knew this moment would come, but hardly the importance of the answer. "There are no secrets in a brothel," replies Mallory, repeating Elise's exact words.

"Elise is a prostitute?" asks Cranston, incredulous.

"No. The Madame," corrects Mallory. "She runs the main brothel in Bray."

Mallory suddenly becomes aware Elles is staring at him, open-mouthed.

"But how would a Madame gain access to secrets?" asks Cranston.

"Have you ever been in a brothel, sir?"

"Certainly *not!*" bristles Cranston.

"Let's just say a bloke will tell a beautiful woman *anything* to impress her."

"Even if he's paying for services?"

"Oh, yes."

"Well, I'll be buggered!" exclaims Cranston. "So you think her information comes from the girls' relationships with Hun officers?"

"I'd say it's a certainty, sir."

"That means the intelligence this Elise is providing is probably good stuff?"

"My guess is it's probably of the highest-quality," replies Mallory.

"Jolly good!" chortles Cranston. "We've finally got decent intelligence on Hun movements!"

"François," Mallory asks. "How is your aunt?"

"Très bien, monsieur. She misses you," he replies sheepishly.

"Yes," sighs Mallory. "I miss her, also."

Mallory and Elles descend silently into the lobby of the headquarters building.

"Sir..." begins Mallory.

Elles raises a cautionary hand. They walk into the bright sunlight past the guards bringing their rifles sharply to present arms. Elles glances around the crowded street and, spotting his staff car parked nearby, waves to the driver. The car arrives and Elles directs Mallory into the vehicle, entering behind him.

"Le Petit Amiens," Elles orders the driver.

As the car pulls away from the headquarters, Elles finally speaks to Mallory. "Why didn't you tell me the truth about Elise earlier?"

"I can't imagine a conversation where *that* would have arisen, can you?" replies Mallory.

"No, I suppose not," acknowledges Elles. "Silly question."

"I didn't think it mattered, sir."

"Didn't *think...?*"

"No."

"Good God, Jack. You're a serving officer! I just nominated you to attend Sandhurst!"

"What's that got to do with Elise?"

"I... I can't send an officer to England's most prestigious military institution when he's consorting with a ... a... prostitute!"

Mallory sees the driver's head jerk upright, his eyes suddenly alert in the rearview mirror.

"Mind the road, Corporal," growls Mallory.

"Yes, sir."

"She's not a prostitute, sir. Her husband was a French officer killed early in the war. She has children to support and just runs the bordello to make a living."

"Hmph!"

"It's not like that, sir!" insists Mallory. "Do you have any idea what it's like to be a war-widow in France? The government pension is a joke and there's no work for her in a war zone – unless she wants to be a prostitute. Which she doesn't! So what's she supposed to do?"

"I suppose I'd never thought of it that way," admits Elles.

"Besides, Sir. Those bordellos are full of our own officers and men. Wouldn't it be hypocritical to judge the girls for providing a service in such high demand by our own people?"

"Yes, yes. I suppose so."

They drive along in silence until the car arrives in front of the hotel bar.

"So, does Sergeant Major James know about this?"

Mallory clears his throat and glances distractedly at the car's ceiling.

"Oh, dear God," moans Elles. "His wife...?"

"... works there. Yes, sir."

The car rolls up in front of Le Petit Amiens. Elles reaches outside the car and turns the door handle. "I need a drink. Are you coming?"

"Certainly, sir." Mallory exits the car and follows Elles up the stairs and into to the bar.

"Two Whiskeys, neat!" shouts Elles and the bartender scrambles for glasses. He locates a marble-topped table and drops exhaustedly into a chair. When the whiskey arrives, Mallory retrieves the glasses from the bar and places them on the table.

Elles seizes both glasses. "Better get one for yourself."

With a grin at Elles' discomfort, Mallory orders himself two whiskeys and takes a seat across from the general.

"Cheers!" toasts Elles and takes a great gulp. Setting down his glass, he peers across the table at Mallory. "So, what are you going to so about these… relationships?"

"*Do*, sir?"

"Well, James is New Army. He's probably not going to remain in the service after the war. So I suppose it doesn't really matter who he's married to. But you! You have a bright future should you decide to pursue it."

"Elise and I discussed getting married, too" reports Mallory and takes a sip from the cut crystal glass.

"No. Now it's totally out of the question," replies Elles with a shudder. "What happens over here – during the war – can be overlooked. But if you want to keep your commission after the war, it's simply unacceptable."

"Then perhaps I don't belong in the army."

"God, you New Army-types are so damned stubborn!"

"Seriously, sir. I… I can't see myself in-garrison back home, or even on a frontier-post in India," explains Mallory. "Constant parades, inspections. I'd lose my mind."

"But what about the tanks?" insists Elles. "Officers like Swinton, Fuller and I are probably going to be retired after the war. Who's going to form the new leadership of the Tank Corps? If we leave it to the Cavalry generals, they'll scrap the tanks and put everyone back on horseback."

"Surely not, sir?"

"Well, why the hell not? They see the tank as a novelty, a toy to punch holes in the line so the cavalry can exploit the breach!"

"Despite our success at Cambrai?"

"Despite it?" scoffs Elles darkly. "I'd say *because* of it!"

CHAPTER 30
Battle of Amiens, France
7 August 1918

"Ours or theirs?" asks James.

The biplane banks gracefully into a turn, the red, white and blue roundel appearing beneath the wings. As the aircraft turns toward them, the sound of the engine fades even as the plane nears. It passes over, the roar erupting in its wake.

"Ours," confirms Mallory. "He's scouting our positions to see if the enemy can spot our preparations."

"What do ya think?"

Mallory glances around the outskirts of Amiens. Between the intact buildings and within the shattered structures are parked dozens of brownish-green Mark Vs and stretched Mark V*s draped in camouflage netting. The crews rest within the shade of the buildings, brewing tea and relaxing in the sweltering afternoon heat. Inexplicably, given the temperature, a group of Australian infantrymen are stripped to their shorts playing football in the courtyard of an abandoned school.

The pitted, cobblestone streets of Amiens are covered with sand and straw to tamp-down the dust and muffle the sounds of tanks, trucks, wagons and artillery moving through the city each night, leaving the streets empty and barren during daylight hours.

"We've done everything we can to make the Hun believe any attack will come up in the Ypres-sector," announces Mallory. "The dangerous part will be when we move-up to the Aussie positions tonight. If we arrive without alerting the Hun, we'll have the element of surprise in the morning."

"And if not?" asks James.

"Then we'll have brought hell down on the Aussies."

"Great."

Mallory checks his watch. "Make sure the crews get a good meal before we move-up this evening. I doubt they'll bring rations to the forward trenches tonight."

"Right, sir," confirms James and turns to leave. He hesitates.

"I don't know, James," replies Mallory before James can ask the question on both their minds. "The girls have been through this before, so I'm sure they'll take cover when the attack begins."

"I hope so," grunts James. "I still can't believe they didn't evacuate when the Germans attacked."

"I do," sighs Mallory. "Elise despises the Germans; she'd do anything to see them defeated."

"Adele, too," replies James. "But…" He shoves his hands into his pockets and stares at the ground, nudging a piece of shattered brick with the tip of his boot.

"What's on your mind, James?"

"Well, it's been botherin' me ever since we heard about the spy-ring."

"You mean, the question of how they're obtaining the information?"

"Yeah. I can't imagine some nasty Hun bastard touchin' my sweet Adele," croaks James. His face is drawn and lined, his voice plaintive as if begging to be told no such thing has taken place.

"You once told me you didn't mind her doing her bit for the war, taking care of our men," insists Mallory as he places a comradely hand on James' shoulder. "By getting information about enemy plans, she's done more to ensure we win this bloody war than either of us. You've just got to keep that in-mind."

"Yeah, I know it in my head, but my heart…"

"Look, for all I know, Elise has been 'consorting with the enemy', too. But I've got to forgive her, because she does it for us. For you and me. For France."

"I know, but…"

"And I'll tell you something else," announces Mallory. He jabs his finger into James' chest. "I am *never* going to ask Elise what she did to get that intelligence!"

Tanks crawl slowly across the rolling hills embracing the left bank of the Somme. Strictly against orders – though orders

General Elles no-doubt suspected he'd violate – Mallory is leading the assault in one of the new Mark V* troop carrying tanks.

He glances back at the sweating crew and Lewis Gun teams huddled at the rear of the extended tank-cum-infantry carrier. Longer and slower than its Mark V counterpart, the infantry carrier is difficult to maneuver and presents an easier target for German gunners. But it allows the infantry to move forward protected within the tank and deploy its machineguns immediately inside the German defenses.

Following a ground-guide through a moonless, humid night, his driver maneuvers the tanks into a deep cut to hide them from enemy observation until the attack begins tomorrow morning. On Mallory's order, the engine sputters to a halt. He emerges through the commander's hatch into darkness. The side doors creak open, the gun crews dismount with a relieved sigh and collapse, soaked with sweat and exhausted along the wall of the natural trench. Matches and trench lighters flare, illuminating young, nervous faces as the men share in the ample supply of Woodbines. In a collective first exhale, a cloud of gray smoke wafts from the trench like a cloud of gas before dissipating in the warm evening breeze.

Mallory slides down the front of the sloping armor and lands on his feet. Groping through the darkness, he seeks out the Australian command bunker and discovers the battalion commander in a log-reinforced dugout calmly sipping tea from a chipped cup. He introduces himself.

"Infantry carriers, huh?" Lieutenant Colonel Andrew Fox acknowledges with a smile. "What wonderful modern times we live-in." Just a few years older than Mallory, he appears to be a much older man.

"Indeed," replies Mallory. "I suppose we can all go home now and let the machines finish the war for us."

Fox hooks the heel of his boot on the edge of a chair and shoves it away from the table. "Take a seat Jack," he offers. Mallory scoops the helmet from his head and complies.

"Murray!" calls Fox. His batman appears with a second chipped cup. He places it on the plank-topped table and departs. Andy reaches into his pocket and withdraws a flask.

"Do you drink?"

Mallory nudges the cup toward his host. "You bet!"

Fox pours a healthy dose into Mallory's cup and empties the remainder into his own. "I hate this part," admits Fox. "This is where a battalion commander feels most useless. The plans are laid, the troops are primed. Now it's up to the Lieutenants and NCOs."

"Well, if you're bored, you're welcome to come with me," offers Mallory.

Fox sits-up in surprise. "You're going forward with your tanks?"

Mallory nods conspiratorially. "Each of my carriers has a Vickers gun crew and two Lewis Gun teams. We're going to roll right into the Hun lines and plant them there to support your advance."

"Well, you may have to catch-up with us," replies Fox. "Our first wave starts off at 4.20. Your infantry carriers don't join the show until 10.00."

"Are you sure?" asks Mallory in surprise. "We're still awaiting final orders."

"I'm afraid so. The plan is for your tanks and the cavalry to exploit any breakthrough we're able to provide."

"That turns our tank tactics on their head," groans Mallory.

"I know. But we should be taking the Hun by surprise. If we can topple his forward defenses, your tanks should have smooth sailing."

"Dare we hope it's so simple?"

Fox shakes his head sadly. "I've been in this damned war since Gallipoli. Though I've discovered that in war everything is simple, but the simplest things are the most difficult."

"Well, I'll be buggered. You're a philosopher," chuckles Mallory.

"No, a plagiarist – I borrowed that from Clauswitz," admits Fox. "All we had to do at Gallipoli is get to the top of the bloody hill before the Turks, but someone thought digging-in on the beaches was a good idea…"

His voice fades as if there is nothing left to say.

Mallory sits in silence as Fox stares vaguely into the darkness. Finally, he breaks the silence.

"See here, Andrew. I'm curious about your plans for Bray."

"Bray?" snorts Fox. "Bray-sur-Somme? My God, that's ten miles from here. You don't think we're planning that far ahead, do you?"

"I'd hoped," admits Mallory.

"It's of no strategic value," replies Fox.

"What about the Somme crossings, aren't they important?"

"Not if I'm heading east."

"*But*... You've got to liberate Bray!"

"You, er, have some attachment there?"

Mallory clears his throat and stares down at his hands, hoping his eyes don't betray him.

"Bit of skirt?" suggests Fox.

"Something like that."

"Look, Jack old-boy," Fox begins, placing his cup on the table and leaning forward solemnly. "My orders are to enter Bray only if the Germans abandon her. We can't waste troops in house-to-house fighting."

"But that'll leave the Germans on your flank," insists Mallory.

"My orders are to keep moving east. This is the 'Big Push' we've been waiting for. We're going to bypass the towns and keep putting pressure on the Hun until his lines break. I'm sorry, but there it is."

"Who goes there?" asks a quivering voice. The metallic clack of a round being chambered echoes through the darkness. Before the sentry can fire, Mallory drops into the trench beside the trembling boy and brushes aside his rifle. "Careful where you point that thing," he advises.

"I... I thought you was a German," blurts the sentry.

"Clearly," replies Mallory. "Now go find the Sar' Major and bring him here."

"Y... yes sir."

"On your way."

Rifle hanging from his right hand, the sentry salutes left handed and scurries away, leaving Mallory alone in the traverse.

Mallory starts down the trench but is suddenly overcome with weariness. Taking a seat on the fire step, he sags against the dirt wall and slides his helmet from his head, plopping it down beside him. His eyes roll back and he stares up into the night sky. Artillery rumbles in the distance. He can't tell if the guns are German or Allied, but realizes it really doesn't matter.

The air is thick and still; a damp blanket, it surrounds him like a claustrophobic shroud. He exhales raggedly, the sound rattles in his chest. His ribs ache. Raising a hand, he realizes he's trembling. He grasps his fingers and squeezes them tightly. A crushing sense of loneliness overwhelms him. Breaking the silence, an anguished sob erupts from deep within. He swallows the pressure building in his chest, strangling the follow-on gasp. Head pounding, he buries his face in his hands and weeps silently. The release is cathartic, cleansing.

After a few minutes, he clears his throat and glances up, startled to find himself still alone in the trench.

"Don't lose it now, Colonel," he whispers to himself. He wipes his eyes and places his helmet back on his head. Making his way down the trench, he runs into the Sergeant Major.

"Where the hell have you been?" blurts James. "The Aussies are getting' ready to go o'er the top!"

"They're going without us," Mallory replies. "We're delayed until 10.00."

"That's the middle of the bleedin' day!"

"It's orders," snaps Mallory. "We're supposed to let the infantry breach the Hun defenses, no matter how many get killed doing it."

James peers at his commander in the darkness, noting the damp, bloodshot eyes and pale, sweating face.

"What are you looking at?" asks Mallory sharply.

"Noffin," grumbles James. "'Cept you look like hell."

Mallory chuckles darkly. "Well and truly, my friend. Well and truly."

The sun is crawling toward midday when the battalion receives orders to advance. Mallory stands in the hatch of his lumbering Mark V*, sweat streaming down his face as he scans the horizon with his binoculars. Despite his initial forecast, the infantry rapidly swept aside the German defenses and are still advancing miles ahead of the tank column.

Rolling across an abandoned battlefield, he orders the tank's hatches be opened to provide air flow through the stifling interior. James appears from the commander's hatch of a parallel tank and gives an enthusiastic thumbs-up.

As yet unwilling to display such confidence, Mallory merely returns a nod and receives a discreet middle finger in response.

A roar of a straining engine draws his attention away from James. He discovers one of his troop carrying tanks struggling to emerge from a collapsed German dugout a hundred yards away. As the battalion continues east, he watches the struggling tank finally surrender to its doom and troops pour from the open hatches to stand staring at the stricken tank. To his satisfaction, the crew immediately mounts the roof and begins to affix the unditching beam. If they're successful, the tank and its infantry passengers will catch-up to the battalion over-night. If not, the stricken Mark V* will remain just another casualty of war.

Mallory retrieves his map. Tracing the planned line of advance, he locates a road running parallel to the Somme.

Banging on the cupola to gain the driver's attention, he yells inside. "Bear left Twenty Degrees! We're looking for a road." He displays the map and points to the heavy black line slashing across the rolling hills.

The driver acknowledges the order and the beast veers northeast. Like a school trailing the pilot fish, the remaining tanks turn in unison to follow.

Within a few minutes, Mallory spots a dusty column of horse-drawn artillery advancing east. As the tanks approach, military police fan-out to halt the Australian troops clogging the road. The red caps signal the tanks to proceed onto the rutted track ahead of the paused artillery. Artillerymen stand upright on their caissons to watch the long green beasts queue-up, mount the berm and swing onto the road. Leaning through open hatches, the Mark V*s crews wave imperiously at the gunners, receiving good-natured cat-calls and rude gestures in response.

After an hour traveling down the dusty road, Bray appears several miles distant. Mallory's heart skips a beat as they approach; *will the Germans defend?* As if reading his mind, a rumble gives way to the crescendo of a dozen hurtling freight trains descending upon them.

"Hard right!" screams Mallory. "Get us off the road!"

The Mark V* churns right and careens down the embankment into the field beside the road. Mallory glances over his shoulder and spots the remainder of the battalion disbursing as artillery rounds drop around them. He ducks inside the tank as huge black, V-shaped bursts of dirt and smoke erupt from the fresh earth. One blast catches the rear of his tank, lifts the stern into the air and drops it back to earth with a crash. Mallory's face collides with the instrument panel. Adrenaline pumping, he barely tastes the blood dripping from his lips.

"Keep moving!" he screams to the driver, who leans into his steering levers with renewed intensity.

He glances back at the infantry riding at the rear of the tank; their pale, sweaty faces gawk back at him as they grapple for handholds to steady themselves against the rollicking ride across the churned field.

Inside the tank with the roar of the straining engine, Mallory is no longer able to make-out the moan of incoming projectiles, learning of the arrival only by the jarring impact of near misses. Shrapnel pings off the armor like gravel flung by an angry child.

Something clangs loudly off the overhead. The crew cringes in unison, fear turning to relief as the projectile fails to explode.

"Thank God!" exclaims a crewman.

The crew's relief is short-lived as the faint aroma of garlic begins to filter through the gun ports. A yellow haze invades the interior.

"GAS!" screams one of the gunners.

"Respirators!" orders Mallory and gropes frantically for the rubberized canvas mask connected to the respirator suspended from the canvas satchel on his chest. The crewmen grapple with their masks in a frantic attempt to defeat the gas before blisters begin to fill their lungs. Some are more successful than others as the irritant attacks exposed, moist parts of the skin.

Panicking, one crewman screams, flings his mask to the deck and tries to rip open the side hatch.

"Stop that man!" yells Mallory and the nearby crewmembers bolt from their positions to tackle the flailing man. Struggling against his terror, the crewmen force the rubberized canvas mask over his face and pull the straps over his head. Energy exhausted, the crewman ceases struggling and curls into the fetal position beneath the port-side gun, arms wrapped around his torso, trembling hysterically.

The gunner-sergeant examines the crewman and flashes Mallory a reassuring thumbs-up.

"Which way, sir?" calls the driver, his voice muffled through the mask.

Mallory thrusts open the visor and peers around rapidly. "Keep going as you are. We've got to get beyond this barrage." Peering through his mask's foggy lenses, the crew appears to move like ghosts around the hazy interior of the tank. Light penetrating the darkness through the gun slits cuts across the compartment, slicing the crew into dismembered arms and legs moving as if dangling from invisible strings. Unable to contribute to the fight, the infantry passengers in the rear steady their Lewis guns between their knees, heads bowed as if in silent prayer.

Within several minutes, the tank passes beyond the barrage and the air slowly clears. Mallory nudges open the hatch and tentatively removes his mask, sniffing the air.

"All clear!" he announces and the rest of the crew gratefully unmask. The artillery has ceased. Rising through the overhead hatch, he realizes they're alone in a pristine green field. Mallory glances back toward the direction from which they came. Smoke rises in the distance with the greasy black consistency of burning fuel and ammo. A yellowish haze clings to the periphery of the battlefield.

"Stop," he mumbles. The tank continues. "Stop, damn it!"

The tank jerks to a stop, its engine sputtering to a halt.

Mallory dumps the helmet from his head and peers around in wonder. Birds are singing, a light summer breeze whips the tall grass that waves like rippling waves upon a green sea. A church steeple stands majestically in the east. He breathes-in the fresh air with an overwhelming feeling of contentment. He leans inside.

"Open the hatches," he orders. "Let's get this thing aired-out."

The hatches creak open and grimy faces appear in the openings.

"I want to go back to the infantry," announces one of the Lewis gunners.

"What? You ain't never had it so good," chides a crewman.

Mallory sighs and glances contentedly around at the lush green field. Something moves among the tall grass. Peering intently, he spots a camouflaged position a few dozen yards behind the tank. The crew of Australian machine gunners gawk up at him from over the barrel of their Vickers machinegun. The loader gestures straight ahead and mouths the word, "G-E-R-M-A-N-S."

Mallory glances abruptly in the direction of the gesture and spots gray-clad uniforms skittering among the wood line a hundred yards away. *CRACK!* A round pings off the open hatch cover. "Shit!" blurts Mallory and drops inside.

"Davy," he calls to the driver. "Get us the hell out of here!"

"Which way?" asks the driver.

"Backwards. We're ahead of our forward line of troops!"

CHAPTER 31
Battle of Amiens, Outskirts of Bray-sur-Somme, France
12 August 1918

"Looks far too peaceful," grunts Mallory, sweeping the countryside with his binoculars. To his right flows the Somme. To his front spread rolling hills capped by the steeple of St. Nicholas Church at a mile's distance. "The Hun may be collapsing, but we're damned unable to exploit it," sighs Mallory.

James flips open his notebook. "Of the forty-two tanks we started with three days ago, we're down to four operational Mark Vs and two Mark V*s."

"Casualties?"

"Not as bad as all that," replies James. "Most of the tanks were ditched or disabled by mechanical problems. Only a few hit by Hun artillery."

"I don't want a bloody excuses, I want numbers," snaps Mallory.

"Eighteen dead, forty-six wounded," replies James in a wounded voice.

"Nearly ten-percent casualties," sighs Mallory.

"I've already sent up the list," responds James. "Do you want to see it?"

Mallory shakes his head. "No," he replies wistfully. "Not right now."

James reaches into his haversack and withdraws a bottle of Scotch. He pours a healthy portion into a tin cup and hands it to Mallory, who takes it gratefully.

"You not having any?" he asks.

"You've got me cup."

"That never stopped you before."

"True," admits James and takes a long gulp from the bottle. "Ahhhh," he sighs and wipes his mouth with his sleeve. "Mother's milk."

As Mallory takes a sip, he spots Fourth Army's intelligence chief, Colonel Cranston, picking his way among the battle-scarred tanks.

Cranston catches Mallory's eye and strides over to the Mark V*. "Ah, there you are Mallory. I was afraid you'd become a casualty."

"No such luck," snorts Mallory.

"I should be checkin' the crews are fed," announces James. "Sir." He nods to Cranston and skulks away.

"So, what brings you up here to the pointy-end of the stick?" asks Mallory.

"A matter of some sensitivity, I'm afraid," admits Cranston.

"Sounds ominous," replies Mallory.

Cranston seizes Mallory's sleeve and leads him away from the crews lounging around their tanks. "I don't suppose you've heard from your gal in Bray, have you?"

Mallory glances around to see if anyone else is listening. "No. Why?"

"Her nephew, François," replies Cranston. "He hasn't returned to our lines for more than three weeks. We were counting on his communications from Parisienne for the next phase of the offensive."

"Parisienne?"

"Er, your friend," clarifies Cranston. "That's her code-name."

"Maybe he's been captured," offers Mallory. "It's not easy to pass back and forth through the lines."

"Or Parisienne has been discovered and put out of commission."

"Put out of commission? You mean killed."

"… Or arrested," offers Cranston.

"… And shot," replies Mallory.

"Or not," concludes Cranston. "My point is, we don't know."

"Is that what you've come here to tell me?"

"The gist of it."

The two officers stand in awkward silence.

"You want something, Colonel," declares Mallory finally. "I can feel it and it's coming straight right at me."

"The thing is – I understand you speak French," replies Cranston.

"Well enough," confirms Mallory, a hint of suspicion in his voice. "But not enough to pass for a native, if that's what you're implying."

"No, but you could probably pass for one in the eyes of a German."

"A German?"

"You see. We need to know precisely who is holding Bray and what his intentions are."

"And you think they'll tell me if I ask politely in French?"

"Don't be dense," snaps Cranston. "I want you to go to Bray and ask Parisienne."

"You want me to become a spy," observes Mallory.

"Let's just call it a reconnaissance."

"Dressed as a Frenchman…"

"Well, yes."

"That *is* a spy," replies Mallory. "The Germans would put me up against a wall and shoot me – same as we would do to one of them."

"Perhaps," concedes Cranston. "But then again, you have a vested interest in our forces not bypassing Bray."

Mallory glances up sharply. "Vested interest? What the *hell* are you trying to say?"

"I'm just offering you the chance to save Bray," replies Cranston reasonably. "If you'd rather not risk it, I certainly understand."

Mallory sighs. "So if I was 'interested', how would I get through to the city?"

"We've identified a thinly-held portion of the Hun line through which you could pass relatively unobserved."

"With what object?"

"Sorry?"

"What do you expect to gain from my making contact with Elise… er… Parisienne?"

"We believe she's well-positioned to obtain the German order of battle north of the Somme."

"And you want me to bring the information back to Allied lines?"

"Yes."

"By when?"

"End of the week," replies Cranston. "But in no case later than August 20th."

"And if I don't volunteer?"

"Absent mitigating intelligence, we'll have to recommend bypassing Bray."

"And it'll be flattened by our artillery," concludes Mallory.

"If the Germans resist. Yes, I suppose so."

"And you'd call that a victory?" growls Mallory.

"Lieutenant Colonel Mallory, this 'push' is our last, best hope for ending the war before winter. We'll do whatever necessary to ensure this thing drags-on no longer!"

"Well, if everyone's dead, I suppose the war will have to end. Won't it?"

Growing angry, Cranston thrusts a finger in Mallory's face. "Need I remind you the opening day of our offensive saw the largest single-day haul of Hun prisoners ever?" demands Cranston. "We tore a hole fifteen miles wide and seven miles deep. Communications intercepts indicate Field Marshal Ludendorf refers to August 8th as the 'Black Day for the German Army'?"

"No, *WE* tore a hole in the German lines," snaps Mallory, motioning vaguely toward the troops dug-in in the surrounding darkness. "*You and your staff* were sitting back in Amiens sipping tea and writing each other commendations. Just how black a day do you estimate it will be for the villagers when we destroy Bray?"

"I've seen you flatten villages with your tanks without giving it a second thought," snorts Cranston, waving a dismissive hand. "It only matters to you now because of your little whore …"

Cranston's comment is cut short when Mallory's fist collides with the older man's face, knocking him to the ground. Shocked, Cranston stares disbelievingly up at Mallory, his wispy gray hair mussed, hand rubbing his jaw.

"*I could have you shot!*"

"That's your privilege," growls Mallory, standing over the prostrate officer, fists clenched to strike again.

Cranston rises to a sitting position and stares up at Mallory, head cocked as if studying him. "You're a queer duck," he announces. "But you're a fighter, I'll give you that. Besides, I suppose my comment *was* a bit out-of-line."

"Yes, it was," replies Mallory flatly.

"So?"

"So, what?"

"Are you going into Bray, or not?"

A flare rises lazily over the German positions, casting the wood line in long shadows. Mallory shelters in a forward trench, dressed as a French civilian. A dozen Tommies surround him, the glow of burning embers illuminating their young faces.

"What are we waiting for?" asks Mallory.

"The company commander," replies the sergeant. "He's warnin' the sentries so's we don' get shot at."

"Good idea," chuckles Mallory nervously.

The sergeant looks him up-and-down. "You really a colonel?"

"Lieutenant-Colonel," corrects Mallory. "Yes."

The sergeant shrugs. "Ain't used to seein' colonels do stuff like this."

"You and I both," agrees Mallory.

A tall, mustachioed officer appears around the traverse. "Sir, it's time to go now," announces the captain. "You'll go out with our routine patrol so it won't appear that we're up to anything unusual. You can take leave once they've got you near enough the wood."

"Right," responds Mallory and dashes his cigarette butt to the floor of the trench. He slings his satchel, checks to ensure his pistol is loaded and shoves it into the side pouch.

"It's probably best if you go unarmed," advises the captain. "If you're captured with a weapon, you'll be shot."

"I'm taking this to ensure than I'm not captured – not alive anyway."

"Good point," replies the captain. "Can't imagine Fritz'd be very pleased with you."

"No, I dare say," replies Mallory dryly. "So, I'll be coming back this way before the end of the week. Will your unit still be here?"

"Probably not. We're due to rotate out of the line in a few days," replies the captain with a shrug.

"Oh, great. So, if I obtain the required information, I'm likely to be shot coming back through the line?"

"Ha! No sir. We're not so rigid. Patrols will be sent out between Midnight and two nightly until the twentieth. The challenge will be 'flash', to which you'll reply 'thunder'. They'll bring you back through the lines."

"Flash. Thunder. Right."

The captain checks his watch. "Off you go, then."

The twelve-man patrol ascends the ladder; Mallory follows them into the darkness. Working its way slowly across the grassy field, the group makes its way to the edge of the woods.

"Head directly east, sir," whispers the sergeant. "There's a gap in the Hun lines between the woods and the river that'll allow you to reach Bray directly."

"Thank you Sergeant," Mallory replies earnestly. "I'll be back in a few days."

Due to the speed of the advance, the woods north of the Somme remain largely intact. Eerie, dark and alive with strange noises, the woods seem haunted. Despite the moonless night, Mallory feels as if he is walking naked in broad daylight, the entire world able to see and hear him trampling through the uncut woods. Shaking-off the chill running up his spine, he squints at his hand-held compass and proceeds cautiously eastward.

After a half mile, the woods thin and he stumbles-upon several lines of open, sparsely-manned trenches. Finding no way around them, he slithers up to the edge of the nearest trench and peers down into the darkness. It appears abandoned. He slides into the trench, withdraws the pistol from his ruck and squats by a traverse. It suddenly occurs to him mufti is a poor ruse; there isn't likely to be a military-aged French peasant within a hundred miles of the front. Any that is, will likely be either a deserter or a spy. A light suddenly appears at the end of the trench and disappears almost immediately. Someone has pulled-back the gas cape covering the entrance to a dugout and let it flop closed behind him.

Mallory raises his pistol and waits. No one appears. Mist and fog mask his movement as he carefully climbs up the backside of the trench.

"Wer da?"

Mallory freezes, hand sweaty on his pistol's grip.

"Sind sie das, Ernst?"

"Ja," rasps Mallory.

"Ja? Kommst du hier," demands the voice irritably.

"*Shit!*" growls Mallory and drops back into the trench. Landing in a squat, he springs to his feet and thrusts his pistol into the startled face. The German gasps and stumbles backward. Mallory places his finger to his lips. "Shhhhh."

The German nods, his mouth moving dumbly as he raises his arms in resignation.

Mallory shoves the man against the back wall of the trench, eyes cutting rabidly in all directions as he considers his next move.

"Sorry, Fritz," mumbles Mallory and pistol whips the petrified German across the side of his face, knocking him unconscious; the man slides to the ground. Realizing he can leave no witness, Mallory reverses the pistol in his grip, grasping the barrel he raises the butt of the weapon over his head to strike again. He hesitates. *Do it!* his mind screams, though his conscience searches desperately for a way-out. "Oh, you're going to Hell for this," he mumbles. He brings the butt down sharply against the man's skull. There's a sickening *crack*, a moan, a cough. Mallory strikes again and again until no further sound emerges.

Grasping the German's collar, he drags the body into a nearby funk hole. Stripping the boots and pants from the corpse, he discards his peasant's clothing and dresses in the dead man's uniform. Examining the bloody feldmützen, he casts aside the cap and rummages around the dugout for replacement headgear. Atop a makeshift bunk, he discovers a coal-scuttle helmet and slips it on, fastening the strap beneath his chin. Unfamiliar with German rank insignia, he examines his shoulder strap and determines he's at least a corporal. He rolls the corpse beneath a cot and packs blankets and equipment against the opening to hide the body. Seizing the German's abandoned rifle, he cautiously draws the bolt partway to the rear and ensures there's a round in the chamber then leaves the bunker.

The rumble of artillery echoes through the trench, projectiles falling in harassing fire along the German lines. Under the clamor of the barrage, he slips from the dugout and darts up the communications trench at a trot. The remaining defenders have taken cover inside protective dugouts, leaving only the occasional sentry to weather the storm of steel. Mallory hurries past the cowering sentries without making eye-contact.

As he nears a rear of the position, he spots a half-completed sap leading off toward the woods. He dodges into the slit and emerges a dozen feet from the trees. Dashing the final few yards, he heaves himself onto the forest floor, gasping for breath. Lying in silence for several minutes, he awaits indication he's been discovered. Finally, hearing no alarm, he climbs to his feet, brushes the leaves from his tunic, and starts down an overgrown path toward Bray.

Entering the town, he discovers a confused melee of rear-area troops, transport personnel and the young, pale faces of under-aged draftees, eyes peering in fear from beneath the brims of over-sized helmets. Steel-wheeled trucks rattle along the cobblestone streets. Scrawny, gun-shy horses drag gray wooden carts laden with food and ammunition. Beside the road, a cast-iron mobile kitchen belches smoke from a wood-fired stove as sausages and cabbage boil in huge pots, the aroma mixing with the odor of sweating men and stench of horse manure sharing the street. A cook stirs a cauldron of ersatz coffee that reeks of boiling tree bark.

Rifle slung casually over his shoulder, Mallory dodges across the crowded street and enters a darkened alley. He discovers the French street signs have been supplemented with Gothic-looking German declarations of occupation. Navigating from memory, he finally locates the familiar alley. He approaches the rear of a gray stone house, trying the handle and finding the door locked. He knocks. Claire, the nearly blind housekeeper, enters the kitchen and waves him away with an impatient flip of her hand.

He taps insistently on the glass. She sets aside her broom and shuffles irritably across the room. Removing the key from the hook, she unlocks the door and cracks it open a few inches.

"Nous sommes fermés! Allez-vous en!" She growls.

"Claire! It's me, Jack!" He hastily removes his helmet and smiles at her.

She squints at him, studying his face in the flickering light of the candle-lit room. A veined hand springs to cover her mouth. "Why are you dressed like les Boches?"

"It's not important. Où est Elise?"

She gasps and glances back over her shoulder. "Le Boche are everywhere. You must leave!" she blurts and attempts to shut the door. Mallory shoves his foot between the door and jamb.

"What the hell is wrong with you?" he rasps. "I need to see Elise!"

With gentle pressure, he overcomes Claire's resistance and forces his way into the kitchen.

"Is she here?"

Claire nods apprehensively.

"Can you get her for me?" he presses. "S'il vous plaît?"

She gazes at him pitifully. "Oui, Jack," she sighs. "Une minute." Motioning for him to sit, she shuffles from the room, the kitchen door swinging closed behind her.

Mallory draws a chair from beneath the scrubbed kitchen table and drops his pack on the floor beside it. He takes a seat and places the rifle across his lap, his right foot tapping nervously on the stone floor. He hears the familiar squeaks and thumps emanating from the floors above and shakes his head sadly.

Within a few minutes, he detects footfalls on the stairs leading down the rear of the house into the kitchen. His grip tightens on the rifle, finger brushing the trigger guard as he directs the muzzle toward the door. The door creaks open and Elise's face appears around the edge.

"Mon Dieu! C'est toi," she moans.

He rises awkwardly and rests the rifle against the table. "Oui. C'est moi."

She glances back over her shoulder, steps into the room and closes the door behind her. "What are you doing 'ere?" she demands.

He steps toward her; she backs away, arms crossed defiantly.

"I'm looking for you," he replies. "We've haven't heard from François in several weeks. We were… concerned…"

"Yes, he told me he'd made contact."

"So…?"

Her face darkens. "François is dead," she croaks. "He was killed trying to cross the lines two weeks ago."

"Oh, Elise..." Mallory steps forward and reaches out for her.

She raises her hands, blocking him.

"What's wrong?" he asks gently.

"He was killed by the British."

"My God," groans Mallory. "Elise, I'm so sorry."

"It doesn't matter," she sighs dismissively. "If not the English, then the Boche. Ce n'est pas important."

"I'm certain it was an accident," he offers lamely.

"As I said, it does not matter…"

Again he steps toward her and she again shrugs from his embrace, pulling her bulky robe tightly around her as if fending off a sudden chill.

"Why won't you let me hold you?"

"*Are you joking?*" she snaps. "I'm a spy, you're a British officer – in a Boche uniform – and the house is full of les alemans! This is not time pour la romance!"

"But…"

"You must leave," she insists firmly.

"Then come with me," he insists. "Bring Adele and come with me. I know a way through the lines."

"C'est impossible! If I leave with you, what will happen to my girls?"

"You're not safe here," he insists.

"None of us are safe! You were insane to come here," she blurts. "You could be killed. You could get us *all killed!*"

"We have to know if the Germans are going to defend the city," he explains. "If so, our armies will bypass it and artillery will flatten the place."

"But they can't..."

"They can and they will. So...?"

"I don't know," she sighs. "The Forty-Third Infanterie Division occupies the city. Many of its veterans died of the Flu and Typhoid over the past months, so it's manned mostly by young replacements."

"But will they fight if we approach in-force?"

Elise shrugs miserably. "Many of the new soldiers are sympathetic to the Bolsheviks and resent their officers. They sing songs of revolution and disobey orders."

"So you think they'll surrender?" he asks hopefully.

"*I don't know*. Now, *go!*" She pushes him toward the door.

Sweeping her hand away, he wraps his arm around her, hand against the small of her back, and pulls her to him. Lips meeting, he can taste the sweetness of her breath, feel the softness of her lips.

He freezes.

Slowly his hand slips from her hip and drops to his side; he draws away.

"No..."

CHAPTER 32
Battle of Amiens, Bray-sur-Somme, France
23 August 1918

"Get the battalion ready," barks Mallory as he approaches a half-dozen parked Mark V*s. "We move before first light."

"I wish you'd tell me what's bothering you," grumbles James. "You've been actin' diff'rent ever since you returned from Bray."

"Nothing's 'wrong', James. Other than I don't know if we can take the town without killing the girls."

"The Aussies tried to take it last night, but they were driven back by artillery and gas."

"Yeah, I know. But they managed to get a battalion of Pioneers on the heights southwest of town. They've got good observation and will cover our advance with Stokes Mortars. The Aussies are going to throw three battalions at Bray in the morning behind a rolling barrage right up to the edge of town. If they can't take it, IV Corps artillery will level the place."

"Jeezus," breathes James. "What are their chances?"

"I don't know. But I'm assigning a company of Mark V*s to accompany the push."

"I can't see a damned thing!" calls the driver over the thunder of artillery.

Mallory squints into his periscope. A hundred yards ahead, explosions erupt in rapid succession, lighting-up the pre-dawn sky. Amid the flashes, he can just detect the silhouettes of flat Brody helmets and fixed bayonets of the Australian battalions advancing on the city.

"Bear right five degrees," he orders. "In this darkness, we can't see the Aussies so they'll have to watch out for *us*."

The driver stares back at Mallory open-mouthed. The expression on Mallory's face is unlike any he's ever seen. Beyond grim, there is coldness in Mallory's hardened features.

God help the Germans – and the Aussies.

As they near the edge of town, fire from a dozen Maxims send the infantry diving for cover. Flat, metallic slaps echo through the tank as bullets strike the frontal armor. Spall showers the interior; the driver releases his levers and flings his arms over his face, the molten steel chips burning holes through his woolen sleeves.

The tank shudders to a stop.

Mallory grasps the driver's shoulder roughly. "Keep moving!" he snarls. "Straight ahead! Keep your eyes fixed on that bloody steeple and park this damned thing right in front of it!"

"Y-yes sir!"

The driver shoves the levers forward.

As the tank resumes its advance, Mallory drops from the commander's seat and mans the forward-mounted Lewis Gun. He rips back the charging handle and leans into the stock, eyes fixed over the sights, looking for targets.

There! He squeezes the trigger. *Thut-thut-thut.* Empty shell casings spew onto the deck as he rakes the edge of town, tracers drawing laser-like lines paths to the German positions.

"Gunners!" he shouts. "There are your targets! Take out those bloody guns!"

A cannon erupts beside him, the blast sucking the wind from his lungs. A corresponding flash bursts at the edge of town, followed by another and another as the battalion's remaining tanks concentrate their firepower on the Bray's defenses.

Adrenaline pumping, Mallory's hearing fades, peripheral vision narrowing as he fixates on muzzle flashes from the defending Maxims. Overheating, oil evaporates off his Lewis Gun's receiver, clouding his vision as he walks .303 caliber rounds along the dark shrubbery at the edge of town.

Abruptly, the supporting artillery ceases, leaving the village backlit solely by the sun inching its way over the horizon.

"Sir! We're outrunning our infantry!" reports a gearsman.

Mallory turns on the gearsman, his face a mask of revulsion. He glares at the crewman and remains mute.

The rest of the crew members glance warily at each other.

"What the *hell* is he doing?" shouts James as the remainder of the battalion slows to await the infantry.

"Maybe he doesn't see us," replies the lieutenant commanding James' tank.

Slowly it dawns on James. "Oh, mother of God. He knows! He's going in alone."

"That's suicide!"

"Damned right," snarls James.

"What do we do Sar' Major?"

"Bloody well catch-up!"

"But the battalion…?"

"He *is* the battalion!" barks James. "Now get us up there or Fritz is gonna swamp him!"

The lieutenant studies the burly sergeant major for a moment then nods. "Right. Edmonds," he orders the driver. "Catch up with the colonel! Dawson!" he shouts to his signaler. "Signal the rest of the battalion to continue the advance. We're going in with the Colonel!"

CRACK! THUMP!

Over open sights, a German 10 Centimeter gun fires at Mallory's Mark V*. The round shrieks past the tank and explodes fifty yards behind.

"Get that bloody gun!" yells Mallory to the gunners.

Drenched in sweat, the loaders retrieve shells from the rack, heave them into the gun's breach and slam the receiver with a loud *clang!* "Round up!"

Gunners lean into push bars and swivel the cannons forward.

"No target!" announces the port-side gunner.

A flash erupts from the edge of the road, the round landing twenty yards ahead of the tank and showering it with mud and debris.

"I've got 'im," The port side gunner shouts. "He's hidin' in the bocage beside the road." He nudges the gun slightly to align the sights and squeezes the trigger. *CRACK!* The round erupts from the gun and plows into the German gun position. Bricks and sandbags burst into the air; surviving gun crews scatter, running and stumbling frantically away from the smoking position.

"Again!" Mallory screams. "Keep hitting them until the gun's destroyed."

"Sah!"

"Port-side," growls Mallory. "Find a target and engage! I don't care what the hell it is. *Engage!*"

"Right!" replies the gunner and begins sweeping his sight along the edge of town. Locating a Maxim, he quickly dispatches the crew with a single, well-placed round.

As the tank rumbles toward the village, Mallory realizes the main entrance is blocked by a makeshift barricade. Maxims pour fire on the tank from either side.

"Get onto the road!" orders Mallory. "We're going through the front door."

The tank jerks left, angles up the embankment and swivels onto the carriageway.

"Gunners…!"

Before he completes the order, the tank's gunners pour rounds into the barricade and machinegun positions behind the hedgerows on either side of the road. As they reach the damaged barricade, the Mark V* claws over the top of the wrecked ox carts and stacked furniture, wood cracking like firecrackers beneath its steel tracks. With a lurch, the tank crashes down on the other side of the barricade, clipping a small building and collapsing the outer wall in a cloud of bricks and dust.

Gray uniforms scatter in all directions as rounds from the tank's Lewis Guns chase Germans fleeing down the intersecting alleys. A pair of panicked draft horses breaks loose from their handler and take flight into the town, ammo and supplies spilling from the dray cart onto the cobblestone street.

"Which way, sir?" the driver calls frantically.

"The church! Head for the church! Just keep moving whatever you do. If they regroup and counterattack, we're buggered!"

Shocked administrative troops stationed in the center of town flee the tank's approach. The church looms into view. "Gunners," Mallory calls to the infantrymen riding in the tank. "Here's your chance to make 'em pay!"

"Bloody good!" and "Good on ya, sir!" come the eager replies. "Anything to get out of this contraption!"

The tank jerks to a halt.

"*Now!*"

The steel doors spring open and a dozen machine gunners leap through the openings. Lewis Guns at their hips, they dash into the square engaging the confused Germans with short bursts of fire. Fleeing defenders stumble and collapse in sad heaps. Last out, Mallory surveys the square and directs placement of the gun crews.

"Take cover behind the fences," he shouts. Glancing up at the bell tower, he points. "Get a couple of guns up there, too!"

As the gunners deploy, a roar draws Mallory's attention to a column of Mark V*s approaching down the main road into the town center. Mallory steps into the street and waves them forward. A hatch pops open on the lead tank and a familiar face appears.

"About damn time you got here!" calls Mallory.

"You... bloody... ," sputters James. "Were you *tryin'* to get killed?"

"Oh, don't be such a mother! Now get these tanks dispersed!"

James points to each tank and directs it toward differing locations around the square, establishing a 360-degree defensive position in the center of town. Lewis gunners disgorge from the arriving tanks and take up positions behind stone walls and fences.

James emerges from the side hatch and approaches Mallory, who stands in the open pointing-out targets to the gunners. "Might want to take a bit 'o cover," he advises.

THWACK!

A bullet strikes the cobblestones at Mallory's feet, showering him with chipped rock.

"Right you are!" agrees Mallory and the two of them dash for cover beside James' tank.

"What now?" asks James.

"As soon as the infantry arrives to secure the area, we'll head down to the house."

"Think they'll be okay?"

"How the hell would I know?" snaps Mallory.

"Here they come!" yells one of the gunners.

Australian infantry begin to appear from the alleys and arrive in the square. An officer glances around and, determining it's safe, holsters his pistol and approaches Mallory. Snapping to attention, he announces. "Captain Caffey, sir. Fortieth Battalion, AIF, at your service!"

Mallory offers his hand. "Well done, Captain. Glad to see you."

"Well done, *sir*," he replies. "What a marvelous charge!"

"Where are the other battalions?"

"Dispursed throughout the village, sir. We captured Hun stores at the railroad station on the edge of town. The men are passing out food to the few locals remaining in the area. Anything we can do for you?"

James clears his throat.

"Yes," replies Mallory. "I need a squad for security. Sergeant Major James and I need to check-out a couple of these buildings."

"My men can do that, sir!" blurts the captain. "No need riskin' your own lives."

"It's all right, Captain," assures Mallory. "This is a personal matter."

"As you wish, sir." He turns and surveys his troops. "Slattery! Gather your squad and report to the colonel!"

"Sah!"

Within a few minutes, Mallory and James start up Rue Gambetta, a squad of heavily-armed Aussies in-tow. Covering each other, they dash, one-by-one, across the street and enter the alley. Rubble and debris of battle are strewn across their paths. Weaving between the detritus, they cautiously approach the end of the passage.

"Wait here," hisses Mallory to the Australians. He and James approach the end of the alley. James peers around the corner and draws-back quickly.

"Germans!"

"What?" blurts Mallory and chances a quick peek. Abandoned hospital wagons and stretcher cases litter the courtyard. Beside the kitchen door are stacked corpses beneath blood-drenched sheets. From the front of the building hangs a torn Red Cross flag.

"They turned the house into a *hospital?*"

"Well, we've taken the town, so I say we claim the spoils."

"Sergeant," calls Mallory to the squad leader. "Take a look."

The sergeant peers around the corner.

"I need your men to secure the courtyard," explains Mallory. "Can you do it?"

"Sure, sir."

"Then get on with it."

The sergeant waves his squad to join him. After a quick huddle, the Aussies fan out across the courtyard and rush into the midst of the abandoned stretchers, disarming the few wounded showing signs of resistance. Pistol drawn, Mallory dashes to the front door with James in pursuit. They crash through the door and find the foyer crowded with more wounded. The aroma of women's perfume mixes repulsively with the coppery smell of blood and pungent, cheesy stench of putrefying wounds.

A hand grasps his ankle. "Wasser," croaks a blinded German. "Bitte…"

Mallory shakes his ankle from the man's grip and pushes past dead and dying Germans. He discovers the living room has been turned into an operating theater. Once elegant rugs are rolled-up and stacked against the wall, the dining and kitchen tables have been dragged into the middle of the room to serve as operating tables. A blood-spattered surgeon glances up from his work, his long-handled mustache quivering as sweat rolls down his large, pale forehead. Several masked nurses stand astride him, bloodied instruments poised in mid-air.

"If you are going to shoot," growls the doctor in a heavy German accent. "Do it now and save me the trouble of amputating this man's leg."

Mallory lowers his pistol. "Where are the girls?"

"Girls?"

"The one's working here at the house. Where are they?"

The doctor glances at the nurses on either side of him. "Fräuleins?"

Both lay aside their instruments and pull-down their masks.

James recognizes one of them. "Adele!"

"Hello husband," she replies with a wan smile. Her eyes are bloodshot and tired; her once youthful face lined and gray.

"Husband?" asks the doctor in surprise. "You didn't tell me you were married to a Britisher."

"I…," James starts. He holsters his pistol and picks his way clumsily between the wounded littering the floor.

"May I, Herr Doctor?" asks Adele.

"Ja, ja. Make haste, though. We have surgery to perform."

She drops the saw on the table and dashes the remaining few feet to meet James. They collide, lips locked passionately together as tears mix on their cheeks. They release each other and immediately re-embrace.

"I thought I'd never see you again!" sobs Adele.

"I know, darling. I know," gasps James and kisses her again. "We'll never be apart again."

"Ah, ah," cautions the doctor. "You need to separate long enough for her to help me before the ether wears off."

"Yeah, right," replies James. He releases Adele and she returns reluctantly to the operating table, eyes glistening as she stares back at him with an enormous smile.

"Where's Elise?" asks James.

Mallory creeps up the stairs, pistol directed toward the darkened hallway. Atop the landing, he discovers Elise's bedroom door ajar. With the muzzle of his pistol, he nudges open the door and steps warily inside. The closet hangs open. Elise's clothes are strewn around the room. Mismatched shoes clutter the floor. A dozen overturned perfume bottles litter her vanity. Her stool and desk chair lay cast aside.

He nods miserably and lowers his pistol. Leaving the room, he trudges down the stairs, encountering James moving the other direction.

"Did you find her?" asks James eagerly.

Mallory shakes his head morosely. "No. She's gone."

"Gone?" blurts James. "What the hell do you mean, *gone?*"

"Packed her stuff and left in a hurry, it seems."

"What the…?" James darts up the remaining stairs as Mallory descends into the foyer.

Mallory stops, holsters his pistol, thrusts his hands in his pockets and glances around the familiar room. Finally, he nods, sighs and wanders out the front door. As he enters the courtyard, an Australian ambulance company draws up before the house.

Medics and orderlies pour from the rear of the trucks dragging crates of medical supplies and equipment into the yard. He walks aimlessly through the busy throng without seeming to notice them.

"*OY!*"

Ignoring the shout, Mallory turns down the alley and wanders toward the tanks parked beside the church.

The sound of boots on the pavement causes him to glance back over his shoulder. James approaches at a trot.

"Where the hell... are you going?" gasps James between breaths.

"I've got a battalion to command," replies Mallory.

"What the hell is going on? Where's Elise?"

Mallory turns and faces his friend. "She's ditched me old boy. She retreated along with the Germans."

Red-faced, James sputters incoherently before finally finding words. "That... absurd!"

Mallory takes a deep breath followed by a shuddering sigh. "When I saw Elise last week, I noticed something unusual. She kept pulling her robe around her like she was cold or something."

"So?"

"James, it's middle of July."

James stares at Mallory as if he's left something unsaid. He shakes his head. "Yeah, so?"

"She's starting to show..."

"... Show?"

"She's pregnant."

Mallory's words hit James like a slap in the face. "Bloody hell!"

"Indeed."

"Well..."

"I'm not the father, James. I haven't been with her in nearly five months. She wasn't so far along."

"How the hell do you know?"

"I confronted her," sighs Mallory. "She told me the father is a German officer she's been sleeping with. That makes her a collaborator. Now that the Germans are retreating, she can hardly remain in the village."

"Blimey..."

Mallory nods in agreement. "So Adele is all right?" he asks finally.

"Well enough," replies James. "Been assistin' the Hun surgeon. Seems she used to be a nurse before the war. Who knew?"

"Yes, 'who knew'?"

CHAPTER 33
Battle of Amiens, Bray-sur-Somme, France
27 August 1918

"Find Sar' Major James and tell him to get over here," snaps Mallory. "We've got movement orders."

"Sah!" The private salutes and takes off at a trot.

Mallory unfolds a map against the scarred front armor of his Mark V*. Several of the surviving company commanders close-in around him.

"We're ordered back to the rear to rest and re-fit," he explains to the officers. "Despite the success of the breakthrough, more than half our tanks are either destroyed or ditched somewhere out there on the battlefield. We've got to recover and repair what we can and prepare to receive new tanks and crews before the next push."

From the corner of his eye, he spots James crossing the street. A second glance reveals Adele rushing alongside him, a robe wrapped around her narrow shoulders. Several of the tank crews gawk at the lovely pale red head, but remain silent, fearing the wrath of their Sergeant Major.

"We've been given west-bound priority on the Albert-Amiens road," continues Mallory as James and Adele arrive at the periphery of the group. "A platoon of Military Police will arrive within the hour to provide escort. It'll be an administrative march, so we'll move in-column unless there are Hun aircraft about. Any questions?"

"Does that mean we can travel with hatches open?" asks a captain.

Mallory glances up at the cloudless summer sky. "God, yes. Looks like it's going to be another scorcher. Anything else?" Hearing nothing, he retrieves the map and begins to re-fold it. "Right. Dismissed."

The officers disperse.

"You heard that, James?" asks Mallory.

"Yes, sir!"

"Then kiss her goodbye and let's get moving." He tucks the map inside his satchel.

"Sir, Adele's got somethin' you need to hear," announces James.

"Look," sighs Mallory. "I know what happened. Elise already told me. I sincerely hope she and her Hun officer will be very happy…"

"*Sir*," interrupts James. "Would you please *shut the hell up* and listen to what she has to say?"

Stunned at James' sudden outburst, Mallory takes a deep breath and sighs. "All right, Sar' Major. Adele, you have something to say?"

"Oui. You are a *bâtard arrogante!*" she blurts.

"My, how original…" He shoves the map into his satchel and retrieves his helmet.

"You are so full of yourself and 'ave so little regard for Elise you are willing – eager – to believe lies!" hisses Adele.

"What the hell are you talking about?"

"Elise! You curse her for betraying you. But you are le traître!"

"Look here," replies Mallory. "I told James I wasn't going to ask how she got her information. But she threw it in my face! Now she's pregnant by her Hun lover…"

"No!"

"I saw her belly," insists Mallory. "She was *definitely* pregnant."

"Yes, but it wasn't the way you believe."

"There's only one way to get pregnant," he scoffs.

He catches her arm in mid-air as she lunges to slap him.

James wraps his ape-like arms around Adele and pulls her way. "There's no need for that, love."

"Vous êtes un cochon!" she shouts.

"It was *her* decision," responds Mallory defensively.

"No, it wasn't. He forced himself on her!"

"*What?*"

"She was raped, you ass!"

Mallory's face pales, a coldness crawling through his chest. "W-when?" he stutters.

"The day after les allemands seized the village." Tears well-up in her eyes as she recounts the story. "We were planning to flee to Amiens, but the British withdrew before we knew what was 'appening."

"A mix-up in orders," mumbles Mallory. "That shouldn't have happened."

Adele wipes her eyes with trembling fingers. "Soon after they occupied the village, a Boche officer came to the house and insisted we reopen it for his men. Elise refused and he struck her. She resisted, but he... he..." Breaking down in tears, she buries her face in James' burly shoulder.

"Why did she lie to me?" croaks Mallory.

"To protect you!" sobs Adele. "She realized if you knew what really happened, you would never leave her behind. She loves you. She couldn't bear to risk you being caught and killed."

"I tried to get her to come with me, but..." Mallory buries his face in his hands. "Why didn't she come?"

"She would not leave her girls defenceless. As long as she remained, we were all under the Boche major's protection!"

"So... where is she?"

"When the attack began, he sent his men to the house. They made her gather her belongings and took her away as a hostage."

"A *hostage?*"

Adele nods miserably. "It is the way of les allemands. It is to prevent provocateurs from attacking them during the retreat."

Mallory's eyes turn eastward. "So, she out there... somewhere..."

"Oui," Adele sighs. "Somewhere..."

Mallory stalks across the courtyard toward a squad of Red Caps guarding a group of dejected-looking German prisoners. Grimy and soot-covered, they've been stripped of personal belongings, medals and field gear. There is a glimmer of relief in their eyes.

"Sah!" reports a sergeant. "What can I do for you?"

"I just want to speak with your prisoners," Mallory announces as he attempts to push-past.

"Hold on! You can't just barge over there by yourself."

Mallory un-holsters his pistol. "Don't worry about me," he growls as he eyes the frightened Germans.

"Sir, I seen that look before. Ya can't kill men after they've surrendered. It ain't right."

"I'll only kill a few. The rest will talk."

Sensing the growing tension, the prisoners begin to fidget uncomfortably.

"Captain!" calls the sergeant to a passing officer. "Could you come 'ere for a moment?"

A nattily-dressed officer marches over. "What is it Sergeant?" he asks irritably.

The sergeant nods toward Mallory.

"Sorry, sir. How may I be of assistance?" asks the captain.

"The... uh... colonel wants to interrogate some of our prisoners, sir," blurts the sergeant.

"Ah, yes. Well. Sir," replies the officer. "Protocol requires we process the prisoners first. We'll turn them over to military intelligence and you can obtain the interrogation reports from them."

"Captain," growls Mallory. "The Hun has taken some of the villagers hostage. We've got to know where they're taking them. We don't have time to follow *protocol*."

"Sir, French civilians are not the concern of His Majesty's forces..."

"They are a concern of *mine*, Captain," snaps Mallory. "That makes them a concern of *yours*. Now are you going to help me find out where the hostages were taken or do I need to relieve you of your prisoners?"

The captain's eyes wander down to the pistol in Mallory's hand then back to the wild, slightly deranged look in his eyes. "Right." The captain peers across the throng of prisoners. "Sergeant, bring me the tall bastard over there? I'm just going by height, but he looks to be in charge of something."

"Right, sir," replies the sergeant. He seizes a tall, blond officer and leads him over to Mallory. "Here ya go, sir. One slightly soiled Allyman."

"Do you speak English?" asks Mallory.

The officer stares back at him with a bored, slightly superior expression.

"Sprechen Sie Englisch?"

The man rolls his eyes and snorts.

Mallory swings the butt of his pistol across the officer's jaw, knocking him against the stone wall. He slides to the ground. Blood oozing from his lips, he stares back defiantly.

The captain steps between Mallory and the German. "I say, steady old man. He doesn't speak English."

"Smug bastard probably understands every word we're saying."

A nasty smirk crawls across the German's lips.

"So you *do* speak English," snorts Mallory.

"Ja," the officer replies and spits blood.

"Your unit took hostages," declares Mallory. "Where did they take them?"

"How do I know?"

Mallory squats in front of the officer and dangles his pistol threateningly across his lap. "Every unit has contingency plans. To where were they supposed to withdraw if overrun?"

"Why should I tell you?"

Mallory shifts the pistol's muzzle toward the German and thumbs the hammer rearward. "Because you've lost the war and you don't want any more civilian deaths on your head."

"Do you want more deaths on *your* head?" asks the German warily.

"Maybe just one more..."

"They're retreating toward Peronne," announces Mallory as he strides to the tank and spreads a dog-eared map. He checks his watch. "Are the MPs here yet?"

"Yes, but..." replies James.

"Good. Get the battalion on the road to Amiens." Mallory squints at the map, tracing the road eastward with his finger.

"All right, but..."

He taps the black dot labeled Peronne. "Have you left enough supplies for the girls at the house?"

"Yes, but..."

Mallory folds the map, shoves it into his pocket. "I'll be back in a few days. Get the crews billeted and hand out some passes. They've earned it."

"Right, but..."

"But *what*, James?"

"Well... where the hell are you going?" asks James.

"Peronne."

"You can't just leave your command," blurts James. "You'll be a deserter!"

"Not if my sergeant major covers for me. Just tell the General I've gone ahead to conduct an advanced reconnaissance."

James purses his lips and shakes his head sadly.

"Look, I'll be back in a few days," insists Mallory. "If I'm not back by Tuesday, just report me missing." Stepping toward the tank, he reaches up in the roof and retrieves his kit.

"*Sir*," replies James desperately. "She's in German hands, there's nothing you can do for her."

"Dammit, James!" swears Mallory. "If they had Adele, what would *you* do?" He peers into his friend's eyes.

James pulls on his chin. "Prob'ly the same thing. But you'd 'ave the good sense to stop me."

"Fortunately, you don't have the same good sense."

"No, I don't."

"So?"

"So, I'll see you in a few days. Good luck with your 'reconnaissance'."

CHAPTER 34
Battle of Amiens, Outskirts of Peronne, France
12 September 1918

"This is highly irregular," snorts Brigadier Cameron.

"I understand, sir. But as you can see," Mallory explains as he unfolds a single, hand-written page and hands it to the colonel. "I've been sent as an observer. I'm to evaluate tank-infantry cooperation as we approach the Hindenburg Line."

Cameron raises the paper to the light and squints at the note. "Can't make-out the signature…"

"Major General Ernest Swinton," explains Mallory. "War Office."

Cameron returns the paper. "And he wants you to go in with the first wave? Seems a tad reckless."

Mallory folds the paper and places it back in his pocket. "Well, sir. You know how these staff officers are, they've no idea what it's like up here at the front." He leans-in and whispers conspiratorially, "probably thinks we'll just walk right into Peronne without a fight."

"Hmm, damned red tabs."

"Truly,"

"Well, I'll assign you to 3rd Battalion. They'll be assaulting Peronne in the morning." He jots a quick hand-written order and passes Mallory a flimsy. "Present that to Lieutenant Colonel Busby and he'll place you with one of the assaulting companies."

"Thank you sir."

Mallory walks from the command post, flimsy in-hand. He pulls the orders from his pocket, glances down at the paper in his other hand and crumples it into a wad. Dropping them to the ground, he continues toward the front line trenches with his new orders.

A scream like an onrushing freight train concludes with an earsplitting *WHUMP!* The earth beneath the Australians' feet jolts and trembles. Clods of dirt shake loose from the berm and cascade into the shallow trench. Aussies balancing on the fire step steady themselves with the butts of their rifles as trains continue to arrive at regular intervals.

"Whoa! Ain't tha' a little close to our own boys?"

Mallory steadies his Brodie helmet with one hand. "A walking barrage," he shouts to a group of pale-faced infantrymen. "When it begins to lift, we'll leave the trench and follow on its heels. Should put us at the Hun positions in no-time!" he assures them with a confidence he doesn't feel.

The Company commander crawls up the berm and peers over the top of the trench, brass whistle dangling from his quivering lip. The tenor of the barrage changes as gunners adjust elevation and extend the barrage fifty yards. The captain's face reddens as he blows rabidly on the whistle. Sergeants begin pushing troops toward the top of the berm.

Mallory joins the charge and emerges atop the ditch, ground still trembling beneath his feet and he jogs forward through the openings in the sparse wire. The shallowness of the trenches and scarcity of wire entanglements give evidence to the temporary nature of the hastily-dug positions on the outskirts of town where the previous advance temporarily stalled.

Behind a screen of blasts and smoke, the Aussies advance rapidly into the fringes of Peronne. The German defenders break into retreat as the attackers overwhelm the fragile defenses and burst into the village. Here and there men in tan uniforms crumple as defenders fire from around corners before dropping back to the next building to resume a fighting retreat.

The attackers close rapidly, bayonets slashing as the orderly Germans withdrawal escalates rapidly into a bloody rout.

Mallory emerges from the middle of the pack of advancing Aussies, eyes searching the retreating Germans. Amid a crowd of gray helmets, he spots a peaked cap.

"Sergeant!" he yells to a passing NCO. "Catch that Hun officer!"

The sergeant glances around in confusion before locating the subject of Mallory's attention. "Sah!" he shouts. Grasping several of his men by the sleeves, he tugs them toward the alley into which the officer disappeared. Mallory overtakes them and leads the advance up the narrow stone pathway. The sound of gunfire fades as they submerge ever deeper into the winding alley.

From behind the haze an object tumbles through the air, bounces off the wall and lands at Mallory's feet.

It takes a moment before anyone reacts.

"*Grenade!*" shrieks the sergeant; men fling themselves to the ground, arms covering the tops of their helmets.

"Christ!" With nowhere to turn, Mallory grabs the grenade and hurls it back into the mist where it explodes mid-flight. *Crump!* A wave of heat washes over him, the blast hurling him onto his back. The air explodes from his lungs and he struggles to regain his breath. He lay amid the debris staring skyward; muffled voices call to him. The accents are strange and slurred. A face hovers above him, the helmet's wide brim casting a shadow over the face beneath.

"Keep going," the faceless man orders his troops. "I've got the Colonel!" The Aussies push past and charge down the alley.

"I'm all right," gasps Mallory and attempts to rise.

"You got a face full of shrapnel," announces the sergeant. He strips off Mallory's kit and gingerly opens his tunic. "Took some in the chest, too."

"It's all right," insists Mallory. "I've got to get that Hun!"

The sergeant shakes his head. "No sir. You stay here and we'll get your Hun."

"Right," Mallory agrees through blood-smeared lips. "Go!"

The sergeant lowers Mallory to his back and takes-off in pursuit of his section.

Wiping blood from his face, Mallory struggles to his feet and recovers his pistol. He staggers drunkenly down the alley in pursuit and passes the mangled body of the German soldier killed by the grenade's blast. Shouts echo through the haze ahead; a mix of New South Wales brogue and guttural Bavarian dialects intermixing in a confused melee. Mallory stumbles through the mist and discovers a half-dozen gray-clad bodies lying in pathetic heaps, Australian infantry standing over them with blood dripping from their long, sword bayonets.

The officer sits pinned against the wall, blood oozing from a shoulder wound, an Aussie bayonet held threateningly to his throat.

"Your Hun officer, sir!" announces the sergeant and passes Mallory the officer's Luger.

Mallory shoves the pistol into his belt, stoops before the prostrate officer and sweeps the bayonet aside gently. "Sprechen Sie Englisch?" he asks.

The officer stares back and shakes his head emphatically.

"I speak some Allyman, sir," announces the sergeant. "We had some Hun vinedressers in Camden. Whatcha' want to know?"

"Ask him where they took the hostages," demands Mallory.

"Wo sind die Geiseln?"

Eyes widening with panic, the German shakes his head rabidly and blurts a string of guttural denials.

"Says they ain't got no hostages. Just some French collaborators fleein' our forces."

"Bullshit," hisses Mallory. He presses the barrel of his pistol against the German's wounded shoulder. Blood oozes around the barrel. The German gasps, fear reflecting in his startlingly blue eyes. He squirms and Mallory relents.

"Ask again."

"Wo sind die collaborateuren?"

The German responds with an emphatic shake of the head.

"I've had enough of this," hisses Mallory. He seizes the front of the man's tunic and drags him to his feet. Shoving him against the wall, he levels his pistol at the Hun officer's face.

The infantrymen back away slowly. "Sir," the sergeant announces reluctantly. "This ain't right."

"No, it's not," seethes Mallory. "*Ask him!*"

"*Wo sind die collaborateuren?*" The fear in the Aussie's voice is infectious. The German drops to his knees, fingers locked in prayer as he babbles hysterically.

"What the hell...?"

"He says it wasn't his men," translates the Aussie. "He said it was the Feldgendarmerie's fault."

"The what?"

"Feldgendarmerie, sir. The Hun military police."
"*What* does he say was the Feldgendarmerie's fault?"

Head bowed, eyes cast downward, the German officer leads Mallory and the Australian patrol to the edge of town. Troops still securing the area swarm around them pursuing German stragglers trapped in the village. A medic stops to check Mallory's wounds; Mallory waves him away.

As they approach the banks of the Somme, the German halts. "Es ist da," the officer croaks, hand trembling as he points toward a smoldering building.

"It's there," translates the soldier.

"What's...?"

"The Feldgendarmerie. Sie ausgeführt, die Geiseln."

Even without translation, the implication is clear. "Oh, God. No," moans Mallory.

Drawn like a moth to the flame, he staggers toward the ruin of what was once a large barn. The charred roof has collapsed, leaving only the skeletal remains of smoke-blackened stone walls. The stench of burnt flesh is overwhelming as a breezeless morning casts a hateful pall over the scene. Mallory stands before the collapsed structure as wisps of smoke drift from between the beams. Holstering his pistol, he lifts several smoldering timbers and heaves them aside. Peering reluctantly inside, he discovers a floor strewn with the corpses of dozens of civilians, many of the bodies charred beyond recognition.

Some died in small clumps, clinging together in their last moments; probably families. Others are strewn around the periphery of the floor as if desperately searching for a way out of the fiery hell. Near the barn door he discovers the form of a pregnant woman, her mangled body clad in the tattered remains of a familiar blue dress.

"*NO!*" he gasps. He staggers backward, reeling as if drunk beyond reason. After several wobbling steps, his legs collapse beneath him. Retching, he vomits violently, back arching as wave after wave of cramps squeeze the contents of his stomach into the dusty French courtyard. He kneels, gasping for air. Slowly recovering his strength, he crawls toward the prisoner. Groping for the Luger in his belt, he thrusts the pistol in the German's face, the pale face growing blurry as his eyes fill with blood. The Australians scatter.

"Nein," begs the German. "Es war *nicht* meine Soldaten."

Click!

The pistol misfires. Mallory squeezes the trigger again and again, but to no avail. Finally he drops the gun and collapses in a heap, an animal wail emerging from deep within.

Hesitantly, the German crawls over and slips his hands beneath Mallory's armpits. Lifting him gently, the Hun officer embraces him; and the two men sag kneeling in the Flanders dust, sobbing.

CHAPTER 35
Resting and Refitting, Bray-sur-Somme, France
30 October 1918

"How are you Jack?" asks General Elles as he draws a chair alongside the iron bedstead. "Getting enough rest?"

Mallory struggles to sit erect, shoving several down pillows behind his back. His face is swollen and covered with tiny scars from the shrapnel removed from his flesh; beneath his hospital gown, his chest is peppered with similar wounds. "Well enough sir. Seems all they want me to do here is rest."

"Well, you've suffered quite a trauma. I'm afraid the concussion from that Hun grenade knocked you back on your heels. And the shrapnel…"

Mallory smiles benignly. "Thank you sir, but I think we both know I'm in a mental ward."

Elles shifts uncomfortably in his seat. "Every man reaches a point where he needs to reorient himself, Jack."

"Reorient," grunts Mallory. "I like the way that sounds."

"Now that your wounds are healing the doctors tell me your mental state has improved dramatically."

"I suppose that's how reorientation works," snorts Mallory. "Tell 'em what they wish to hear and suddenly you're fit for duty."

"Have you told them the truth?" asks Elles. "About what happened, I mean."

"They don't want to hear that," scoffs Mallory. "Collateral damage and all. Civilians are bound to get in the way, *wot?*"

"Don't be sarcastic, Colonel. You and I both know that's not the way it is."

"Yes, sir," replies Mallory sheepishly. "I suppose I'm just feeling sorry for myself."

They sit in awkward silence, the wounded battalion commander and his commanding general eye each other warily. A clock in the hospital's foyer strikes Noon, the bell tolls a dozen times.

"Look, sir. I appreciate the visit…", begins Mallory.

"This isn't a social call," interrupts Elles. "I need to know if you deem *yourself* fit to return to service."

"It's not up to me. It's up to the docs..."

"Yes, yes," replies Elles impatiently. "But I need to know if I can count on your return. A lot of things ride on your answer."

"Such as?"

"Plan 1919, for one. And of course there's that appointment to Sandhurst."

"What's plan 1919?"

"It's Boney Fuller's plan for what he calls an 'attack by paralysation'. It focuses tanks and air support at the German leadership and supply lines. Our tanks will penetrate en masse on a narrow front and run amok in the enemy's rear area. It 'll break up their command and control and precipitate the collapse of the entire front."

Mallory nods thoughtfully. "Not to seem negative, sir. But according to the last report, we haven't enough tanks left to mount a battalion-sized attack, much less conduct a sustainable breakthrough. Besides, if Amiens showed us anything, it's that our tanks aren't fast enough to conduct cavalry-type sweeps."

"True, but we are working on a new Medium Type-D Tank. The prototype came out this month. It's got a new track design system, higher speed…"

"How fast?" asks Mallory hopefully.

"Twenty, twenty-five miles per hour," declares Elles.

"And crews?"

"Yes, and crews. But they'll be draftees, amateurs needing proper leadership."

"Meaning?"

"I want you back."

"*Back???*" Mallory spreads his arms. "Look at me, sir!" he blurts in exasperation. "I'm in the mental ward – *again!* I'm nuts! The M.O. has confirmed it. Who in his right mind wants me commanding troops?"

Elles rises angrily to his feet. "*I* do!" He snaps. "The war's left us damned few good men. I need leaders and, for better or worse, you're the best I've got! If you're barmy, maybe we should clean-out all the lunatic asylums and commission the lot!"

"But the doctor... my medical records..."

"Show nothing of what occurred," replies Elles. "I've spoken with the Command Surgeon and he agrees your mental breakdown was brought on by a concussion attendant to your wounds. The records reflect nothing negative about your mental state."

"So can I return to duty?"

"Do you *want* to?"

"Sir, I've got *a lot* of Germans to kill to make up for what happened at Peronne."

"Yes, well. That's the one thing that concerns me," admits Elles. "Can you kill Germans without wasting the lives of your men? Your single-tank attack on Bray and bayonet charge at Peronne seem to indicate a death wish. Is that true?"

Mallory sighs. "No sir, it reflects a desperate desire to *get on with it!* We're this close," he insists, his thumb and forefinger poised millimeters apart. "One more push and the Hun will collapse. I feel it! But if the fight continues to drag-on..."

"What?"

"Something too awful to contemplate."

"What is?"

"An armistice?"

"*Armistice?* Who said anything about *an armistice?*" replies Elles' in a shrill, defensive voice.

"No one specifically, sir. It's a mood, just something I hear in people's voices. A sort of exhaustion indicating they might accept something short of victory."

"And you wouldn't see an Armistice as victory, even if we forced the Hun into unfavourable terms?"

"Sir, if we allow the Germans to walk away from this war without being properly defeated on the battlefield, God help us!"

"And if we're bankrupt and ruined as a nation by the time we defeat him, what kind of victory would that be?"

Mallory waves his finger. "That's precisely the mood I'm talking about!"

"Yes, well," interrupts Elles. "Policy is not our job, thank God. That's up to the politicians. Our job is to prepare for that victory you so desire. So get yourself sorted, take a spot of leave and report to Bermicourt. Colonel Fuller will be waiting." As he stands and offers his hand, there is a knock at the door.

"Sorry, sir. It's time for the Colonel's medication," announces the nurse.

"It's all right, I'm just leaving." Tucking his cap beneath his arm, he turns to Mallory. "Do as your doctor orders. When you're medically fit, we'll get you back into command, eh?"

"Right, sir," replies Mallory. "And thank you."

"Whatever for?" asks Elles in mild surprise.

"Getting me back in the fight."

"Yes, well…," replies Elles. "Be careful what you ask for."

Mallory rolls the shaving kit into his housewife and shoves it into the valise alongside a change of uniforms. He sorts irritably through his drawers, peering into and slamming each as he finds it empty.

"Sister?" he asks a passing nurse. "Where is my pistol?"

"We don't allow our patients to retain weapons, sir," she replies.

"I'm no longer a patient, so where the hell is it?"

"There's a cupboard downstairs in the foyer, sir. A sergeant maintains the key. I'll fetch him for you."

"Just tell him to meet me at the cupboard."

He finishes dressing and retrieves his lighter and remaining cigarettes from the nightstand. A shrill honk summons him to the window. Glancing down at the arched driveway, he spots James ensconced imperiously in the rear seat of a staff car, a Sergeant serving as chauffer. Mallory catches James' eye and waves his acknowledgement.

As Mallory reaches the bottom of the stairs, the sergeant hands him a Webley Mk. VI. He immediately thumbs the latch, breaks open the pistol and notes the weapon is unloaded.

"Cartridges?"

The sergeant reaches back into the cupboard and scoops a handful of stubby .455 rounds. Mallory glances at the half-dozen cartridges. "That's not all of it," he scolds and receives an additional ration of bullets. He loads six rounds into the cylinder and snaps it shut. Buckling the pistol into the holster at his waist, he pockets the remaining rounds, clamps the peaked cap on his head and shuffles down the stairs to the waiting car.

He tosses his bag in the front seat, climbs over the rear door and collapses in the passenger seat before the chauffer can exit the driver's position and open it for him.

"It's all right, Sergeant," laughs James. "The Colonel ain't much for ceremony."

"Do you have it?" asks Mallory.

James reaches into his satchel and hands Mallory a fifth of Scotch. "Welcome back!"

Mallory peels away the seal, pulls the stopper and takes a gulp. Nodding approvingly, he hands it back to James. "God, I'm glad to see you!"

"You too, sir! Though you look like a bloody lad with them marks all over yer face. That goin' to heal?"

"Every time they think they've got all the shrapnel, something else works its way to the surface. I seem to be on the mend, though."

"So, what's on your mind?"

"I've got a 48-hour pass and no plans," he announces with a slap on the order in his breast pocket.

"Well, good. 'Cause tonight's my weddin' anniversary."

"A year! My God. Has it been so long already?"

"Yep, twelve months of marital bliss."

"Wouldn't you two prefer to be alone?"

"Naw, we spend too much time together as it is. Besides, I think it'd be good for you and Adele to spend some time together. You know, grievin'."

"Is she still in mourning?"

"Aren't you?"

"I suppose."

"Then let's get started."

The car passes through Amiens and continues east toward Bray. As they enter the village, Mallory notices the locals have already begun to reconstruct their battered town. Scaffolds obscure the church tower as new materials are carefully winched in place to be fitted among the ancient stone. Sections of cratered street have been shoveled-out and replaced with fresh cobblestones. As they cross the bridge, James leans forward and whispers to the driver, who nods and veers away from the three storey stone house off Rue Pasteur.

They arrive before a small bakery at dusk. Weaving drunkenly, Mallory retrieves his valise and steps from the car. James passes the driver a few Francs. "Get lost for the night, Ernie," he mumbles. "Won't need ya 'til mornin'." The driver doffs his cap, waves cheerfully and drives away.

"Come on," urges James. "See me new place and say hello to Adele."

Mallory follows James up a creaky staircase to the landing above the bakery. He pushes through the door into a comfortable flat furnished with mismatched furniture apparently gleaned from a dozen destroyed homes.

"It ain't much, but it's ours," announces James with a wink.

"Est ce que toi mon cheri?" comes a voice from the kitchen.

"Oui, baby. It's me." replies James. "And I brought an old friend."

Adele appears through the kitchen door wiping her hands on a faded blue apron. "Mon Dieu!" She dashes across the room and throws her arms around Mallory's neck. He feels tears running down her cheeks as she gasps, sobbing. He wraps his arms around her and finds himself crying gently.

James stands-by, a smile on his face and tears in his eyes. "There ya go, sir. I told ya she'd be glad to see ya."

"Oh, Adele," sighs Mallory. "I'm so sorry."

She pulls away and stares at him through teary eyes. "*You* are sorry? James and I are together and everything is fine for us. But... how are you?"

"James told you?"

"Yes. Alemands damnés!" she swears. "There is a special place in 'ell for them."

He smiles back at her, but his heart sinks. Here stands Adele, alive, in love. But Elise?

She stares at him queerly, as if trying to read his mind.

"Happy anniversary," he announces with a wan smile. "I see you've managed to tame the bear."

"Tame the bear? Ah, c'est pas difficile," she replies with a loving glance toward her husband.

"Now, don't be spreadin' rumours. Love," replies James kindly. He removes his cap and places it on the rough-hewn table. "How about we have another drink?"

Adele sniffs James breath. "I think you are ahead of me." She skitters into the kitchen. They hear her sorting through the cabinet.

"So, how's the battalion?" asks Mallory.

"Trainin'," shrugs James. "We ain't got many tanks left. But we got a draft full of useless sons-of…"

"Pas de blasphème," cautions Adele as she enters with three mismatched wine glasses and a bottle of Scotch.

Mallory glances at James in mild surprise. "No profanity?" he chuckles.

"Ever since we squared our marriage with the army, she's turned into a proper lady," admits James "Even cooks dinner sometimes."

After filling and handing-out the glasses, Adele takes a seat on James' lap and drapes an affectionate arm over his shoulder. "To what shall we drink?" she asks.

"To your anniversary, of course," replies Mallory with raised glass.

"To the end of the war?" adds James.

"No," Adele whispers. "To Elise?"

"To Elise," agrees Mallory.

They drink the toast in silence as Mallory drains his glass in a single gulp.

James glances at Adele and nods.

She refills Mallory's glass.

"Christ!" swears Mallory.

Thump, thump, thump!

"Piss off!" he shouts and pulls the blanket over his pounding head.

Thump, thump, thump!

"Shit," he swears and throws-off the covers. Grabbing the sheet, he pulls it around his naked body and shuffles into the living room.

"James? Adele?" he calls.

There's no reply.

He shuffles to the door and wrenches it open. "*What?*" he demands irritably.

A fresh-faced corporal eyes him with suspicion. "I'm lookin' for Sar Major James."

Mallory shades his eyes against the rising sun and squints at the corporal. "He's not here. What's the message?"

"It's a matter of some importance," responds the corporal.

"I'm Lieutenant-Colonel-bloody-Mallory," snaps Mallory. "You can damned-well trust me to pass along anything you've got to say to my Sar' Major!"

The corporal looks him up and down dubiously.

Mallory glances down at his sheet. "I obviously don't have identification on me at the moment. Now, what the *hell* do you want me to tell him?"

The corporal straightens. "Right. Yes, sir. Please tell 'em it starts at Eleven-Hundred Hours."

"Eleven-Hundred Hours, right," acknowledges Mallory and begins to close the door. He halts. "Er, *what* starts at Eleven Hundred Hours?"

"The Armistice, of course!"

"I'm sorry. *The what?*"

"Armistice, sir. The Germans have agreed to a cease fire starting at Eleven Hundred Hours."

Mallory grabs the front of the corporal's uniform. Shaking the boy, he demands, "*Today?*"

The soldier shifts uncomfortably before the raging colonel. "Yes, sir. November 11th."

Releasing the boy's lapels, Mallory's anger recedes. "Eleven Hundred Hours," he repeats. "Yeah. I'll tell him." He backs inside the flat and starts to close the door.

"But, *sir*," adds the corporal helpfully. "That means the war's over!"

"Uh, oh," groans James as he discovers the flat's door ajar. He steps inside with Adele at his heels. "Sir?" he calls.

No response.

"Where is he?" asks Adele.

"I dunno," replies James.

"Do you think he's heard about the armistice?" she asks.

"Oh, God. No!" James dashes into the guest room and discovers a rumpled tunic on the bed, an empty leather holster on the floor. "Shit!"

"What's wrong?"

"What time is it?"

She checks the wall clock. "Ten forty-five. Why? Where is he?"

James pushes past her and bolts down the stairs.

"*James?*"

"Stay there, love!"

He dashes down the cobblestone street, a damp autumn wind chilling beads of sweat that form on his brow. Rounding the corner, he approaches the abandoned three storey stone house. Halting at the entrance, he takes a deep breath and exhales slowly. With a nudge, he pushes open the door and steps into the unlit foyer. The blood-stained floor remains littered with crusty bandages, shattered splints and remnants of tattered German uniforms. The building reeks of death.

"Sir?" he calls tentatively.

In the darkened parlour, he detects breathing. He enters the room and can barely make-out the shadowy figure of a man reclining in an overstuffed chair. "Jack?"

"What do you want, Gaylord?" responds an exhausted voice.

"Just thought I'd come by and see how you're doin'? Adele and me got back from the market and found you was gone." He steps tentatively toward the seated shadow. His eyes begin to adjust to the darkness. Mallory is sprawled in the chair, a half-empty bottle of Scotch in one hand, his pistol in the other.

"Wha'cha doing here?" he asks.

"Just came to say farewell," rasps Mallory.

"You goin' somewhere?"

"The infernal regions," Mallory replies.

James takes a step.

"No," drawls Mallory. He raises the pistol and cocks the hammer. "Stay away from me!"

"Wha' you gonna do, shoot me?" James takes another step.

"Not you," replies Mallory and raises the barrel to his temple. James halts. "*Why?*" he begs. "The bleedin' war is *over.*"

"*Why?*" snorts Mallory. "*Because* the bleeding war is over!"

"But that don't make sense…"

"Don't you *understand?* It means everything. The war gave me Elise; the war took her away. I have *nothing left* but the war."

"That ain't true."

"How am I supposed to avenge Elise's murder, James? *How?* You said it yourself. *The bloody war is over!*"

"Surely there'll be tribunals…," sputters James.

"Not with an *armistice,*" insists Mallory. "The whole damned German army will march home, flags flying! They'll pass out Iron Crosses and the rest of the world will breathe a collective sigh of relief. There'll be no justice!"

"That ain't right."

"No, it '*ain't,*" agrees Mallory. "And those Hun bastards will spend the next few years figuring out what went wrong then reorganize and do the whole damned thing all over again."

"If that's true, how's killin' yerself gonna change anythin'?" demands James. "It sure as hell ain't gonna avenge Elise!"

"Sure it will."

"Bollocks!"

"James… the Hun isn't the only guilty party."

"You didn't do nothin'."

"I left her here to be raped and killed," slurs Mallory. "I failed her." He raises the bottle in his left hand and glances at his watch. "It's almost Eleven. Now get out of here."

"What's at eleven?"

"The reckoning…"

"I ain't leavin' you."

"You can't stop me."

The conversation is interrupted by the crunch of broken glass underfoot. The silhouette of a woman appears in the doorway.

"What are you *doing?*" snaps Adele.

"What is *she* doing here?" rasps Mallory.

"I didn't bring 'er," insists James. "Stay back Adele…"

"I will not!" She stomps into the room. "Bâtard enfantin!"

"Excuse me?" rasps Mallory.

"Millions 'ave perished. Elise is dead. And this is how you honor their memories?"

"I…"

As she stalks up to him, he presses the barrel to his temple. "Stay back!"

With one, deft move, she snatches the pistol by the barrel and twists the muzzle toward the ceiling. It erupts in her hand, the bullet splintering a board in the ceiling above. "Merde!" she curses. Wrenching the pistol in her burnt hand, she rips the Webley from his grasp and flings it across the room.

He stares up at her in disbelief.

Slapping him across the face, she yells. "Get up!"

Dropping the bottle, he staggers drunkenly to his feet. She wraps her arms around his neck and pulls him to her. Sagging against her narrow frame, he sobs like a lost child. "What am I going to do?' he gasps.

"From now on, live every day for *her*," she sighs. "*Live for Elise,*"

CHAPTER 36
Royal Military College, Sandhurst
Berkshire, United Kingdom
September 1919

"See you on the pitch?" asks Ernie, bright-eyed and full of youth.

Mallory checks the time – Ernie recognizes with envy the snap-back trench watch favored by veterans of the Great War.

"Dunno," replies Mallory. "What time's the match?"

"We'll meet at half-three. But we need a decent bowler. Terry's mum is ill, so he's heading back to Reading for a few days."

"I've got to meet with Colonel Langdon about the course syllabus."

"Well, make it if you can!"

"Right-o."

Feeling slightly silly in his dark blue cadet's uniform and short-brimmed cap, Mallory marches up the marble stairs and enters the main administrative building. Members of the faculty who would have otherwise harassed a first year cadet nod respectfully to the battle scarred gentleman walking briskly toward the faculty offices.

Reaching the mahogany-framed door, he raps vigorously three times and awaits an invitation to enter. Instead, the door swings open and Colonel Langdon answers the knock himself, resplendent in his polished riding boots and breeches.

"Sir," Mallory barks and presents a sharp, backhanded salute. Instead of returning the salute, Langdon offers a hand.

"Lieutenant Colonel Mallory," he replies, beaming. "Forgive me if I find it difficult to address you as 'Cadet Gentleman'. Your reputation precedes you."

Mallory lowers his salute hesitatingly, shakes the firm hand and enters the office.

"Tea?" Asks Langdon and signals for Mallory to take a seat.

"Er, thank you sir."

As Langdon busies himself with the cups, Mallory glances around the dark-paneled office. Above the mantle are mounted a pair of crossed polo mallets, plaques, trophies and framed photographs of nearly thirty-year's worth of colonial wars and punitive expeditions. None of the memorabilia appears to be from the recent Great War.

"Milk?"

"No, thank you."

"Sugar?"

"No, sir."

Langdon hands Mallory a cup and saucer then takes a seat behind his desk. Stirring his tea, he nods. "Now, I understand you have some question about the syllabus."

"Not questions, sir. More like… observations. Am I to understand the College is planning to incorporate lessons from recent operations in Flanders into the new curriculum?"

"That's right."

"Well, I was reviewing the syllabus and it appears, while the infantry tactics manual has been updated, the cavalry course has not. May I ask why?"

"Quite simple, actually. It doesn't need to be updated. Cavalry tactics have developed over centuries and there was little to be learned from operations in the recent war."

"Because cavalry was seldom used…"

"Yes, but that was because of the unusual nature of the war."

"Forgive me, sir. But I don't see it as unusual."

"Well, this was your first war. You really have nothing to compare it to, have you?" A hint of ice begins to creep into the colonel's condescending tone.

"In what course will tank tactics be covered?" asks Mallory.

Langdon grunts derisively. "Tank tactics? What are those?"

"The combined arms strategies developed by Colonel Fuller, for one."

"Colonel Fuller? He's hardly an academician, young man. His ideas were a local expedient to overcome a temporary tactical problem. While suitable to the moment, they really have no practical application for the future."

"Temporary tactical problem?" blurts Mallory before catching himself. "They weren't just ideas, sir. We used them at Cambrai, at Amiens…"

"With limited success…"

"But with great promise! We broke the German lines, crossed their trenches, incapacitated their forward defences."

"Yes, tanks were good for crossing No Man's land, but they were – by the nature of mechanical devices – unable to exploit the breakthrough."

"Which is the privilege of the cavalry," replies Mallory darkly.

"Why, yes!"

"But the cavalry was nowhere to be seen. And the few times they made an appearance, they were slaughtered wholesale."

"Well, those bloody machineguns and artillery…"

"…Are the future of warfare," announces Mallory. "As are tanks. Don't you see, sir?"

"Hmph! Tanks were merely an expedient to overcome the anomaly of trench warfare. Had we utilized cavalry earlier and in greater mass, static warfare would never have occurred and we wouldn't have needed those armoured tractors. With proper cavalry and infantry tactics, in the future, your tanks will be consigned to the rubbish-heap of history.'"

"My, God," sighs Mallory. "General Elles was right."

"Elles?"

"Commander of the Tank Corps."

"Ah, yes. Er, what was he 'right' about?"

"He said the donkey-wallopers would kill the tank."

Langdon places his cup gingerly on the saucer and lowers it to the blotter atop his desk. "We don't use that term, cadet. It's poor form."

Mallory rises to his feet. "So is mass-murder. But *that* seems jolly-good form, eh?"

Clad in mufti, Mallory disembarks the Second Class coach. A shabby one-armed man reaches inside the coach and retrieves his valise. Despite the man's relative youth, his hair is graying but combed. On his threadbare jacket hang three tattered medals, the 1914-1915 Star, British War Medal and the Victory Medal.

"Changing trains, sir?"

"No. This is my destination," replies Mallory.

"Got more luggage?"

"No, that's it. Thank you."

The man limps alongside as Mallory walks self-consciously toward the station's gate. He retrieves the bag and hands the man a shilling.

"Tha's too much, sir!" protests the veteran. "It's only ha'penny per bag."

"What's your regiment, Sergeant?"

The young man straightens and announces, "East Surrey, Sir! Second Battalion, Glasgow Greys!"

"You fought at the Hohenzollern Redoubt?"

"Yessir!"

Mallory offers his hand. "Thank you for your service, Sergeant."

"Sah!"

Mallory tosses a casual half salute and heads into town. As he nears the Corn Exchange, the clinging mist turns to a steady rain. He steps beneath a sheltering balcony and retrieves his umbrella. The war having ended, services at St. Mary-le-More have returned to a more leisurely, peace-time schedule. He strolls past the church and heads to the rectory. Beneath a pounding rain, he peers through the front bay window and spots a familiar gray head bowed over a book. He taps on the window; the head jerks upright. Squinting through thick glasses, the face peers back at him, eyes widening with recognition. He flings the glasses onto the table and disappears from the room, to appear seconds later at the door.

"Jack, my boy!" blurts Fr. Hall. "Come in! Come in!"

Mallory closes the umbrella and enters the foyer. Hall embraces him warmly. "Thank God you're safe! I wondered when you'd return to us!"

"Thanks, Padre. Good to see you too." He strips off his trench coat and hangs it on the coatrack beside the door.

"Step into the den, I'll ring for tea."

"I'd prefer something stronger if you don't mind."

Fr. Hall eyes him warily. "That can be arranged. There's a fire in the hearth. Go and get warm while I fetch the Scotch and some glasses."

Mallory wanders into the familiar Victorian study with its sagging bookshelves and faded red wallpaper. The display encircling Fr. Hall's cavalry sword and Boer War pith helmet has been expanded to add a glossy photo of the two of them standing beside a Mark IV the day before Messines.

"Seems like ages ago, doesn't it?" asks Fr. Hall as he enters the room carrying a cut glass decanter and two matching glasses.

"A long year and a half, yes," agrees Mallory as he retrieves a glass and takes a sip. A satisfying smile creases his lips as he swallows the remainder of the smoky liquid in a single gulp. He hands back the empty glass.

"So, it's like that, eh?" asks Fr. Hall perceptively.

"I'm afraid so. May we sit?"

"Certainly." Fr. Hall refills Mallory's glass and they each settle into facing armchairs. "So, when did you return?"

"I arrived home about six months ago. I've been up at Sandhurst for the past few months."

"Sandhurst?"

"Something Parliament authorized for young officers from the war."

Fr. Hall nods sagely.

"What?"

"Just seems a bit forward-thinking for the politicians – and the army."

"Yes, well…" Mallory fingers the glass in his hand, swirling the liquid and staring at the revolving contents.

"Something tells me it didn't go well."

"No. No, it didn't. According to the College's Chief of Tactics, 'tanks were a local expedient to overcome a temporary tactical problem'. Seems they're to be consigned to the rubbish-heap of history."

"Dear, God. Surely not!"

"Surely so," confirms Mallory. "I took compassionate leave to 'consider my future', as the department head calls it. It seems I've been awakening my roommate with nightmares. The College is concerned I might not be suitable for further service."

"Because of the nightmares, or because of your views on tank warfare?"

"Exactly," agrees Mallory.

Fr. Hall sits watching Mallory's eyes dart about in their sockets. Moving, not seeing, as if watching a battle reflected solely in his mind.

"What happened, Jack?"

Mallory takes a gulp of Scotch. "Elise is dead," he announces.

"I was afraid of that," sighs Fr. Hall. "What happened?"

Mallory rises to his feet and begins pacing rabidly. "Does it matter? I mean, the war's over. She's gone and I don't know where I belong!"

"The war may be over, but you're still fighting it, Jack. You've got to learn how to deal with it so you can get on with your life'."

"*Get on* with it?"

"Yes. You have to deal with those demons in your head. If you don't, you'll find no flask deep enough to drown those memories."

Mallory nods vacantly.

"You were a student before the war, right?"

"So?"

"You were ripped from your placid academic environment and thrust into four years of the bloodiest war even known to mankind. You can't just turn it off."

"No, I suppose not. But the memories... I always thought I would refight the battles in my dreams. But I don't. And it's not just in my dreams. That feeling... It can be triggered by a noise, a smell. Sometimes I feel a sudden chill as if a ghost has just passed through me. And... it... it all comes back to me in a rush, the anxiety, the panic..."

He spins suddenly and blurts, "I see Elise everywhere I look! I was walking down the street in Oxford a few months ago and I caught a glimpse of Elise's black bob. I dashed across the street and grabbed her arm. The poor woman screamed and ran away. Even since then, I catch a passing glance from the corner of my eye and actually double-take to make certain it isn't her."

Fr. Hall rises and retrieves Mallory's glass. Instead of refilling it, he places it back on the tray.

"You've got to go back to France," he announces. "Go visit the battlefields and say farewell to the ghosts that haunt you."

Mallory stares up at the old soldier. "But what if I can't," he croaks. "What if they stay with me?"

Fr. Hall places a fatherly hand on Mallory's shoulder.

"They'll never leave, my son. But you can learn to live with them."

CHAPTER 37
A Year after the Armistice, Cambrai, France
11 November 1919

A damp November rain patters against his civilian overcoat. The hired Renault rocks down a muddy, rutted road newly constructed across what was once no man's land. Names on newly-erected road signs mark the route to towns remaining in name only: Havrincourt, Graincourt, Anneux...

"You fought here?" asks the driver as he squints in the car's rear view mirror.

"Yes. I served in the Tank Corps."

"Ahhh, le Tank Corps," sighs the driver sagely. "Cambrai is a spécial place for you."

"Yes," agrees Mallory. "Cambrai is a very special place."

Through a gray haze appears a looming hulk in the field beside the road. The driver squints into the rain. "Ah, regardez! There is one of your tanks." shouts the driver, pointing across the barren field to the half-buried hulk of a rusting Mark IV.

"Stop!" shouts Mallory and the car slides to a halt. "Un moment," he demands. He pops open the door and descends the car's running board into the muddy field.

"Monsieur! There is unexploded ordnance everywhere!"

"Ça va," replies Mallory and picks his way across the field. *Maybe this is how I will die. Unexploded ordnance from the last war.* The thought is somehow comforting.

He reaches the tank and is disappointed to find the name and hull number have been overtaken by rust. The crew's skeletal remains have long since been recovered and buried. Ordnance crews have stripped the hulk, removing the salvageable cannons and Lewis guns, leaving lonely mounts corroding on site.

On the opposite side he discovers the recently-scratched names of eight crew members, beneath which is etched in epitaph, "They gave their lives that others might live." He removes his glove, places a bare hand on the cold steel and draws his fingertips lightly across the unfamiliar names. Closing his eyes, he bows his head and recites the final phrases of Siegfried Sassoon's "Poet as Hero":

"... But now I've said good-bye to Galahad, And am no more the knight of dreams and show: For lust and senseless hatred make me glad, And my killed friends are with me where I go. Wound for red wound I burn to smite their wrongs; And there is absolution in my songs."

Patting the icy steel, he mumbles, "Rest in peace, mates."

He picks his way back to the car across the sodden field.

"Mon Dieu! It's getting cold!" announces the driver through clattering teeth. "Where next?" he asks.

"Cambrai. Service des Archives Municipales."

Within the hour, the rattletrap Renault sedan arrives in Cambrai before a dilapidated building temporarily serving as the municipal records department. Mallory hands the driver a wad of Francs and asks him to return in a half-hour.

As the driver pulls-away, Mallory mounts the steps and enters the old stone building. A lone clerk glances up at him, notes the English attire and lowers his eyes disinterestedly.

"Ou peut-on trouver les registres fonciers?" asks Mallory.

The clerk glances up with renewed interest. "Business or family property?"

"Family," replies Mallory. "I'm looking for a particular farm."

"What is the name?" inquires the clerk.

"Fousard," replies Mallory. "Captain Henri and Madame Elise Fousard."

"Ah, le Capitaine Fousard! He was a friend of yours?"

"I... uh... knew his family. Did you know him?"

"Oui, he was a wonderful man! And his wife... ah, so beautiful! But... quelle tragédie."

Mallory's face flushes. "Indeed. Is the farm nearby?"

"Just on the edge of town. About, ten minutes from 'ere. Down Route d'Arras." He points west. "There are the remains of a crashed Boche triplane in front of the farm house. You cannot miss it."

"Thank you," replies Mallory gratefully and hands the clerk a five Franc note. With an ingratiating smirk, the clerk palms the note and slips it expertly into his waistcoat pocket.

"Au revoir, monsieur!"

Mallory steps into the rain and paces the sidewalk. Checking his watch, he realizes the driver is nearly fifteen minutes late returning. "Shit," he curses and claps his hands together, rubbing them for warmth.

After ten more minutes, he gives-up on the driver and walks west down the shattered road leading toward Arras. Along the way, he encounters small groups of workmen clearing rubble from demolished buildings to be used in the rebuilding effort. Hat pulled down and collar turned up against a bitter wind, he leans into the stiff breeze and hastens westward.

In the fading light, he discovers what appears at first to be a rubbish pile. On closer examination, he discovers a Maltese cross painted on what remains of an aircraft tail-section. Beyond the wreckage is a farm. Fields fallow, the once grand stone farmhouse seems to sag beneath the weight of history. A section of the thatched roof has burned away, exposing bare, charred beams. Emaciated cows wander carelessly across the barren landscape, stopping to nibble tufts of grass here and there. A plow sits rusting beside the skeleton of a barn long stripped of siding to provide fuel for the invaders – and perhaps the survivors.

He detects the faint aroma of burning wood. A wisp of smoke floats lazily from the kitchen chimney. He walks hesitantly up the walkway to the kitchen door. Tentatively, he raps lightly on the glass pane. A young girl replies.

"Oui?"

Dumbfounded, he stares into familiar brown eyes.

"Monsieur?"

"My, God. You look just like…" he mumbles.

"You are English?" she asks.

"Y-yes. Are your parents home?"

"Tante Louise," she shouts into the kitchen. "Nous avons un visiteur anglais!"

A middle aged woman shuffles to the door. She's plain, a little plump, and bears a passing resemblance to Elise.

"May I 'elp you?" she asks pleasantly.

"Madame...?" he asks uncertainly.

"Louise Durant."

"Madame Durant, of course," Mallory sighs as he realizes this must be Elise's elder sister. "You don't know me, but my name is Jack Mallory," he announces, removing his hat. "I..."

"Mon Dieu!" Louise's hand leaps to her mouth to cover a startled gasp.

"You know who I am?" he asks uncertainly.

"Of course! Elise spoke of you many times! Please, mon colonel, come inside out of the rain. You must be freezing!" She grasps his arm and urges him inside.

The home's interior is warm and inviting. The aroma of freshly baked bread pervades the kitchen. Two young girls eye him shyly, their brown eyes twinkling playfully.

"I... I've been traveling through France," he explains. "Visiting some of the places..."

"Oui," confirms Louise. "We are starting to see many former soldiers voyager en pèlerinage."

"Yes, of course there would be many of us. I just wanted to see the farm," he stammers. "I heard it was beautiful. I didn't get to see it during the war.'`

"Les Boches occupied the area until l'Armistice."

"Yes, I know. You see..."

Unable to endure the playful glances from the girls, he blurts, "See here, are these Elise's daughters?"

"Oui," beams Louise. "Anastasie, Paulette. Ceci est le colonel Mallory," she announces to the girls.

"Bonjour, mon colonel," they reply in unison.

"Bonjour Anastasie; bonjour Paulette," replies Mallory, squatting and offering his scarred hand. Taking his hand, they smile and curtsey in response.

"God, they're as beautiful as their mother," he sighs.

He glances up at Louise's tearing eyes. Rising to his feet, he places an affectionate hand on her arm. "Madame Durant, I just realized François must have been your son."

"Oui," she declares stoutly, her voice clear despite the sudden flash of pain in her eyes.

"I knew him," insists Mallory. "He knew how dangerous it was crossing through German lines. He was a fine and courageous young man."

"Thank you, mon colonel," she replies gratefully. "He will always be remembered as such in our family."

Mallory nods firmly.

"But surely you are here for other reasons, no?" Louise asks.

He fingers his hat awkwardly. "I'm not sure. I suppose I just wanted to pay my respects…"

"Louise, pourquoi parlez-tu anglais?" comes a voice from another room.

"We have un visiteur," beams Louise.

The kitchen door swings open. He finds himself face-to-face with familiar liquid brown eyes, a porcelain face framed by a short bob coming to points beneath an elegant jawline.

In the woman's arms struggles a blond baby boy.

"Elise…"

IPILOGUE
Twenty-Two Years Later, Cambrai, France
10 May 1940

"Hurry, papa," insists Lieutenant James Mallory, tank platoon leader in the newly formed French 4e Division cuirassée. "The train leaves at 1000."

"Where's the rest of your kit?" asks Mallory as he reaches into the Renault's boot and retrieves his son's single canvas duffel bag.

Lieutenant Mallory impatiently retrieves the bag from his father's grasp and mounts the stairs leading to the railway station. "My orderly sent everything ahead. Colonel DeGaulle insisted we travel as light as possible now that the Germans have broken through at Sedan. We'll meet up with the regiment's tanks at the railhead and attack toward Montcornet."

"De Gaulle isn't parceling-out your tanks to the infantry divisions, is he?"

"No, papa. I told you, he agrees with Colonel Fuller's principes de manoeuvre. We'll slice through First Panzer Division's supply lines and leave his tanks to wither on the vine."

"Guderian's Panzers are fast and light, son. Your Char B's are slow and ponderous."

"This isn't Poland, father. We're not going to counter-attack armour with horse cavalry. We've got more than three thousand tanks. Besides, the Germans will never get past the Maginot Line."

"Just don't let the Hun get behind you."

Lieutenant Mallory glances around the crowded platform. "Where's mama? She said she'd be here."

"I wish she wasn't coming," grumbles Mallory. "This sort of thing is hard on a mother."

The train's whistle shrills. Steel wheels squealing, the boxcars bump and begin moving slowly down the track. Poilus crowded into the cattle cars wave their rifles and call out to the civilians cheering from the platform.

"Vive la France!"

"Vive la victoire!"

"I can't wait, father. I've got to go!" He extends his hand formally.

Mallory glances at his adopted son's pale white hand, so reminiscent of his mother's. He reaches out and grasps his son in a strong embrace. "I love you, son," gasps Mallory.

The young French officer is taken aback at his stoic British step-father's sudden display of affection.

"I love you, too, papa," he replies. "Tell mother I'll be home by Christmas," he announces. He turns and hops aboard the running board. Eager hands reach out, retrieve his duffel and pull him aboard the accelerating train.

Mallory doffs his hat and watches the train depart in a cloud of steam. He remains standing, staring eastward until the train fades from sight. He replaces his hat and walks slowly toward the ticket office.

As the crowd of weeping mothers and grizzled veteran poilus of the First World War thins, he spots Elise, a look of utter despair on her face as she stares at the empty tracks. Beside her stand the elegant red-headed Adele and a paunchy, middle-aged James. Mallory takes Elise in his arms.

"He's gone?" she asks.

"Yes, darling," sighs Mallory. "Military trains keep very strict schedules."

She limply raises a wicker hamper. "But I brought him food for his trip," she mutters.

"Damned Police Militaire blocked-off the bloody road or we would've been on time," swears James.

Mallory pats his friend on the arm. "Couldn't be helped," he assures. "Did Pierre get off to his regiment all right?"

"Yeah, left yesterday afternoon. Broke poor Adele's heart," replies James with an affectionate squeeze of his wife's shoulder. She glances up at him with adoring gaze so reminiscent of those distant summer days in 1916.

"I cannot believe they would take a family's only son," insists Adele. "It isn't right."

"The lads are officers in good regiments," replies James. "They'll be all right with their mates."

"How can this be happening again?" Elise demands. Mallory runs his hand through her graying black hair and kisses her lightly on the forehead.

"Because we didn't finish it in 1918," he replies.

"I can't help thinking the first German he kills may be his cousin," sighs Elise.

Mallory smiles and squeezes her pale hand. "I know..."

"I'd feel better if the lads were in the British Army," James grumbles.

"The boys were born in France, James," Mallory reminds his friend. "This is their country to defend."

"The Nazis is takin' the same bloody path they took in 1914," scoffs James. "What makes 'em think it'll work better this time?"

"Blitzkrieg," replies Mallory.

"What the hell is that?" asks James.

"Plan 1919," replies Mallory - "Boney Fuller's strategy to win the last war."

GLOSSARY

ADC	Aide de Camp. A senior officer's personal aide.
Baled Charge	Six grenades bundled around a single stick grenade. Used at close range to attack British tanks.
BEF	British Expeditionary Force – the 6-division, all-volunteer professional army sent to fight in France at the beginning of the war. Between August and December 1914, the BEF was all but wiped-out halting the German advance.
Blighty	Affectionate slang for England; also denotes a wound that gets a soldier sent home.
Boche	Derogatory slang for Germans, generally.
Brody Helmet	Rimmed, soup-bowl-shaped helmet worn by Commonwealth and U.S. soldiers.
Case-Shot	Cannon round filled with steel or lead balls that spread out from the bore of the gun like a shotgun, peppering infantry in the open with thousands of projectiles (a.k.a. grape-shot).
Chauchat (pronounced Sho-sho)	French Chauchat M-1915 is an 8mm light machinegun meant to be fired by a single operator. One of the first true "automatic rifles", it was poorly manufactured and jammed frequently due to the introduction of dust into its exposed magazine and open-bolt firing mechanism. Cheap to produce in large quantities, its presence on the battlefield had more to do with availability than desirability.
Company Sergeant Major	Senior non-commissioned officer (NCO) responsible for administration standards and discipline at Company-level. Actually a Warrant Officer, he is typically addressed as "Sir" by the enlisted men and "Sar' Major" by officers.
DCM	Distinguished Conduct Medal. A decoration for valor awarded to enlisted soldiers in the British Army. Discontinued in 1993.
Devil Dodger	Nickname for Army Chaplain.
Digger	Slang for an Australian Soldier; similar to "Tommy" in the British army and "Yank" in the American.
Ditch	Also "ditching" or "ditched". Occurs when a tank sinks up to its belly in the mud and loses traction, often in a water-filled crater.

Dixie	Oval pot in which hot food is transported.
Donkey Walloper	Derogatory nickname for a Cavalryman.
Estaminet	French tavern or pub.
Feldmützen	Brimless service cap worn by German enlisted men.
Fire Step	Ledge on which soldiers stand to see and shoot over the top of the trench.
Fizzer	Disciplinary charges.
Flimsy	Message recorded on a thin piece of paper between which carbon paper provides an exact copy on the paper beneath.
Fritz	Nickname for the invading Germans. Most commonly used by the enlisted men, it reflects a more humanized view of an enemy that shared similar burdens of war.
Grey Hen	Earthenware jar marked 'SRD' (Service Rum Department), used to carry rum to the trenches.
HBMGC	Heavy Branch, Machine Gun Corps – the predecessor name for the Tank Corps, which was finally established as its own branch 28 June 1917.
High-port	A rifle raised to chest-level, the weapon carried diagonally across the torso during an advance.
Hun	Derogatory nickname for the invading Germans. Most commonly used by officers.
Iron Ration	Emergency ration of preserved meat, cheese, biscuit, tea, sugar and salt. Eating one's Iron Ration without orders was a chargeable offense.
Jumping the bags	Going 'over the top' of the trench or parapet to assault across no-man's land.
Kitchener's Mob	Also known as "Kitchener's Army" or "New Army". It initially began as an all-volunteer force of new recruits formed by Secretary of War Lord Kitchener to replace the original BEF wiped-out in 1914. New battalions were formed beneath existing Army Regiments and eventually became indistinguishable from the Old Army by the end of the war.
Left-Footer	Scot-Irish slang for a Catholic.
Lieutenant	Lowest officer grade in the British Army
Loophole	An opening in fortifications through which machineguns or snipers fired at attackers.

Maxim	German redesign of American Hiram Maxim's water cooled machinegun. Designated Maschinengewehr 08, or MG08, it was the German Army's standard heavy machine gun in World War I.
Minnie	Projectile launched from a 7.5 cm German trench mortar, referred to in German as a Minenwerfer (mine thrower).
No Man's Land	Area of land between two enemy trench systems into which neither side wishes to move openly or to seize due to fear of being attacked by the enemy in the process. Interestingly, the term was coined for World War One by then war correspondent, Colonel Earnest Swinton, a central character in this story.
M.O.	Medical Officer; doctor.
NCO	Non-Commissioned Officer; enlisted leaders with a rank of sergeant and above.
Ooja	Slang for a 190-pound gas canister used to transport and release chlorine gas in vapor form.
Other Ranks	Refers to an enlisted soldier lower than the rank of Sergeant.
OTC	Officer Training Corps, a university-based commissioning program that provided more than 30,000 British officers during the war.
Ox & Bucks	Oxfordshire and Buckinghamshire Light Infantry, Est. in 1881.
Plonk	Slang for French vin blanc (white wine)
Potato Masher	Model 24 Stielhandgranate – German-made stick-grenade introduced in 1915.
PBI	Poor Bloody Infantry, referred to simply as 'the PBI'.
Poilu	Literally 'hairy ones'; a nickname for French troops in the First World War. They preferred to be called 'les bonhommes' (good men).
Red Tab	Derogatory reference to a staff (planning), rather than combat, officer; identifiable by red collar tabs and hatbands.
RFC	Royal Flying Corps – forerunner to the Royal Air Force (RAF)

SMLE	Short-Magazine Lee Enfield, the excellent .303 caliber rifle of the British Army in both World Wars. A bolt-action rifle, it fired 10 rounds from a detachable box magazine.
Smoke Hood	Early gas mask created by soaking a khaki-colored flannel bag in Glycerin and Sodium Thiosulphate and breathing through the material.
Sponson	Naval term for a bulging protrusion containing a cannon or other armament.
Tommy	Slang for an individual British soldier, similar to the American 'Yank' or 'Doughboy'.
Tracer	Projectiles with a small pyrotechnic charge in the base. When fired from a weapon, the pyrotechnic composition burns brightly, making the projectiles trajectory visible to the naked eye during flight.
Victoria Cross	Awarded by the King, it is the highest decoration for valor in the British Army. It is the rough equivalent of the American Congressional Medal of Honor.
Vin Blanc	French white wine.
Vin Rouge	French red wine.
Vin Blanc Anglais	Literally "English white wine". Nickname the French used to describe English Whiskey.
Webley	The .455 caliber Webley Mark VI is a six-shot, double action revolver that served as the standard issue sidearm for officers in commonwealth armies.
Wound Stripe	In the British Army, a brass bar attached to the forearm of the battle dress uniform indicating the recipient was wounded in action. U.S. military wore a chevron on the lower sleeve during the First World War, but this was later converted to the Purple Heart Medal and ribbon.

About the Author

Steve Howery is a reserve Lieutenant Colonel in U.S. Army Intelligence and veteran of Iraq, Afghanistan, and other lesser-known theaters of 21st Century conflict. In his civilian capacity, he is a technology transfer attorney, adjunct college professor and author of *Without Reserve: a Novel of the War on Terror* (Khukuri Publishing, 2007).